CRIME
in a
COLD
CLIMATE

CRIME
in a
COLD
CLIMATE

AN ANTHOLOGY *of*
CLASSIC CANADIAN CRIME

——— *edited by* ———
DAVID SKENE-MELVIN

Simon & Pierre
Toronto, Canada

Editor: Jean Paton
Designer: Andy Tong
Printed and bound in Canada by Metrolitho Inc., Quebec

The writing of this manuscript and the publication of this book were made possible by support from several sources. We would like to acknowledge the generous assistance and ongoing support of the **Canada Council, The Book Publishing Industry Development Program** of the **Department of Canadian Heritage, The Ontario Arts Council,** and **The Ontario Publishing Centre** of the **Ministry of Culture, Tourism and Recreation.**

J. Kirk Howard, President

ISBN 0-88924-260-7
1 2 3 4 5 . 9 8 7 6 5

Canadian Cataloguing in Publication Data

Main entry under title:

Crime in a cold climate

Includes bibliographical references.
ISBN 0-88924-260-7
1. Detective and mystery stories, Canadian (English).*
I. Skene Melvin, David, 1936- .

PS8323.D4C7 1994   C813'.087208   C94-932201-6
PR9197.35.D4C7 1994

Order from Simon & Pierre Publishing Co. Ltd.

2181 Queen Street East	73 Lime Walk	1823 Maryland Avenue
Suite 301	Headington, Oxford	P.O. Box 1000
Toronto, Canada	England	Niagara Falls, N.Y.
M4E 1E5	0X3 7AD	U.S.A. 14302-1000

DEDICATION

As the noted author Robert A. Heinlein stated: "just as mathematics is the key to all knowledge, library science is the foundation, and our civilization will rise or fall depending on how well librarians do their job." My fellow professional librarians at the Metropolitan Toronto Central Reference Library, specifically the Inter-Library Loan service and particularly in the Literature Section, are doing their job very well indeed and justly deserve my appreciation and thanks.

And above all my wife Ann without whose love and support in my many many hours of pain I could not endure.

CONTENTS

PREFACE

It is my hope in compiling this anthology that it will not only give a few hours' pleasure to readers, but will also resurrect from unjustified oblivion some Canadian crime writers from the late nineteenth and early twentieth centuries, and be a small contribution toward rekindling Canada's national spirit and sense of cultural identity. The selections are all "good reads" and worthy of inclusion on their own merits; I am vain enough to hope that my critical analysis placing them in their historical context and the associated biographical information on the authors may add to the reader's enjoyment.

I offer neither apology nor explanation for my selections other than personal preference and my belief that those selected reflect my argument. Additionally, I hold that a narrative can be in either prose or verse; that it is the content that matters, not the form. In response to those purists who would reject poetry or consider the selections included unworthy of the label, and readers who are furious that authors they would have selected are ignored in favour of writers they believe to be utterly boring, best-forgotten nonentities, I quote Dr. Jowett, Master of Balliol College: "Never retreat. Never explain. Get it done and let them howl."

Others may howl for a different reason. A word of warning – here and there throughout these stories are phrases and expressions of attitudes and racial terms that are not in these neo-Puritan times "politically correct." No attempt has been made to bowdlerize these passages. The tales are historical documents and reflect their times and customs. One does not correct current social injustice by denying the past and telling lies, but by facing it squarely and accepting it, like Cromwell's portrait, "warts and all."

The format of the book is thus: a general introduction; a biography of the author of the story; an introduction to the selection; the story; and a bibliography of the author's criminous and other works. Occasionally I slip into librarian's jargon and use abbreviations such as "ss," meaning short stories, which identify a work as a collection rather than a novel, and phrases like "inter alia" (meaning among others), but generally I have tried to avoid such esoterica (see – there I go again).

INTRODUCTION

The detective-story (despite those literary genealogists who insist on finding ancestors for it at least back to Edgar Allan Poe) was the invention of Arthur Conan Doyle, who created Sherlock Holmes, although Conan Doyle, like all inventors, founded his invention on experiments that had gone before. Prior to Conan Doyle and alongside him were the sensational novelists and storytellers, with many Canadian authors among this company.

From late in the nineteenth century until well into the twentieth, Canadian crime writing in particular, and Canadian literature in general, suffered from a serious problem: the slighting of Canadian authors due to economic reasons. It was too expensive to produce small numbers of domestic editions when the country was swamped with American culture and had to compete with imported British culture as well.

Yet some authors made it as Canadians, while others masqueraded as either Americans or British. Crime writing – adventure, crime, detective, espionage, intrigue, mystery, suspense, and thriller fiction – as a field of endeavour for contemporary Canadian crime writers was not a virgin land waiting for the plough. More than trails had been blazed, from the late nineteenth century onward, through this country of the mind. Clearings had been made in the bush, crops sown and gathered. Even before the genre had formulated itself under its current rubric, Canadians were contributing to this bountiful harvest.

Canadian criminous literature falls into five fairly distinct periods: from the earliest begetters to 1880; 1880 to 1920; 1920 to 1940; 1940 to 1980; and 1980 to date. The authors whose poetry and short fiction has been selected for this anthology come from the second and third periods: 1880 to 1920 – the heyday of the "Northern" and the literary exploration of Canada's remote and romantic frontiers, and 1920 to 1940 – the "Golden Age" of detection, when private sector professional and amateur sleuths abounded.

John Dent, Grant Allan, Robert Barr, William Fraser, Pauline Johnson, Roger Pocock, Robert W. Service, and Robert Stead exemplify the "frontier" period of 1880-1920; the work of Arthur Stringer, Harvey O'Higgins, Frank L. Packard, Hulbert Footner, and R.T.M. Scott lies mainly in the inter-war period, although there is in actuality much overlap between the two. Fraser and Service, for example, wrote mystery thrillers in the 1920s, and Stringer and Footner began their careers before World War I with "Northerns" before settling with urban detectives, while the foundations of Packard's career rest on the now forgotten sub-genre of "railroad" fiction, once immensely popular, but now disappeared like the steam locomotives that inspired it.

These writers were the entertainment of a literate age, the age of reading. They were the explorers of that country of the mind that the reader entered at his or her own peril, a country of infinite geography, for each time it was encountered it was individually interpreted.

The ancient Greeks said a person is immortal as long as his or her name is remembered. So by perpetuating a record of their one-time existence we are serving to preserve the immortality of these writers. It is an immortality they deserve. They would have been the last to claim they wrote great literature – they wrote to entertain. They were storytellers, spinning yarns to be printed and read, just as their predecessors, minstrels, recited and were listened to. And entertain they did! Through their countless tales of adventure and derring-do they brought romance and colour to the drab lives of countless millions who could do no more than dream.

When Canada was a young country, London, England, was the world's literary centre; and for ambitious young men and women there were only two metropolises to head for: London or New York City. Consequently, many aspiring Canadian writers went into voluntary exile: of the writers in this book, John Dent, Grant Allen, and Robert Barr returned to their British roots and settled in London, although Dent subsequently returned to Canada where he found his fame and fortune. Arthur Stringer, Harvey O'Higgins, Hulbert Footner, and R.T.M. Scott all sooner or later made their careers in New York City; Stringer returned to his homeland for a significant period of his creative life before moving again to the USA. Roger Pocock and Robert W. Service came and went, but the productive part of their literary endeavours was performed while they were in Canada, and is rooted in our Northern clime. William Fraser, Pauline Johnson, and Frank L. Packard did their writing in Canada and succeeded both at home and abroad.

It is not true that there was no market abroad for Canadian heroes and Canadian settings. John Dent's too few stories bring to life a Toronto no less adventurous and just as romantic as Robert Louis Stevenson's Edinburgh transmogrified into London. Although Grant Allen and Robert Barr set the bulk of their romances in Britain, Barr made a significant contribution to Canadian letters with two of his non-criminous novels, *In the midst of alarms*, set in the Niagara region of Canada in 1866 during the Fenian invasion, and *The measure of the rule*, an autobiographical novel about the author's training at the Toronto Normal School. The latter is a minor classic. William Fraser chose two frontier Canadas as the locales for some of his criminous fictions, and the Western and Northern frontiers served Pauline Johnson, Roger Pocock, Robert W. Service, Frank L. Packard, and Robert Stead for some of theirs.

Arthur Stringer utilized New York City as the "city" for much of his criminous writing, but also wrote of Canadians in this city as well as of Canada. Harvey O'Higgins looked to New York City as the setting for his detective stories, but the author's first novel, *Don-a-dreams; a story of love and youth*, is an autobiographical story about student days at the University of Toronto that is one of the best ever written about life at the Varsity. Frank L. Packard also used

New York City as his "city" for the saga of Jimmie Dale, but set many of his adventure thrillers in Canadian wilds, as did Hulbert Footner.

Robert Stead was a stay-at-home, writing about Canadians, save for one egregious aberration, *The copper disc*, which was set in England, with Morley Kent as the sleuth. R.T.M. Scott emulated Stringer, O'Higgins, Packard, and Footner in ultimately choosing New York City as the milieu for his detective hero, although Aurelius Smith begins his career in India, with which Scott was familiar, and Fraser utilized his work experience there as a setting for *The eye of a god; and other tales of East and West, The three sapphires*, and *Caste. Caste* tells of Captain Barlow and British operations against Indian highwaymen. A review of the book in the *Canadian Bookman* said: "a masterpiece in colour, intrigue, and dramatic love, laid in the old India. The facts of the story are authentic, having been turned over to Fraser by the India Office."[1]

It was a custom for authors of the late Victorian era who wrote short stories about a single character to compose what in effect was a serial novel: a collection of short stories centred on one main character, linked by a common thread that has both a discernible beginning and end, and that flows through a specific chronological period of time. Rather than merely chapters in a book, each episode can stand alone as an individual exploit. This is the pattern followed by Grant Allen in *The adventures of an African millionaire*, Arthur Stringer in *The man who could not sleep*, and Harvey O'Higgins with *The adventures of detective Barney*. In each of these instances we have chosen the initial story that introduces the character and sets the scene for the adventures that follow, all leading to a happy denouement.

As Alberto Manguel pointed out in *Out of place*, "From abroad, Canada has been perceived as a land of noble savages (mainly among French novelists), as a place of redemption (countless are the books in which fallen sinners find a new life in the Frozen North), as utopia (the setting for many fantastic stories)."[2]

In all of such stories about Canada, the common thread is the assertion of national authority, the compulsive driving force within the Canadian psyche, represented particularly by the scarlet tunics of the North-West, later Royal North-West, still later Royal Canadian, Mounted Police.

Edgar Friedenberg, an American professor resident in Canada, theorized in 1980 that "Canadians defer to authority; Americans submit to force."[3] That divergence is borne out in our respective constitutions: Canada's calls for "peace, order, and good government"; the American Declaration of Independence proclaims a person's right to "life, liberty, and the pursuit of happiness." The two constitutions are mutually incompatible, and explain the real, even if hidden, gulf between Canadians and their southern neighbours.

Canadians want the rule of law and the presence of law and order; Americans strive to escape it. American popular culture is replete with frontiersmen moving West as settlement follows them. As Natty Bumppo and his literary descendants moved across the continent they changed into the cowboys and gunslingers of the "Wild" West and eventually became the hardboiled private eyes in the mean streets of San Francisco and Los Angeles. The defiance of law was enshrined in the American Revolution and Americans have rebelled against authority ever since. Hence the prevalence of the outlaw as hero in American popular culture: Jesse James, Billy the Kid, and W. R. Burnett's "Little Caesar."

Canada never had a Wild West, because the Mounties got there first. As Margaret Atwood points out:

> No outlaws or lawless men for Canada; if one appears, the Mounties always get their man ... It both reflects and reinforces a view of the universe based not on the eighteenth-century American version of "freedom" in which man is supposedly free to shape his own destiny ... but on a vision of order as inherent in the universe.... And it does indicate why the first presence of the Mounties and the absence of a Wild West are neither omissions nor accidents: law is first because the universe is conceived as being already under its sway. The presence or absence of law is not thought of as something determined more or less arbitrarily by a shoot-em-out or display of strength at High Noon.[4]

It is said that Canada has no heroes and hence no popular culture, a theme best explored and expressed by George Grant, George Woodcock, B. K. Sandwell, and Charles Taylor. Indeed, as the latter points out in his *Six journeys*, "More than most peoples, Canadians are prejudiced in favour of the ordinary ... It might almost be said that something in us hates a hero."[5] There are no national figures in Canadian folk-consciousness. We lack our Daniel Boones, our Davy Crocketts, our Ned Kellys. Not that we did not have characters even more colourful than these. But in our abnegation and modesty, we forbear to glorify Dollard des Ormeaux, Sir Guy Carleton, Isaac Brock, Tecumseh, Charles de Salaberry, or Inspectors Walsh and MacLeod of the North-West Mounted Police.

If there is a Canadian hero, it is one that has been manufactured for us, but which we willingly adopted, a symbol rather than a persona: "the manly, taciturn Mountie who imposes law and order on the peoples of the wilderness, making it safer for the settlers, the traders and the missionaries." Instead of the individual Mountie, the Mounted Police in the Canadian tradition of collective heroism.

The sub-genre of the "Mountie" novel gave Canada and the world British North America's own unique and most enduring image: a stalwart, red-coated, fur-hatted policeman on snowshoes, accompanied by his trusty husky, pursuing mad trappers across the trackless wastes of the Barren Lands, or exchanging his ear-flapped winter headgear for a Boy Scout Stetson, riding alone into a camp of hostile Indians. Stereotypical, perhaps, but stereotypes exist because they reflect reality and serve as guideposts to the truth.

"Where are the rest of you?" said the American cavalry colonel at the head of his regiment, to the lone Mountie escorting the fugitive Amerindian warband back across the border. "Oh, he's back at camp cooking breakfast," was the reply.

Around the world, readers thrilled to these tales of the Mounted Police.

Two parallel streams of Canadian crime fiction developed: the Mountie/Northern, and the detective mystery in the classical tradition. The dichotomy was that it was mostly foreigners who wrote about Canada in the Mountie/Northern, while Canadians primarily wrote about foreigners in the classic detective tales they essayed. Hence a paradox: British and American writers searching for a more remote and romantic locale had their characters adventure in Canada; Canadian authors seeking market acceptance geared their output to their audiences and set their stories in Great Britain and the United States, with occasional forays to the Continent and the more exotic places of the world.

But Canadians did not completely ignore the possibilities of their own land.

The "Mountie" novel, the "Northern," and the romantic adventures set in the Great Lone Land entwine to rival the Gordian knot. Roger Pocock led the way with *The blackguard* in 1896, a humourous portrayal of the NWMP circa 1885, adumbrated by his short story, "The lean man," the first appearance of a Mountie in fiction. It appeared in *Tales of Western life, Lake Superior and the Canadian Prairies* in 1888. Pocock's lead was followed by John Mackie, William Alexander Fraser, Ridgwell Cullum, "Ralph Connor," and Hiram A. Cody, among others.

It was "Connor" who gave us the first series character in Canadian crime fiction, in two of his Mountie novels. In 1912, he published *Corporal Cameron; a tale of the Macleod Trail,* re-titled in the USA *Corporal Cameron of the North West Mounted Police,* to ensure that readers knew that the hero, Allen Cameron, was a corporal of the NWMP. This tale was so popular that "Connor," like Conan Doyle before him, was forced by popular demand to bring back his hero, whom he had retired from the Force and married off; to promote him to Sergeant; and to set him on *The patrol of the Sun Dance Trail.*[6]

The "Mountie" novel has been enduring: as recently as 1988 adventures of the Force such as Ian Anderson's *The flying patrol*[7] were still being published about the exploits of the NWMP.

The Mountie, the Horseman, the Rider of the Plains, the Scarlet Rider – all these soubriquets have had their common usage – and his deeds are an integral part of the "Matter" of Canada. A concept in a popular culture can be measured in proportion to the number of names by which it is known; the Force has roots deep in the Canadian psyche.

So, Canadian popular fiction created, nurtured, and developed the Northern, and because the Mountie was and is so much a part of the North, the Mountie novel bulks large in Canadian crime fiction.

Even today, the Mountie novel is not extinct, because one cannot write crime fiction set outside of Ontario and Quebec, save for a few large urban centres, without writing about the Force: the RCMP under contract polices Canada's other eight provinces as well as its territories. Part of the attraction of the Force for novelists is that the Mounties can be promoted and transferred from one end of the country to the other and all points in between. In British Columbia, L.R. Wright's protagonist is S/Sgt Karl Alberg of the Force; in New Brunswick, RCMP Inspector Madoc Rhys performs for Charlotte MacLeod writing as "Alisa Craig"; in the Northwest Territories Inspector Matthew "Matteesie" Kitologitak investigates at the bidding of Scott Young.

Canada would not be Canada had the NWMP not made its long march from Fort Garry to Fort MacLeod – from Winnipeg to Edmonton – tying this country together by a scarlet thread of outposts and patrols. The human thread bound it well, until the country had coalesced and could replace the bands of flesh with the bands of steel of the railroad. There would have been no railroad to build, for there would have been no nation to build it over, had not the Scarlet Riders of the Plains held it together.

An essay on Canadian fiction from 1880 to 1920 tells us:

> Most of these books are now out of print, and are no longer read by the reading public. They are not regarded as serious literature by the literary critics of our day; the pictures of Canadian life they present have been overlooked by cultural historians. Yet the Canadian fiction-writers between 1880 and 1920 were read more widely by their contemporaries, inside and outside Canada, than have been the Canadian fiction-writers – collectively – since. Because they wrote in the grain of the dominant feeling of their Anglo-North-American world, their fiction had a significant reciprocal relation with their times. It reflects, through direct representation or through fantasy, many aspects of the pluralistic life in Canada between 1880 and 1920; it also provided images of Canadian life which formed a definition of Canadian identity, at home and abroad.[8]

From the plethora of "Northerns" that proliferated between 1880 and 1920, besides the authors represented in this anthology and those already mentioned, a few others used Canada as a setting for their criminous fiction. Among them were Joseph Edmund Collins, who wrote *The story of Louis Riel; the rebel chief*[9] which gave rise to the curious legend that Riel had ordered the execution of Thomas Scott because they were rivals in love – a story that took such a hold in Eastern Canada that Collins had to issue a disclaimer. Collins also wrote *Annette, the Metis spy; a heroine of the North West Rebellion*, concerning the exploits of a Duck Lake Mata Hari.[10] Thomas Stinson Jarvis was the author of *Geoffrey Hampstead*, a detective thriller with psychological overtones set in Toronto that was the most widely reviewed novel of its time in the USA.[11] Also popular were Bertrand W(illiam) Sinclair and *The land of frozen suns*;[12] the Rev. Hiram A(lfred) Cody with his adventurous tales of "muscular Christianity" in the Far North such as *The long patrol; a tale of the Mounted Police* [13] and *Rod of the Lone Patrol*.[14]

This is but a sampling of the lush variety of sensational novels of romantic intrigue set in the glittering metropolises of the fashionable world, and tales of adventure in the Frozen North produced by Canadian crime writers between 1880 and 1920.

Crime came to Canada. Perhaps the most notable crime writer was Arthur Stringer, who in 1914 created *The perils of Pauline*, which brought early moviegoers back to the cinema and to the edge of their seats once there, as week after week the heroine fell victim to one diabolical plot after another. Packard (does anyone today remember Jimmie Dale, "The Gray Seal"?); Footner; O'Higgins; Scott; and Stead: in this period of the 1920s and '30s, some of the most popular and most prolific writers were Canadians.

These were the years when Canadians writing crime fiction masqueraded as either Americans or British. Even members of the Arts & Letters Club were not above such subterfuge. Though he set his "Mountie/Northern" "Blue Pete" series in Canada, William Lacey Amy, who wrote as "Luke Allen," set all his detective/mystery stories in either the USA or Great Britain, with the exception of *The black opal*,[15] which, although its setting is never named, gives itself away in its reference to the "Provincial Police." John De Navarre Kennedy, having told Lacey Amy in the Club that "anyone could write that stuff" and been challenged to do so, produced three thrillers, all set in Continental Europe. Bertram Brooker, alias the improbable "Huxley Herne," published *The tangled miracle* in 1936,[16] the year he won the first Governor General's Award for Fiction for *Think of the earth;*[17]his criminous contribution was set in the remote and enchanted land of Hollywood.

Another hidden Canadian from this period was Guy (Eugene) Morton, (1884-1948), a reporter for the Toronto *Star* and *Globe and Mail*, who never left Canada, yet published a slew of Edgar Wallace-like thrillers in the inter-war years, fourteen under his own name and twenty by "Peter Traill"; every one was set in either England or New York City.

The two decades between the World Wars were a rich time for popular culture. The period has been called the "Golden Age" of detective fiction and was dominated by Dorothy L. Sayers, Agatha Christie, and Ngaio Marsh.

Competing with this dazzling trio, and holding their own, were a number of Canadians, many of whom wrote about what they knew and set their mysteries in Canada, and were published regardless, even in Great Britain and the USA. Foremost were the authors anthologized in this volume.

Among the others, a few at random were "S. Carleton" (i.e., Susan Carleton Jones): *The LaChance Mine mystery*,[18] "Hopkins Moorhouse," (i.e., (Arthur) Herbert Joseph Moorhouse): *Every man for himself*, set along the North Shore of Lake Superior,[19] and *The gauntlet of Alceste*,[20] and its sequel, *The golden scarab*,[21] which at least have a Canadian hero, "popular novelist and hard-working Canadian newspaper youth Addison Kent," even if set in New York City.

Also finding an audience were Victor Lauriston: *The twenty-first burr*,[22] set in Goderich, Ontario, regrettably his only novel, although he was a prolific local historian of Southwestern Ontario; Charles C. Jenkins: *The timber pirate*,[23] and *The reign of brass*,[24] both set along the North Shore of Lake Superior; Pearl (Beatrix) Foley who in addition to a couple of pseudo-American mysteries under her own name wrote as "Paul De Mar": *The Gnome Mine mystery; a Northern mining story*,[25] set in the Kirkland Lake district of Northern Ontario, in which the villains are thwarted by an amazingly accurate knowledge of the *Ontario Mining Act* on the part of their opponents. (Charles) Leslie McFarlane was the first ghost writer of the Hardy Boys; under his own name he wrote for adults *Streets of shadow*,[26] set in Montreal. These are but a few of the good, solid, Canadian crime writers who were interpreting their society for their fellow Canadians and for readers abroad.

Within the poems and stories anthologized in *Crime in a Cold Climate* can be found the critical definitions of Canadian fiction: the ambivalent hero; the equivocal results of heroism; and the disinclination to believe in "happily-ever-after."

Canadians today are telling their own stories, no longer feeling obliged to hide their nationality nor pretending to be British or American; and those stories are being listened to. Neither as class-conscious as the British nor as egalitarian as the Americans, Canadian crime writers have developed a voice and manner all their own, built on the foundation laid by the authors represented here. Out of these contemporary stories shall come our true national heroes.

David Skene-Melvin
Toronto, 1994

Endnotes

1. *Canadian Bookman,* Vol. 4: no. 10, (October 1922), p.268.
2. Alberto Manguel. "Introduction" in *Out of Place; stories and poems.* Ed. by Ven Begammudre and Judith Krause. Regina, Sask.: Coteau, 1991.
3. Edgar Zodiaq Friedenberg. *Deference to authority; the case of Canada.* White Plains, New York: M.E. Sharpe, 1980.
4. Margaret Atwood. *Survival; a thematic guide to Canadian literature.* Toronto: Anansi, 1972.
5. Charles Taylor. *Six journeys: a Canadian pattern.* Toronto: Anansi, 1977.
6. Ralph Connor. *Corporal Cameron; a tale of the MacLeod Trail.* London: Hodder & Stoughton, 1912, and *The patrol of the Sun Dance Trail.* London: Hodder & Stoughton, 1914.
7. Ian Anderson. *The flying patrol.* New York: Zebra, "Scarlet Rider" series, no. 6.
8. Gordon Roper, S. Ross Beharriell, and Rupert Schieder. "Writers of fiction 1880-1920." In *Literary history of Canada; Canadian literature in English,* 2nd ed. Toronto: University of Toronto Press, 1976.
9. Joseph Edmund Collins. *The story of Louis Riel; the rebel chief.* Toronto: Robertson, 1885.
10. —. *Annette, the Metis spy; a heroine of the North West Rebellion.* Toronto: Rose, 1886.
11. Thomas Stinson Jarvis. *Geoffrey Hampstead.* New York: Appleton, 1890.
12. Bertrand W. Sinclair. *The land of frozen suns.* New York: Dillingham, 1910.
13. Rev. Hiram A. Cody. *The long patrol; a tale of the Mounted Police.* Toronto: Briggs/New York: Doran/London: Hodder & Stoughton 1912.
14. Cody. *Rod of the Lone Patrol.* Toronto: McClelland & Stewart, 1916.
15. William Lacey Amy. *The black opal.* London: Arrowsmith, 1935.
16. Huxley Herne. *The tangled miracle.* London: Nelson, 1936.
17. Bertram Brooker. *Think of the earth.* Toronto: Nelson, 1936.
18. S. Carleton. *The LaChance Mine mystery.* Boston: Little, Brown, 1920; London: Duckworth, 1921.
19. Hopkins Moorhouse. *Every man for himself.* London: Hodder & Stoughton/Toronto: Musson, 1920.
20. Moorhouse. *The gauntlet of Alceste.* Toronto: Musson; 1921/London: Hodder & Stoughton; New York: McCann; 1922.
21. Moorhouse. *The golden scarab.* London: Hodder & Stoughton/Toronto: Musson, 1926.
22. Victor Lauriston. *The twenty-first burr.* New York: Doran/Toronto: McClelland & Stewart, 1922.
23. Charles C. Jenkins: *The timber pirate.* New York: Doran, 1922/Toronto: McClelland & Stewart, 1923.
24. Jenkins. *The reign of brass.* Toronto: Ryerson, 1927.
25. Pearl (Beatrix) Foley, aka Paul De Mar. *The Gnome Mine mystery; a Northern mining story.* London: John Hamilton/Toronto: McLean & Smithers, 1933.
26. (Charles) Leslie McFarlane. *Streets of shadow.* New York: Dutton, 1930/London: Paul, 1931.

JOHN DENT

The Gerrard Street Mystery
The Gerrard Street mystery; and other weird tales.
Toronto: Rose, 1888.

DENT, John Charles, 1841-1888

John Dent was born in Kendal, Westmoreland, England, on 8 November 1841, and brought as a child to Upper Canada, where he was educated and called to the bar in 1865. He found the practice of law profitable enough, but uncongenial. Nursing literary aspirations, he relinquished his practice as soon as he could afford to do so, and returned to his native English to become a journalist. He prospered, and soon was writing for several of the better periodicals, most notably *Once A Week*, for which he was a regular contributor.

After several years in England he and his family moved to Boston, Massachusetts, where he worked on the *Globe*. In 1876 he returned to Ontario as editor of the new Toronto *Evening Telegram*, and later as a member of the staff of the *Globe*. Dent again became a free-lance writer and for a brief period in 1887 the editor of the short-lived historical and literary weekly, *Arcturus*.

Shortly after the murder of the Hon. George Brown, proprietor of the *Globe*, Dent left newspaper work entirely to devote himself to Canadian biography and history. His first ambitious undertaking was the four volume *Canadian Portrait Gallery*, followed by *The last forty years; Canada since the Union of 1841*. Dent also collaborated with the Rev. Henry Scadding on his very important 1884 volume, *Toronto: past and present*.

Dent's magnum opus was *History of the Rebellion in Upper Canada*; which severely criticized William Lyon Mackenzie. Dent suffered opprobrium from all quarters. John King, Mackenzie's son-in-law and the father of Canada's longest serving Prime Minster, was disturbed enough to publish his own biased and subjective rebuttal. Dent's reaction to his critics was to let them fulminate; as he knew, the controversy only stimulated interest in his own work.

In addition to his biographical and historical works, Dent produced one collection of criminous short fiction, *The Gerrard Street mystery; and other weird tales*.

He died in Toronto on 27 September 1888.

THE GERRARD STREET MYSTERY
The Gerrard Street mystery; and other weird tales. Toronto: Rose, 1888.

The stories in Dent's only collection of criminous and supernatural fiction give a glimpse of a talent that could have made Dent the fantasist of his age.

The *Catalogue of crime** describes the title story as "the most interesting, with its blend of the supernatural (a ghostly uncle) and the very natural and absconding forger." In style, it is reminiscent of the best of Robert Louis Stevenson, and besides being an excellent yarn, it is a valuable snapshot of middle-class commercial life in mid-nineteenth century Toronto. Toronto comes alive on Dent's pages as a city in which anything can happen – and does.

Walk with William Francis Furlong as he progresses from Union Station to his uncle's home, and steps into "The Gerrard Street mystery."

---

* Jacques Barzun and Wendell Hertig Taylor. *Catalogue of crime; [being a reader's guide to the literature of mystery, detection & related genres]* (2nd imp. corr.). New York: Harper & Row, 1971.

THE GERRARD STREET MYSTERY

My name is William Francis Furlong. My occupation is that of a commission merchant, and my place of business is on St. Paul Street, in the City of Montreal. I have resided in Montreal ever since shortly after my marriage, in 1862, to my cousin, Alice Playter, of Toronto. My name may not be familiar to the present generation of Torontonians, though I was born in Toronto, and passed the early years of my life there. Since the days of my youth my visits to the Upper Province have been few, and – with one exception – very brief; so that I have doubtless passed out of the remembrance of many persons with whom I was once on terms of intimacy. Still there are several residents of Toronto whom I am happy to number among my warmest personal friends at the present day. There are also a good many persons of middle age, not in Toronto only, but scattered here and there throughout various parts of Ontario, who will have no difficulty in recalling my name as that of one of their fellow-students at Upper Canada College. The name of my late uncle, Richard Yardington, is of course well known to all residents of Toronto, where he spent the last thirty-two years of his life. He settled there in the year 1829, when the place was still known as Little York. He opened a small store on Yonge Street, and his commercial career was a reasonably prosperous one. By steady degrees the small store developed into what, in those times, was regarded as a considerable establishment. In the course of years the owner acquired a competency, and in 1854 retired from business altogether. From that time up to the day of his death he lived in his own house on Gerrard Street.

After mature deliberation, I have resolved to give to the Canadian public an account of some rather singular circumstances connected with my residence in Toronto. Though repeatedly urged to do so, I have hitherto refrained from giving any extended publicity to those circumstances, in consequence of my inability to see any good to be served thereby. The only person, however, whose reputation can be injuriously affected by the details has been dead for some years. He has left behind him no one whose feelings can be shocked by the disclosure, and the story is in itself sufficiently remarkable to be worth the telling. Told, accordingly, it shall be; and the only fictitious element introduced into the narrative shall be the name of one of the persons most immediately concerned in it.

At the time of taking up his abode in Toronto – or rather in Little York – my uncle Richard was a widower, and childless; his wife having died several months previously. His only relatives on this side of the Atlantic were two maiden sisters, a few years younger than himself. He never contracted a second matrimonial alliance, and for some time after his arrival here his sisters lived in his house, and were dependent upon him for support. After the lapse of a few years both of them married and settled down in homes of their own. The elder of them subsequently became my mother. She was left a widow when I was a mere boy, and survived my father only a few months. I was an only child, and as my parents had been in humble circumstances, the charge of my maintenance devolved upon my uncle, to whose kindness I am indebted for such educational training as I have received. After sending me to school and college for several years, he took me into his store, and gave me my first insight into commercial life. I lived with him, and both then and always received at his hands the kindness of a father, in which light I eventually almost came to regard him. His younger sister, who was married to a watchmaker called Elias Playter, lived at Quebec from the time of her marriage until her death, which took place in 1846. Her husband had been unsuccessful in business, and was moreover of dissipated habits. He was left with one child – a daughter – on his hands; and as my uncle was averse to the idea of his sister's child remaining under the control of one so unfit to provide for her welfare, he proposed to adopt the little girl as his own. To this proposition Mr. Elias Playter readily assented, and little Alice was soon domiciled with her uncle and myself in Toronto.

Brought up, as we were, under the same roof, and seeing each other every day of our lives, a childish attachment sprang up between my cousin Alice and myself. As the years rolled by, this attachment ripened into a tender affection, which eventually resulted in an engagement between us. Our engagement was made with the full and cordial approval of my uncle, who did not share the prejudice entertained by many persons against marriages between cousins. He stipulated, however, that our marriage should be deferred until I had seen somewhat more of the world, and until we had both reached an age when we might reasonably be presumed to know our own minds. He was also, not unnaturally, desirous that before taking upon myself the responsibility of marriage I should give some evidence of my ability to provide for a wife, and for other contingencies usually consequent upon matrimony. He made no secret of his intention to divide his property between Alice and myself at his death; and the fact that no actual division would be necessary in the event of our marriage with each other was doubtless one reason for his ready acquiescence in our engagement. He was, however, of a vigorous constitution, strictly regular and methodical in all his habits, and likely to live to an advanced age. He could hardly be called parsimonious, but, like most men who have successfully fought their own way through life, he was rather fond of authority, and little disposed to divest himself of his wealth until he should have no further occasion for it. He expressed his willingness to establish me in business, either in Toronto or elsewhere, and to give me the benefit of his experience in all mercantile transactions.

When matters had reached this pass I had just completed my twenty-first year, my cousin being three years younger. Since my uncle's retirement I had engaged in one or two little speculations on my own account, which had turned out fairly successful, but I had not devoted myself to any regular or fixed pursuit. Before any definite arrangements had been concluded as to the course of my future life, a circumstance occurred which seemed to open a way for me to turn to good account such mercantile talent as I possessed. An old friend of my uncle's opportunely arrived in Toronto from Melbourne, Australia, where, in the course of a few years, he had risen from the position of a junior clerk to that of senior partner in a prominent commercial house. He painted the land of his adoption in glowing colours, and assured my uncle and myself that it presented an inviting field for a young man of energy and business capacity, more especially if he had a small capital at his command. The matter was carefully debated in our domestic circle. I was naturally averse to a separation from Alice, but my imagination took fire at Mr. Redpath's glowing account of his own splendid success. I pictured myself returning to Canada after an absence of four or five years with a mountain of gold at my command, as the result of my own energy and acuteness. In imagination, I saw myself settled down with Alice in a palatial mansion on Jarvis Street, and living in affluence all the rest of my days. My uncle bade me consult my own judgment in the matter, but rather encouraged the idea than otherwise. He offered to advance me £500, and I had about half that sum as the result of my own speculations. Mr. Redpath, who was just about returning to Melbourne, promised to aid me to the extent of his power with his local knowledge and advice. In less than a fortnight from that time he and I were on our way to the other side of the globe.

We reached our destination early in the month of September, 1857. My life in Australia has no direct bearing upon the course of events to be related, and may be passed over in a very few words. I engaged in various enterprises, and achieved a certain measure of success. If none of my ventures proved eminently prosperous, I at least met with no serious disasters. At the end of four years – that is to say, in September, 1861 – I made up my account with the world, and found I was worth ten thousand dollars. I had, however, become terribly homesick, and longed for the termination of my voluntary exile. I had, of course, kept up a regular correspondence with Alice and Uncle Richard, and of late they had both pressed me to return home. "You have enough," wrote my uncle, "to give you a start in Toronto, and I see no reason why Alice and you should keep apart any longer. You will have no housekeeping expenses, for I intend you to live with me. I am getting old, and shall be glad of your companionship in my declining years. You will have a comfortable home while I live and when I die you will get all I have between you. Write as soon as you receive this, and let us know how soon you can be here – the sooner the better."

The letter containing this pressing invitation found me in a mood very much disposed to accept it. The only enterprise I had on hand which would be likely to delay me was a transaction in wool, which, as I believed, would be closed by the end of January or the beginning of February. By the first of

March I should certainly be in a condition to start on my homeward voyage, and I determined that my departure should take place about that time. I wrote both to Alice and my uncle, apprising them of my intention, and announcing my expectation to reach Toronto not later than the middle of May.

The letters so written were posted on the 19th of September, in time for the mail which left on the following day. On the 27th, to my huge surprise and gratification, the wool transaction referred to was unexpectedly concluded, and I was at liberty, if so disposed, to start for home by the next fast mail steamer, the *Southern Cross,* leaving Melbourne on the 11th of October. I *was* so disposed, and made my preparations accordingly. It was useless, I reflected, to write to my uncle or to Alice, acquainting them with the change in my plans, for I should take the shortest route home, and should probably be in Toronto as soon as a letter could get there. I resolved to telegraph from New York, upon my arrival there, so as not to take them altogether by surprise.

The morning of the 11th of October found me on board the *Southern Cross,* where I shook hands with Mr. Redpath and several other friends who accompanied me on board for a last farewell. The particulars of the voyage to England are not pertinent to the story, and may be given very briefly. I took the Red Sea route, and arrived at Marseilles about two o'clock in the afternoon of the 29th of November. From Marseilles I travelled by rail to Calais, and so impatient was I to reach my journey's end without loss of time, that I did not even stay over to behold the glories of Paris. I had a commission to execute in London, which, however, delayed me there only a few hours, and I hurried down to Liverpool, in the hope of catching the Cunard Steamer for New York. I missed it by about two hours, but the *Persia* was detailed to start on a special trip to Boston on the following day. I secured a berth, and at eight o'clock the next morning steamed out of the Mersey on my way homeward.

The voyage from Liverpool to Boston consumed fourteen days. All I need say about it is, that before arriving at the latter port I formed an intimate acquaintance with one of the passengers – Mr. Junius H. Gridley, a Boston merchant, who was returning from a hurried business trip to Europe. He was – and is – a most agreeable companion. We were thrown together a good deal during the voyage, and we then laid the foundation of a friendship which has ever since subsisted between us. Before the dome of the State House loomed in sight he had extracted a promise from me to spend a night with him before pursuing my journey. We landed at the wharf in East Boston on the evening of the 17th of December, and I accompanied him to his house on West Newton Street, where I remained until the following morning. Upon consulting the time-table, we found that the Albany express would leave at 11.30 a.m. This left several hours at my disposal, and we sallied forth immediately after breakfast to visit some of the lions of the American Athens.

In the course of our peregrinations through the streets, we dropped into the post office, which had recently been established in the Merchant's Exchange

Building, on State Street. Seeing the countless piles of mail-matter, I jestingly remarked to my friend that there seemed to be letters enough there to go around the whole human family. He replied in the same mood, whereupon I banteringly suggested the probability that among so many letters, surely there ought to be one for me.

"Nothing more reasonable," he replied. "We Bostonians are always bountiful to strangers. Here is the General Delivery, and here is the department where letters addressed to the Furlong family are kept in stock. Pray inquire for yourself."

The joke I confess was not a very brilliant one; but with a grave countenance I stepped up to the wicket and asked the young lady in attendance:

"Anything for W.F. Furlong?"

She took from a pigeon-hole a handful of correspondence, and proceeded to run her eye over the addresses. When about half the pile had been exhausted she stopped, and propounded the usual inquiry in the case of strangers:

"Where do you expect letters from?"

"From Toronto," I replied.

To my no small astonishment she immediately handed me a letter, bearing the Toronto post-mark. The address was in the peculiar and well-known handwriting of my uncle Richard.

Scarcely crediting the evidence of my senses I tore open the envelope, and read as follows: –

> "TORONTO, 9th December, 1861.
> "MY DEAR WILLIAM – I am so glad to know that you are coming home so much sooner than you expected when you wrote last, and that you will eat your Christmas dinner with us. For reasons which you will learn when you arrive, it will not be a very merry Christmas at our house, but your presence will make it much more bearable than it would be without you. I have not told Alice that you are coming. Let it be a joyful surprise for her, as some compensation for the sorrows she has had to endure lately. You needn't telegraph. I will meet you at the G.W.R. station.
> "Your affectionate uncle,
> "RICHARD YARDINGTON."

"Why, what's the matter?" asked my friend, seeing the blank look of surprise on my face. "Of course the letter is not for you; why on earth did you open it?"

"It *is* for me," I answered. "See here, Gridley, old man; have you been playing me a trick? If you haven't, this is the strangest thing I ever knew in my life."

Of course he hadn't been playing me a trick. A moment's reflection showed me that such a thing was impossible. Here was the envelope, with the Toronto post-mark of the 9th of December, at which time he had been with me on board the *Persia,* on the Banks of Newfoundland. Besides, he was a gentleman, and would not have played so poor and stupid a joke upon a guest. And, to put the matter beyond all possibility of doubt, I remembered that I had never mentioned my cousin's name in his hearing.

I handed him the letter. He read it carefully through twice over, and was as much mystified at its contents as myself; for during our passage across the Atlantic I had explained to him the circumstance under which I was returning home.

By what conceivable means had my uncle been made aware of my departure from Melbourne? Had Mr. Redpath written to him as soon as I acquainted that gentleman with my intentions? But even if such were the case, the letter could not have left before I did, and could not possibly have reached Toronto by the 9th of December. Had I been seen in England by some one who knew me, and had not one written from there? Most unlikely; and even if such a thing had happened, it was impossible that the letter could have reached Toronto by the 9th. I need hardly inform the reader that there was no telegraphic communication at that time. And how could my uncle know that I would take the Boston route? And if he *had* known, how could he foresee that I would do anything so absurd as to call at the Boston post office and inquire for letters? *"I will meet you at the G.W.R. station."* How was he to know by what train I would reach Toronto, unless I notified him by telegraph? And that he expressly stated to be unnecessary.

We did no more sight-seeing. I obeyed the hint contained in the letter, and sent no telegram. My friend accompanied me down to the Boston and Albany station, where I waited in feverish impatience for the departure of the train. We talked over the matter until 11.30, in the vain hope of finding some clue to the mystery. Then I started on my journey. Mr. Gridley's curiosity was aroused and I promised to send him an explanation immediately upon my arrival at home.

No sooner had the train glided out of the station than I settled myself in my seat, drew the tantalizing letter from my pocket, and proceeded to read and re-read it again and again. A very few perusals sufficed to fix its contents in my memory, so that I could repeat every word with my eyes shut. Still I continued to scrutinize the paper, the penmanship, and even the tint of the ink. For what purpose, do you ask? For no purpose, except that I hoped, in some mysterious manner, to obtain more light on the subject. No light came, however. The more I scrutinized and pondered, the greater was my mystification. The paper was a simple sheet of white letter-paper, of the kind ordinarily used by my uncle in his correspondence. So far as I could see, there was nothing peculiar about the ink. Anyone familiar with my uncle's writing could have sworn that no hand but his had penned the lines. His well-known signature, a masterpiece of involved hieroglyphics, was there in all its indistinctness, written as no one but himself could ever have written it. And yet, for some unaccountable reason,

I was half disposed to suspect forgery. Forgery! What nonsense. Anyone clever enough to imitate Richard Yardington's handwriting would have employed his talents more profitably than indulging in a mischievous and purposeless jest. Not a bank in Toronto but would have discounted a note with that signature affixed to it.

Desisting from all attempts to solve these problems, I then tried to fathom the meaning of other points in the letter. What misfortune had happened to mar the Christmas festivities at my uncle's house? And what could the reference to my cousin Alice's sorrows mean? She was not ill. *That,* I thought, might be taken for granted. My uncle would hardly have referred to her illness as "one of the sorrows she had to endure lately." Certainly, illness may be regarded in the light of a sorrow; but "sorrow" was not precisely the word which a straightforward man like Uncle Richard would have applied to it. I could conceive of no other cause of affliction in her case. My uncle was well, as was evinced by his having written the letter, and by his avowed intention to meet me at the station. Her father had died long before I started for Australia. She had no other near relation except myself, and she had no cause for anxiety, much less for "sorrow," on my account. I thought it singular, too, that my uncle, having in some strange manner become acquainted with my movements, had withheld the knowledge from Alice. It did not square with my pre-conceived ideas of him that he would derive any satisfaction from taking his niece by surprise.

All was a muddle together, and as my temples throbbed with the intensity of my thoughts, I was half disposed to believe myself in a troubled dream from which I should presently awake. Meanwhile, on glided the train.

A heavy snow-storm delayed us for several hours, and we reached Hamilton too late for the mid-day express for Toronto. We got there, however, in time for the accommodation leaving at 3.15 p.m., and we would reach Toronto at 5.05. I walked from one end of the train to the other in hopes of finding some one I knew, from whom I could make enquiries about home. Not a soul. I saw several persons whom I knew to be residents of Toronto, but none with whom I had ever been personally acquainted, and none of them would be likely to know anything about my uncle's domestic arrangements. All that remained to be done under these circumstances was to restrain my curiosity as well as I could until reaching Toronto. By the by, would my uncle really meet me at the station, according to his promise? Surely not. By what means could he possibly know that I would arrive by this train? Still, he seemed to have such accurate information respecting my proceedings that there was no saying where his knowledge began or ended. I tried not to think about the matter, but as the train approached Toronto my impatience became positively feverish in its intensity. We were not more than three minutes behind time, as we glided in front of the Union Station, I passed out on to the platform of the car, and peered intently through the darkness. Suddenly my heart gave a great bound. There, sure enough, standing in front of the door of the waiting-room, was my uncle, plainly discernible by the fitful glare of the overhanging lamps. Before the train came to a stand-still, I sprang from the car and advanced towards him. He was looking out for me, but his eyes not being as young as mine, he did not recognize me until I grasped him by the hand. He greeted me warmly, seizing me by the waist, and almost raising me from the ground. I at once noticed several changes in his appearance; changes for which I was wholly unprepared. He had aged very much since I had last seen him, and the lines about his mouth had deepened considerably. The iron-grey hair which I remembered so well had disappeared; its place being supplied with a new and rather dandified-looking wig. The oldfashioned great-coat which he had worn ever since I could remember, had been supplanted by a modern frock of spruce cut, with seal-skin collar and cuffs. All this I noticed in the first hurried greetings that passed between us.

"Never mind your luggage, my boy," he remarked. "Leave it till tomorrow, when we will send down for it. If you are not tired we'll walk home instead of taking a cab. I have a good deal to say to you before we get there."

I had not slept since leaving Boston, but was too much excited to be conscious of fatigue, and as will readily be believed, I was anxious enough to hear what he had to say. We passed from the station, and proceeded up York Street, arm in arm.

"And now, Uncle Richard," I said, as soon as we were well clear of the crowd, "keep me no longer in suspense. First and foremost, is Alice well?"

"Quite well, but for reasons you will soon understand, she is in deep grief. You must know that – "

"But," I interrupted, "tell me, in the name of all that's wonderful, how you knew I was coming by this train; and how did you come to write to me at Boston?"

Just then we came to the corner of Front Street, where was a lamp-post. As we reached the spot where the light of the lamp was most brilliant, he turned half round, looked me full in the face, and smiled a sort of wintry smile. The expression of his countenance was almost ghastly.

"Uncle," I quickly said, "What's the matter? Are you not well?"

"I am not as strong as I used to be, and I have had a good deal to try me of late. Have patience and I will tell you all. Let us walk more slowly, or I shall not finish before we get home. In order that you may clearly understand how matters are, I had better begin at the beginning, and I hope you will not interrupt me with any questions till I have done. How I knew you would call 'at the Boston post-office, and that you would arrive in Toronto by this train, will come last in order. By the by, have you my letter with you?"

"The one you wrote to me at Boston? Yes, here it is," I replied, taking it from my pocket-book.

"Let me have it."

I handed it to him, and he put it into the breast pocket of his inside coat. I wondered at this proceeding on his part, but made no remark upon it.

We moderated our pace, and he began his narration. Of course I don't pretend to remember his exact words, but they were to this effect. During the winter following my departure to Melbourne, he had formed the acquaintance of a gentleman who had then recently settled in Toronto. The name of this gentleman was Marcus Weatherley, who had commenced business as a wholesale provision merchant immediately upon his arrival, and had been engaged in it ever since. For more than three years the acquaintance between him and my uncle had been very slight, but during the last summer they had had some real estate transactions together, and had become intimate. Weatherley, who was comparatively a young man and unmarried, had been invited to the house on Gerrard Street, where he had more recently become a pretty frequent visitor. More recently still, his visits had become so frequent that my uncle suspected him of a desire to be attentive to my cousin, and had thought proper to enlighten him as to her engagement with me. From that day his visits had been voluntarily discontinued. My uncle had not given much consideration to the subject until a fortnight afterwards, when he had accidently become aware of the fact that Weatherley was in embarrassed circumstances.

Here my uncle paused in his narrative to take breath. He then added, in a low tone, and putting his mouth almost close to my ear:

"And, Willie, my boy, I have at last found out something else. He has forty-two thousand dollars falling due here and in Montreal within the next ten days, and *he has forged my signature to acceptances for thirty-nine thousand seven hundred and sixteen dollars and twenty-four cents.*"

Those, to the best of my belief, were his exact words. We had walked up York Street to Queen, and then had gone down Queen to Yonge, when we turned up the east side on our way homeward. At the moment when the last words were uttered we had got a few yards north of Crookshank Street, immediately in front of a chemist's shop which was, I think, the third house from the corner. The window of this shop was well lighted, and its brightness was reflected on the sidewalk in front. Just then, two gentlemen walking rapidly in the opposite direction to that we were taking brushed by us; but I was too deeply absorbed in my uncle's communication to pay much attention to passers-by. Scarcely had they passed, however, ere one of them stopped and exclaimed:

"Surely that is Willie Furlong!"

I turned, and recognised Johnny Grey, one of my oldest friends. I relinquished my uncle's arm for a moment and shook hands with Grey, who said:

"I am surprised to see you. I heard only a few days ago, that you were not to be here till next spring."

"I am here," I remarked, "somewhat in advance of my own expectation." I then hurriedly enquired after several of our common friends, to which enquiries he briefly replied.

"All well," he said; "but you are in a hurry, and so am I. Don't let me detain you. Be sure and look in on me tomorrow. You will find me at the old place, in the Romain Buildings."

We again shook hands, and he passed on down the street with the gentleman who accompanied him. I then turned to re-possess myself of my uncle's arm. The old gentleman had evidently walked on, for he was not in sight. I hurried along, making sure of overtaking him before reaching Gould Street, for my interview with Grey had occupied barely a minute. In another minute I was at the corner of Gould Street. No signs of Uncle Richard. I quickened my pace to a run, which soon brought me to Gerrard Street. Still no signs of my uncle. I had certainly not passed him on my way, and he could not have got farther on his homeward route than here. He must have called in at one of the stores; a strange thing for him to do under the circumstances. I retraced my steps all the way to the front of the chemist's shop, peering into every window and doorway as I passed along. No one in the least resembling him was to be seen.

I stood still for a moment, and reflected. Even if he had run at full speed – a thing most unseemly for him to do – he could not have reached the corner of Gerrard Street before I had done so. And what should he run for? He certainly did not wish to avoid me, for he had more to tell me before reaching home. Perhaps he had turned down Gould Street. At any rate, there was no use waiting for him. I might as well go home at once. And I did.

Upon reaching the old familiar spot, I opened the gate, passed on up the steps to the front door, and rang the bell. The door was opened by a domestic who had not formed part of the establishment in my time, and who did not know me; but Alice happened to be passing through the hall and heard my voice as I inquired for Uncle Richard. Another moment and she was in my arms. With a strange foreboding at my heart I noticed that she was in deep mourning. We passed into the dining-room, where the table was laid for dinner.

"Has Uncle Richard come in?" I asked, as soon as we were alone. "Why did he run away from me?"

"Who?" exclaimed Alice, with a start; "what do you mean, Willie? Is it possible you have not heard?"

"Heard what?"

"I see you have *not* heard," she replied. "Sit down, Willie, and prepare yourself for painful news. But first tell me what you meant by saying what you did just now, – who was it that ran away from you?"

"Well, perhaps I should hardly call it running away, but he certainly disappeared most mysteriously, down here near the corner of Yonge and Crookshank Streets."

"Of whom are you speaking?"

"Of Uncle Richard, of course."

"Uncle Richard! The corner of Yonge and Crookshank Streets! When did you see him there?"

"When? A quarter of an hour ago. He met me at the station and we walked up together till I met Johnny Grey. I turned to speak to Johnny for a moment, when –"

"Willie, what on earth are you talking about? You are labouring under some strange delusion. *Uncle Richard died of apoplexy more than six weeks ago, and lies buried in St. James's Cemetery.*"

II

I don't know how long I sat there, trying to think, with my face buried in my hands. My mind had been kept on a strain during the last thirty hours, and the succession of surprises to which I had been subjected had temporarily paralyzed my faculties. For a few moments after Alice's announcement I must have been in a sort of stupor. My imagination, I remember, ran riot about everything in general, and nothing in particular. My cousin's momentary impression was that I had met with an accident of some kind, which had unhinged my brain. The first distinct remembrance I have after this is, that I suddenly awoke from my stupor to find Alice kneeling at my feet, and holding me by the hand. Then my mental powers came back to me, and I recalled all the incidents of the evening.

"When did uncle's death take place?" I asked.

"On the 3rd of November, about four o'clock in the afternoon. It was quite unexpected, though he had not enjoyed his usual health for some weeks before. He fell down in the hall, just as he was returning from a walk, and died within two hours. He never spoke or recognised any one after his seizure."

"What has become of his old overcoat?" I asked.

"His old overcoat, Willie – what a question," replied Alice, evidently thinking that I was again drifting back into insensibility.

"Did he continue to wear it up to the day of his death?" I asked.

"No. Cold weather set in very early this last fall, and he was compelled to don his winter clothing earlier than usual. He had a new overcoat made within a fortnight before he died. He had it on at the time of his seizure. But why do you ask?"

"Was the new coat cut by a fashionable tailor, and had it a fur collar and cuffs?"

"It was cut at Stovel's, I think. It had a fur collar and cuffs."

"When did he begin to wear a wig?"

"About the same time that he began to wear his new overcoat. I wrote you a letter at the time, making merry over his youthful appearance and hinting – of course only in jest – that he was looking out for a young wife. But you surely did not receive my letter. You must have been on your way home before it was written."

"I left Melbourne on the 11th of October. The wig, I suppose, was buried with him?"

"Yes."

"And where is the overcoat?"

"In the wardrobe upstairs, in uncle's room."

"Come and show it to me."

I led the way upstairs, my cousin following. In the hall on the first floor we encountered my old friend Mrs. Daly, the housekeeper. She threw up her hands in surprise at seeing me. Our greeting was brief; I was too intent on solving the problem which had exercised my mind ever since receiving the letter at Boston, to pay much attention to anything else. Two words, however, explained to her where we were going, and at our request she accompanied us. We passed into my uncle's room. My cousin drew the key of the wardrobe from a drawer where it was kept, and unlocked the door. There hung the overcoat. A single glance was sufficient. It was the same.

The dazed sensation in my head began to make itself felt again. The atmosphere of the room seemed to oppress me, and closing the door of the wardrobe, I led the way down stairs again to the dining-room, followed by my cousin. Mrs. Daly had sense enough to perceive that we were discussing family matters, and retired to her own room.

I took my cousin's hand in mine, and asked:

"Will you tell me what you know of Mr. Marcus Weatherley?"

This was evidently another surprise for her. How could I have heard of Marcus Weatherley? She answered, however, without hesitation:

"I know very little of him. Uncle Richard and he had some dealings a few months since, and in that way he became a visitor here. After a while he began to call pretty often, but his visits suddenly ceased a short time before uncle's death. I need not affect any reserve with you. Uncle Richard thought he came after me, and gave him a hint that you had a prior claim. He never called afterwards. I am rather glad that he didn't, for there is something about him that I don't quite like. I am at a loss to say what the something is; but his manner always impressed me with the idea that he was not exactly what he seemed to be on the surface. Perhaps I misjudged him. Indeed, I think I must have done so, for he stands well with everybody, and is highly respected."

I looked at the clock on the mantel piece. It was ten minutes to seven. I rose from my seat.

"I will ask you to excuse me for an hour or two, Alice. I must find Johnny Grey."

"But you will not leave me, Willie, until you have given me some clue to your unexpected arrival, and to the strange questions you have been asking? Dinner is ready, and can be served at once. Pray don't go out again till you have dined."

She clung to my arm. It was evident that she considered me mad, and thought it probable that I might make away with myself. This I could not bear. As for eating any dinner, that was simply impossible in my then frame of mind, although I had not tasted food since leaving Rochester. I resolved to tell her all. I resumed my seat. She placed herself on a stool at my feet, and listened while I told her all that I have set down as happening to me subsequently to my last letter to her from Melbourne.

"And now, Alice, you know why I wish to see Johnny Grey."

She would have accompanied me, but I thought it better to prosecute my inquiries alone. I promised to return some time during the night, and tell her the result of my interview with Grey. That gentleman had married and become a householder on his own account during my absence in Australia. Alice knew his address, and gave me the number of his house, which was on Church Street. A few minutes' rapid walking brought me to his door. I had no great expectation of finding him at home, as I deemed it probable he had not returned from wherever he had been going when I met him; but I should be able to find out when he was expected, and would either wait or go in search of him. Fortune favored me for once, however; he had returned more than an hour before. I was ushered into the drawing-room, where I found him playing cribbage with his wife.

"Why, Willie," he exclaimed, advancing to welcome me, "this is kinder than I expected. I hardly looked for you before tomorrow. All the better; we have just been speaking of you. Ellen, this is my old friend, Willie Furlong, the returned convict, whose banishment you have so often heard me deplore."

After exchanging brief courtesies with Mrs. Grey, I turned to her husband.

"Johnny, did you notice anything remarkable about the old gentleman who was with me when we met on Yonge Street this evening?"

"Old gentleman? Who? There was no one with you when I met you."

"Think again. He and I were walking arm in arm, and you had passed us before you recognized me, and mentioned my name."

He looked hard in my face for a moment, and then said positively:

"You are wrong, Willie. You were certainly alone when we met. You were walking slowly, and I must have noticed if any one had been with you."

"It is you who are wrong," I retorted, almost sternly. "I was accompanied by an elderly gentleman, who wore a great coat with fur collar and cuffs, and we were conversing earnestly together when you passed us."

He hesitated an instant, and seemed to consider, but there was no shade of doubt on his face.

"Have it your own way, old boy," he said. "All I can say is, that I saw no one but yourself, and neither did Charley Leitch, who was with me. After parting from you we commented upon your evident abstraction, and the sombre expression of your countenance, which we attributed to your having only recently heard of the sudden death of your Uncle Richard. If any old gentleman had been with you we could not possibly have failed to notice him."

Without a single word by way of explanation or apology, I jumped from my seat, passed out into the hall, seized my hat, and left the house.

III

Out into the street I rushed like a madman, banging the door after me. I knew that Johnny would follow me for an explanation so I ran like lightning round the next corner, and thence down to Yonge Street. Then I dropped into a walk, regained my breath, and asked myself what I should do next.

Suddenly I bethought me of Dr. Marsden, an old friend of my uncle's. I hailed a passing cab, and drove to his house. The doctor was in his consultation-room, and alone.

Of course he was surprised to see me, and gave expression to some appropriate words of sympathy at my bereavement. "But how is it that I see you so soon?" he asked – "I understood that you were not expected for some months to come."

Then I began my story, which I related with great circumstantiality of detail, bringing it down to the moment of my arrival at his house. He listened with the closest attention, never interrupting me by a single exclamation until I had finished. Then he began to ask questions, some of which I thought strangely irrelevant.

"Have you enjoyed your usual good health during your residence abroad?"

"Never better in my life. I have not had a moment's illness since you last saw me."

"And how have you prospered in your business enterprises?"

"Reasonably well; but pray doctor, let us confine ourselves to the matter in hand. I have come for friendly, not professional, advice."

"All in good time, my boy," he calmly remarked. This was tantalizing. My strange narrative did not seem to have disturbed his serenity in the least degree.

"Did you have a pleasant passage?" he asked, after a brief pause. "The ocean, I believe, is generally rough at this time of year."

"I felt a little squeamish for a day or two after leaving Melbourne," I replied, "but I soon got over it, and it was not very bad even while it lasted. I am a tolerably good sailor."

"And you have had no special ground of anxiety of late? At least not until you received this wonderful letter" – he added, with a perceptible contraction of his lips, as though trying to repress a smile.

Then I saw what he was driving at.

"Doctor," I exclaimed, with some exasperation in my tone – "pray dismiss from your mind the idea that what I have told you is the result of diseased imagination. I am as sane as you are. The letter itself affords sufficient evidence that I am not quite such a fool as you take me for."

"My dear boy, I don't take you for a fool at all, although you are a little excited just at present. But I thought you said you returned the letter to – ahem – your uncle."

For a moment I had forgotten that important fact. But I was not altogether without evidence that I had not been the victim of a disordered brain. My friend Gridley could corroborate the receipt of the letter and its contents. My cousin could bear witness that I had displayed an acquaintance with facts which I would not have been likely to learn from any one but my uncle. I had referred to his wig and overcoat, and had mentioned to her the name of Mr. Marcus Weatherley – a name which I had never heard before in my life. I called Dr. Marsden's attention to these matters, and asked him to explain them if he could.

"I admit," said the doctor, "that I don't quite see my way to a satisfactory explanation just at present. But let us look the matter squarely in the face. During an acquaintance of nearly thirty years, I always found your uncle a truthful man, who was cautious enough to make no statements about his neighbours that he was not able to prove. Your informant, on the other hand, does not seem to have confined himself to facts. He made a charge of forgery against a gentleman whose moral and commercial integrity are unquestioned by all who know him. I know Marcus Weatherley pretty well, and am not disposed to pronounce him a forger and a scoundrel upon the unsupported evidence of a shadowy old gentleman who appears and disappears in the most mysterious manner, and who cannot be laid hold of and held responsible for his slanders in a court of law. And it is not true, as far as I know and believe, that Marcus Weatherley is embarrassed in his circumstances. Such confidence have I in his solvency and integrity that I would not be afraid to take up all his outstanding paper without asking a question. If you will make inquiry, you will find that my opinion is shared by all the bankers in the city. And I have no hesitation in saying that you will find no acceptances with your uncle's name to them, either in this market or elsewhere."

"That I will try to ascertain tomorrow," I replied. "Meanwhile, Dr. Marsden, will you oblige your old friend's nephew by writing to Mr. Junius Gridley, and asking him to acquaint you with the contents of the letter, and the circumstances under which I received it?"

"It seems an absurd thing to do," he said, "but I will if you like. What shall I say?" and he sat down at his desk to write the letter.

It was written in less than five minutes. It simply asked for the desired information, and requested an immediate reply. Below the doctor's signature I added a short postscript in these words: –

"My story about the letter and its contents is discredited. Pray answer fully, and at once. – W.F.F."

At my request the doctor accompanied me to the post office, on Toronto Street, and dropped the letter into the box with his own hands. I bade him good night, and repaired to the Rossin House. I did not feel like encountering Alice again until I could place myself in a more satisfactory light before her. I dispatched a messenger to her with a short note stating that I had not discovered anything important, and requesting her not to wait up for me. Then I engaged a room and went to bed.

But not to sleep. All night long I tossed about from one side of the bed to the other; and at daylight, feverish and unrefreshed, I strolled out. I returned in time for breakfast, but ate little or nothing. I longed for the arrival of ten o'clock, when the banks would open.

After breakfast I sat down in the reading-room of the hotel, and vainly tried to fix my attention upon the local columns of the morning's paper. I remember reading over several items time after time, without any comprehension of their meaning. After that I remember – nothing.

Nothing? All was blank for more than five weeks. When consciousness came back to me I found myself in bed in my own old room, in the house on Gerrard Street, and Alice and Dr. Marsden were standing by my bedside.

No need to tell how my hair had been removed, nor about the bags of ice that had been applied to my head. No need to linger over any details of the "pitiless fever that burned in my brain." No need, either, to linger over my progress back to convalescence, and thence to complete recovery. In a week from the time I have mentioned, I was permitted to sit up in bed, propped up by a mountain of pillows. My impatience would brook no further delay, and I was allowed to ask questions about what had happened in the interval which had elapsed since my over-wrought nerves gave way under the prolonged strain upon them. First, Junius Gridley's letter in reply to Dr. Marsden was placed in my hands. I have it still in my possession, and I transcribe the following copy from the original now lying before me: –

BOSTON, Dec. 22nd, 1861.
DR. MARSDEN:

"In reply to your letter, which has just been received, I have to say that Mr. Furlong and myself became acquainted for the first time during our recent passage from Liverpool to Boston, in the *Persia,* which arrived here Monday last. Mr. Furlong accompanied me home, and remained until Tuesday morning, when I took him to see the Public Library, the State House, the Athenaeum, Faneuil Hall, and other points of interest. We casually dropped into the post-office, and he remarked upon the great number of letters there. At my instigation – made, of course, in jest – he applied at the General Delivery for letters for himself. He received one bearing the Toronto post-mark. He was naturally very much surprised at receiving it, and was not less so at its contents. After reading it he handed it to me, and I also read it carefully. I cannot recollect it word for word, but it professed to come from his affectionate uncle, Richard Yardington. It expressed pleasure at his coming home sooner than had been anticipated, and hinted in rather vague terms at some calamity. He referred to a lady called Alice, and stated that she had not been informed of Mr. Furlong's intended arrival. There was something too, about his presence at home being a recompense to her for recent grief which she had sustained. It also expressed the writer's intention to meet his nephew at the Toronto railway station upon his arrival, and stated that no telegram need be sent. This, as nearly as I can remember, was about all there was in the letter. Mr. Furlong professed to recognise the handwriting as his uncle's. It was a cramped hand, not easy to read, and the signature was so peculiarly formed that I was hardly able to decipher it. The peculiarly consisted of the extreme irregularity in the formation of the letters, no two of which were of equal size; and capitals were interspersed promiscuously, more especially throughout the surname.

"Mr. Furlong was much agitated by the contents of the letter, and was anxious for the arrival of the time of his departure. He left by the B. & A. train at 11.30. This is really all I know about the matter, and I have been anxiously expecting to hear from him ever since he left. I confess that I feel curious, and should be glad to hear from him – that is, of course, unless something is involved which it would be impertinent for a comparative stranger to pry into.

Yours, &c.,

"JUNIUS H. GRIDLEY."

So that my friend has completely corroborated my account, so far as the letter was concerned. My account, however, stood in no need of corroboration, as will presently appear.

When I was stricken down, Alice and Dr. Marsden were the only persons to whom I had communicated what my uncle had said to me during our walk from the station. They both maintained silence in the matter, except to each other. Between themselves, in the early days of my illness, they discussed it with a good deal of feeling on each side. Alice implicitly believed my story from first to last. She was wise enough to see that I had been made acquainted with matters that I could not possibly have learned through any ordinary channels of communication. In short, she was not so enamoured of professional jargon as to have lost her common sense. The doctor, however, with the mole-blindness of many of his tribe, refused to believe. Nothing of this kind had previously come within the range of his own experience, and it was therefore impossible. He accounted for it all upon the hypothesis of my impending fever. He is not the only physician who mistakes cause for effect, and *vice versa*.

During the second week of my prostration, Mr. Marcus Weatherley absconded. This event so totally unlooked for by those who had had dealings with him, at once brought his financial condition to light. It was found that he had been really insolvent for several months past. The day after his departure a number of his acceptances became due. These acceptances proved to be four in number, amounting to exactly forty-two thousand dollars. So that that part of my uncle's story was confirmed. One of the acceptances was payable in Montreal, and was for $2,283.76. The other three were payable at different banks in Toronto. These last had been drawn at sixty days, and each of them bore a signature presumed to be that of Richard Yardington. One of them was for $8,972.11; another was for $10,114.63; and the third and last was for $20,629.50. A short sum in simple addition will show us the aggregate of these three amounts –

$$\begin{array}{r} \$8,972\ 11 \\ 10,114\ 63 \\ 20,629\ 50 \\ \hline \$39,716\ 24 \end{array}$$

which was the amount for which my uncle claimed that his name had been forged.

Within a week after these things came to light a letter addressed to the manager of one of the leading banking institutions of Toronto arrived from Mr. Marcus Weatherley. He wrote from New York, but stated that he should leave there within an hour from the time of posting his letter. He voluntarily admitted having forged the name of my uncle to three of the acceptances above referred to and entered into other details about his affairs, which, though interesting enough to his creditors at that time, would have no special interest to the public at the present day. The banks where the acceptances had been discounted were wise after the fact, and detected numerous little details wherein the forged signatures differed from the genuine signatures of my Uncle Richard. In each case they pocketed the loss and held their tongues, and I dare say they will not thank me for calling attention to the matter, even at this distance of time.

There is not much more to tell. Marcus Weatherley, the forger, met his fate within a few days after writing his letter from New York. He took passage at New Bedford, Massachusetts, in a sailing vessel called the *Petrel* bound for Havana. The *Petrel* sailed from port on the 12th of January, 1862, and went down in mid-ocean with all hands on the 23rd of the same month. She sank in full sight of the captain and crew of the *City of Baltimore* (Inman Line), but the hurricane prevailing was such that the latter were unable to render any assistance, or to save one of the ill-fated crew from the fury of the waves.

At an early stage in the story I mentioned that the only fictitious element should be the name of one of the characters introduced. The name is that of

Marcus Weatherley himself. The person whom I have so designated really bore a different name – one that is still remembered by scores of people in Toronto. He has paid the penalty of his misdeeds, and I see nothing to be gained by perpetuating them in connection with his own proper name. In all other particulars the foregoing narrative is as true as a tolerably retentive memory has enabled me to record it.

I don't propose to attempt any psychological explanation of the events here recorded, for the very sufficient reason that only one explanation is possible. The weird letter and its contents, as has been seen, do not rest upon my testimony alone. With respect to my walk from the station with Uncle Richard, and the communication made by him to me, all the details are as real to my mind as any other incidents of my life. The only obvious deduction is, that I was made the recipient of a communication of the kind which the world is accustomed to regard as supernatural.

Mr. Owen's publishers have my full permission to appropriate this story in the next edition of his "Debatable Land between this World and the Next." Should they do so, their readers will doubtless be favoured with an elaborate analysis of the facts, and with a pseudo-philosophic theory about spiritual communion with human beings. My wife, who is an enthusiastic student of electro-biology, is disposed to believe that Weatherley's mind, overweighted by the knowledge of his forgery, was in some occult manner, and unconsciously to himself, constrained to act upon my own senses. I prefer, however, simply to narrate the facts. I may or may not have my own theory about those facts. The reader is at perfect liberty to form one of his own if he so pleases. I may mention that Dr. Marsden professes to believe to the present day that my mind was disordered by the approach of the fever which eventually struck me down, and that all I have described was merely the result of what he, with delightful periphrasis, calls "an abnormal condition of the system, induced by causes too remote for specific diagnosis."

It will be observed that, whether I was under an hallucination or not, the information supposed to be derived from my uncle was strictly accurate in all its details. The fact that the disclosure subsequently became unnecessary through the confession of Weatherley does not seem to me to afford any argument for the hallucination theory. My uncle's communication was important at the time when it was given to me; and we have no reason for believing that "those who are gone before" are universally gifted with a knowledge of the future.

It was open to me to make the facts public as soon as they became known to me, and had I done so, Marcus Weatherley might have been arrested and punished for his crime. Had not my illness supervened, I think I should have made discoveries in the course of the day following my arrival in Toronto which would have led to his arrest.

Such speculations are profitless enough, but they have often formed the topic of discussion between my wife and myself. Gridley, too, whenever he pays us a visit, invariably revives the subject, which he long ago christened "The Gerrard Street Mystery," or, "The Mystery of the Union Station." He has urged me a hundred times over to publish the story; and now, after all these years, I follow his counsel, and adopt his nomenclature in the title.

BIBLIOGRAPHY - JOHN CHARLES DENT

Criminous works

The Gerrard Street mystery; and other weird tales. Toronto: Rose, 1888. Set: Toronto.

Other works

Arcturus; a Canadian journal of literature and life. Toronto: 1887. Vol. 1 (1 January-25 June 1887).
The Canadian portrait gallery, 4 vols. Toronto: Magurn, 1880-1881.
The last forty years; Canada since the union of 1841, 2 vols. Toronto: Geo. Virtue, 1881.
The story of the Upper Canadian Rebellion. Toronto: Robinson, 1885.
Toronto; past and present: historical and descriptive – a memorial volume for the semi-centennial of 1884. By the Rev. Henry Scadding and John Charles Dent. Toronto: Hunter Rose, 1884.

GRANT ALLEN

The Episode of the Mexican Seer

An African millionaire; episodes in the life of the illustrious Colonel Clay.
New York: Richards/London: Arnold, 1897.

ALLEN, (Charles) Grant (Blairfindie), 1848-1899

An author, philosopher, and scientist, who also wrote non-criminous works under the pseudonyms Cecil Power and J. Arbuthnot Wilson, Grant Allen was born in 1848 near Kingston, Ontario, at his family home "Alwington House," on Wolfe Island. He was the second son of Joseph Antisell Allen, a minister of the Church of Ireland, the first minister on Wolfe Island and himself the author of two books of poetry, and Catharine Ann (Grant) Allen, only daughter of Charles William Grant, 5th Baron de Longueuil. The family was described by historian Francis Parkman as "the most truly eminent in Canada."

Allen was educated privately in Kingston, then at Edwards' School in Birmingham, England and Merton College, Oxford, where he graduated in 1871. He married while still attending school and had to work while studying because his wife was an invalid. In 1873 he was appointed Professor of Mental and Moral Philosophy at a new university for negroes in Spanish Town, Jamaica. When the college closed three years later because of lack of students, Allen returned to England to pursue a writing career. But success eluded him. His several scientific and philosophical books on evolution and the physiology of aesthetics gave him a reputation for scholarship, but little money.

In 1880, he turned to writing the magazine fiction that brought him a large readership. He assiduously published about thirty non-fiction works and forty novels, sometimes as many as four titles a year. His two most important works were literary breakthroughs. The first, *The woman who did*, (1895), created a sensation in late Victorian England and brought Allen notoriety because of its candid and much-imitated discussion of sex, as implied in the title. The other, *An African millionaire*, guarantees Allen a lasting place in the annals of detective fiction.

Although Allen lived his adult life in England and never set any of his novels in his native Canada, he is the first Canadian to seriously essay criminous literature professionally, and he made a significant contribution to the genre.

Always himself in poor health, Allen died at the age of 51, leaving behind an uncompleted novel, *Hilda Wade*. It was completed by Sir Arthur Conan Doyle, who was a neighbour, and published posthumously in 1900. Sir Arthur did not do his late friend a favour; the book was not worth finishing.

THE EPISODE OF THE MEXICAN SEER
An African millionaire; episodes in the life of the illustrious Colonel Clay. New York: Richards/London: Arnold, 1897.

An African millionaire is a collection of stories about Colonel Clay, the first important rogue in crime fiction who is the hero, rather than a subsidiary character, villain, or antihero. The Colonel precedes A. J. Raffles by two years. The eponymous millionaire of the title is Sir Charles Vandrift, who is repeatedly cheated, duped, tricked, fooled, and robbed by Clay, a consummate actor and master of disguise.

In the opinion of Ellery Queen, this Adam of yeggmen – the first great thief on the criminaliterary scene – has been shamefully neglected.* Clay falls into the class of Master Criminals – "Napoleons of Crime." The exemplar is, of course, Professor Moriarty, but in reality the class goes back into the Newgate novels and their successor "penny dreadfuls and shilling shockers" where can be found such exquisite villains as "Sweeney Todd the Barber" and Dick Turpin. Clay is a species of the larger genus of "Masters of the World" and in this capacity adumbrates Carl Peterson who caused so much trouble to "Sapper's" Bull-dog Drummond.

In "The episode of the Mexican seer" we meet for the first time the notorious Colonel Clay and the unfortunate Sir Charles Vandrift, who does so much, albeit unintentionally, to keep the Colonel in the style in which he is accustomed.

---

* Ellery Queen. *Queen's Quorum; a history of the detective-crime short story as revealed in the 106 most important books published in this field since 1845.* [With] Supplements through 1967. New York: Biblo and Tannen, 1969.

THE EPISODE OF
THE MEXICAN SEER

My name is Seymour Wilbraham Wentworth. I am brother-in-law and secretary to Sir Charles Vandrift, the South African millionaire and famous financier. Many years ago, when Charlie Vandrift was a small lawyer in Cape Town, I had the (qualified) good fortune to marry his sister. Much later, when the Vandrift estate and farm near Kimberley developed by degrees into the Cloetedorp Golcondas, Limited, my brother-in-law offered me the not unremunerative post of secretary; in which capacity I have ever since been his constant and attached companion.

He is not a man whom any common sharper can take in, is Charles Vandrift. Middle height, square build, firm mouth, keen eyes – the very picture of a sharp and successful business genius. I have only known one rogue impose upon Sir Charles, and that one rogue, as the Commissary of Police at Nice remarked, would doubtless have imposed upon a syndicate of Vidocq, Robert Houdin, and Cagliostro.

We had run across to the Riviera for a few weeks in the season. Our object being strictly rest and recreation from the arduous duties of financial combination, we did not think it necessary to take our wives out with us. Indeed, Lady Vandrift is absolutely wedded to the joys of London, and does not appreciate the rural delights of the Mediterranean littoral. But Sir Charles and I, though immersed in affairs when at home, both thoroughly enjoy the complete change from the City to the charming vegetation and pellucid air on the terrace at Monte Carlo. We *are* so fond of scenery. That delicious view over the rocks of Monaco, with the Maritime Alps in the rear, and the blue sea in front, not to mention the imposing Casino in the foreground, appeals to me as one of the most beautiful prospects in all Europe. Sir Charles has a sentimental attachment for the place. He finds it restores and freshens him, after the turmoil of London, to win a few hundreds at roulette in the course of an afternoon among the palms and cactuses and pure breezes of Monte Carlo. The country, say I, for a jaded intellect! However, we never on any account actually stop in the Principality itself. Sir Charles thinks Monte Carlo is not a sound address for a financier's letters. He prefers a comfortable hotel on the Promenade des Anglais at Nice, where he recovers health and renovates his nervous system by taking daily excursions along the coast to the Casino.

This particular season we were snugly ensconced at the Hôtel des Anglais. We had capital quarters on the first floor – salon, study, and bedrooms – and found on the spot a most agreeable cosmopolitan society. All Nice, just then, was ringing with talk about a curious imposter, known to his followers as the Great

Mexican Seer, and supposed to be gifted with supernatural powers. Now, it is a peculiarity of my able brother-in-law's that, when he meets with a quack, he burns to expose him; he is so keen a man of business himself that it gives him, so to speak, a disinterested pleasure to unmask and detect imposture in others. Many ladies at the hotel, some of whom had met and conversed with the Mexican Seer, were constantly telling us strange stories of his doings. He had disclosed to one the present whereabouts of a runaway husband; he had pointed out to another the numbers that would win at roulette next evening; he had shown a third the image on a screen of the man she had for years adored without his knowledge. Of course, Sir Charles didn't believe a word of it; but his curiosity was roused; he wished to see and judge for himself of the wonderful thought-reader.

"What would be his terms, do you think, for a private *séance?*" he asked of Madame Picardet, the lady to whom the Seer had successfully predicted the winning numbers.

"He does not work for money," Madame Picardet answered, "but for the good of humanity. I'm sure he would gladly come and exhibit for nothing his miraculous faculties."

"Nonsense!" Sir Charles answered. "The man must live. I'd pay him five guineas, though, to see him alone. What hotel is he stopping at?"

"The Cosmopolitan, I think," the lady answered. "Oh no; I remember now, the Westminster."

Sir Charles turned to me quietly. "Look here, Seymour," he whispered. "Go round to this fellow's place immediately after dinner, and offer him five pounds to give a private *séance* at once in my rooms, without mentioning who I am to him; keep the name quite quiet. Bring him back with you, too, and come straight upstairs with him, so that there may be no collusion. We'll see just how much the fellow can tell us."

I went as directed. I found the Seer a very remarkable and interesting person. He stood about Sir Charles's own height, but was slimmer and straighter, with an aquiline nose, strangely piercing eyes, very large black pupils, and a finely-chiselled close-shaven face, like the bust of Antinous in our hall in Mayfair. What gave him his most characteristic touch, however, was his odd head of hair, curly and wavy like Paderewski's, standing out in a halo round his high white forehead and his delicate profile. I could see at a glance why he succeeded so well in impressing women; he had the look of a poet, a singer, a prophet.

"I have come round," I said, "to ask whether you will consent to give a *séance* at once in a friend's rooms; and my principal wishes me to add that he is prepared to pay five pounds as the price of the entertainment."

Señor Antonio Herrera — that was what he called himself — bowed to me with impressive Spanish politeness. His dusky olive cheeks were wrinkled with a smile of gentle contempt as he answered gravely —

"I do not sell my gifts; I bestow them freely. If your friend – your anonymous friend – desires to behold the cosmic wonders that are wrought through my hands, I am glad to show them to him. Fortunately, as often happens when it is necessary to convince and confound a sceptic (for that your friend is a sceptic I feel instinctively), I chance to have no engagements at all this evening." He ran his hand through his fine, long hair reflectively. "Yes, I go," he continued, as if addressing some unknown presence that hovered about the ceiling; "I go; come with me!" Then he put on his broad sombrero, with its crimson ribbon, wrapped a cloak round his shoulders, lighted a cigarette, and strode forth by my side towards the Hôtel des Anglais.

He talked little by the way, and that little in curt sentences. He seemed buried in deep thought; indeed, when we reached the door and I turned in, he walked a step or two farther on, as if not noticing to what place I had brought him. Then he drew himself up short, and gazed around him for a moment. "Ha, the Anglais," he said – and I may mention in passing that his English, in spite of a slight southern accent, was idiomatic and excellent. "It is here, then; it is here!" He was addressing once more the unseen presence.

I smiled to think that these childish devices were intended to deceive Sir Charles Vandrift. Not quite the sort of man (as the City of London knows) to be taken in by hocus-pocus. And all this, I saw, was the cheapest and most commonplace conjurer's patter.

We went upstairs to our rooms. Charles had gathered together a few friends to watch the performance. The Seer entered, wrapt in thought. He was in evening dress, but a red sash round his waist gave a touch of picturesqueness and a dash of colour. He paused for a moment in the middle of the salon, without letting his eyes rest on anybody or anything. Then he walked straight up to Charles, and held out his dark hand.

"Good-evening," he said. "You are the host. My soul's sight tells me so."

"Good shot," Sir Charles answered. "These fellows have to be quick-witted, you know, Mrs. Mackenzie, or they'd never get on at it."

The Seer gazed about him and smiled blankly at a person or two whose faces he seemed to recognise from a previous existence. Then Charles began to ask him a few simple questions, not about himself, but about me, just to test him. He answered most of them with surprising correctness. "His name? His name begins with an S I think: – You call him Seymour." He paused long between each clause, as if the facts were revealed to him slowly. "Seymour – Wilbraham – Earl of Strafford. No, not Earl of Strafford! Seymour Wilbraham Wentworth. There seems to be some connection in somebody's mind now present between Wentworth and Strafford. I am not English. I do not know what it means. But they are somehow the same name, Wentworth and Strafford."

He gazed around, apparently for confirmation. A lady came to his rescue.

"Wentworth was the surname of the great Earl of Strafford," she murmured gently; " and I was wondering, as you spoke, whether Mr. Wentworth might possibly be descended from him."

"He is," the Seer replied instantly, with a flash of those dark eyes. And I thought this curious; for though my father always maintained the reality of the relationship, there was one link wanting to complete the pedigree. He could not make sure that the Hon. Thomas Wilbraham Wentworth was the father of Jonathan Wentworth, the Bristol horse-dealer, from whom we are descended.

"Where was I born?" Sir Charles interrupted, coming suddenly to his own case.

The Seer clapped his two hands to his forehead and held it between them, as if to prevent it from bursting. "Africa," he said slowly, as the facts narrowed down, so to speak. "South Africa; Cape of Good Hope; Jansenville; De Witt Street. 1840."

"By Jove, he's correct," Sir Charles muttered. "He seems really to do it. Still he may have found me out. He may have known where he was coming."

"I never gave a hint," I answered; "till he reached the door, he didn't even know to what hotel I was piloting him."

The Seer stroked his chin softly. His eye appeared to me to have a furtive gleam in it. "Would you like me to tell you the number of a bank-note inclosed in an envelope?" he asked casually.

"Go out of the room," Sir Charles said, "while I pass it round the company."

Señor Herrera disappeared. Sir Charles passed it round cautiously, holding it all the time in his own hand, but letting his guests see the number. Then he placed it in an envelope and gummed it down firmly.

The Seer returned. His keen eyes swept the company with a comprehensive glance. He shook his shaggy mane. Then he took the envelope in his hands and gazed at it fixedly. "AF, 73549," he answered, in a slow tone. "A Bank of England note for fifty pounds – exchanged at the Casino for gold won yesterday at Monte Carlo."

"I see how he did that," Sir Charles said triumphantly. "He must have changed it there himself; and then I changed it back again. In point of fact, I remember seeing a fellow with long hair loafing about. Still, it's capital conjuring."

"He can see through matter," one of the ladies interposed. It was Madame Picardet. "He can see through a box." She drew a little gold vinaigrette, such as our grandmothers used, from her dress-pocket. "What is in this?" she inquired, holding it up to him.

Señor Herrera gazed through it. "Three gold coins," he replied, knitting his brows with the effort of seeing into the box: "one, an American five dollars; one a French ten-franc piece; one, twenty marks, German, of the old Emperor William."

She opened the box and passed it round. Sir Charles smiled a quiet smile.

"Confederacy!" he muttered, half to himself. "Confederacy!"

The Seer turned to him with a sullen air. "You want a better sign?" he said, in a very impressive voice. "A sign that will convince you! Very well: you have a letter in your left waistcoat pocket – a crumpled-up letter. Do you wish me to read it out? I will, if you desire it."

It may seem to those who know Sir Charles incredible, but, I am bound to admit, my brother-in-law coloured. What that letter contained I cannot say; he only answered, very testily and evasively, "No, thank you; I won't trouble you. The exhibition you have already given us of your skill in this kind more than amply suffices." And his fingers strayed nervously to his waistcoat pocket, as if he was half afraid, even then, Señor Herrera would read it.

I fancied, too, he glanced somewhat anxiously towards Madame Picardet.

The Seer bowed courteously. "Your will, señor, is law," he said. "I make it a principle, though I can see through all things, invariably to respect the secrecies and sanctities. If it were not so, I might dissolve society. For which of us is there who could bear the whole truth being told about him?" He gazed around the room. An unpleasant thrill supervened. Most of us felt this uncanny Spanish American knew really too much. And some of us were engaged in financial operations.

"For example," the Seer continued blandly, "I happened a few weeks ago to travel down here from Paris by train with a very intelligent man, a company promoter. He had in his bag some documents – some confidential documents:" he glanced at Sir Charles. "You know the kind of thing, my dear sir: reports from experts – from mining engineers. You may have seen some such; marked *strictly private.*"

"They form an element in high finance," Sir Charles admitted coldly.

"Pre-cisely," the Seer murmured, his accent for a moment less Spanish than before. "And, as they were marked *strictly private*, I respect, of course, the seal of confidence. That's all I wish to say. I hold it a duty, being intrusted with such powers, not to use them in a manner which may annoy or incommode my fellow-creatures."

"Your feeling does you honour," Sir Charles answered, with some acerbity. Then he whispered in my ear: "Confounded clever scoundrel, Sey; rather wish we hadn't brought him here."

Señor Herrera seemed intuitively to divine this wish, for he interposed, in a lighter and gayer tone –

"I will now show you a different and more interesting embodiment of occult power, for which we shall need a somewhat subdued arrangement of surrounding lights. Would you mind, señor host – for I have purposely abstained from reading your name on the brain of any one present – would you mind my turning down this lamp just a little? ... So! That will do. Now, this one; and this one. Exactly! that's right." He poured a few grains of powder out of a packet into a saucer. "Next, a match, if you please. Thank you!" It burnt with a strange green light. He drew from his pocket a card, and produced a little ink-bottle.

"Have you a pen?" he asked.

I instantly brought one. He handed it to Sir Charles. "Oblige me," he said, "by writing your name there." And he indicated a place in the centre of the card, which had an embossed edge, with a small middle square of a different colour.

Sir Charles has a natural disinclination to signing his name without knowing why. "What do you want with it?" he asked. (A millionaire's signature has so many uses.)

"I want you to put the card in an envelope," the Seer replied, "and then to burn it. After that, I shall show you your own name written in letters of blood on my arm, in your own handwriting."

Sir Charles took the pen. If the signature was to be burned as soon as finished, he didn't mind giving it. He wrote his name in his usual firm clear style – the writing of a man who knows his worth and is not afraid of drawing a cheque for five thousand.

"Look at it long," the Seer said, from the other side of the room. He had not watched him write it.

Sir Charles stared at it fixedly. The Seer was really beginning to produce an impression.

"Now, put it in that envelope," the Seer exclaimed.

Sir Charles, like a lamb, placed it as directed.

The Seer strode forward. "Give me the envelope," he said. He took it in his hand, walked over towards the fireplace, and solemnly burnt it. "See – it crumbles into ashes," he cried. Then he came back to the middle of the room, close to the green light, rolled up his sleeve, and held his arm before Sir Charles. There, in blood-red letters, my brother-in-law read the name, "Charles Vandrift," in his own handwriting!

"I see how that's done," Sir Charles murmured, drawing back. "It's a clever delusion; but still I see through it. It's like that ghost-book. Your ink was deep green; your light was green; you made me look at it long; and then I saw the same thing written on the skin of your arm in complementary colours."

"You think so?" the Seer replied, with a curious curl of the lip.

"I'm sure of it," Sir Charles answered.

Quick as lightning the Seer again rolled up his sleeve. "That's your name," he cried, in a very clear voice, "but not your whole name. What do you say, then, to my right? Is this one also a complementary colour?" He held his other arm out. There, in sea-green letters, I read the name, "Charles O'Sullivan Vandrift." It is my brother-in-law's full baptismal designation; but he has dropped the O'Sullivan for many years past, and, to say the truth, doesn't like it. He is a little bit ashamed of his mother's family.

Charles glanced at it hurriedly. "Quite right," he said, "quite right!" But his voice was hollow. I could guess he didn't care to continue the *séance*. He could see through the man, of course; but it was clear the fellow knew too much about us to be entirely pleasant.

"Turn up the lights," I said, and a servant turned them. "Shall I say coffee and benedictine?" I whispered to Vandrift.

"By all means," he answered. "Anything to keep this fellow from further impertinences! And, I say, don't you think you'd better suggest at the same time that the men should smoke? Even these ladies are not above a cigarette – some of them."

There was a sigh of relief. The lights burned brightly. The Seer for the moment retired from business, so to speak. He accepted a partaga with a very good grace, sipped his coffee in a corner, and chatted to the lady who had suggested Strafford with marked politeness. He was a polished gentleman.

Next morning, in the hall of the hotel, I saw Madame Picardet again, in a neat tailor-made travelling dress, evidently bound for the railway-station.

"What, off, Madame Picardet?" I cried.

She smiled, and held out her prettily-gloved hand. "Yes, I'm off," she answered archly. "Florence, or Rome, or somewhere. I've drained Nice dry – like a sucked orange. Got all the fun I can out of it. Now I'm away again to my beloved Italy."

But it struck me as odd that, if Italy was her game, she went by the omnibus which takes down to the *train de luxe* for Paris. However, a man of the world accepts what a lady tells him, no matter how improbable; and I confess, for ten days or so, I thought no more about her, or the Seer either.

At the end of that time our fortnightly pass-book came in from the bank in London. It is part of my duty, as the millionaire's secretary, to make up this book once a fortnight, and to compare the cancelled cheques with Sir Charles's counterfoils. On this particular occasion I happened to observe what I can only describe as a very grave discrepancy, – in fact, a discrepancy of £5000. On the wrong side, too. Sir Charles was debited with £5000 more than the total amount that was shown on the counterfoils.

I examined the book with care. The source of the error was obvious. It lay in a cheque to Self or Bearer, for £5000, signed by Sir Charles, and evidently paid across the counter in London, as it bore on its face no stamp or indication of any other office.

I called in my brother-in-law from the salon to the study. "Look here, Charles," I said, "there's a cheque in the book which you haven't entered." And I handed it to him without comment, for I thought it might have been drawn to settle some little loss on the turf or at cards, or to make up some other affair he didn't desire to mention to me. These things will happen.

He looked at it and stared hard. Then he pursed up his mouth and gave a long low "Whew!" At last he turned it over and remarked, "I say, Sey, my boy, we've just been done jolly well brown, haven't we?"

I glanced at the cheque. "How do you mean?" I inquired.

"Why, the Seer," he replied, still staring at it ruefully. "I don't mind the five thou., but to think the fellow should have gammoned the pair of us like that –

ignominious, I call it!"

"How do you know it's the Seer?" I asked.

"Look at the green ink," he answered. "Besides, I recollect the very shape of the last flourish. I flourished a bit like that in the excitement of the moment, which I don't always do with my regular signature."

"He's done us," I answered, recognising it. "But how the dickens did he manage to transfer it to the cheque? This looks like your own handwriting, Charles, not a clever forgery."

"It is," he said. "I admit it – I can't deny it. Only fancy his bamboozling me when I was most on my guard! I wasn't to be taken in by any of his silly occult tricks and catch-words; but it never occurred to me he was going to victimise me financially in this way. I expected attempts at a loan or an extortion; but to collar my signature to a blank cheque – atrocious!"

"How did he manage it?" I asked.

"I haven't the faintest conception. I only know those are the words I wrote. I could swear to them anywhere."

"Then you can't protest the cheque?"

"Unfortunately, no; it's my own true signature."

We went that afternoon without delay to see the Chief Commissary of Police at the office. He was a gentlemanly Frenchman, much less formal and red-tapey than usual, and he spoke excellent English with an American accent, having acted, in fact, as a detective in New York for about ten years in his early manhood.

"I guess," he said slowly, after hearing our story, "you've been victimised right here by Colonel Clay, gentlemen."

"Who is Colonel Clay?" Sir Charles asked.

"That's just what I want to know," the Commissary answered, in his curious American-French-English. "He is a colonel, because he occasionally gives himself a commission; he is called Colonel Clay, because he appears to possess an india-rubber face, and he can mould it like clay in the hands of the potter. Real name, unknown. Nationality, equally French and English. Address, usually Europe. Profession, former maker of wax figures to the Musée Grévin. Age, what he chooses. Employs his knowledge to mould his own nose and cheeks, with wax additions, to the character he desires to personate. Aquiline this time, you say. *Hein!* Anything like these photographs?"

He rummaged in his desk and handed us two.

"Not in the least," Sir Charles answered. "Except, perhaps, as to the neck, everything here is quite unlike him."

"Then that's the Colonel!" the Commissary answered, with decision, rubbing his hands in glee. "Look here," and he took out a pencil and rapidly sketched the outline of one of the two faces – that of a bland-looking young man, with no expression worth mentioning. "There's the Colonel in his simple disguise. Very good. Now watch me: figure to yourself that he adds here a tiny patch of wax to his nose – an aquiline bridge – just so; well, you have him right there; and the chin, ah, one touch: now, for hair, a wig: for complexion, nothing easier: that's the profile of your rascal, isn't it?"

"Exactly," we both murmured. By two curves of the pencil, and a shock of false hair, the face was transmuted.

"He had very large eyes, with very big pupils, though," I objected, looking close; "and the man in the photograph here has them small and boiled-fishy."

"That's so," the Commissary answered. "A drop of belladonna expands – and produces the Seer; five grains of opium contract – and give a dead-alive, stupidly innocent appearance. Well, you leave this affair to me, gentlemen. I'll see the fun out. I don't say I'll catch him for you; nobody ever yet has caught Colonel Clay; but I'll explain how he did the trick; and that ought to be consolation enough to a man of your means for a trifle of five thousand!"

"You are not the conventional French office-holder, M. le Commissaire," I ventured to interpose.

"You bet!" the Commissary replied, and drew himself up like a captain of infantry. "Messieurs," he continued, in French, with the utmost dignity, "I shall devote the resources of this office to tracing out the crime, and, if possible, to effectuating the arrest of the culpable."

We telegraphed to London, of course, and we wrote to the bank, with a full description of the suspected person. But I need hardly add that nothing came of it.

Three days later the Commissary called at our hotel. "Well, gentlemen," he said, "I am glad to say I have discovered everything!"

"What? Arrested the Seer?" Sir Charles cried.

The Commissary drew back, almost horrified at the suggestion.

"Arrested Colonel Clay?" he exclaimed. "*Mais,* monsieur, we are only human! Arrested him? No, not quite. But tracked out how he did it. That is already much – to unravel Colonel Clay, gentlemen!"

"Well, what do you make of it?" Sir Charles asked, crestfallen.

The Commissary sat down and gloated over his discovery. It was clear a well-planned crime amused him vastly. "In the first place, monsieur," he said, "disabuse your mind of the idea that when monsieur your secretary went out to fetch Señor Herrera that night, Señor Herrera didn't know to whose rooms he was coming. Quite otherwise, in point of fact. I do not doubt myself that Señor Herrera, or Colonel Clay (call him which you like), came to Nice this winter for no other purpose than just to rob you."

"But I sent for him," my brother-in-law interposed.

"Yes; he *meant* you to send for him. He forced a card, so to speak. If he couldn't do that I guess he would be a pretty poor conjurer. He had a lady of his own – his wife, let us say, or his sister – stopping here at this hotel; a certain Madame Picardet. Through her he induced several ladies of your circle to attend his *séances*. She and they spoke to you about him, and aroused your curiosity. You may bet your bottom dollar that when he came to this room he came ready primed and prepared with endless facts about both of you."

"What fools we have been, Sey," my brother-in-law exclaimed. "I see it all now. That designing woman sent round before dinner to say I wanted to meet him; and by the time you got there he was ready for bamboozling me."

"That's so," the Commissary answered. "He had your name ready painted on both his arms; and he had made other preparations of still greater importance."

"You mean the cheque. Well, how did he get it?"

The Commissary opened the door. "Come in," he said. And a young man entered whom we recognised at once as the chief clerk in the Foreign Department of the Crédit Marseillais, the principal bank all along the Riviera.

"State what you know of this cheque," the Commissary said, showing it to him, for we had handed it over to the police as a piece of evidence.

"About four weeks since –" the clerk began.

"Say ten days before your *séance*," the Commissary interposed.

"A gentleman with very long hair and an aquiline nose, dark, strange, and handsome, called in at my department and asked if I could tell him the name of Sir Charles Vandrift's London banker. He said he had a sum to pay in to your credit, and asked if we would forward it for him. I told him it was irregular for us to receive the money, as you had no account with us, but that your London bankers were Darby, Drummond, and Rothenberg, Limited."

"Quite right," Sir Charles murmured.

"Two days later a lady, Madame Picardet, who was a customer of ours, brought in a good cheque for three hundred pounds, signed by a first-rate name, and asked us to pay it in on her behalf to Darby, Drummond, and Rothenberg's, and to open a London account with them for her. We did so, and received in reply a cheque-book."

"From which this cheque was taken, as I learn from the number, by telegram from London," the Commissary put in. "Also, that on the same day on which your cheque was cashed, Madame Picardet, in London, withdrew her balance."

"But how did the fellow get me to sign the cheque?" Sir Charles cried. "How did he manage the card trick?"

The Commissary produced a similar card from his pocket. "Was that the sort of thing?" he asked.

"Precisely! A facsimile."

"I thought so. Well, our Colonel, I find, bought a packet of such cards, intended for admission to a religious function, at a shop in the Quai Masséna. He cut out the centre, and, see here –" The Commissary turned it over, and showed a piece of paper pasted neatly over the back; this he tore off, and there, concealed behind it, lay a folded cheque, with only the place where the signature should be written showing through on the face which the Seer had

presented to us. "I call that a neat trick," the Commissary remarked, with professional enjoyment of a really good deception.

"But he burned the envelope before my eyes," Sir Charles exclaimed.

"Pooh!" the Commissary answered. "What would he be worth as a conjurer, anyway, if he couldn't substitute one envelope for another between the table
and the fireplace without your noticing it? And Colonel Clay, you must
remember, is a prince among conjurers."

"Well, it's a comfort to know we've identified our man, and the woman
who was with him," Sir Charles said, with a slight sigh of relief. "The next
thing will be, of course, you'll follow them up on these clues in England and
arrest them?"

The Commissary shrugged his shoulders. "Arrest them!" he exclaimed,
much amused. "Ah, monsieur, but you are sanguine. No officer of justice has
ever succeeded in arresting le Colonel Caoutchouc, as we call him in French.
He is as slippery as an eel, that man. He wriggles through our fingers. Suppose
even we caught him, what could we prove? I ask you. Nobody who has seen
him once can ever swear to him again in his next impersonation. He is
impayable, this good Colonel. On the day when I arrest him, I assure you,
monsieur, I shall consider myself the smartest police-officer in Europe."

"Well, I shall catch him yet," Sir Charles answered, and relapsed into
silence.

BIBLIOGRAPHY - GRANT ALLEN

Criminous works

An African millionaire; episodes in the life of the illustrious Colonel Clay. New York: Richards/London: Arnold, 1897.

An army doctor's romance. New York: Tuck, 1893/London: Tuck, 1894.

At market value. London: Chatto & Windus/Chicago: Neely, 1894.

Babylon. By "Cecil Power." London: Chatto & Windus/New York: Munro, 1885.

The backslider. London/New York: Lewis Scribner, 1901. ss.

The beckoning hand; and other stories. London: Chatto & Windus, 1887. ss.

Blood Royal. New York: Cassell, 1892/London: Chatto & Windus, 1893.

A bride from the desert. New York: Fenno, 1896. ss.

Desire of the eyes; and other stories. London: Digby/New York: Fenno, 1895. ss.

The Devil's die. London: Chatto & Windus/New York: Lovell, 1888.

The Duchess of Powysland. New York: U.S. Book Co., 1891/London: Chatto & Windus, 1892.

Dr. Palliser's patient. London: Mullen, 1889.

Dumaresq's daughter. London: Chatto & Windus/New York: Harper, 1891.

For Mamie's sake; a tale of love and dynamite. London: Chatto & Windus/New York: Munro, 1886.

The general's will. London: Butterworth, 1892. ss.

Hilda Wade; a woman with great tenacity of purpose. Completed by Sir Arthur Conan Doyle. London: Richards/New York: Putnam, 1900. ss. Despite the efforts of booksellers and other bibliographers of the genre, this collection of short stories has nothing to do with detection and is not even barely criminous. It is a lacklustre example of the tales of romantic intrigue typical of the period, and the only thing that has kept this particular specimen from sinking into deserved obscurity is the adventitious posthumous completion of the final chapter, "The Episode of the Dead Man Who Spoke," which was running in serial form in the *Strand* at the time of Allen's death, of the eponymous story by the creator of Sherlock Holmes, who was Allen's friend and neighbour in Hindhead, where Conan Doyle had moved on Allen's recommendation.

In all shades. London: Chatto & Windus, 1886/New York: Rand, 18??.

The incidental bishop. London: Pearson/New York: Appleton, 1898.

Ivan Greet's masterpiece. London: Chatto & Windus, 1893. ss.

The jaws of death. London: Simpkin Marshall, 1889/New York: New Amsterdam, 1896.

Kalee's shrine. With May Cotes. Bristol: Arrowsmith, 1886/New York: New Amsterdam, 1897. Also publ. as: *The Indian mystery; or, Kalee's shrine.* New York: New Amsterdam, 1902.

Linnet. London: Richards, 1898/New York: New Amsterdam, 1900.

Michael's crag. London: Leadenhall/Chicago: Rand McNally, 1893.

Miss Cayley's adventures. London: Richards/New York: Putnam, 1899. ss. Char: Miss Lois Cayley.

Recalled to life. London: Arrowsmith/New York: Holt, 1891.

The reluctant hangman; and other stories of crime. Boulder, Colorado: Aspen Press, 1975. ss.

The scallywag. London: Chatto & Windus/New York: Cassell, 1893.

Sir Theodore's guest; and other stories. Bristol: Arrowsmith, 1902. ss.

A splendid sin. London: White, 1896/New York(?): Buckles, 1899.

Strange stories. London: Chatto & Windus, 1884. ss.

The tents of Shem; a novel. London: Chatto & Windus/Chicago: Rand McNally, 1889.

A terrible inheritance. London: SPCK, 1887/New York: Crowell, 18??.

This mortal coil; a novel. London: Chatto & Windus, 1888/New York: Appleton, 1889.

Twelve tales. London: Richards, 1899. ss.

Under sealed orders. New York: Collier, 1894/London: Chatto & Windus, 1895.

Wednesday the tenth. Boston: Lothrop, 1890. Also publ. as: *The cruise of the 'Albatross'; a story of the South Pacific.* Boston: Lothrop, 1898.

What's bred in the bone. London: Tit-bits/New York: Tucker, 1891.

Other works

Anglo-Saxon Britain. 1881.

The British barbarians. New York: Putnam, 1895.

Colin Clout's calendar. 1883.

The colour sense. 1879.

Colours of flowers. 1882.

The evolution of the idea of God. 1897.

The evolutionist at large. 1881.

Flowers and their pedigrees. 1884.

The great taboo. London: Chatto, 1890.

Philistia. By "Cecil Power." New York: Munro, 1884.

Physiological aesthetics. 1877.

Rosalba; the story of her development. By "Olive Pratt Rayner." New York: Putnam, 1899.

The typewriter girl. By "Olive Pratt Rayner." London: Pearson, 1897/New York: Street & Smith – as by: Grant Allen, 1900.

Vignettes from nature. 1881.

The white man's foot. London: Hatchards, 1888.

The woman who did. Boston: Roberts, 1895.

—, (ed.). Catullus. *The Attis of Caius Valerius Catullus, translated into English verse by Grant Allen, with dissertations on the myth of Attis, on the origins of tree-worship, and on the galliambic metre.* By Grant Allen, B.A., formerly Postmaster of Merton College, Oxford. London: David Nutt, 1892. (Bibliotheque de Carabas, Vol. VI). "As I did so I struck against an elderly deformed man, who had been behind me, and I knocked down several books which he was carrying. I remember that as I picked them up I observed the title of one of them, *The origin of tree worship* ..." ("The Empty House," *Strand,* October 1903). So Sir Arthur Conan Doyle paid posthumous tribute to his good friend and neighbour who had died four years before.

ROBERT BARR

The Absent-Minded Coterie
The triumphs of Eugène Valmont.
New York: Appleton/London: Hurst, 1906.

The Adventures of Sherlaw Kombs
London: *The Idler Magazine*, 1892.

BARR, Robert, 1850-1912

Only two Canadian authors make the honour roll of *The Haycraft-Queen List of Detective-Crime-Mystery Fiction: two centuries of cornerstones.** One is Robert Barr, for *The triumphs of Eugène Valmont.*

Born in Glasgow, Scotland, on 16 September 1850, the eldest child of Robert and June Barr, Robert Barr junior was brought to Canada when he was four. By education and upbringing Barr was a Canadian. The family settled first in Wallacetown, Ontario, and then, after living in other Ontario towns, finally moved to Windsor, Ontario, where Barr spent much of his childhood and was educated. He taught in Windsor on a temporary certificate until 1873, when he entered the Toronto Normal School to obtain his permanent teaching licence.

His 1907 book, *The measure of the rule,* recounts his days at the Normal School in the 1870s; this autobiographical novel is a serious contribution to Canadian literature.

Barr returned to Windsor in 1875 as principal of Windsor Central School, but in 1876 he abandoned teaching for journalism, taking a job as a reporter on the *Detroit Free Press* and quickly becoming editor.

In 1881, Barr moved to England where he remained until 1911, achieving success as a magazine editor, short-story writer, and novelist; twenty of his novels were published. His numerous short stories were good, fast-moving tales that were immensely popular with mass audiences. His first novel, *In the midst of alarms,* which is set in Canada and centres around the Fenian invasion of 1866, was published in 1894, preceded by two collections of short stories.

In 1892, in association with Jerome K. Jerome, author of the classic *Three men in a boat,* Barr established and edited *The Idler,* which was vastly popular for a few years until destroyed by a lawsuit. He died aged 62 of heart failure at Woldingham, Surrey, England, on 22 October 1912.

---

* *The Haycraft-Queen List of Detective-Crime-Mystery Fiction; two centuries of cornerstones.* In Howard Haycraft. *Murder for Pleasure; the life and times of the detective story.* Rev. ed. New York: Biblo & Tannen, 1968.

THE ABSENT-MINDED COTERIE
The triumphs of Eugène Valmont. New York: Appleton/London: Hurst, 1906.

Eugène Valmont is the first humorous detective in English literature, and the first of many comic French sleuths. Among his "triumphs" is one of the most famous and ingenious stories in the genre, "The absent-minded coterie."

Jacques Barzun and Wendell Hertig Taylor admire the story: "A tale of elegant swindling, achieved by simple yet well-jointed means, this little masterpiece outstrips all the author's other efforts and has deservedly been reprinted over and over again."*

Ellery Queen in *Queen's quorum* states that "The real purpose behind [this book] has long been misunderstood. Some critics think of Eugène Valmont simply as a comic criminologist; other critics consider him merely a forerunner of Agatha Christie's Hercule Poirot. The truth is deeper: what Robert Barr intended was a satirization of the nationalistic differences between French and English police systems and, as such, the book is a trenchant, if generally unrecognized, tour de force. The humor, warmth, and ingenuity, especially in the classic story, 'The absent-minded coterie,' are extra dividends."**

* Jacques Barzun and Wendell Hertig Taylor. *Catalogue of crime; [being a reader's guide to the literature of mystery, detection & related genres]* (2nd imp. corr.). New York: Harper & Row, 1971.

** Ellery Queen. *Queen's Quorum; a history of the detective-crime short story as revealed in the 106 most important books published in this field since 1845.* [With] Supplements through 1967. New York: Biblo and Tannen, 1969.

THE ABSENT-MINDED COTERIE

The question of lighting is an important one in a room such as mine, and electricity offers a good deal of scope to the ingenious. Of this fact I have taken full advantage. I can manipulate the lighting of my room so that any particular spot is bathed in brilliancy, while the rest of the space remains in comparative gloom, and I arranged the lamps so that the full force of their rays impinged against the door that Wednesday evening, while I sat on one side of the table in semi-darkness and Hale sat on the other, with a light beating down on him from above which gave him the odd, sculptured look of a living statue of Justice, stern and triumphant. Any one entering the room would first be dazzled by the light, and next would see the gigantic form of Hale in the full uniform of his order.

When Angus Macpherson was shown into this room he was quite visibly taken aback, and paused abruptly on the threshold, his gaze riveted on the huge policeman. I think his first purpose was to turn and run, but the door closed behind him and he doubtless heard, as we all did, the sound of the bolt being thrust in its place, thus locking him in.

"I – I beg your pardon," he stammered, "I expected to meet Mr. Webster."

As he said this, I pressed the button under my table, and was instantly enshrouded with light. A sickly smile overspread the countenance of Macpherson as he caught sight of me, and he made a very creditable attempt to carry off the situation with nonchalance.

"Oh, there you are, Mr. Webster; I did not notice you at first."

It was a tense moment. I spoke slowly and impressively.

"Sir, perhaps you are not unacquainted with the name of Eugène Valmont."

He replied brazenly –

"I am sorry to say, sir, I never heard of the gentleman before."

At this came a most inopportune "Haw-haw" from that blockhead Spenser Hale, completely spoiling the dramatic situation I had elaborated with such thought and care. It is little wonder the English possess no drama, for they show scant appreciation of the sensational moments in life.

"Haw-haw," brayed Spenser Hale, and at once reduced the emotional atmosphere to a fog of commonplace. However, what is a man to do? He must handle the tools with which it pleases Providence to provide him. I ignored Hale's untimely laughter.

"Sit down, sir," I said to Macpherson, and he obeyed.

"You have called on Lord Semptam this week," I continued sternly.

"Yes, sir."

"And collected a pound from him?"

"Yes, sir."

"In October, 1893, you sold Lord Semptam a carved antique table for fifty pounds?"

"Quite right, sir."

"When you were here last week, you gave me Ralph Summertrees as the name of a gentleman living in Park Lane. You knew at the time that this man was your employer?"

Macpherson was now looking fixedly at me, and on this occasion made no reply. I went on calmly: –

"You also knew that Summertrees, of Park Lane, was identical with Simpson, of Tottenham Court Road?"

"Well, sir," said Macpherson, "I don't exactly see what you're driving at, but it's quite usual for a man to carry on a business under an assumed name. There is nothing illegal about that."

"We will come to the illegality in a moment, Mr. Macpherson. You, and Rogers, and Tyrrel, and three others, are confederates of this man Simpson."

"We are in his employ; yes sir, but no more confederates than clerks usually are."

"I think, Mr. Macpherson, I have said enough to show you that the game is, what you call, up. You are now in the presence of Mr. Spenser Hale, from Scotland Yard, who is waiting to hear your confession."

Here the stupid Hale broke in with his –

"And remember, sir, that anything you say will be – "

"Excuse me, Mr. Hale," I interrupted hastily, "I shall turn over the case to you in a very few moments, but I ask you to remember our compact, and to leave it for the present entirely in my hands. Now, Mr. Macpherson, I want your confession, and I want it at once."

"Confession? Confederates?" protested Macpherson with admirably simulated surprise. "I must say you use extraordinary terms, Mr. – Mr. – What did you say the name was?"

"Haw-haw," roared Hale. "His name is Monsieur Valmont."

"I implore you, Mr. Hale, to leave this man to me for a very few moments. Now, Macpherson, what have you to say in your defence?"

"Where nothing criminal has been alleged, Monsieur Valmont, I see no necessity for defence. If you wish me to admit that somehow you have acquired a number of details regarding our business, I am perfectly willing to do so, and to subscribe to their accuracy. If you will be good enough to let me know of what you complain, I shall endeavour to make the point clear to you if I can. There has evidently been some misapprehension, but for the life of me, without further explanation, I am as much in a fog as I was on my way coming here, for it is getting a little thick outside."

Macpherson certainly was conducting himself with great discretion, and presented, quite unconsciously, a much more diplomatic figure than my friend,

Spenser Hale, sitting stiffly opposite me. His tone was one of mild expostulation, mitigated by the intimation that all misunderstanding speedily would be cleared away. To outward view he offered a perfect picture of innocence, neither protesting too much nor too little. I had, however, another surprise in store for him, a trump card, as it were, and I played it down on the table.

"There!" I cried with vim, "have you ever seen that sheet before?"

He glanced at it without offering to take it in his hand.

"Oh yes," he said, "that has been abstracted from our file. It is what I call my visiting list."

"Come, come, sir," I cried sternly, "you refuse to confess, but I warn you we know all about it. You never heard of Dr. Willoughby, I suppose?"

"Yes, he is the author of the silly pamphlet on Christian Science."

"You are in the right, Mr. Macpherson; on Christian Science and Absent-Mindedness."

"Possibly. I haven't read it for a long while."

"Have you ever met this learned doctor, Mr. Macpherson?"

"Oh, yes. Dr. Willoughby is the pen-name of Mr. Summertrees. He believes in Christian Science and that sort of thing, and writes about it."

"Ah, really. We are getting your confession bit by bit, Mr. Macpherson. I think it would be better to be quite frank with us."

"I was just going to make the same suggestion to you, Monsieur Valmont. If you will tell me in a few words exactly what is your charge against either Mr. Summertrees or myself, I will know then what to say."

"We charge you, sir, with obtaining money under false pretences, which is a crime that has landed more than one distinguished financier in prison."

Spenser Hale shook his fat forefinger at me, and said,

"Tut, tut, Valmont; we mustn't threaten, we mustn't threaten, you know;" but I went on without heeding him.

"Take for instance, Lord Semptam. You sold him a table for fifty pounds, on the instalment plan. He was to pay a pound a week, and in less than a year the debt was liquidated. But he is an absent-minded man, as all your clients are. That is why you came to me. I had answered the bogus Willoughby's advertisement. And so you kept on collecting and collecting for something more than three years. Now do you understand the charge?"

Mr. Macpherson's head during this accusation was held slightly inclined to one side. At first his face was clouded by the most clever imitation of anxious concentration of mind I had ever seen, and this was gradually cleared away by the dawn of awakening perception. When I had finished, an ingratiating smiled hovered about his lips.

"Really, you know," he said, "that is rather a capital scheme. The absent-minded league, as one might call them. Most ingenious. Summertrees, if he had any sense of humour, which he hasn't, would be rather taken by the idea that his innocent fad for Christian Science had led him to be suspected of obtaining money under false pretences. But, really, there are no pretensions about the matter at all. As I understand it, I simply call and receive the money through the forgetfulness of the persons on my list, but where I think you would have both Summertrees and myself, if there was anything in your audacious theory, would be an indictment for conspiracy. Still, I quite see how the mistake arises. You have jumped to the conclusion that we sold nothing to Lord Semptam except that carved table three years ago. I have the pleasure in pointing out to you that his lordship is a frequent customer of ours, and has had many things from us at one time or another. Sometimes he is in our debt; sometimes we are in his. We keep a sort of running contract with him by which he pays us a pound a week. He and several other customers deal on the same plan, and in return for an income that we can count upon, they get the first offer of anything in which they are supposed to be interested. As I have told you, we call these sheets in the office our visiting lists, but to make the visiting lists complete you need what we term our encyclopaedia. We call it that because it is in so many volumes; a volume for each year, running back I don't know how long. You will notice little figures here from time to time above the amount stated on this visiting list. These figures refer to the page of the encyclopaedia for the current year, and on that page is noted the new sale, and the amount of it, as it might be set down, say, in a ledger."

"That is a very entertaining explanation, Mr. Macpherson. I suppose this encyclopaedia, as you call it, is in the shop at Tottenham Court Road?"

"Oh, no, sir. Each volume of the encyclopaedia is self-locking. These books contain the real secret of our business, and they are kept in the safe at Mr. Summertrees' house in Park Lane. Take Lord Semptam's account, for instance. You will find in faint figures under a certain date, 102. If you turn to page 102 of the encyclopaedia for that year, you will then see a list of what Lord Semptam has bought, and the prices he was charged for them. It is really a very simple matter. If you will allow me to use your telephone for a moment, I will ask Mr. Summertrees, who has not yet begun dinner, to bring with him here the volume for 1893, and, within a quarter of an hour, you will be perfectly satisfied that everything is quite legitimate."

I confess that the young man's naturalness and confidence staggered me, the more so as I saw by the sarcastic smile on Hale's lips that he did not believe a single word spoken. A portable telephone stood on the table, and as Macpherson finished his explanation, he reached over and drew it towards him. Then Spenser Hale interfered.

"Excuse *me,*" he said, "I'll do the telephoning. What is the call number of Mr. Summertrees?"

"140 Hyde Park."

Hale at once called up Central, and presently was answered from Park Lane. We heard him say –

"Is this the residence of Mr. Summertrees? Oh, is that you, Podgers? Is Mr.

Summertrees in? Very well. This is Hale. I am in Valmont's flat – Imperial Flats – you know. Yes, where you went with me the other day. Very well, go to Mr. Summertrees, and say to him that Mr. Macpherson wants the encyclopaedia for 1893. Do you get that? Yes, encyclopaedia. Oh, he'll understand what it is. Mr. Macpherson. No, don't mention my name at all. Just say Mr. Macpherson wants the encyclopaedia for the year 1893, and that you are to bring it. Yes, you may tell him that Mr. Macpherson is at Imperial Flats, but don't mention my name at all. Exactly. As soon as he gives you the book, get into a cab, and come here as quickly as possible with it. If Summertrees doesn't want to let the book go, then tell him to come with you. If he won't do that, place him under arrest, and bring both him and the book here. All right. Be as quick as you can; we're waiting."

Macpherson made no protest against Hale's use of the telephone; he merely sat back in his chair with a resigned expression on his face which, if painted on canvas, might have been entitled "The Falsely Accused." When Hale rang off, Macpherson said,

"Of course you know your own business best, but if your man arrests Summertrees, he will make you the laughing-stock of London. There is such a thing as unjustifiable arrest, as well as getting money under false pretences, and Mr. Summertrees is not the man to forgive an insult. And then, if you will allow me to say so, the more I think over your absent-minded theory, the more absolutely grotesque it seems, and if the case ever gets into the newspaper, I am sure, Mr. Hale, you'll experience an uncomfortable half-hour with your chiefs at Scotland Yard."

"I'll take the risk of that, thank you," said Hale stubbornly.

"Am I to consider myself under arrest," inquired the young man.

"No, sir."

"Then, if you will pardon me, I shall withdraw. Mr. Summertrees will show you everything you wish to see in his books, and can explain his business much more capably than I, because he knows more about it; therefore, gentlemen, I bid you good-night."

"No you don't. Not just yet awhile," exclaimed Hale, rising to his feet simultaneously with the young man.

"Then I *am* under arrest," protested Macpherson.

"You're not going to leave this room until Podgers brings that book."

"Oh, very well," and he sat down again.

And now, as talking is dry work, I set out something to drink, a box of cigars, and a box of cigarettes. Hale mixed his favourite brew, but Macpherson, shunning the wine of his country, contented himself with a glass of plain mineral water, and lit a cigarette. Then he awoke my high regard by saying pleasantly as if nothing had happened –

"While we are waiting, Monsieur Valmont, may I remind you that you owe me five shillings?"

I laughed, took the coin from my pocket, and paid him, whereupon he thanked me.

"Are you connected with Scotland Yard, Monsieur Valmont?" asked Macpherson, with the air of a man trying to make conversation to bridge over a tedious interval; but before I could reply, Hale blurted out,

"Not likely!"

"You have no official standing as a detective, then, Monsieur Valmont?"

"None whatever," I replied quickly, thus getting in my oar ahead of Hale.

"This is a loss to our country," pursued this admirable young man, with evident sincerity.

I began to see I could make a good deal of so clever a fellow if he came under my tuition.

"The blunders of our police," he went on, "are something deplorable. If they would but take lessons in strategy, say, from France, their unpleasant duties would be so much more acceptably performed, with much less discomfort to their victims."

"France," snorted Hale in derision, "why, they call a man guilty there until he's proven innocent."

"Yes, Mr. Hale, and the same seems to be the case in Imperial Flats. You have quite made up your mind that Mr. Summertrees is guilty, and will not be content until he proves his innocence. I venture to predict that you will hear from him before long in a manner that may astonish you."

Hale grunted and looked at his watch. The minutes passed very slowly as we sat there smoking, and at last even I began to get uneasy. Macpherson, seeing our anxiety, said that when he came in the fog was almost as thick as it had been the week before, and that there might be some difficulty in getting a cab. Just as he was speaking the door was unlocked from the outside, and Podgers entered, bearing a thick volume in his hand. This he gave to his superior, who turned over its pages in amazement, and then looked at the back, crying –

"*Encyclopaedia of Sport*, 1893! What sort of a joke is this, Mr. Macpherson?"

There was a pained look on Mr. Macpherson's face as he reached forward and took the book. He said with a sigh –

"If you had allowed me to telephone, Mr. Hale, I should have made it perfectly plain to Summertrees what was wanted. I might have known this mistake was liable to occur. There is an increasing demand for out-of-date books of sport, and no doubt Mr. Summertrees thought this was what I meant. There is nothing for it but to send your man back to Park Lane and tell Mr. Summertrees that what we want is the locked volume of accounts for 1893, which we call the encyclopaedia. Allow me to write an order that will bring it. Oh, I'll show you what I have written before your man takes it," he said, as Hale stood ready to look over his shoulder.

On my notepaper he dashed off a request such as he had outlined, and handed it to Hale, who read it and gave it to Podgers.

"Take that to Summertrees, and get back as quickly as possible. Have you a cab at the door?"

"Yes, sir."

"Is it foggy outside?"

"Not so much, sir, as it was an hour ago. No difficulty about the traffic now, sir."

"Very well, get back as soon as you can."

Podgers saluted, and left with the book under his arm. Again the door was locked, and again we sat smoking in silence until the stillness was broken by the tinkle of the telephone. Hale put the receiver to his ear.

"Yes, this is the Imperial Flats. Yes. Valmont. Oh, yes; Macpherson is here. What? Out of what? Can't hear you. Out of print. What, the encyclopaedia's out of print? Who is that speaking? Dr. Willoughby; thanks."

Macpherson rose as if he would go to the telephone, but instead (and he acted so quietly that I did not notice what he was doing until the thing was done), he picked up the sheet which he called his visiting list, and walking quite without haste, held it in the glowing coals of the fireplace until it disappeared in a flash of flame up the chimney. I sprang to my feet indignant, but too late to make even a motion towards saving the sheet. Macpherson regarded us both with that self-deprecatory smile which had several times lighted up his face.

"How dare you burn that sheet?" I demanded.

"Because, Monsieur Valmont, it did not belong to you; because you do not belong to Scotland Yard; because you stole it; because you had no right to it; and because you have no official standing in this country. If it had been in Mr. Hale's possession I should not have dared, as you put it, to destroy the sheet, but as this sheet was abstracted from my master's premises by you, an entirely unauthorised person, whom he would have been justified in shooting dead if he had found you housebreaking and you had resisted him on his discovery, I took the liberty of destroying the document. I have always held that these sheets should not have been kept, for, as has been the case, if they fell under the scrutiny of so intelligent a person as Eugène Valmont, improper inferences might have been drawn. Mr. Summertrees, however, persisted in keeping them, but made this concession, that if I ever telegraphed him or telephoned him the word 'Encyclopaedia,' he would at once burn these records, and he, on his part, was to telegraph or telephone to me 'The *Encyclopaedia* is out of print,' whereupon I would know that he had succeeded.

"Now, gentlemen, open this door, which will save me the trouble of forcing it. Either put me formally under arrest, or cease to restrict my liberty. I am very much obliged to Mr. Hale for telephoning, and I have made no protest to so gallant a host as Monsieur Valmont is, because of the locked door. However, the farce is now terminated. The proceedings I have sat through were entirely illegal, and if you will pardon me, Mr. Hale, they have been a little too French to go down here in old England, or to make a report in the newspapers that would be quite satisfactory to your chiefs. I demand either my formal arrest, or the unlocking of that door."

In silence I pressed a button, and my man threw open the door. Macpherson walked to the threshold, paused, and looked back at Spenser Hale, who sat there silent as a sphinx.

"Good-evening, Mr. Hale."

There being no reply, he turned to me with the same ingratiating smile,

"Good-evening, Monsieur Eugène Valmont," he said, "I shall give myself the pleasure of calling next Wednesday at six for my five shillings."

THE ADVENTURES OF SHERLAW KOMBS
London: *The Idler Magazine*, 1892.

Robert Barr is also noted as the author of the first Holmesian parody, "Detective stories gone wrong; the adventures of Sherlaw Kombs," which first appeared in *The Idler Magazine* under the pseudonym "Luke Sharp" and in book form as "The Great Pegram mystery," in *The face and the mask.**

Ronald Burt De Waal, the great Sherlockian bibliographer and scholar has called it "the finest and one of the funniest Sherlockian parodies ever written."**

---

* *The Idler Magazine*, 1 May 1892, pp.413-424; *The face and the mask.* London: Hutchinson, 1894/New York: Stokes, 1895.

** R.B. De Waal. *The world bibliography of Sherlock Holmes and Dr. Watson; a classified and annotated list of materials relating to their lives and adventures.* Boston: New York Graphic Society, 1974.

THE ADVENTURES OF
SHERLAW KOMBS

I dropped in on my friend, Sherlaw Kombs, to hear what he had to say about the Pegram mystery, as it had come to be called in the newspapers. I found him playing the violin with a look of sweet peace and serenity on his face, which I never noticed on the countenances of those within hearing distance. I knew this expression of seraphic calm indicated that Kombs had been deeply annoyed about something. Such, indeed, proved to be the case, for one of the morning papers had contained an article eulogizing the alertness and general competence of Scotland Yard. So great was Sherlaw Kombs' contempt for Scotland Yard that he never would visit Scotland during his vacations, nor would he ever admit that a Scotchman was fit for anything but export.

He generously put away his violin, for he had a sincere liking for me, and greeted me with his usual kindness.

"I have come," I began, plunging at once into the matter on my mind, "to hear what you think of the great Pegram mystery."

"I haven't heard of it," he said quietly, just as if all London were not talking of that very thing. Kombs was curiously ignorant on some subjects, and abnormally learned on others. I found, for instance, that political discussion with him was impossible, because he did not know who Salisbury and Gladstone were. This made his friendship a great boon.

"The Pegram mystery has baffled even Gregory, of Scotland Yard."

"I can well believe it," said my friend, calmly. "Perpetual motion, or squaring the circle, would baffle Gregory. He's an infant, is Gregory."

This was one of the things I always liked about Kombs. There was no professional jealousy in him, such as characterizes so many other men.

He filled his pipe, threw himself into his deep-seated armchair, placed his feet on the mantel, and clasped his hands behind his head.

"Tell me about it," he said simply.

"Old Barrie Kipson," I began, "was a stock-broker in the City. He lived in Pegram, and it was his custom to —"

"Come in!" shouted Kombs, without changing his position, but with a suddenness that startled me. I had heard no knock.

"Excuse me," said my friend, laughing, "my invitation to enter was a trifle premature. I was really so interested in your recital that I spoke before I thought, which a detective should never do. The fact is, a man will be here in a moment who will tell me all about this crime, and so you will be spared further effort in that line."

"Ah, you have an appointment. In that case I will not intrude," I said, rising.

"Sit down; I have no appointment. I did not know until I spoke that he was coming."

I gazed at him in amazement. Accustomed as I was to his extraordinary talents, the man was a perpetual surprise to me. He continued to smoke quietly, but evidently enjoyed my consternation.

"I see you are surprised. It is really too simple to talk about, but, from my position opposite the mirror, I can see the reflection of objects in the street. A man stopped, looked at one of my cards, and then glanced across the street. I recognized my card, because, as you know, they are all in scarlet. If, as you say, London is talking of this mystery, it naturally follows that *he* will talk of it, and the chances are he wished to consult with me upon it. Anyone can see that, besides there is always – *Come* in!"

There was a rap at the door this time.

A stranger entered. Sherlaw Kombs did not change his lounging attitude.

"I wish to see Mr. Sherlaw Kombs, the detective," said the stranger, coming within the range of the smoker's vision.

"This is Mr. Kombs," I remarked at last, as my friend smoked quietly, and seemed half-asleep.

"Allow me to introduce myself," continued the stranger, fumbling for a card.

"There is no need. You are a journalist," said Kombs.

"Ah," said the stranger, somewhat taken aback, "you know me, then."

"Never saw or heard of you in my life before."

"Then how in the world –"

"Nothing simpler. You write for an evening paper. You have written an article condemning the book of a friend. He will feel bad about it, and you will condole with him. He will never know who stabbed him unless I tell him."

"The devil!" cried the journalist, sinking into a chair and mopping his brow, while his face became livid.

"Yes," drawled Kombs, "it is a devil of a shame that such things are done. But what would you, as we say in France."

When the journalist had recovered his second wind he pulled himself together somewhat. "Would you object to telling me how you know these particulars about a man you say you have never seen?"

"I rarely talk about these things," said Kombs with great composure. "But as the cultivation of the habit of observation may help you in your profession, and thus in a remote degree benefit me by making your paper less deadly dull, I will tell you. Your first and second fingers are smeared with ink, which shows that you write a great deal. This smeared class embraces two subclasses, clerks or accountants, and journalists. Clerks have to be neat in their work. The ink smear is slight in their case. Your fingers are badly and carelessly smeared;

therefore, you are a journalist. You have an evening paper in your pocket. Anyone might have any evening paper, but yours is a Special Edition, which will not be on the streets for half an hour yet. You must have obtained it before you left the office, and to do this you must be on the staff. A book notice is marked with a blue pencil. A journalist always despises every article in his own paper not written by himself; therefore, you wrote the article you have marked, and doubtless are about to send it to the author of the book referred to. Your paper makes a specialty of abusing all books not written by some member of its own staff. That the author is a friend of yours, I merely surmised. It is all a trivial example of ordinary observation."

"Really, Mr. Kombs, you are the most wonderful man on earth. You are the equal of Gregory, by Jove, you are."

A frown marred the brow of my friend as he placed his pipe on the sideboard and drew his self-cocking six-shooter.

"Do you mean to insult me, sir?"

"I do not – I – I assure you. You are fit to take charge of Scotland Yard tomorrow – I am in earnest, indeed I am, sir."

"Then heaven help you," cried Kombs, slowly raising his right arm.

I sprang between them.

"Don't shoot!" I cried. "You will spoil the carpet. Besides, Sherlaw, don't you see the man means well? He actually thinks it is a compliment!"

"Perhaps you are right," remarked the detective, flinging his revolver carelessly beside his pipe, much to the relief of the third party. Then, turning to the journalist, he said, with his customary bland courtesy –

"You wanted to see me, I think you said. What can I do for you, Mr. Wilber Scribbings?"

The journalist started.

"How do you know my name?" he gasped.

Kombs waved his hand impatiently.

"Look inside your hat if you doubt your own name."

I then noticed for the first time that the name was plainly to be seen inside the top-hat Scribbings held upside down in his hands.

"You have heard, of course, of the Pegram mystery –"

"Tush," cried the detective; "do not, I beg of you, call it a mystery. There is no such thing. Life would become more tolerable if there ever *was* a mystery. Nothing is original. Everything has been done before. What about the Pegram affair?"

"The Pegram – ah – case has baffled everyone. The *Evening Blade* wishes you to investigate, so that it may publish the result. It will pay you well. Will you accept the commission?"

"Possibly. Tell me about the case."

"I thought everybody knew the particulars. Mr. Barrie Kipson lived at Pegram. He carried a first-class season ticket between the terminus and that station. It was his custom to leave for Pegram on the 5:30 train each evening. Some weeks ago, Mr. Kipson was brought down by the influenza. On his first visit to the City after his recovery, he drew something like three hundred pounds in notes, and left the office at his usual hour to catch the 5:30. He was never seen again alive, as far as the public have been able to learn. He was found at Brewster in a first-class compartment on the Scotch Express, which does not stop between London and Brewster. There was a bullet in his head, and his money was gone, pointing plainly to murder and robbery."

"And where is the mystery, might I ask?"

"There are several unexplainable things about the case. First, how came he on the Scotch Express, which leaves at six, and does not stop at Pegram? Second, the ticket examiners at the terminus would have turned him out if he showed his season ticket; and all the tickets sold for the Scotch Express on the 21st are accounted for. Third, how could the murderer have escaped? Fourth, the passengers in two compartments on each side of the one where the body was found heard no scuffle and no shot fired."

"Are you sure the Scotch Express on the 21st did not stop between London and Brewster?"

"Now that you mention the fact, it did. It was stopped by signal just outside of Pegram. There was a few moments' pause, when the line was reported clear, and it went on again. This frequently happens, as there is a branch line beyond Pegram."

Mr. Sherlaw Kombs pondered for a few moments, smoking his pipe silently.

"I presume you wish the solution in time for tomorrow's paper?"

"Bless my soul, no. The editor thought if you evolved a theory in a month you would do well."

"My dear sir, I do not deal with theories, but with facts. If you can make it convenient to call here tomorrow at 8 a.m. I will give you the full particulars early enough for the first edition. There is no sense in taking up much time over so simple an affair as the Pegram case. Good afternoon, sir."

Mr. Scribbings was too much astonished to return the greeting. He left in a speechless condition, and I saw him go up the street with his hat still in his hand.

Sherlaw Kombs relapsed into his old lounging attitude, with his hands clasped behind his head. The smoke came from his lips in quick puffs at first, then at longer intervals. I saw he was coming to a conclusion, so I said nothing.

Finally he spoke in his most dreamy manner. "I do not wish to seem to be rushing things at all, Whatson, but I am going out tonight on the Scotch Express. Would you care to accompany me?"

"Bless me!" I cried, glancing at the clock. "You haven't time, it is after five now."

"Ample time, Whatson – ample," he murmured, without changing his position. "I give myself a minute and a half to change slippers and dressing-gown for boots and coat, three seconds for hat, twenty-five seconds to the street, forty-two seconds waiting for a hansom, and then seven minutes at the terminus before the express starts. I shall be glad of your company."

I was only too happy to have the privilege of going with him. It was most interesting to watch the workings of so inscrutable a mind. As we drove under the lofty iron roof of the terminus I noticed a look of annoyance pass over his face.

"We are fifteen seconds ahead of our time," he remarked, looking at the big clock. "I dislike having a miscalculation of that sort occur."

The great Scotch express stood ready for its long journey. The detective tapped one of the guards on the shoulder.

"You have heard of the so-called Pegram mystery, I presume?"

"Certainly, sir. It happened on this very train, sir."

"Really? Is the same carriage still on the train?"

"Well, yes, sir, it is," replied the guard, lowering his voice, "but of course, sir, we have to keep very quiet about it. People wouldn't travel in it, else, sir."

"Doubtless. Do you happen to know if anybody occupies the compartment in which the body was found?"

"A lady and gentleman, sir; I put 'em in myself, sir."

"Would you further oblige me," said the detective, deftly slipping half a sovereign into the hand of the guard, "by going to the window and informing them in an offhand casual sort of way that the tragedy took place in that compartment?"

"Certainly, sir."

We followed the guard, and the moment he had imparted his news there was a suppressed scream in the carriage. Instantly a lady came out, followed by a florid-faced gentleman, who scowled at the guard. We entered the now empty compartment, and Kombs said:

"We would like to be alone here until we reach Brewster."

"I'll see to that, sir," answered the guard, locking the door.

When the official moved away, I asked my friend what he expected to find in the carriage that would cast any light on the case.

"Nothing," was his brief reply.

"Then why do you come?"

"Merely to corroborate the conclusions I have already arrived at."

"And might I ask what those conclusions are?"

"Certainly," replied the detective, with a touch of lassitude in his voice. "I beg to call your attention, first, to the fact that this train stands between two platforms, and can be entered from either side. Any man familiar with the station for years would be aware of that fact. This shows how Mr. Kipson entered the train just before it started."

"But the door on this side is locked," I objected, trying it.

"Of course. But every season ticket holder carries a key. This accounts for the guard not seeing him, and for the absence of a ticket. Now let me give you some information about the influenza. The patient's temperature rises several degrees above normal, and he has a fever. When the malady has run its course, the temperature falls to three-quarters of a degree below normal. These facts are unknown to you, I imagine, because you are a doctor."

I admitted such was the case.

"Well, the consequence of this fall in temperature is that the convalescent's mind turns towards thoughts of suicide. Then is the time he should be watched by his friends. Then was the time Mr. Barrie Kipson's friends did *not* watch him. You remember the 21st, of course. No? It was a most depressing day. Fog all around and mud underfoot. Very good. He resolves on suicide. He wishes to be unidentified, if possible, but forgets his season ticket. My experience is that a man about to commit a crime always forgets something."

"But how do you account for the disappearance of the money?"

"The money has nothing to do with the matter. If he was a deep man, and knew the stupidness of Scotland Yard, he probably sent the notes to an enemy. If not, they may have been given to a friend. Nothing is more calculated to prepare the mind for self-destruction than the prospect of a night ride on the Scotch Express, and the view from the windows of the train as it passes through the northern part of London is particularly conducive to thoughts of annihilation."

"What became of the weapon?"

"That is just the point on which I wish to satisfy myself. Excuse me for a moment."

Mr. Sherlaw Kombs drew down the window on the right-hand side, and examined the top of the casing minutely with a magnifying glass. Presently he heaved a sigh of relief, and drew up the sash.

"Just as I expected," he remarked, speaking more to himself than to me. "There is a slight dent on the top of the window frame. It is of such a nature as to be made only by the trigger of a pistol falling from the nerveless hand of a suicide. He intended to throw the weapon far out of the window, but had not the strength. It might have fallen into the carriage. As a matter of fact, it bounced away from the line and lies among the grass about ten feet six inches from the outside rail. The only question that now remains is where the deed was committed, and the exact position of the pistol reckoned in miles from London, but that, fortunately, is too simple even to need explanation."

"Great heavens, Sherlaw!" I cried. "How can you call that simple? It seems to me impossible to compute."

We were now flying over northern London, and the great detective leaned back with every sign of *ennui,* closing his eyes. At last he spoke warily:

"It is really too elementary, Whatson, but I am always willing to oblige a friend. I shall be relieved, however, when you are able to work out the A B C of detection for yourself, although I shall never object to helping you with the words of more than three syllables. Having made up his mind to commit suicide, Kipson naturally intended to do it before he reached Brewster, because tickets are again examined at that point. When the train began to stop at the signal near Pegram, he came to the false conclusion that it was stopping at Brewster. The fact that the shot was not heard is accounted for by the screech of the air-brake, added to the noise of the train. Probably the whistle was also sounding at the same moment. The train being a fast express would stop as near the signal as possible. The air-brake will stop a train in twice its own length. Call it three times in this case. Very well. At three times the length of this train from the signal-post towards London, deducting half the length of the train, as this carriage is in the middle, you will find the pistol."

"Wonderful!" I exclaimed.

"Commonplace," he murmured.

At this moment the whistle sounded shrilly, and we felt the grind of the air-brakes.

"The Pegram signal again," cried Kombs, with something almost like enthusiasm. "This is indeed luck. We will get out here, Whatson, and test the matter."

As the train stopped, we got out on the right-hand side of the line. The engine stood panting impatiently under the red light, which changed to green as I looked at it. As the train moved on with increasing speed, the detective counted the carriages, and noted down the number. It was now dark, with the thin crescent of the moon hanging in the western sky throwing a weird half-light on the shining metals. The rear lamps of the train disappeared around a curve, and the signal stood at baleful red again. The black magic of the lonesome night in that strange place impressed me, but the detective was a most practical man. He placed his back against the signal-post, and paced up the line with even strides, counting his steps. I walked along the permanent way beside him silently. At last he stopped, and took a tape-line from his pocket. He ran it out until the ten feet six inches were unrolled, scanning the figures in the wan light of the new moon. Giving me the end, he placed his knuckles on the metals, motioning me to proceed down the embankment. I stretched out the line, and then sank my hand in the damp grass to mark the spot.

"Good God!" I cried, aghast. "What is this?"

"It is the pistol," said Kombs quietly.

It was!

* * *

Journalistic London will not soon forget the sensation that was caused by the record of the investigations of Sherlaw Kombs, as printed at length in the next day's *Evening Blade*. Would that my story ended here. Alas! Kombs contemptuously turned over the pistol to Scotland Yard. The meddlesome officials, actuated, as I always hold, by jealousy, found the name of the seller upon it. They investigated. The seller testified that it had never been in the possession of Mr. Kipson, as far as he knew. It was sold to a man whose description tallied with that of a criminal long watched by the police. He was arrested, and turned Queen's evidence in the hope of hanging his pal. It seemed that Mr. Kipson, who was a gloomy, taciturn man, and usually came home in a compartment by himself, thus escaping observation, had been murdered in the lane leading to his house. After robbing him, the miscreants turned their thoughts towards the disposal of the body – a subject that always occupies a first-class criminal mind after the deed is done. They agreed to place it on the line, and have it mangled by the Scotch Express, then nearly due. Before they got the body halfway up the embankment the express came along and stopped. The guard got out and walked along the other side to speak with the engineer. The thought of putting the body into an empty first-class carriage instantly occurred to the murderers. They opened the door with the deceased's key. It is supposed that the pistol dropped when they were hoisting the body in the carriage.

The Queen's evidence dodge didn't work, and Scotland Yard ignobly insulted my friend Sherlaw Kombs by sending him a pass to see the villains hanged.

BIBLIOGRAPHY - ROBERT BARR

Criminous works

The adventures of Sherlaw Kombs. Boulder, Colorado: Aspen Press, 1979. An edition of the
story as a separate.
Cardillac. London: Mills and Boon/New York: Stokes, 1909.
A Chicago princess. New York: Stokes 1904/London: Methuen – as: *The tempetuous petticoat,*
1905.
From whose bourne? London: Chatto & Windus, 1893, as by "Luke Sharp"/New York:
Stokes, 1896. Char: William Brenton, deceased. ss.
The girl in the case. New York: Nash, 1910.
Jennie Baxter, journalist. New York: Stokes/London: Methuen, 1899.
The King dines. London: McClure, 1901/London: Chatto & Windus/ New York: McClure
– as: *A prince of good fellows,* 1902.
Lady Eleanor, lawbreaker. Chicago: Rand McNally, 1911.
The mutable many. New York: Stokes, 1896/London: Methuen, 1897.
Over the border. New York: Stokes/London: Isbister, 1903.
Revenge! New York: Stokes/London: Chatto & Windus, 1896. ss.
A rock in the Baltic. New York: Authors & Newspapers, 1906/London: Hurst & Blackett,
1907.
Strange happenings. As by "Luke Sharp." London: Dunkerley, 1883. ss.
The strong arm. New York: Stokes, 1899/London: Methuen, 1900. A selection therein was
published as: *Gentlemen, the King!* – New York: Stokes, [n.d.] ss.
Tales of two continents. London: Mills and Boon, 1920. ss.
The triumphs of Eugène Valmont. New York: Appleton/London: Hurst, 1906.
The victors; a romance of yesterday morning and this afternoon. New York: Stokes,
1901/London: Methuen, 1902. Set: New York City. A study of political corruption.
The Watermead Affair. Philadelphia: Altemus, 1906.
A woman intervenes; or, The mistress of the mine. New York: Stokes/ London: Chatto &
Windus, 1896.
The woman wins. New York: Stokes/London: Methuen – as: *The Lady Electra,* 1904. ss.

Other works

The helping hand; and other stories. London: Mills and Boon, 1920. ss.
I travel the road. London: Quality, 1945.
In a steamer chair; and other shipboard stories. London: Chatto & Windus/New York:
Cassell, 1892. ss.
In the midst of alarms. London: Methuen/New York: Stokes, 1894. Set in the Niagara region
of Canada in 1866 during the Fenian invasion.
Lord Stranleigh abroad. London: Ward, Lock, 1913.
Lord Stranleigh, philanthropist. London: Ward, Lock, 1911.
The measure of the rule. London: Constable, 1907/New York: Appleton, 1908. Set: Toronto.
Char: Tom Prentis. An autobigraphical novel of the author's training at the Toronto
Normal School.
My enemy Jones; an extravaganza. London: Nash/London: Hodder & Stoughton – as:
Unsentimental journey, 1913.

One day's courtship; and, The heralds of fame. New York: Stokes, 1896. Set in Canada.

The O'Ruddy. With Stephen Crane. New York: Stokes, 1903/London: Methuen, 1904. A picaresque tale.

The palace of logs. London: Mills and Boon, 1912.

The speculations of John Steele. London: Chatto & Windus/New York: Stokes, 1905.

Stranleigh's millions. London: Nash, 1909.

The sword maker. London: Mills and Boon/New York: Stokes, 1910.

Tekla; a romance of love and war. New York: Stokes, 1898/London: Methuen – as: *The Countess Tekla,* 1899.

The unchanging East. London: Chatto & Windus/Boston: Page, 1900.

A woman in a thousand. London: Hodder & Stoughton, 1913.

Young Lord Stranleigh. London: Ward, Lock/New York: Appleton, 1908.

WILLIAM FRASER

Bulldog Carney
Bulldog Carney.
Toronto: McClelland & Stewart, 1919.

Wild Oats
Red Meekins.
New York: Doran/Toronto: McClelland & Stewart, 1921.

FRASER, William Alexander, 1859-1933

Born at River John in Pictou County, Nova Scotia, in 1859, William Fraser received his early education in New York and Boston. At the age of fourteen he returned to Canada to live with an uncle in Elgin County in Southwestern Ontario. He graduated in engineering and helped to develop the early oil wells in Western Ontario. Subsequently he spent seven years prospecting for oil in Burma and India, where he met and became a life-long friend of Rudyard Kipling.

On his return to Canada Fraser prospected for oil in Western Canada: in the employ of the Canadian Government, he sank the first well at Pelican Falls, Alberta. He also prospected for precious metals in the Cobalt District of Northern Ontario in its roaring days, using his experiences as a setting for *Red Meekins*.

Due to illness, Fraser gave up field work and settled in Georgetown, Ontario, where he lived for many years. It was Fraser who suggested and saw into realization the Silver Cross for mothers whose sons had died in war. Fraser died at his Toronto residence on 9 November 1933, in his 75th year.

Fraser spun exciting tales with a humorous touch about exotic places like India and Burma. Such a story is *Caste*, which is set in India and tells about Captain Barlow and British operations against Indian highwaymen. A review in the *Canadian Bookman* in 1922 called it "... a masterpiece in colour, intrigue, and dramatic love, laid in the old India. The facts of the story are authentic, having been turned over to Fraser by the India Office."

Fraser is also known for the novels *The eye of a god; and other tales of East and West; Thirteen men;* and *The three sapphires*, as well as more sophisticated mysteries about horse-racing: *Brave hearts, Delilah plays the ponies*, and *Thoroughbreds*. He was also a prolific writer of short stories, with over 250 to his credit.

BULLDOG CARNEY
Bulldog Carney. Toronto: McClelland & Stewart, 1919.

Fraser gets two stories in this collection because he explored two of Canada's frontiers: the West and the mining country of north-eastern Ontario.

Bulldog Carney is a collection of skilfully told Western tales about a Robin Hood-like smuggler in the Alberta foothills.

Bulldog Carney, the hero, is not the only knave-turned-thief-taker to come out of Canada's Northwest Territories. Contemporaneously, there was "Blue Pete," a reformed cattle rustler who worked as an agent for the North West Mounted Police, and was created by "Luke Allen," (i.e., [William] Lacey Amy). "Blue Pete" originally appeared as a character in "Blue Pete, the sentimental half-breed,"* and made his full-length-novel debut in *Blue Pete: half-breed; a story of the cowboy West* ** in 1920, the first of a series of twenty titles.

There is no indication which character inspired which: did the initial appearance of "Blue Pete" in 1911 plant the seed of "Bulldog Carney" in Fraser's mind? Did the publication of *Bulldog Carney* in 1919 spur Amy to resurrect his cowboy-cum-police-agent? Such speculation is one with the song the sirens sang. What is important is that we have two originals who each bring us a picture of life in the Canadian West in the early days of the twentieth century, and provide us with good entertainment as well.

---

* In *The Canadian Magazine,* January 1911.

** Lacey Amy. *Blue Pete: half-breed; a story of the cowboy West.* London: Jenkins, 1920/New York: James A. McCann, 1921.

BULLDOG CARNEY

I've thought it over many ways and I'm going to tell this story as it happened, for I believe the reader will feel he is getting a true picture of things as they were but will not be again. A little padding up of the love interest, a little spilling of blood, would, perhaps, make it stronger technically, but would it lessen his faith that the curious thing happened? It's beyond me to know – I write it as it was.

To begin at the beginning, Cameron was peeved. He was rather a diffident chap, never merging harmoniously into the western atmosphere; what saved him from rude knocks was the fact that he was lean of speech. He stood on the board sidewalk in front of the Alberta Hotel and gazed dejectedly across a trench of black mud that represented the main street. He hated the sight of squalid, ramshackle Edmonton, but still more did he dislike the turmoil that was within the hotel.

A lean-faced man, with small piercing gray eyes, had ridden his buckskin cayuse into the bar and was buying. Nagel's furtrading men, topping off their spree in town before the long trip to Great Slave Lake, were enthusiastically, vociferously naming their tipple. A freighter, Billy the Piper, was playing the "Arkansaw Traveller" on a tin whistle.

When the gray-eyed man on the buckskin pushed his way into the bar, the whistle had almost clattered to the floor from the piper's hand; then he gasped, so low that no one heard him, "By cripes! Bulldog Carney!" There was apprehension trembling in his hushed voice. Well he knew that if he had clarioned the name something would have happened to Billy the Piper. A quick furtive look darting over the faces of his companions told him that no one else had recognized the horseman.

Outside, Cameron, irritated by the rasping tin whistle groaned, "My God! a land of bums!" Three days he had waited to pick up a man to replace a member of his gang down at Fort Victor who had taken a sudden chill through intercepting a plug of cold lead.

Diagonally across the lane of ooze two men waded and clambered to the board sidewalk just beside Cameron to stamp the muck from their boots. One of the two, Cayuse Gray, spoke:

"This feller'll pull his freight with you, boss, if terms is right; he's a hell of a worker."

Half turning, Cameron's Scotch eyes took keep cognizance of the "feller": a shudder twitched his shoulders. He had never seen a more wolfish face set atop a man's neck. It was a sinister face; not the thin, vulpine sneak visage of a thief, but lowering: black sullen eyes peered boldly up from under shaggy brows that almost met a mop of black hair, the forehead was so low. It was a hungry face, as if its owner had a standing account against the world. But Cameron wanted a strong worker, and his business instinct found strength and endurance in that heavy-shouldered frame, and strong, wide-set legs.

"What's your name?" he asked.

"Jack Wolf," the man answered.

The questioner shivered; it was as if the speaker had named the thought that was in his mind.

Cayuse Gray tongued a chew of tobacco into his cheek, spat, and added, "Jack the Wolf is what he gets most oftenest."

"From damn broncho-headed fools," Wolf retorted angrily.

At that instant a straggling Salvation Army band tramped around the corner into Jasper Avenue, and, forming a circle, cut loose with brass and tambourine. As the wail from the instruments went up, the men in the bar, led by Billy the Piper, swarmed out.

A half-breed roared out a profane parody on the Salvation hymn:—

"There are flies on you, and there're flies on
me,
But there ain't no flies on Je-e-e-sus."

This crude humor appealed to the men who had issued from the bar; they shouted in delight.

A girl who had started forward with her tambourine to collect stood aghast at the profanity, her blue eyes wide in horror.

The breed broke into a drunken laugh: "That's damn fine new songs for de Army bums, Miss," he jeered.

The buckskin cayuse, whose mouse-colored muzzle had been sticking through the door, now pushed to the sidewalk, and his rider, stooping his lithe figure, took the right ear of the breed in lean bony fingers with a grip that suggested he was squeezing a lemon. "You dirty swine!" he snarled; "you're insulting the two greatest things on earth – God and a woman. Apologize, you hound!"

Probably the breed would have capitulated readily, but his river-mates' ears were not in a death grip, and they were bellicose with bad liquor. There was an angry yell of defiance, events moved with alacrity. Profanity, the passionate profanity of anger, smote the air; a beer bottle hurtled through the open door, missed its mark – the man on the buckskin – but, end on, found a bull's-eye between the Wolf's shoulder blades, and that gentleman dove into the black mud of Jasper Avenue.

A silence smote the Salvation Army band. Like the Arab it folded its instruments and stole away.

A Mounted Policeman, attracted by the clamour, reined his horse to the sidewalk to quiet with a few words of admonition this bar-room row. He slipped from the saddle; but at the second step forward he checked as the thin face of the horseman turned and the steel-gray eyes met his own. "Get down off that cayuse, Bulldog Carney – I want you!" he commanded in sharp clicking tones.

Happenings followed this. There was the bark of a 6-gun, a flash, the Policeman's horse jerked his head spasmodically, a little jet of red spurted from his forehead, and he collapsed, his knees burrowing into the black mud and as the buckskin cleared the sidewalk in a leap, the half-breed, two steel-like fingers in his shirt band, was swung behind the rider.

With a spring like a panther the policeman reached his fallen horse, but as he swung his gun from its holster he held it poised silent; to shoot was to kill the breed.

Fifty yards down the street Carney dumped his burden into a deep puddle, and with a ringing cry of defiance sped away. Half-a-dozen guns were out and barking vainly after the escaping man.

Carney cut down the bush-road that wound its sinuous way to the river flat, some two hundred feet below the town level. The ferry, swinging from the steel hawser, that stretched across the river, was snuggling the bank.

"Some luck," the rider of the buckskin chuckled. To the ferryman he said in a crisp voice: "Cut her out; I'm in a hurry!"

The ferryman grinned. "For one passenger, eh? Might you happen to be the Gov'nor General, by any chanct?"

Carney's handy gun held its ominous eye on the boatman, and its owner answered, "I happen to be a man in a hell of a hurry. If you want to travel with me get busy."

The thin lips of the speaker had puckered till they resembled a slit in a dried orange. The small gray eyes were barely discernible between the half-closed lids; there was something devilish compelling in the lean parchment face; it told of demoniac concentration in the brain behind.

The ferryman knew. With a pole he swung the stern of the flat barge down stream, the iron pulleys on the cable whined a screeching protest, the hawsers creaked, the swift current wedged against the tangented side of the ferry, and swiftly Bulldog Carney and his buckskin were shot across the muddy old Saskatchewan.

On the other side he handed the boatman a five dollar bill, and with a grim smile said: "Take a little stroll with me to the top of the hill; there's some drunken bums across there whose company I don't want."

At the top of the south bank Carney mounted his buckskin and melted away into the poplar-covered landscape; stepped out of the story for the time being.

Back at the Alberta the general assembly was rearranging itself. The Mounted Policeman, now set afoot by the death of his horse, had hurried down to the barracks to report; possibly to follow up Carney's trail with a new mount.

The half-breed had come back from the puddle a thing of black ooze and profanity.

Jack the Wolf, having dug the mud from his eyes, and ears, and neck band, was in the hotel making terms with Cameron for the summer's work at Fort Victor.

Billy the Piper was revealing intimate history of Bulldog Carney. From said narrative it appeared that Bulldog was as humorous a bandit as ever slit a throat. Billy had freighted whisky for Carney when that gentleman was king of the booze runners.

"Why didn't you spill the beans, Billy?" Nagel queried; "there's a thousand on Carney's head all the time. We'd've tied him horn and hoof and copped the dough."

"Dif'rent here," the Piper growled; "I've saw a man flick his gun and pot at Carney when Bulldog told him to throw up his hands, and all that cuss did was laugh and thrown his own gun up coverin' the other broncho; but it was enough – the other guy's hands went up too quick. If I'd set the pack on him, havin' so to speak no just cause, well, Nagel, you'd been lookin' round for another freighter. He's the queerest cuss I ever stacked up agen. It kinder seems as if jokes is his religion; an' when he's out to play he's plumb hostile. Don't monkey none with his game, is my advice to you fellers."

Nagel stepped to the door, thrust his swarthy face through it, and, seeing that the policeman had gone, came back to the bar and said: "Boys, the drinks is on me cause I see a man, a real man."

He poured whisky into a glass and waited with it held high till the others had done likewise; then he said in a voice that vibrated with admiration:

"Here's to Bulldog Carney! Gad, I love a man! When that damn trooper calls him, what does he do? You or me would've quit cold or plugged Mister Khaki-jacket – we'd had to. Not so Bulldog. He thinks with his nut, and both hands, and both feet; I don't need to tell you boys what happened; you see it, and it were done pretty. Here's to Bulldog Carney!" Nagel held his hand out to the Piper: "Shake, Billy. If you'd give that cuss away I'd've kicked you into kingdom come, knowin' him as I do now."

* * *

The population of Fort Victor, drawing the color line, was four people: the Hudson's Bay Factor, a missionary minister and his wife, and a school teacher, Lucy Black. Half-breeds and Indians came and went, constituting a floating population; Cameron and his men were temporary citizens.

Lucy Black was lathy of construction, several years past her girlhood, and not an animated girl. She was a professional religionist. If there were seeming voids in her life they were filled with this dominating passion of moral reclamation; if she worked without enthusiasm she made up for it in insistent persistence. It was as if a diluted strain of the old Inquisition had percolated down through the blood of centuries and found a subdued existence in this pale-haired, blue-eyed woman.

When Cameron brought Jack the Wolf to Fort Victor it was evident to the little teacher that he was morally an Augean stable: a man who wandered in mental darkness; his soul was dying for want of spiritual nourishment.

On the seventy-mile ride in the Red River buck-board from Edmonton to Fort Victor the morose Wolf had punctuated every remark with virile oaths, their original angularity suggesting that his meditative moments were spent in coining appropriate expressions for his perfervid view of life. Twice Cameron's blood had surged hot as the Wolf, at some trifling perversity of the horses, had struck viciously.

Perhaps it was the very soullessness of the Wolf that roused the religious fanaticism of the little school teacher; or perhaps it was the strange contrariness in nature that causes the widely divergent to lean eachotherward. At any rate a miracle grew in Fort Victor. Jack the Wolf and the little teacher strolled together in the evening as the great sun swept down over the rolling prairie to the west; and sometimes the full-faced moon, topping the poplar bluffs to the east, found Jack slouching at Lucy's feet while she, sitting on a camp stool, talked Bible to him.

At first Cameron rubbed his eyes as if his Scotch vision had somehow gone agley; but, gradually, whatever incongruity had manifested at first died away.

As a worker Wolf was wonderful; his thirst for toil was like his thirst for moral betterment – insatiable. The missionary in a chat with Cameron explained it very succinctly: "Wolf, like many other Westerners, had never had a chance to know the difference between right and wrong; but the One who missed not the sparrow's fall had led him to the port of salvation, Fort Victor – Glory to God!" The poor fellow's very wickedness was but the result of neglect. Lucy was the worker in the Lord's vineyard who had been chosen to lead this man into a better life.

It did seem very simple, very all right. Tough characters were always being saved all over the world – regenerated, metamorphosed, and who was Jack the Wolf that he should be excluded from salvation.

At any rate Cameron's survey gang, vitalized by the abnormal energy of Wolf, became a high-powered machine.

The half-breeds, when couraged by bad liquor, shed their religion and became barbaric, vulgarly vicious. The missionary had always waited until this condition had passed, then remonstrance and a gift of bacon with, perhaps, a bag of flour, had brought repentance. This method Jack the Wolf declared was all wrong; the breeds were like train-dogs, he affirmed, and should be taught respect for God's agents in a proper muscular manner. So the first time three French half-breeds, enthusiastically drunk, invaded the little log school house and declared school was out, sending the teacher home with tears of shame in her blue eyes, Jack reëstablished the dignity of the church by generously walloping the three backsliders.

It is wonderful how the solitude of waste places will blossom the most ordinary woman into a flower of delight to the masculine eye; and the lean, anæmic, scrawny-haired school teacher had held as admirers all of Cameron's gang, and one Sergeant Heath of the Mounted Police whom she had known in the Klondike, and who had lately come to Edmonton. With her negative nature she had appreciated them pretty much equally; but when the business of salvaging this prairie derelict came to hand the others were practically ignored.

For two months Fort Victor was thus; the Wolf always the willing worker and well on the way, seemingly, to redemption.

Cameron's foreman, Bill Slade, a much-whiskered, wise old man, was the only one of little faith. Once he said to Cameron:

"I don't like it none too much; it takes no end of worry to make a silk purse out of a sow's ear; Jack has blossomed too quick; he's a booze fighter, and that kind always laps up mental stimulants to keep the blue devils away."

"You're doing the lad an injustice, I think," Cameron said. "I was prejudiced myself at first."

Slade pulled a heavy hand three times down his big beard, spat a shaft of tobacco juice, took his hat off, straightened out a couple of dents in it, and put it back on his head:

"You best stick to that prejudice feeling, Boss – first guesses about a feller most gener'ly pans out pretty fair. And I'd keep an eye kinder skinned if you have any fuss with Jack; I see him look at you once or twice when you corrected his way of doin' things."

Cameron laughed.

"'Tain't no laughin' matter, Boss. when a feller's been used to cussin' like hell he can't keep healthy bottlin' it up. And all that dirtiness that's in the Wolf'll bust out some day same's you touched a match to a tin of powder; he'll throw back."

"There's nobody to worry about except the little school teacher," Cameron said meditatively.

This time it was Slade who chuckled. "The school mam's as safe as houses. She ain't got a pint of red blood in 'em veins of hers, 'tain't nothin' but vinegar. Jack's just tryin' to sober up on her religion, that's all; it kind of makes him forget horse stealin' an' such while he makes a stake workin' here."

Then one morning Jack had passed into perihelion.

Cameron took his double-barreled shot gun, meaning to pick up some prairie chicken while he was out looking over his men's work. As he passed the shack where his men bunked he noticed the door open. This was careless, for train dogs were always prowling about for just such a chance for loot. He stepped through the door and took a peep into the other room. There sat the Wolf at a pine table playing solitaire.

"What's the matter?" the Scotchman asked.

"I've quit," the Wolf answered surlily.

"Quit?" Cameron queried. "The gang can't carry on without a chain man."

"I don't care a damn. It don't make no dif'rence to me. I'm sick of that tough bunch – swearin' and cussin,' and tellin' smutty stories all day; a man can't keep decent in that outfit."

"Ma God!" Startled by this, Cameron harked back to his most expressive Scotch.

"You needn't swear 'bout it, Boss; you yourself ain't never give me no square deal; you've treated me like a breed."

This palpable lie fired Cameron's Scotch blood; also the malignant look that Slade had seen was now in the wolfish eyes. It was a murder look, enhanced by the hypocritical attitude Jack had taken.

"You're a scoundrel!" Cameron blurted; "I wouldn't keep you on the work. The sooner Fort Victor is shut of you the better for all hands, especially the women folks. You're a scoundrel."

Jack sprang to his feet; his hand went back to a hip pocket; but his blazing wolfish eyes were looking into the muzzle of the double-barrel gun that Cameron had swung straight from his hip, both fingers on the triggers.

"Put your hands flat on the table, you blackguard," Cameron commanded. "If I weren't a married man I'd blow the top of your head off; you're no good on earth; you'd be better dead, but my wife would worry because I did the deed."

The Wolf's empty hand had come forward and was placed, palm downward, on the table.

"Now, you hound, you're just a bluffer. I'll show you what I think of you. I'm going to turn my back, walk out, and send a breed up to Fort Saskatchewan for a policeman to gather you in."

Cameron dropped the muzzle of his gun, turned on his heel and started out.

"Come back and settle with me," the Wolf demanded.

"I'll settle with you in jail, you blackguard!" Cameron threw over his shoulder, stalking on.

Plodding along, not without nervous twitchings of apprehension, the Scotchman heard behind him the voice of the Wolf saying, "Don't do that, Mr. Cameron; I flew off the handle and so did you, but I didn't mean nothin'."

Cameron, ignoring the Wolf's plea, went along to his shack and wrote a note, the ugly visage of the Wolf hovering at the open door. He was humbled, beaten. Gun-play in Montana, where the Wolf had left a bad record, was one thing, but with a cordon of Mounted Police between him and the border it was a different matter; also he was wanted for a more serious crime than a threat to shoot, and once in the toils this might crop up. So he pleaded. But Cameron was obdurate; the Wolf had no right to stick up his work and quit at a moment's notice.

Then Jack had an inspiration. He brought Lucy Black. Like woman of all time her faith having been given she stood pat, a flush rouging her bleached cheeks as, earnest in her mission, she pleaded for the "wayward boy," as she euphemistically designated this coyote. Cameron was to let him go to lead the better life; thrown into the pen of the police barracks, among bad characters, he would become contaminated. The police had always persecuted her Jack.

Cameron mentally exclaimed again, "Ma God!" as he saw tears in the neutral blue-tinted eyes. Indeed it was time that the Wolf sought a new runway. He had a curious Scotch reverence for women, and was almost reconciled to the loss of a man over the breaking up of this situation.

Jack was paid the wages due; but at his request for a horse to take him back to Edmonton the Scotchman laughed. "I'm not making presents of horses today," he said; "and I'll take good care that nobody else here is shy a horse when you go, Jack. You'll take the hoof express – it's good enough for you."

So the Wolf tramped out of Fort Victor with a pack slung over his shoulder; and the next day Sergeant Heath swung into town looking very debonaire in his khaki, sitting atop the bright blood-bay police horse.

He hunted up Cameron, saying: "You've a man here that I want – Jack Wolf. They've found his prospecting partner dead up on the Smoky River, with a bullet hole in the back of his head. We want Jack at Edmonton to explain."

"He's gone."

"Gone! When?"

"Yesterday."

The Sergeant stared helplessly at the Scotchman.

A light dawned upon Cameron. "Did you, by any chance, send word that you were coming?" he asked.

"I'll be back, mister," and Heath darted from the shack, swung to his saddle, and galloped toward the little log school house.

Cameron waited. In half an hour the Sergeant was back, a troubled look in his face.

"I'll tell you," he said dejectedly, "women are hell; they ought to be interned when there's business on."

"The little school teacher?"

"The little fool!"

"You trusted her and wrote you were coming, eh?"

"I did."

"Then, my friend, I'm afraid you were the foolish one."

"How was I to know that rustler had been 'making bad medicine' – had put the evil eye on Lucy? Gad, man, she's plumb locoed; she stuck up for him; spun me the most glimmering tale – she's got a dime novel skinned four ways of the pack. According to her the police stood in with Bulldog Carney on a train holdup, and made this poor innocent lamb the goat. They persecuted him, and he had to flee. Now he's given his heart to God, and gone away to buy a ranch and send for Lucy, where the two of them are to live happy ever after."

"Ma God!" the Scotchman cried with vehemence.

"That bean-headed affair in calico gave him five hundred she's pinched up against her chest for years."

Cameron gasped and stared blankly; even his reverent exclamatory standby seemed inadequate.

"What time yesterday did the Wolf pull out?" the Sergeant asked.

"About three o'clock."

"Afoot?"

"Yes."

"He'll rustle a cayuse the first chance he gets, but if he stays afoot he'll hit Edmonton to-night, seventy miles."

"To catch the morning train for Calgary," Cameron suggested.

"You don't know the Wolf, Boss; he's got his namesake of the forest skinned to death when it comes to covering up his trail – no train for him now that he knows I'm on his track; he'll just touch civilization for grub till he makes the border for Montana. I've got to get him. If you'll stake me to a fill-up of bacon and a chew of oats for the horse I'll eat and pull out."

In an hour Sergeant Heath shook hands with Cameron saying: "If you'll just not say a word about how that cuss got the message I'll be much obliged. It would break me if it dribbled to headquarters."

Then he rode down the ribbon of roadway that wound to the river bed, forded the old Saskatchewan that was at its summer depth, mounted the south bank and disappeared.

* * *

When Jack the Wolf left Fort Victor he headed straight for a little log shack, across the river, where Descoign, a French half-breed, lived. The family was away berry picking, and Jack twisted a rope into an Indian bridle and borrowed a cayuse from the log corral. The cayuse was some devil, and that evening, thir-ty miles south, he chewed loose the rope hobble on his two front feet, and left the Wolf afoot.

Luck set in against Jack just there, for he found no more borrowable horses till he came to where the trail forked ten miles short of Fort Saskatchewan. To the right, running southwest, lay the well beaten trail that passed through Fort Saskatchewan to cross the river and on to Edmonton. The trail that switched to the left, running southeast, was the old, now rarely-used one that stretched away hundreds of miles to Winnipeg.

The Wolf was a veritable Indian in his slow cunning; a gambler where money was the stake, but where his freedom, perhaps his life, was involved he could wait, and wait, and play the game more than safe. The Winnipeg trail would be deserted – Jack knew that; a man could travel it the round of the clock and meet nobody, most like. Seventy miles beyond he could leave it, and heading due west, strike the Calgary railroad and board a train at some small station. No notice would be taken of him, for trappers, prospectors, men from distant ranches, morose, untalkative men, were always drifting toward the rails, coming up out of the silent solitudes of the wastes, unquestioned and unquestioning.

The Wolf knew that he would be followed; he knew that Sergeant Heath would pull out on his trail and follow relentlessly, seeking the glory of capturing his man single-handed. That was the *esprit de corps* of these riders of the prairies, and Heath was, *par excellence,* large in conceit.

A sinister sneer lifted the upper lip of the trailing man until his strong teeth glistened like veritable wolf fangs. He had full confidence in his ability to outguess Sergeant Heath or any other Mounted Policeman.

He had stopped at the fork of the trail long enough to light his pipe, looking down the Fort Saskatchewan-Edmonton road thinking. He knew the old Winnipeg trail ran approximately ten or twelve miles east of the railroad south for a hundred miles or more; where it crossed a trail running into Red Deer, half-way between Edmonton and Calgary, it was about ten miles east of that town.

He swung his blanket pack to his back and stepped blithely along the Edmonton chocolate-colored highway muttering: "You red-coated snobs, you're waiting for Jack. A nice baited trap. And behind, herding me in, my brave Sergeant. Well, I'm coming."

Where there was a matrix of black mud he took care to leave a footprint; where there was dust he walked in it, in one or the other of the ever persisting two furrow-like paths that had been worn through the strong prairie turf by the hammering hoofs of two horses abreast, and grinding wheels of wagon and buckboard. For two miles he followed the trail till he sighted a shack with a man chopping in the front yard. Here the Wolf went in and begged some matches and a drink of milk; incidentally he asked how far it was to Edmonton. Then he went back to the trail – still toward Edmonton. The Wolf had plenty of matches, and he didn't need the milk, but the man would tell Sergeant Heath when he came along of the one he had seen heading for Edmonton.

For a quarter of a mile Jack walked on the turf beside the road, twice putting down a foot in the dust to make a print; then he walked on the road for a short distance and again took to the turf. He saw a rig coming from behind, and popped into a cover of poplar bushes until it had passed. Then he went back to the road and left prints of his feet in the black soft dust, that would indicate that he had climbed into a waggon here from behind. This accomplished he turned east across the prairie, reaching the old Winnipeg trail, a mile away; then he turned south.

At noon he came to a little lake and ate his bacon raw, not risking the smoke of a fire; then on in that tireless Indian plod – toes in, and head hung forward, that is so easy on the working joints – hour after hour; it was not a walk, it was more like the dog-trot of a cayuse, easy springing short steps, always on the balls of his wide strong feet.

At five he ate again, then on. He travelled till midnight, the shadowy gloom having blurred his path at ten o'clock. Then he slept in a thick clump of saskatoon bushes.

At three it was daylight, and screened as he was and thirsting for his drink of hot tea, he built a small fire and brewed the inspiring beverage. On forked sticks he broiled some bacon; then on again.

All day he travelled. In the afternoon elation began to creep into his veins; he was well past Edmonton now. At night he would take the dipper on his right hand and cut across the prairie straight west; by morning he would reach steel; the train leaving Edmonton would come along about ten, and he would be in Calgary that night. Then he could go east, or west, or south to the Montana border by rail. Heath would go on to Edmonton; the police would spend two or three days searching all the shacks and Indian and half-breed camps, and they would watch the daily outgoing train.

There was one chance that they might wire Calgary to look out for him; but there was no course open without some risk of capture; he was up against that possibility. It was a gamble, and he was playing his hand the best he knew how. Even approaching Calgary he would swing from the train on some grade, and work his way into town at night to a shack where Montana Dick lived. Dick would know what was doing.

Toward evening the trail gradually swung to the east skirting muskeg country. At first the Wolf took little notice of the angle of detour; he was thankful he followed a trail, for trails never led one into impassable country; the muskeg would run out and the trail swing west again. But for two hours he plugged along, quickening his pace, for he realized now that he was covering miles which had to be made up when he swung west again.

Perhaps it was the depressing continuance of the desolate muskeg through which the shadowy figures of startled hares darted that cast the tiring man into foreboding. Into his furtive mind crept a suspicion that he was being trailed. So insidiously had this dread birthed that at first it was simply worry, a feeling as if the tremendous void of the prairie was closing in on him, that now and then a white boulder ahead was a crouching wolf. He shivered, shook his wide shoulders and cursed. It was that he was tiring, perhaps.

Then suddenly the thing took form, mental form – something *was* on his trail. This primitive creature was like an Indian – gifted with the sixth sense that knows when somebody is coming though he may be a day's march away; the mental wireless that animals possess. He tried to laugh it off to dissipate the unrest with blasphemy; but it wouldn't down.

The prairie was like a huge platter, everything stood out against the luminous evening sky like the sails of a ship at sea. If it were Heath trailing, and that man saw him, he would never reach the railroad. His footprints lay along the trail, for it was hard going on the heavily-grassed turf. To cut across the muskeg that stretched for miles would trap him. In the morning light the Sergeant would discover that his tracks had disappeared, and would know just where he had gone. Being mounted the Sergeant would soon make up for the few hours of darkness – would reach the railway and wire down the line.

The Wolf plodded on for half a mile, then he left the trail where the ground was rolling, cut east for five hundred yards, and circled back. On the top of a cut-bank that was fringed with wolf willow he crouched to watch. The sun had slipped through purple clouds, and dropping below them into a sea of greenish-yellow space, had bathed in blood the whole mass of tesselated vapour; suddenly outlined against this glorious background a horse and man silhouetted, the stiff erect seat in the saddle, the docked tail of the horse, square cut at the hocks, told the watcher that it was a policeman.

When the rider had passed the Wolf trailed him keeping east of the road where his visibility was low against the darkening side of the vast dome. Half a mile beyond where the Wolf had turned, the Sergeant stopped, dismounted, and, leading the horse, with head low hung searched the trail for the tracks that had now disappeared. Approaching night, creeping first over the prairie, had blurred it into a gigantic rug of sombre hue. The trail was like a softened stripe; footprints might be there, merged into the pattern till they were indiscernible.

A small oval lake showed in the edge of the muskeg beside the trail, its sides festooned by strong-growing blue-joint, wild oats, wolf willow, saskatoon bushes, and silver-leafed poplar. Ducks, startled from the nests, floating nests built of interwoven rush leaves and grass, rose in circling flights, uttering plaintive rebukes. Three giant sandhill cranes flopped their sail-like wings, folded their long spindle shanks straight out behind, and soared away like kites.

Crouched back beside the trail the Wolf watched and waited. He knew what the Sergeant would do; having lost the trail of his quarry he would camp there, beside good water, tether his horse to the picket pin by the hackamore rope, eat, and sleep till daylight, which would come about three o'clock; then he would cast about for the Wolf's tracks, gallop along the southern trail, and when he did not pick them up would surmise that Jack had cut across the muskeg land; then he would round the southern end of the swamp and head for the railway.

"I must get him," the Wolf muttered mercilessly; "gentle him if I can, if not – get him."

He saw the Sergeant unsaddle his horse, picket him, and eat a cold meal; this rather than beacon his presence by a glimmering fire.

The Wolf, belly to earth, wormed closer, slithering over the gillardias, crunching their yellow blooms beneath his evil body, his revolver held between his strong teeth as his grimy paws felt the ground for twigs that might crack.

If the Sergeant would unbuckle his revolver belt, and perhaps go down to the water for a drink, or even to the horse that was at the far end of the picket line, his nose buried deep in the succulent wild-pea vine, then the Wolf would rush his man, and the Sergeant, disarmed, would throw up his hands.

The Wolf did not want on his head the death of a Mounted Policeman, for then the "Redcoats" would trail him to all corners of the earth. All his life there would be someone on his trail. It was too big a price. Even if the murder thought had been paramount, in that dim light the first shot meant not overmuch.

So Jack waited. Once the horse threw up his head, cocked his ears fretfully, and stood like a bronze statue; then he blew a breath of discontent through his spread nostrils, and again buried his muzzle in the pea vine and sweet-grass.

Heath had seen this movement of the horse and ceased cutting at the plug of tobacco with which he was filling his pipe; he stood up, and searched with his eyes the mysterious gloomed prairie.

The Wolf, flat to earth, scarce breathed.

The Sergeant snuffed out the match hidden in his cupped hands over the bowl, put the pipe in his pocket, and, revolver in hand, walked in a narrow circle; slowly, stealthily, stopping every few feet to listen; not daring to go too far lest the man he was after might be hidden somewhere and cut out his horse. He passed within ten feet of where the Wolf lay, just a gray mound against the gray turf.

The Sergeant went back to his blanket and with his saddle for a pillow lay down, the tiny glow of his pipe showing the Wolf that he smoked. He had not removed his pistol belt.

The Wolf lying there commenced to think grimly how easy it would be to kill the policeman as he slept; to wiggle, snake-like, to within a few feet and then the shot. But killing was a losing game, the blundering trick of a man who easily lost control; the absolutely last resort when a man was cornered beyond escape and saw a long term at Stony Mountain ahead of him, or the gallows. The Wolf would wait till all the advantage was with him. Besides, the horse was like a watch-dog. The Wolf was down wind from them now, but if he moved enough to rouse the horse, or the wind shifted – no, he would wait. In the morning the Sergeant, less wary in the daylight, might give him his chance.

Fortunately it was late in the summer and that terrible pest, the mosquito, had run his course.

The Wolf slipped back a few yards deeper into the scrub, and, tired, slept. He knew that at the first wash of gray in the eastern sky the ducks would wake him. He slept like an animal, scarce slipping from consciousness; a stamp of the horse's hoof on the sounding turf bringing him wide awake. Once a gopher raced across his legs, and he all but sprang to his feet thinking the Sergeant had grappled with him. Again a great horned owl, at a twist of Jack's head as he dreamed, swooped silently and struck, thinking it a hare.

Brought out of his sleep by the myriad noises of the waterfowl the Wolf knew that night was past, and the dice of chance were about to be thrown. He crept back to where the Sergeant was in full view, the horse, his sides ballooned by the great feed of sweet-pea vine, lay at rest, his muzzle on the earth, his drooped ears showing that he slept.

Waked by the harsh cry of a loon that swept by rending the air with his death-like scream, the Sergeant sat bolt upright and rubbed his eyes sleepily. He rose, stretched his arms above his head, and stood for a minute looking off toward the eastern sky that was now taking on a rose tint. The horse, with a little snort, canted to his feet and sniffed toward the water; the Sergeant pulled the picket pin and led him to the lake for a drink.

Hungrily the Wolf looked at the carbine that lay across the saddle, but the Sergeant watered his horse without passing behind the bushes. It was a chance; but still the Wolf waited, thinking, "I want an ace in the hole when I play this hand."

Sergeant Heath slipped the picket pin back into the turf, saddled his horse, and stood mentally debating something. Evidently the something had to do with Jack's whereabouts, for Heath next climbed a short distance up a poplar, and with his field glasses scanned the surrounding prairie. This seemed to satisfy him; he dropped back to earth, gathered some dry poplar branches and built a little fire, hanging by a forked stick he drove in the ground his copper tea pail half full of water.

Then the thing the Wolf had half expectantly waited for happened. The Sergeant took off his revolver belt, his khaki coat, rolled up the sleeves of his gray flannel shirt, turned down its collar, took a piece of soap and a towel from the roll of his blanket and went to the water to wash away the black dust of the prairie trail that was thick and heavy on his face and in his hair. Eyes and ears full of suds, splashing and blowing water, the noise of the Wolf's rapid creep to the fire was unheard.

When the Sergeant, leisurely drying his face on the towel, stood up and turned about he was looking into the yawning maw of his own heavy police revolver, and the Wolf was saying: "Come here beside the fire and strip to the buff – I want them duds. There won't nothin' happen you unless you get hostile, then you'll get yours too damn quick. Just do as you're told and don't make no fool play; I'm in a hurry."

Of course the Sergeant, not being an imbecile, obeyed.

"Now get up in that tree and stay there while I dress," the Wolf ordered. In three minutes he was arrayed in the habiliments of Sergeant Heath; then he said, "Come down and put on my shirt."

In the pocket of the khaki coat that the Wolf now wore were a pair of steel handcuffs; he tossed them to the man in the shirt commanding, "Click these on."

"I say," the Sergeant expostulated, "can't I have the pants and coat and your boots?"

The Wolf sneered: "Dif'rent here my bounder; I got to make a get-away. I'll tell you what I'll do – I'll give you your choice of three ways: I'll stake you to the clothes, bind and gag you; or I'll rip one of these 44 plugs through you; or I'll let you run foot loose with a shirt on your back; I reckon you won't go far on this wire grass in bare feet."

"I don't walk on my pants."

"That's just what you would do; the pants and coat would cut up into about four pairs of moccasins; they'd be as good as duffel cloth."

"I'll starve."

"That's your look-out. You'd lie awake nights worrying about where Jack Wolf would get a dinner – I guess not. I ought to shoot you. The damn police are nothin' but a lot of dirty dogs anyway. Get busy and cook grub for two – bacon and tea, while I sit here holdin' this gun on you."

The Sergeant was a grotesque figure cooking with the manacles on his wrists, and clad only in a shirt.

When they had eaten the Wolf bridled the horse, curled up the picket line and tied it to the saddle horn, rolled the blanket and with the carbine strapped it to the saddle, also his own blanket.

"I'm going to grubstake you," he said, "leave you rations for three days; that's more than you'd do for me. I'll turn your horse loose near steel, I ain't horse stealin', myself – I'm only borrowin'."

When he was ready to mount a thought struck the Wolf. It could hardly be pity for the forlorn condition of Heath; it must have been cunning – a play against the off chance of the Sergeant being picked up by somebody that day. He said:

"You fellers in the force pull a gag that you keep your word, don't you?"

"We try to."

"I'll give you another chance, then. I don't want to see nobody put in a hole where there ain't no call for it. If you give me your word, on the honor of a Mounted Policeman, swear it, that you'll give me four days' start before you squeal I'll stake you to the clothes and boots; then you can get out in two days and be none the worse."

"I'll see you in hell first. A Mounted Policeman doesn't compromise with a horse thief – with a skunk who steals a working girl's money."

"You'll keep palaverin' till I blow the top of your head off," the Wolf snarled. "You'll look sweet trampin' in to some town in about a week askin' somebody to file off the handcuffs Jack the Wolf snapped on you, won't you?"

"I won't get any place in a week with these handcuffs on," the Sergeant objected; "even if a pack of coyotes tackled me I couldn't protect myself."

The Wolf pondered this. If he could get away without it he didn't want the death of a man on his hands – there was nothing in it. So he unlocked the handcuffs, dangled them in his fingers debatingly, and then threw them far out into the bushes, saying, with a leer: "I might get stuck up by somebody, and if they clamped these on to me it would make a get-away harder."

"Give me some matches," pleaded the Sergeant.

With this request the Wolf complied saying, "I don't want to do nothin' mean unless it helps me out of a hole."

Then Jack swung to the saddle and continued on the trail. For four miles he rode, wondering at the persistence of the muskeg. But now he had a horse and twenty-four hours ahead before train time; he should worry.

Another four miles, and to the south he could see a line of low rolling hills that meant the end of the swamps. Even where he rode the prairie rose and fell, the trail dipping into hollows, on its rise to sweep over higher land. Perhaps some of these ridges ran right through the muskegs; but there was no hurry.

Suddenly as the Wolf breasted an upland he saw a man leisurely cinching a saddle on a buckskin horse.

"Hell!" the Wolf growled as he swung his mount; "that's the buckskin that I see at the Alberta; that's Bulldog; I don't want no mix-up with him."

He clattered down to the hollow he had left, and raced for the hiding screen of the bushed muskeg. He was almost certain Carney had not seen him, for the other had given no sign; he would wait in the cover until Carney had gone; perhaps he could keep right on across the bad lands, for his horse, as yet, sunk but hoof deep. He drew rein in thick cover and waited.

Suddenly the horse threw up his head, curved his neck backward, cocked his ears and whinnied. The Wolf could hear a splashing, sucking sound of hoofs back on the tell-tale trail he had left.

With a curse he drove his spurs into the horse's flanks, and the startled animal sprang from the cutting rowels, the ooze throwing up in a shower.

A dozen yards and the horse stumbled, almost coming to his knees; he recovered at the lash of Jack's quirt, and struggled on; now going half the depth of his cannon bones in the yielding muck, he was floundering like a drunken man; in ten feet his legs went to the knees.

Quirt and spur drove him a few feet; then he lurched heavily, and with a writhing struggle against the sucking sands stood trembling; from his spread mouth came a scream of terror – he knew.

And now the Wolf knew. With terrifying dread he remembered – he had ridden into the "Lakes of the Shifting Sands." This was the country they were in and he had forgotten. The sweat of fear stood out on the low forehead; all the tales that he had heard of men who had disappeared from off the face of the earth, swallowed up in these quicksands, came back to him with numbing force. To spring from the horse meant but two or three wallowing strides and then to be sucked down in the claiming quicksands.

The horse's belly was against the black muck. The Wolf had drawn his feet up; he gave a cry for help. A voice answered, and twisting his head about he saw, twenty yards away, Carney on the buckskin. About the man's thin lips a smile hovered. He sneered:

"You're up against it, Mister Policeman; what name'll I turn in back at barracks?"

Jack knew that it was Carney, and that Carney might know Heath by sight, so he lied:

"I'm Sergeant Phillips; for God's sake help me out."

Bulldog sneered. "Why should I – God doesn't love a sneaking police hound."

The Wolf pleaded, for his horse was gradually sinking; his struggles now stilled for the beast knew that he was doomed.

"All right," Carney said suddenly. "One condition – never mind, I'll save you first – there isn't too much time. Now break your gun, empty the cartridges out and drop it back into the holster," he commanded. "Unsling your picket line, fasten it under your armpits, and if I can get my cow-rope to you tie the two together."

He slipped from the saddle and led the horse as far out as he dared, seemingly having found firmer ground a little to one side. Then taking his cowrope, he worked his way still farther out, placing his feet on the tufted grass that stuck up in little mounds through the treacherous ooze. Then calling, "Look out!" he swung the rope. The Wolf caught it at the first throw and tied his own to it. Carney worked his way back, looped the rope over the horn, swung to the saddle, and calling, "Flop over on your belly – look out!" he started his horse, veritably towing the Wolf to safe ground.

The rope slacked; the Wolf, though half smothered with muck, drew his revolver and tried to slip two cartridges into the cylinder.

A sharp voice cried, "Stop that, you swine!" and raising his eyes he was gazing into Carney's gun. "Come up here on the dry ground," the latter commanded. "Stand there, unbuckle your belt and let it drop. Now take ten paces straight ahead." Carney salvaged the weapon and belt of cartridges.

"Build a fire, quick!" he next ordered, leaning casually against his horse, one hand resting on the butt of his revolver.

He tossed a couple of dry matches to the Wolf when the latter had built a little mound of dry poplar twigs and birch bark.

When the fire was going Carney said: "Peel your coat and dry it; stand close to the fire so your pants dry too – I want that suit."

The Wolf was startled. Was retribution so hot on his trail? Was Carney about to set him afoot just as he had set afoot Sergeant Heath? His two hundred dollars and Lucy Black's five hundred were in the pocket of that coat also. As he took it off he turned it upside down, hoping for a chance to slip the parcel of money to the ground unnoticed of his captor.

"Throw the jacket here," Carney commanded; "seems to be papers in the pocket."

When the coat had been tossed to him, Carney sat down on a fallen tree, took from it two packets – one of papers, and another wrapped in strong paper. He opened the papers, reading them with one eye while with the other he watched the man by the fire. Presently he sneered: "Say, you're some liar – even for a government hound; your name's not Phillips, it's Heath. You're the waster who fooled the little girl at Golden. You're the bounder who came down from the Klondike to gather Bulldog Carney in; you shot off your mouth all along the line that you were going to take him singlehanded. You bet a man in Edmonton a hundred you'd tie him hoof and horn. Well, you lose, for I'm going to rope you first, see? Turn you over to the Government tied up like a bag of spuds; that's just what I'm going to do Sergeant Liar. I'm going to break you for the sake of that little girl at Golden, for she was my friend and I'm Bulldog Carney. Soon as that suit is dried a bit you'll strip and pass it over; then you'll get into my togs and I'm going to turn you over to the police as Bulldog Carney. D'you get me, kid?" Carney chuckled. "That'll break you, won't it, Mister Sergeant Heath? You can't stay in the Force a joke; you'll never live it down if you live to be a thousand – you've boasted too much."

The Wolf had remained silent – waiting. He had an advantage if his captor did not know him. Now he was frightened; to be turned in at Edmonton by Carney was as bad as being taken by Sergeant Heath.

"You can't pull that stuff, Carney," he objected; "the minute I tell them who I am and who you are they'll grab you too quick. They'll know me; perhaps some of them'll know you."

A sneering "Ha!" came from between the thin lips of the man on the log. "Not where we're going they won't, Sergeant. I know a little place over on the rail" – and he jerked his thumb toward the west – "where there's two policemen that don't know much of anything; they've never seen either of us. You ain't been at Edmonton more'n a couple of months since you came from the Klondike. But they do know that Bulldog Carney is wanted at Calgary and that there's a thousand dollars to the man that brings him in."

At this the Wolf pricked his ears; he saw light – a flood of it. If this thing went through, and he was sent on to Calgary as Bulldog Carney, he would be turned loose at once as not being the man. The police at Calgary had cause to know just what Carney looked like for he had been in their clutches and escaped.

But Jack must bluff – appear to be the angry Sergeant. So he said: "They'll know me at Calgary, and you'll get hell for this."

Now Carney laughed out joyously. "I don't give a damn if they do. Can't you get it through your wooden police head that I just want this little pleasantry driven home so that you're the goat of that nanny band, the Mounted Police; then you'll send in your papers and go back to the farm?"

As Carney talked he had opened the paper packet. Now he gave a crisp "Hello! what have we here?" as a sheaf of bills appeared.

The Wolf had been watching for Carney's eyes to leave him for five seconds. One hand rested in his trousers pocket. He drew it out and dropped a knife treading it into the sand and ashes.

"Seven hundred," Bulldog continued. "Rather a tidy sum for a policeman to be toting. Is this police money?"

The Wolf hesitated; it was a delicate situation. Jack wanted that money but a slip might ruin his escape. If Bulldog suspected that Jack was not a policeman he would jump to the conclusion that he had killed the owner of the horse and clothes. Also Carney would not believe that a policeman on duty wandered about with seven hundred in his pocket; if Jack claimed it all Carney would say he lied and keep it as Government money.

"Five hundred is Government money I was bringin' in from a post, and two hundred is my own," he answered.

"I'll keep the Government money," Bulldog said crisply; "the Government robbed me of my ranch – said I had no title. And I'll keep yours, too; it's coming to you."

"If luck strings with you, Carney, and you get away with this dirty trick, what you say'll make good – I'll have to quit the Force; an' I want to get home down east. Give me a chance; let me have my own two hundred."

"I think you're lying – a man in the Force doesn't get two hundred ahead, not honest. But I'll toss you whether I give you one hundred or two," Carney said, taking a half dollar from his pocket. "Call!" and he spun it in the air.

"Heads!" the Wolf cried.

The coin fell tails up. "Here's your hundred," and Bulldog passed the bills to their owner.

"I see here," he continued, "your order to arrest Bulldog Carney. Well, you've made good, haven't you. And here's another for Jack the Wolf; you missed him, didn't you? Where's he – what's he done lately? He played me a dirty trick once; tipped off the police as to where they'd get me. I never saw him, but if you could stake me to a sight of the wolf I'd give you this six hundred. He's the real hound that I've got a low down grudge against. What's his description – what does he look like?"

"He's a tall slim chap – looks like a breed, 'cause he's got nigger blood in him," the Wolf lied.

"I'll get him some day," Carney said; "and now them duds are about cooked – peel!"

The Wolf stripped, gray shirt and all.

"Now step back fifteen paces while I make my toilet," Carney commanded, toying with his 6-gun in the way of emphasis.

In two minutes he was transformed into Sergeant Heath of the N.W.M.P., revolver belt and all. He threw his own clothes to the Wolf, and lighted his pipe.

When Jack had dressed Carney said: "I saved your life, so I don't want you to make me throw it away again. I don't want a muss when I turn you over to the police in the morning. There ain't much chance they'd listen to you if you put up a holler that you were Sergeant Heath – they'd laugh at you, but if they did make a break at me there'd be shooting, and you'd be plumb in line of a careless bullet – see? I'm going to stay close to you till you're on that train."

Of course this was just what the Wolf wanted; to go down the line as Bulldog Carney, handcuffed to a policeman, would be like a passport for Jack the Wolf. Nobody would even speak to him – the policeman would see to that.

"You're dead set on putting this crazy thing through, are you?" he asked.

"You bet I am – I'd rather work this racket than go to my own wedding."

"Well, so's you won't think your damn threat to shoot keeps me mum, I'll just tell you that if you get that far with it I ain't going to give myself away. You've called the turn, Carney; I'd be a joke even if I only got as far as the first barracks a prisoner. If I go in as Bulldog Carney I won't come out as Sergeant Heath – I'll disappear as Mister Somebody. I'm sick of the Force anyway. They'll never know what happened to Sergeant Heath from me – I couldn't stand the guying. But if I ever stack up against you, Carney, I'll kill you for it." This last was pure bluff – for fear Carney's suspicions might be aroused by the other's ready compliance.

Carney scowled; then he laughed, sneering: "I've heard women talk like that in the dance halls. You cook some bacon and tea at that fire – then we'll pull out."

As the Wolf knelt beside the fire to blow the embers into a blaze he found a chance to slip the knife he had buried into his pocket.

When they had eaten they took the trail, heading south to pass the lower end of the great muskegs. Carney rode the buckskin, and the Wolf strode along in front, his mind possessed of elation at the prospect of being helped out of the country, and depression over the loss of his money. Curiously the loss of his own one hundred seemed a greater enormity than that of the school teacher's five hundred. That money had been easily come by, but he had toiled a month for the hundred. What right had Carney to steal his labor – to rob a workman. As they plugged along mile after mile, a fierce determination to get the money back took possession of Jack. If he could get it he could get the horse. He would fix Bulldog some way so that the latter would not stop him. He must have the clothes, too. The khaki suit obsessed him; it was a red flag to his hot mind.

They spelled and ate in the early evening; and when they started for another hour's tramp Carney tied his cow-rope tightly about the Wolf's waist, saying: "If you'd tried to cut out in these gloomy hills I'd be peeved. Just keep that line taut in front of the buckskin and there won't be no argument."

In an hour Carney called a halt, saying: "We'll camp by this bit of water, and hit the trail in the early morning. We ain't more than ten miles from steel, and we'll make some place before train time."

Carney had both the police picket line and his own. He drove a picket in the ground, looped the line that was about the Wolf's waist over it, and said:

"I don't want to be suspicious of a mate jumping me in the dark, so I'll sleep across this line and you'll keep to the other end of it; if you so much as wink at it I guess I'll wake. I've got a bad conscience and sleep light. We'll build a fire and you'll keep to the other side of it same's we were neighbors in a city and didn't know each other."

Twice, as they ate, Carney caught a sullen, vicious look in Jack's eyes. It was as clearly a murder look as he had ever seen; and more than once he had faced eyes that thirsted for his life. He wondered at the psychology of it; it was not like his idea of Sergeant Heath. From what he had been told of the policeman he had fancied him a vain, swaggering chap who had had his ego fattened by the three stripes on his arm. He determined to take a few extra precautions, for he did not wish to lie awake.

"We'll turn in," he said when they had eaten; "I'll hobble you, same's a sly cayuse, for fear you'd walk in your sleep, Sergeant."

He bound the Wolf's ankles, and tied his wrists behind his back, saying, as he knotted the rope, "What the devil did you do with your handcuffs – thought you johnnies always had a pair in your pocket?"

"They were in the saddle holster and went down with my horse," the Wolf lied.

Carney's nerves were of steel, his brain worked with exquisite precision. When it told him there was nothing to fear, that his precautions had made all things safe, his mind rested, untortured by jerky nerves; so in five minutes he slept.

The Wolf mastered his weariness and lay awake, waiting to carry out the something that had been in his mind. Six hundred dollars was a stake to play for; also clad once again in the police suit, with the buckskin to carry him to the railroad, he could get away; money was always a good thing to bribe his way through. Never once had he put his hand in the pocket where lay the knife he had secreted at the time he had changed clothes with Carney, as he trailed hour after hour in front of the buckskin. He knew that Carney was just the cool-nerved man that would sleep – not lie awake through fear over nothing.

In the way of a test, he shuffled his feet and drew from the half-dried grass a rasping sound. It partly disturbed the sleeper; he changed the steady rhythm of his breathing; he even drew a heavy-sighing breath; had he been lying awake watching the Wolf he would have stilled his breathing to listen.

The Wolf waited until the rhythmic breaths of the sleeper told that he had lapsed again into the deeper sleep. Slowly, silently the Wolf worked his hands to the side pocket, drew out the knife and cut the cords that bound his wrists. It took time, for he worked with caution. Then he waited. The buckskin, his nose deep in the grass, blew the pollen of the flowered carpet from his nostrils.

Carney stirred and raised his head. The buckskin blew through his nostrils again, ending with a luxurious sigh of content; then was heard the clip-clip of his strong teeth scything the grass. Carney, recognizing what had waked him, turned over and slept again.

Ten minutes, and the Wolf, drawing up his feet slowly, silently, sawed through the rope on his ankles. Then with spread fingers he searched the grass for a stone the size of a goose egg, beside which he had purposely lain down. When his fingers touched it he unknotted the handkerchief that had been part of Carney's make-up and which was now about his neck, and in one corner tied the stone, fastening the other end about his wrist. Now he had a slung shot that with one blow would render the other man helpless.

Then he commenced his crawl.

A pale, watery, three-quarter moon had climbed listlessly up the eastern sky changing the sombre prairie into a vast spirit land, draping with ghostly garments bush and shrub.

Purposely Carney had tethered the buckskin down wind from where he and the Wolf lay. Jack had not read anything out of this action, but Carney knew the sensitive wariness of his horse – the scent of the stranger in his nostrils would keep him restless, and any unusual move on the part of the prisoner would agitate the buckskin. Also he had only pretended to drive the picket pin at some distance away; in the dark he had trailed it back and worked it into the loose soil at his very feet. This was more a move of habitual care than a belief that the bound man could work his way, creeping and rolling, to the picket pin, pull it, and get away with the horse.

At the Wolf's first move the buckskin threw up his head, and, with ears cocked forward, studied the shifting blurred shadow. Perhaps it was the scent of his master's clothes which the Wolf wore that agitated his mind, that cast him to wondering whether his master was moving about; or, perhaps as animals instinctively have a nervous dread of a vicious man he distrusted the stranger; perhaps, in the dim uncertain light, his prairie dread came back to him and he thought it a wolf that had crept into camp. He took a step forward; then another, shaking his head irritably. A vibration trembled along the picket line that now lay across Carney's foot and he stirred restlessly.

The Wolf flattened himself to earth and snored. Five minutes he waited, cursing softly the restless horse. Then again he moved, so slowly that even the watchful animal scarce detected it.

He was debating two plans: a swift rush and a swing of his slung shot, or the silent approach. The former meant inevitably the death of one or the other – the crushed skull of Carney, or, if the latter were by any chance awake, a bullet through the Wolf. He could feel his heart pounding against the turf as he scraped along, inch by inch. A bare ten feet, and he could put his hand on the butt of Carney's gun and snatch it from the holster; if he missed, then the slung shot.

The horse, roused, was growing more restless, more inquisitive. Sometimes he took an impatient snap at the grass with his teeth; but only to throw his head up again, take a step forward, shake his head, and exhale a whistling breath.

Now the Wolf had squirmed his body five feet forward. Another yard and he could reach the pistol; and there was no sign that Carney had wakened – just the steady breathing of a sleeping man.

The Wolf lay perfectly still for ten seconds, for the buckskin seemingly had quieted; he was standing, his head low hung, as if he slept on his feet. Carney's face was toward the creeping man and was in shadow. Another yard, and now slowly the Wolf gathered his legs under him till he rested like a sprinter ready for a spring; his left hand crept forward toward the pistol stock that was within reach; the stone-laden handkerchief was twisted about the two first fingers of his right.

Yes, Carney slept.

As the Wolf's fingers slid along the pistol butt the wrist was seized in fingers of steel, he was twisted almost face to earth, and the butt of Carney's own gun, in the latter's right hand, clipped him over the eye and he slipped into dreamland. When he came to workmen were riveting a boiler in the top of his head; somebody with an augur was boring a hole in his forehead; he had been asleep for ages and had wakened in a strange land. He sat up groggily and stared vacantly at a man who sat beside a camp fire smoking a pipe. Over the camp fire a copper kettle hung and a scent of broiling bacon came to his nostrils. The man beside the fire took the pipe from his mouth and said: "I hoped I had cracked your skull, you swine. Where did you pick up that thug trick of a stone in the handkerchief? As you are troubled with insomnia we'll hit the trail again."

With the picket line around his waist once more Jack trudged ahead of the buckskin, in the night gloom the shadowy cavalcade cutting a strange, weird figure as though a boat were being towed across sleeping waters.

The Wolf, groggy from the blow that had almost cracked his skull, was wobbly on his legs – his feet were heavy as though he wore a diver's leaden boots. As he waded through a patch of wild rose the briars clung to his legs, and, half dazed he cried out, thinking he struggled in the shifting sands.

"Shut up!" The words clipped from the thin lips of the rider behind.

They dipped into a hollow and the played-out man went half to his knees in the morass. A few lurching steps and overstrained nature broke; he collapsed like a jointed doll – he toppled head first into the mire and lay there.

The buckskin plunged forward in the treacherous going, and the bag of a man was skidded to firm ground by the picket line, where he sat wiping the mud from his face, and looking very all in.

Carney slipped to the ground and stood beside his captive. "You're soft, my bucko – I knew Sergeant Heath had a yellow streak," he sneered; "boasters generally have. I guess we'll rest till daylight. I've a way of hobbling a bad man that'll hold you this time, I fancy."

He drove the picket pin of the rope that tethered the buckskin, and ten feet away he drove the other picket pin. He made the Wolf lie on his side and fastened him by a wrist to each peg so that one arm was behind and one in front.

Carney chuckled as he surveyed the spread-eagle man: "you'll find some trouble getting out of that, my bucko; you can't get your hands together and you can't get your teeth at either rope. Now I *will* have a sleep."

The Wolf was in a state of half coma; even untethered he probably would have slept like a log; and Carney was tired; he, too, slumbered, the soft stealing gray of the early morning not bringing him back out of the valley of rest till a glint of sunlight throwing over the prairie grass touched his eyes, and the warmth gradually pushed the lids back.

He rose, built a fire, and finding water made a pot of tea. Then he saddled the buckskin, and untethered the Wolf, saying: "We'll eat a bite and pull out."

The rest and sleep had refreshed the Wolf, and he plodded on in front of the buckskin feeling that though his money was gone his chances of escape were good.

At eight o'clock the square forms of log shacks leaning groggily against a sloping hill came into view; it was Hobbema; and, swinging a little to the left, in an hour they were close to the Post.

Carney knew where the police shack lay, and skirting the town he drew up in front of a log shack, an iron-barred window at the end proclaiming it was the Barracks. He slipped from the saddle, dropped the rein over the horse's head, and said quietly to the Wolf: "Knock on the door, open it, and step inside," the muzzle of his gun emphasizing the command.

He followed close at the Wolf's heels, standing in the open door as the latter entered. He had expected to see perhaps one, not more than two constables, but at a little square table three men in khaki sat eating breakfast.

"Good morning, gentlemen," Carney said cheerily; "I've brought you a prisoner, Bulldog Carney."

The one who sat at table with his back to the door turned his head at this; then he sprang to his feet, peered into the prisoner's face and laughed.

"Bulldog nothing, Sergeant; you've bagged the Wolf."

The speaker thrust his face almost into the Wolf's. "Where's my uniform – where's my horse? I've got you now – set me afoot to starve, would you, you damn thief – you murderer! Where's the five hundred dollars you stole from the little teacher at Fort Victor?"

He was trembling with passion; words flew from his lips like bullets from a gatling – it was a torrent.

But fast as the accusation had come, into Carney's quick mind flashed the truth – the speaker was Sergeant Heath. The game was up. Still it was amusing. What a devilish droll blunder he had made. His hands crept quietly to his two guns, the police gun in the belt and his own beneath the khaki coat.

Also the Wolf knew his game was up. His blood surged hot at the thought that Carney's meddling had trapped him. He was caught, but the author of his evil luck should not escape.

"*That's Bulldog Carney!*" he cried fiercely; "don't let him get away."

Startled, the two constables at the table sprang to their feet.

A sharp, crisp voice said: "The first man that reaches for a gun drops." They were covered by two guns held in the steady hands of the man whose small gray eyes watched from out narrowed lids.

"I'll make you a present of the Wolf," Carney said quietly; "I thought I had Sergeant Heath. I could almost forgive this man, if he weren't such a skunk, for doing the job for me. Now I want you chaps to pass, one by one, into the pen," and he nodded toward a heavy wooden door that led from the room they were in to the other room that had been fitted up as a cell. "I see your carbines and gunbelts on the rack – you really should have been properly in uniform by this time; I'll dump them out on the prairie somewhere, and you'll find them in the course of a day or so. Step in, boys, and you go first, Wolf."

When the four men had passed through the door Carney dropped the heavy wooden bar into place, turned the key in the padlock, gathered up the fire arms, mounted the buckskin, and rode into the west.

A week later the little school teacher at Fort Victor received through the mail a packet that contained five hundred dollars, and this note:–

DEAR MISS BLACK:–

I am sending you the five hundred dollars that you bet on a bad man. No woman can afford to bet on even a *good* man. Stick to the kids, for I've heard they love you. If those Indians hadn't picked up Sergeant Heath and got him to Hobbema before I got away with your money I wouldn't have known, and you'd have lost out.

Yours delightedly,
BULLDOG CARNEY.

WILD OATS

Red Meekins. New York: Doran/Toronto: McClelland & Stewart, 1921.

The eponymous hero of "Wild Oats," Red Meekins, is an amiable chap, not above venality, but on the side of the angels when the chips are down.

This selection is from a collection of stories set in Cobalt, Ontario during the town's silver boom. In those boom times, Cobalt and other mining towns in the district, Kirkland Lake, Haileybury, New Liskeard, were as dramatic and romantic as the Klondike. In this area Harry Oakes made the great strike that led eventually to his murder in the Bahamas during the Second World War. It was an exciting time of high-graders and four-flushers, yet has been sadly neglected as a time and place for Canadian novelists and story tellers. This is a pity, for here is a rich mother-lode of plot and incident.

WILD OATS

Red Meekins had his collection of antique silver hidden under a large boulder of conglomerate rock half a mile from the Silver Ledge shaft-house. When even the professors of geology and mineralogy had disputed with heat the age of these samples of ancient art, Red had troubled little over the matter, being more largely interested in the subtle endeavour of acquiring his contorted slabs of pure silver quietly and the equally difficult business of finding a secretive purchaser.

In short, Red was "high grading," assimilating the precious metal from the sorting board of his employers, the Silver Ledge Company.

This high grading was a peculiarly fine point in the ethics of stealing; it was looked upon as something akin to beating the customs. Meekins found a touch of exhilaration in outwitting the company's two detectives. The detectives worked as ordinary miners; they slept in the one big room of the bunkhouse, which contained thirty beds; they ate at the table with the men, and fancied that they were unsuspected; but Red knew. A massive-jawed fighting bulldog was turned loose nightly in the ore-house to guard the sacks of high grade ore; but Red Meekins rubbed shoulders with the two detectives as fellow workmen, shied a rock at the bulldog if he saw him nosing about alone, and went on high grading.

It was a species of woodsman's instinct, something akin to a sixth sense, that told Meekins somebody had found his cache of silver under the big rock. For two sweet moonlight nights he watched Farren and Riley, the detectives, as they sat in vigil near his cache waiting to pounce upon the unknown depositor. On the third night dark clouds smothered the moon, and Meekins took his little bag of ore from under the very noses of the watchers and hid it in a badger hole a mile away.

In the way of establishing an alibi should his absence from the bunkhouse cause an inquiry, Meekins , after he had hidden the silver, called at the log shack of Jack Gray, owner of the Little Star mining claim.

"How's she showin' up?" Red asked as he took a seat on Gray's bunk. "How's the vein lookin'?"

"Not too bad," Gray answered, with the conservative caution of an old-time prospector.

"I heered you shootin' today," Meekins offered. "Hope you ripped up a silver sidewalk – you had calcite enough before."

Gray ignored the matter of silver sidewalks and passed the speaker a plug of tobacco, saying, "Fill your pipe, Red."

Red lighted the pipe and drew at it with tantalizing deliberation. He was thinking. Evidently Gray's shot had discovered no bonanza; his whole manner held the sombreness of defeat. Meekins finally hazarded, "I heerd you'd sold the Little Star, Jack."

"Well," Gray answered, shuffling about the shack as he spoke, "I've sold it, an' I ain't. Two hundred thousand if the vein shows native silver; that's the bargain, Red. Mr. Downs was to come tomorrow to look at the vein."

"An' the mineral, Jack, got it?"

"Well, we're hopin.' She looks good to me."

"He ain't got it yet," Meekins muttered to himself. And somehow a thought of his own little silver horde came tangently into his mind like a correlative factor. Here was a trinity of holdings that, concreted into one, would certainly be advantageous.

"Say," he ejaculated as he fussed at the pipe bowl with his knife, loosening the tobacco, "I'd like to see you soak that Englishman that's bluffin' round here 'bout buyin' a mine. A mine! It's a pup Bank of England that Bloater Bangs wants."

"Boultbee Downs is the gent's name, Red; you've got his handle sorter twisted," Gray advised.

"His name don't cut no ice, Jack; he's a porky little stiff! I meets him kinder offhand like at the Nugget Hotel last night an' makes a play to boost the Little Star for you, Jack, an' what d'you think Bolster & Co. hands out to me?"

Gray chuckled. "Said he hadn't been introduced; gave you the wall eye an' cut away, eh?"

"Kinder like that, Jack, only wuss, more cold blooded. Says he, takin' a cigarette case from his pocket an' lightin' one of 'em coffin nails, 'I have in my service an engineer quite competent to advise me of the desirability of such properties as I wish to purchase.' Holy Snakes! Could you beat it?"

Gray chuckled again; then his face relaxed into its habitual solemnity. "English is no dub, Red; he knows what o'clock it is. He's got the coin at his back, an' I'd like to sell him the Little Star for two hundred thousand. I don't know nothin' about floatin' a company – an' God knows some of the veins about here is as lean as a razorback hog! The Little Star has got mighty good indications of silver; but –" Gray walked over to a cupboard, swung the door open, brought a black bottle forth by the neck, and, handing a glass to Meekins, added, "By the hokey! If I clean up this time, farmin' for mine! No more minin,' never no more again!"

Meekins laughed disagreeably.

"Heerd a man talk like that afore, eh, Red?" Gray growled sarcastically.

"Sorter that way; but they gener'lly held a better hand."

"You ain't seen none of my cards. What d'you know about the Little Star?" Gray snapped.

"Nothin,' nothin.' Jus' kinder mind readin,' that's all."

Gray vouchsafed no answer to this sally; but stood looking, a suspicion of sullen anger in his heavy eyes, at Meekins. After a little he spoke. "If you're good at mind readin',' p'r'aps you could tell the fortune of the Little Star, whether there's a big vein like the Lawson or the Crown Reserve in her."

"I can tell you how to put that Cockney's two hundred thousand in your pocket, if you want to know," Meekins answered.

"Tellin' is one thing, an' figurin' the dollars is another."

"You ripped up the vein today, didn't you, Jack?" Meekins asked.

"I opened her up some."

"An' you didn't find nothin' but calcite, with p'r'aps a few colours of cobalt; ain't that right, Jack?"

"S'posin' it is, that ain't your business, Red! You didn't grubstake me, did you?"

Meekins ignored the irrelevant aftermath. "Well, when Johnny Bull cocks his one-eyed winder at that hole, he don't buy; he just says, 'Ah, by Jove! Not quite up to the mark, me dear feller,' an' skins back to the hotel for a bath." Meekins grinned as he heard Gray cursing under his breath. "But if he sees some nice fat chunks of silver there, then he 'diplomatically opens negotiations,' don't he? – that's the way he puts it – an' it ends by you gettin' the dough."

"An' if in the mornin' I get a letter sayin' an aunt's left me a million dollars, Red, I'll buy you a bottle of whisky an' a monkey on a stick, an' you can have a high old time. See?"

"Now what I propose," Meekins shoved both hands into his pockets in utter contempt of Gray's misplaced humour, "is to let the gent from Londonderry see enough silver to knock that glass plumb out of his eye."

Gray stared in astonishment at Meekins. "He's only had one drink," he muttered; then he added aloud, in heavy sarcasm, "That's a good idea, Red. You can come over in the mornin',' turn this forty acres upside down, an' just let the silver spill out. I'll give you ten per cent. Kinder wish I'd talked this over with you afore."

"I'll take the ten per cent," Meekins offered in fee simple for the whole statement; "an' as to how, it's this wise. We just fill that calcite vein up with cement an' gravel carryin' about three thousand ounces of silver to the ton, an' on the day as specified by Johnny Bull you put in a shot an' loosen her up. There can't be no deception, gentlemen, 'cause you have your sleeves rolled up. See?"

Gray leaned back in his chair and laughed. "Meekins, you've got a great head – for hammerin' a drill. You oughter've been a revivalist, 'cause the people don't ask too many questions in the perfession. What d'you s'pose they'd say when they know I'd been round buyin' cement an' pieces of silver to stick in a vein, eh?"

"I got the silver right enough," Meekins said quietly; "got her cached within ten minutes totin' of this spot. An' I'll jus' borrow the cement from the Silver Ledge. They're puttin' in a new engine bed on vein fourteen, an' there's tons of cement lyin' round there loose. All you've got to do is lend me a bag to bring the stuff. It wouldn't do to hook a full bag, 'cause they're all tallied up."

Red's cold blooded scheme of knavery was like a heavy blow to Gray. He sat for a long time pulling at his pipe; the pop-pop of his lips as he shot forth the smoke crackled on the heavy silence of the room like the bursting of horse chestnuts in a fire of leaves. Through twenty years of scorching heat and blizzard cold he had sought the pot of gold at the foot of the rainbow. Twice he had touched the hem of the purple robe of wealth and had been well kicked in the ribs by the foot of adversity hidden beneath. At that very link in his chain of thought he worded this somewhat more prosaically for Meekins, "I got a raw deal twice in my life, Red –"

"I know," Meekins interrupted. "When Hardy beat you out of the Golden Oriole."

"Yes, that was 'bout the only time I was chuck full of murder. I'd've killed Hardy if he hadn't skun out, I'd've ripped him up like an ol' rubber boot! Then I sold the One Horse mine to a bunch from Pittsburgh – But what's the use of talkin'? It makes me dead sore! I never got nothin' out of it 'cept the first payment."

"Well, you got yer chance to break more than even with the game now."

"I don't call it gettin' even to turn crook just because you've been bunkoed yerself," Gray argued.

There was a lack of fire in his tone that Meekins caught; there was a dragging intonation as if the speaker was uttering an abstract thought with his mind dwelling on something more impressive.

"Bein' a crook is gettin' caught, I figger," Meekins declared doggedly. "You've heerd, an' I've heerd, of a good many deals up in this field, an' the whole boilin' of lawyers an' Gov'men legal department is jus' up to their armpits tryin' to give somebody some kind of a square deal. Minin's kinder like swimmin' – you leave your Sunday clo'es to home when you go at it."

"That's right enough, Red; but I don't lose no sleep 'cause the other feller's crooked."

"No; an' they don't lose no sleep if you ain't got a nickel in your pocket. The gent as gets your mine for two hundred thousand will soak the public with it as a million-dollar company – or perhaps five."

Gray sat sullenly silent, a heavy frown on his face, and Meekins asked abruptly, "Ain't the Little Star no good, Jack? It's close up to the Silver Ledge, an' the veins there is packed like herrin's in a bar'l."

"Why, it's sure got to turn out a good mine," Gray answered; "but a feller can't cross trench forty acres of land in a month, an' I just ain't dropped onto no big vein yet."

"Then don't be a fool!" Meekins advised. "You ain't cheatin' nobody by lettin' 'em have the Little Star at two hundred thousand; only if you had that money in the bank I guess you an' the wife'd feel you could afford a little holi-day an' be set up for life."

Gray rose and paced the floor. In an aimless manner he wandered to the cupboard and brought forth the black bottle again. Meekins was considerable of a drinker himself but he gasped as Gray tossed off half a tumbler of the raw whisky.

"That'll brace you, Jack," he ventured. "You've got yer chance right now to make yer pile. I'll bet you've swore a dozen times, since you've been minin' an' seen all the crooked work that's bein' done, that if you ever got a chance to make a big stake you'd make it! Didn't you, Jack?"

"Yes, I've got hot under the collar when I knowed the fellers was playin' me fer a sucker when I got done up; but I ain't never lied about a mine yet. Them's two things I never shot off hot air about yet, a woman or a mine."

"Course you didn't, Jack. An' you'll go on jus' that way, an' the fellers as makes the pile'll give you a job when you're old sortin' ore on the dump. An' as for lyin', you ain't got to do none. I'll fix up that vein, an' when Bleater-Down comes here to see there ain't no deception, you put the shot in an' let him take the samples of ore away to get an assay. When his assay man hands him out two or three big buttons of silver he'll be that sure he's cheatin' you in gettin' the Little Star at that price, he won't sleep till he's got you to accept a check."

Meekins rose in his eagerness and put his hand on Gray's arm, saying, "Get me a grain bag out of your stable, Jack. I'm dashed if I don't work all night pluggin' that vein! Two hundred thousand dollars ain't made every night. Now, don't get grouchy, Jack," he coaxed, as Gray drew his arm away; "you've got a chance at two hundred thousand sure, an' if you turn it down p'r'aps your claim'll peter out same's the Lone Pine claim did. It broke ol' Saunders, broke his pockets an' broke his heart. Ain't he now in the asylum diggin' little ditches in a wooden table with a pocketknife, swearin' he's got the biggest silver mine in the world? He could've sold for half a million, an' wouldn't."

Rugged and strong as Gray appeared, yet there was pliability to his moral fibre. In the lesser matter of taking a drink – too many drinks – he had always yielded to the friendly, "Come on, Jack, old boy!" Hardly acquiescing in the scheme, still rebelling weakly against it, Gray yielded to the pressure of Red's hand on his arm, and the two went out to a little log stable that held Gray's hoisting gear, the bucket horse.

"Here's an empty!" Meekins exclaimed, as he peered about by the light of his miner's candle. "I'll take this bag an' get busy, Jack. I'll be back in an hour." Suddenly a thought struck him. "Say, where's the two fellers that works on the vein?"

"They're boardin' over to McCann's bunkhouse."

"Well, you give 'em a day off tomorrow. Say the ol' hoss's sick an' can't hoist none. Keep 'em away from the vein till the cement gets sot good an' hard. Now I'm off!"

Meekins turned at the door, and, scanning Gray's face, asked, "D'you want to put a hand to this job? 'Cause if you don't I can do it alone."

"There ain't no call for you to do it alone, Red. I don't see no difference 'tween helpin' an knowin' it's done. Guess I never was learned in them fine points of lyin'. I'll help salt the mine – 'cause that's what it is, Red – and if the Englishman gets wise to it an' asks me, I won't hand him out no fairy tale; I'll just get riled an' buffalo him off the forty acres by the seat of his pants. I feel sorter mad at him myself now."

"You ain't weakenin,' Jack?"

"No, I ain't weakenin.' It's a kind of disease I never get. I've been bunkoed, an' made use of by fellers with money for more'n twenty years, an' I'm goin' to see this through. P'r'aps I can sorter square it by doin' more good with that money – if I get it – than them rich promoters. I know a slue of poor people down in my county that'll throw a powerful lot of prayers after I've done with 'em. I've jus' been itchin' to help some of 'em out!"

Meekins stood for a second scratching the tangled mop of red bristling hair; then he said, "Takin' one thing with another, Jack, I figger I'd best do this job all by myself."

"I don't want to shirk –"

"Shirk nothin'! I wasn't nursin' your feelin's, Jack; but that silver I've got is dead set again' lettin' anybody see it, an' as long as nobody's got to swear in court they see me with it, why I've got a good alibi, haven't I, if the Silver Ledge people gits on my trail? You jus' go by-by in your little bed, Jack, an' in the mornin' you'll find that tear in the vein all nice healed up."

Then Meekins slipped into the scant forest of birch and poplar and his shadow was soon merged with its gloom.

Gray went back to his shack and the toiler's sleep, and from the storehouse of his mind stalked forth grim entanglements. One time he was lying helpless while Meekins, with sardonic deliberation, incased him in a fast solidifying sarcophagus of cement. Again he was throwing a shower of silver coins to a rabble of starvelings. All night his dreams, with chameleon-like affiliation, draped their hideous forms in the drab of guilt. Yes, all night he dreamed; for at dawn with a mighty effort he swept aside the avalanche of banknotes that, a foot deep, were smothering him, and sprang to the floor, his blanket still in his trembling grasp.

Then he dressed and went down to the little pit, six feet deep, that had been sunk on the vein. Where yesterday the jagged gash left by the dynamite shot had disfigured the bottom of the pit now a smooth dull gray surface met his eye. Meekins had done a neat job of concrete work.

Gray threw a shovelful of loose sand down to cover the evidence of Red's handicraft and took his way to McCann's to tell his men there would be no work for that day.

"Now for Boultbee Downs of London!" Gray muttered.

A telephone message from the office of the Black Rock mine, giving the sick horse excuse, brought much imperious expostulation from Boultbee Downs, and the latter's visit of inspection was postponed for two days.

On the second day Boultbee Downs, with an engineer and a secretary, drove over to the Little Star. He was rotund of body and manner. As Red Meekins had described him he seemed to think the Lord had built a straight-away chute through the world for him with all rights preserved.

"I've been trenchin' for a couple of days," Gray explained, "tryin' to see how far the mineralized vein I picked up ran."

"Ah, my dear fellow!" Boultbee Downs condescended. "By 'mineralized' just what do you mean, now? There's cobalt, and nickel, and smaltite, and tremendous lot of other 'ites, while all I'm interested in is silver. Now, definitely speaking, Mr. – ah– Gray, will you be good enough to inform Mr. Forsythe here just what you found?"

"Well," Gray answered slowly, "I kinder thought it'd be a good idee for you to see the shot put in, and –"

Boultbee Downs interrupted fussily. "Sample the veins ourselves, eh, Gray? Seems deuced fair, Forsythe, eh?"

"Yes, sir," the engineer answered deferentially.

"I say, Forsythe, by Jove! Quite an innovation finding one of these mining fellows wanting to play the game fair!"

"I drilled a hole," Gray advised, "and I'll have Jorgsen put the dynamite in."

"Quite right, quite right," Downs declared. "Expeditiously, of course, for I have a stupendous number of things to attend to."

Just as the charge was rammed home, the fuse lighted, and the men were scuttling to places of safety, Red Meekins drifted casually on the scene.

"Thought I'd kinder like to see the fun," he said as he crouched behind a rock with Gray. "I want to see that Cheapside chap bulge his eyes just for onct when he cuddles one of my nuggets. I'll bet he tells you the vein doesn't run to more'n two hundred ounces to the ton, an' tries to beat you down to a hundred thousand. There she goes!" he exclaimed as the earth trembled under their feet and an explosive roar heralded a shower of rock debris. "I strung the silver pretty well along," Red whispered as they went toward the shaft. "Hope it didn't get mislaid, none of it."

It was Boultbee Downs himself who picked up a slab of silver the size of his own fat palm, to the side of which clung a piece of Red's conglomerate. Meekins saw him pick it up; but turned his back quickly, and Downs, without comment, passed it to Forsythe, who dropped the metal into his leather bag. In the rent the shot had made from two or three places undoubtedly silver protruded.

"Yes," Gray said in answer to a question from Downs, "I got a couple of pieces of silver farder on in the vein an' thought it looked pretty good."

Downs exhibited a tremendous anxiety to get away, also to carry with him as many fragments of conglomerate as might be had. An ore sack that was in his buggy was filled. Quite casually, just as he was about to step into his conveyance, he turned to Gray and said:

"Ah, Mr. Gray, I'm a man of business – yes, sir, of what I might term definite business arrangements. We have found – haven't we, Mr. Forsythe?" he appealed to the engineer – "that bargains in this mining region are like piecrust, made to be broken. Ha-ha! And we waste a great deal of valuable time through having deals repudiated. My secretary, Mr. Smythe, has a little form of sale which you might sign. It simply gives me an option on your mine for forty-eight hours. I may say that in the event of the assay of these samples being satisfactory I shall close the deal at once. Now what figures shall we say, Mr. Gray, twenty thousand pounds?"

Gray felt Meekins kick him in the calf of the leg, and he answered, "Two hundred thousand dollars is what I said I'd sell for; but if that don't go the price of the Little Star is boosted to half a million now."

Boultbee Downs gasped, and hurriedly drawing a pencil from his pocket inserted some figures, saying, "Ah, my dear fellow, you agreed to sell at two hundred thousand."

"An' I gen'rally keep my word," Gray asserted as he signed the paper.

"You'll hear from me within forty-eight hours," Boultbee Downs advised as he clambered into the buggy. "If the assay is satisfactory, I'll have the regular papers and a check waiting for you."

The two miners watched Downs till a turn in the road hid him.

"Somethin'll go wrong," Gray muttered, speaking as if to himself. "'Tain't my luck to make a win like this."

"Hit yourself over the liver, Jack!" Red advised. "That shark thinks he's skinnin' you, an' he'll have the Little Star twinklin' in his shirt front afore tomorrow night. I near bust tryin' to keep from laughin' when I see him palm that chunk of silver. I took a day off from the work just to enjoy the show."

Meekins spent the day and evening with Gray. He had picked out a dozen investments for the twenty thousand he was to get out of the deal.

It was nearly ten o'clock, and he had just finished, to the minutest detail, a description of a dairy business he was going to start in his native town, when there came a sharp rap at the door.

"Say, what did I tell you, Jack?" Meekins whispered. "That's Bolter Jones, I bet a hundred. He just couldn't sleep till he closed the deal."

"Come in!" Gray called sharply.

As the door swung open Red gave an involuntary gasp of delight. It was the secretary, Smythe. He was a thin young man with straw coloured eyebrows. Employment with Boultbee Downs had negatived him into a proper suave humility.

"Mr. Gray?" he said tentatively.

"That's me," Gray answered.

The secretary drew from his pocket a large official envelope.

Meekins stretched his leg under the table and gently rubbed the toe of his boot up and down Gray's shin. It was surely a check for at last half of the two hundred thousand, Red whispered to himself.

"Mr. Boultbee Downs had me drive over to present this letter with his compliments to Mr. Gray," the secretary said. Then he put his hat on and turned to the door.

"Hadn't you best wait and see if there's – he might be wantin' an answer or somethin,'" Gray suggested.

"Mr. Boultbee Downs advised me there would be no answer," Smythe replied, and melted away into the shadows of the night.

"Well, I'm dashed!" Gray ejaculated softly. "That's kinder queer!" He turned the envelope over in his hands, eyeing it apprehensively.

Meekins stretched a big hand which carried on its back a bristle of red hair, saying, "Let me see her, Jack!" Red held the envelope between his eyes and the lamp. "Bet you five dollars there's a check in that, Jack! I can see a pinky end of somethin,'" he said, handing the letter back to Gray.

"What was that straw coloured ink slinger in such a hurry to get away for, Red? Seems to me as though there's somethin' gone wrong."

"Wrong nothin'! Don't you understand! Bloater Brown was afeared you might want to call the deal off to his secretary – don't you see? – an' he'd be a sort of witness – an' me bein' here, too, to hear it. But he's served the check on you – it's like a summons. He didn't want to give you no chance to refuse the money. Oh, you're bound up to the sale now!"

"I hope you're right, Red; but danged if I don't sorter hate to open her up! I got a kinder feelin' that – Well, it's just this way, I never did have no luck!"

"There couldn't nothin' go wrong," Red objected. "He ain't seen the mine since he took them nuggets away. He's just rushed the assay an' was afeared you'd find how rich it had panned out afore he closed the deal. Here's a knife. Slit her open an' see how big the check is. I never felt so sure of anything in my life."

Well, here goes!" Gray drew a big breath, shoved the knife through an end of the envelope, and as he inserted his fingers added, "It sorter makes me creepy."

Red leaned far over the table, his brown eyes electric with excitement, as Gray drew forth a somewhat bulky fold of papers. "What did I say?" yelled Red. "There's the proper agreement an' all, I bet! Hello! What in thunder's this?" A small, neatly folded parcel had fallen from the papers in Gray's hand.

"P'r'aps that's a diamond pin present for you," Red opined as he picked it up. "But first see if there ain't a check there, an' what Bloater says."

Gray opened the papers and discovered the preliminary agreement he had signed earlier in the day.

"That's the old one back," Red advised. "He's got the new ones all drawed up. What does Bloater Jones say, Jack?"

Gray ran his eyes slowly down a typewritten letter, and Meekins saw his face turn to an ashy hue and his heavy lip stiffen to hard lines.

"What does he say, Jack? Old man, there ain't nothin' gone wrong? He ain't squealin,' is he?"

"Gimme that little package, Red!"

Gray with trembling fingers opened the package, and Meekins saw nestling in the white paper half a dozen grains of discoloured oats.

"I don't understand, Jack!" he gasped. "What's it all about? What's that got to do with Bloater Brown an' your mine?"

Gray passed the letter to Meekins, and sat, his head hanging heavily on a limber neck, while Red perused the contents aloud. The letter explained that the assayer had found the samples of ore very rich in silver; the writer might add "suspiciously rich." He had also discovered, in the process of pulverizing the ore, probably half a pint of oats. This curious blend of agricultural product with silver, hitherto unknown in mineralogy, had caused him to examine closely the conglomerate carrying the silver, and he had classed it as manufactured cement, mixed with loose gravel. These startling inconsistencies had induced Mr. Boultbee Downs to decline the purchase of the Little Star mine, and he was returning inclosed the preliminary agreement.

The letter fell from Red's hand. He sat staring helplessly at Gray.

The latter roused himself to say, "I knew I never could have no luck!"

"The oats was in the feed bag!" Red moaned. "Twenty thousand bucks! If I'd only had a clean bag!"

BIBLIOGRAPHY - WILLIAM ALEXANDER FRASER

Criminous works

The blood lilies. New York: Scribner's/Toronto: Briggs, 1903. Set: Fort Donaldson. Mountie.

Brave hearts. New York: Scribner's, 1904. ss.

Bulldog Carney. Toronto: McClelland & Stewart, 1919.

Caste. New York/Toronto: Doran/London: Hodder & Stoughton, 1922.

Delilah plays the ponies. Toronto: Musson, 1927.

The eye of a god; and other tales of East and West. New York: Doubleday, 1899.

Red Meekins. New York: Doran/Toronto: McClelland & Stewart, 1921. Set: Cobalt, Ontario. Char: Red Meekins.

Thirteen men. New York: Appleton, 1906. Set: India and Burma.

Thoroughbreds. New York: McClure, 1902.

The three sapphires. New York: Doran/Toronto, 1918. Set: India and Burma.

Other works

The lone furrow. New York: Appleton, 1907. Partially set in Georgetown, Ontario, thinly disguised as "York."

Mooswa; and others of the boundaries. New York: Scribner's, 1900. ss.

The outcasts. Toronto: Briggs/New York, 1901.

The Sa'Zada tales. New York: Scribner's, 1905. ss.

Sorrow. Philadelphia, 1896.

PAULINE JOHNSON

The Riders of the Plains

Flint and feather; the complete poems of E. Pauline Johnson [Tekahionwake].
Toronto: Musson, 1912 and subsequently.

JOHNSON, E(mily) Pauline, 1862-1913

Canadian First Nation poetess Pauline Johnson, or Tekahionwake, was the youngest child of four, and second daughter of George Henry Martin Johnson, (Onwanonsyshon), Head Chief of the Six Nations (Iroquois), and Emily S. (Howells) Johnson, from Bristol, England. Her father was a member of the Mohawk tribe that along with the Seneca, Cayuga, Oneida, Onondaga, and Tuscarora, forms the Six Nations, and was a scion of one of the fifty families that comprised the then Five Nations founded by Hiawatha, (who was a historical personage despite Henry Wadsworth Longfellow), in the sixteenth century. George Johnson was also a descendant of Sir William Johnson (1715-1774), superintendent of northern Indians in British North America during the Seven Years War, whose second wife was Molly Brant, sister of Canada's famous hero, Joseph Brant.

Pauline Johnson was born on the family estate, "Chiefswood," on the banks of the Grand River near Brantford, Ontario, on March 10, 1861. She was educated at home and locally, her only formal schooling two years at the Brantford Model School.

By the age of thirty-one Johnson was a regular contributor of poetry to a wide range of journals and periodicals, and her work was well received by critics. She is best known for the poem "The song my paddle sings."

From 1882 to 1910 she gave a series of speaking tours, characteristically dressed as a Native princess, in the United States and in England, where she appeared before Queen Victoria. Many remote settlements from coast to coast in Canada and Newfoundland enjoyed her poetry readings, as she traversed Canada at least nineteen times, and appeared at least once in every city and town between Halifax and Vancouver.

A Canadian cultural ambassador throughout her relatively short life, Pauline Johnson was a fervent nationalist who used Canadian themes in much of her writing, and an ardent spokesperson for the position of the Native Peoples in Canadian society.

She died in Vancouver, British Columbia, on 7 March 1913, after a long illness.

THE RIDERS OF THE PLAINS

Flint and feather; the complete poems of E. Pauline Johnson [Tekahionwake].
Toronto: Musson, 1912 and subsequently.

"The Riders of the Plains" was one of Pauline Johnson's favourite poems, and certainly helped to create the romantic image of the Mounted Police.

The title of the poem was the affectionate nickname in the Northwest Territory for the North-West Mounted Police, and was commonly used throughout the West: in Assiniboia, as what is now southern Saskatchewan was then called; in Saskatchewan, which meant the northern half of what is now that province; and in Alberta.

The poetess got the idea for the poem at a dinner party in Boston, when she was asked, "Who are the North-West Mounted Police?" Upon her reply that they were the pride of Canada's fighting men, the American sneered, "Ah! then they are only some of your British Lion's whelps."

This poem was her patriotic response.

THE RIDERS OF THE PLAINS

Who is it lacks the knowledge? Who are the curs that dare
To whine and sneer that they do not fear the whelps in the Lion's lair?
But we of the North will answer, while life in the North remains,
Let the curs beware lest the whelps they dare are the Riders of the Plains;
For these are the kind whose muscle makes the power of the Lion's jaw,
And they keep the peace of our people and the honour of British law.

A woman has painted a picture – 'tis a neat little bit of art
The critics aver, and it roused up for her the love of the big British heart.
'Tis a sketch of an English bulldog that tigers would scarce attack,
And round and about and beneath him is painted the Union Jack.
With its blaze of colour, and courage, its daring in every fold,
And underneath is the title, "What we have we'll hold."
'Tis a picture plain as a mirror, but the reflex it contains
Is the counterpart of the life and heart of the Riders of the Plains;
For like to that flag and that motto, and the power of that bulldog's jaw,
They keep the peace of our people and the honour of British law.

These are the fearless fighters, whose life in the open lies,
Who never fail on the prairie trail 'neath the Territorial skies,
Who have laughed in the face of the bullets and the edge of the rebels' steel,
Who have set their ban on the lawless man with his crime beneath their heel;
These are the men who battle the blizzards, the suns, the rains,
These are the famed that the North has named the "Riders of the Plains,"
And theirs is the might and the meaning and the strength of the bulldog's jaw,
While they keep the peace of the people and the honour of British law.

These are the men of action, who need not the world's renown,
For their valour is known to England's throne as a gem in the British crown;
These are the men who face the front, whose courage the world may scan,
The men who are feared by the felon, but are loved by the honest man;
These are the marrow, the pith, the cream, the best that the blood contains,
Who have cast their days in the valiant ways of the Riders of the Plains;
And theirs is the kind whose muscle makes the power of old England's jaw,
And they keep the peace of her people and the honour of British law.

Then down with the cur that questions – let him slink to his craven den –
For he daren't deny our hot reply as to "who are our mounted men."
He shall honour them east and westward, he shall honour them south and
    north,
He shall bare his head to that coat of red wherever that red rides forth.
'Tis well that he knows the fibre that the great North-West contains,
The North-West pride in her men that ride on the Territorial plains –
For of such as these are the muscles and the teeth in the Lion's jaw,
And they keep the peace of our people and the honour of British law.

BIBLIOGRAPHY - E. PAULINE JOHNSON

Canadian born. Toronto: George Morang, 1903. poems.

Flint and feather; the complete poems of E. Pauline Johnson (Tekahionwake). Toronto: Musson, 1912 and subsequently.

Legends of Vancouver. Vancouver: Thompson Stationery Co., 1911.

The moccasin maker. Toronto: Briggs, 1913. poems.

The Shagganappi. Toronto: Briggs, 1912. Mountie. novel.

The white wampum. London: John Lane, 1895. poems.

ROGER POCOCK

The Lean Man
Tales of Western life, Lake Superior and the Canadian Prairie.
Ottawa: C. W. Mitchell, 1888.

POCOCK, (Henry) Roger (Astell), 1865-1941

Roger Pocock was born in Cookham, Berkshire, England, on 9 November 1865, the second son of Commander Pocock, RN. He left school at fifteen and two years later immigrated to Canada with his father. After a year at the Guelph Agricultural College, he left to work as a surveyor on the building of the Canadian Pacific Railway along the north shore of Lake Superior. At nineteen he enlisted as a constable in the NWMP, serving from 1884 to 1886; his humourous autobiographical account of those years is titled *The blackguard.*

Pocock was disabled by frostbite during the Riel Rebellion and was invalided out of the Force in 1886. He opened a trading post in Kamloops, BC, and tried his hand as a newspaper correspondent, reporting on the Skeena troubles for the Montreal *Witness* and on the Kootenay mines for merchants in Victoria. In 1888 he moved to California, and established himself as a popular novelist.

Pocock returned to Canada in 1897 and immediately became involved in a scandal: a British baronet, Sir Arthur Curtis, engaged Pocock as a guide on an expedition into the interior of British Columbia. Sir Arthur became lost in the bush and died, and Pocock was alleged to have murdered him. Though charges were never laid, the accusation plagued him for the rest of his life.

Trying to put the *cause célèbre* of Curtis's death behind him, Pocock successfully completed one of the great horseback rides in equestrian history, riding from Fort MacLeod, Alberta, to Mexico City in two hundred days. At the outbreak of the Boer War, Pocock enlisted in the British Army and served in South Africa, rising to the rank of Captain.

He settled in England after the war. An ardent imperialist, and highly influenced by the war-scare propaganda of the time, Pocock decided to organize a body of adventurers like himself, men who had proved their mettle in the outposts of the Empire, men who could serve the Empire in a civilian, auxiliary capacity. In 1904 he founded the Legion of Frontiersmen. Within a decade there were branches in all the English-speaking Dominions and Crown Colonies, with a very strong representation in Canada. Many members of the Legion fought in World War I, and casualties were high. Internecine dissension led to a decline in membership during the inter-war period.

Captain Roger Pocock died on 12 November, 1941, in Weston-Super-Mare, Somersetshire, England. The plaque on the family vault reads: *Founder of the Legion of Frontiersmen, adventurer and novelist.* He has a lasting place in the annals of adventure.

THE LEAN MAN

Tales of Western life, Lake Superior and the Canadian Prairie. Ottawa: C. W. Mitchell, 1888.

This story, which originally appeared in the *Toronto World* in 1887, marks what is probably the earliest appearance of a Mountie in fiction.

A very poignant piece, it is quite sympathetic toward and understanding of the Native Peoples of the Prairies immediately following the Northwest Rebellion of 1885, and can stand as a metaphor for their rapidly vanishing way of life and the tragedy of their existence.

THE LEAN MAN

Chapter I

When "The Lean Man" entered his lodge at nightfall, and saw his young squaw adorning her cheeks with vermillion, and braiding her straight black hair in tails after the enlightened manner of the Palefaces; when she had made him a robe for his comfort at night of the skins of over 200 rabbits; when she welcomed him at the door of his tent with good things earned or stolen from the white men: no wonder that the young husband felt that the Great Spirit had been good to him in giving "medicine" to ward off evil times, and to provide for his modest wants during the long winters.

He didn't say much about it however; but, relieved of a great anxiety after the risky perpetration of early marriage, settled down to a life of honorable theft and genteel idleness, leaving "Turkey Legs" to manage his worldly affairs in the shape of a daily meal, which that lady never failed to produce in good season.

"The Lean Man" used to spend much of his time in admiring his red blanket, for which he had wisely traded something that did not belong to him; and in meditating upon the obtuseness of the "Shermogonish" in arresting "the party of the second part" in that transaction instead of himself. For that ingenuous youth, "the Man-Who-Bites-His-Nails," had been arrested on the information of the Indian agent at "Big Child's" reserve; and was now in the guard room at the barracks, and like to be tried for larceny. Our friend was a Sioux; and had come from Montana to the far Saskatchewan after an escapade on the part of his tribe that did not meet with the approval of the United States authorities. This was the glorious victory of "Sitting Bull" over "The Sun Child," Gen. Custer, who, with some four hundred American soldiers, had been slain in a coulee by only about 1400 Sioux. They had then come to the land of the Great Mother, where the white Okemow told them to their great surprise, that their conduct was wicked and disreputable; though, even after the usual largesse of tea and tobacco, they still retained some scepticism about the peculiar views of the white men. Gradually this little band had drifted to the Saskatchewan; and, providing the Great Mother didn't bother them about reserves and treaty – even with the loss of flour and other emoluments – they were fairly content. True, it was a great shame that they couldn't get "treaty payments" like the Crees, without being corralled on a reserve; but they were better off than when badgered and hunted in the south because of their natural proclivities for lifting the wandering cattle on the prairie, such as they had eaten from time immemorial, and which were their rightful prey.

And even if these poor wanderers could not overthrow the hosts of Pharaoh, as they had tried to do last year, they could at least have the satisfaction of spoiling individual Egyptians, and so gain a precarious but honest livelihood in default of larger game.

And so it was that our hero went out to take the air one fine summer morning, and walked down the main trail on the river bank with his blanket held about him with inimitable grace, while he fanned himself with the bedraggled old wing of a crane in great peace and dignity. For in truth it was a hot day, and the sun burned down on the dusty road. He wore his great hat, the abandoned top-hat of a departed Jesuit missionary, from which he had cut the crown, and after cutting battlements from the raw edge, adorned it with a feather and three brass nails. His leggings were of embroidered bead work, beautifully designed by his squaw. He had also well-fitting moccasins and a pipe-tomahawk. Altogether, despite that he felt it was foolish to expose himself to such a hot sun, he was delighted to feel that he looked his best, and that his new "fire bag" showed to perfection. He saw a white man cursing a team in one of the adjoining fields, and felt that his Race was able to look with superior calmness upon the irritable and too talkative whites.

But as he strode leisurely down the trail and was nearing the Hudson Bay Company's Post, he saw a cloud of dust beyond and the glitter of helmets above it. "By the Great Horn Spoon of the Pale-faces," he soliloquised, "here come the Shermogonish," and he went and hid himself. When "The Lean Man" had effaced himself he continued to gaze at the approaching horsemen from a secluded corner. And presently there came up the trail a gallant troop of Mounted Police, the accoutrements and scarlet tunics, their white helmets and rifles across the saddle, resplendent in the sunlight. First came videttes, then twenty mounted men, followed by the rumbling transport. The waggons, loaded with provisions and bedding, carried each three men; and, at the trot, sent clouds of dust to leeward. Then came the rear guard of mounted men; and the commanding officer, the sergeant-major, and the bugler rode beside them. It was a stirring sight to see these splendid horses, the hardy sensitive bronchos of Alberta with their sun-burnt young riders; and all the eclat of military usage, and all the power of good rule over the great land-oceans of the far west.

The Indian followed the party with wistful eyes; these proud careless masters of the plains – these robbers of his people's heritage, who had driven away the buffalo, and sent disease among the tribes, to slowly blight his kindred until they were all dead.

And they went on through the Mission, and out on the rolling prairie beyond, to patrol the country that had last year been the seat of war – when the restless wandering peoples had made one last useless stand against the tide that was overwhelming them. Their leader, Louis Riel, who had seemed their only friend, had turned out but a self-seeking adventurer, and a traitor to them; and now he was dead, and the whites were more powerful than ever.

But "The Lean Man" was not a politician or a sociologist, but only a poor Sioux, who not knowing the meaning of events, was moderately happy. He went to the barracks, where he knew that the troop, having broken up camp, must have left many treasures in the shape of brass buttons, scarlet cloth and old boot-legs, among the refuse. But by the time he arrived at the barracks the camp had been cleared by a fatigue party, and he had to resort to the ash heaps. He was not challenged, save by a half-kindly, half-disdainful, "A wuss nitchie – get away out of this," from the cook; and in the evening he returned home-wards laden with spoil. Now it happened that Const. Anstaye, being on pass that evening, was proceeding up town to see Her, when he remembered that his washing was not contracted for. He therefore turned into a tepee by the wayside and sat down. He knew four words of the language, and pronounced two of these wrong; but had little difficulty in making himself understood, and presently left the tent. So "The Lean Man" saw from the distance a young sol-dier coming out of his tent, and with his boots flashing in the sunlight, his for-age cap balanced on the traditional three hairs, and his white gauntlets and switch and other finery, proceed gaily towards the Mission. Then "The Lean Man's" heart was filled with bad! When he came to the tent he disregarded the vacuous broad smiles of welcome that greeted him, and said to himself that these were full of guile (although they certainly did not look it) and he sat on the robes and sulked.

Later in the evening he crossed the river to where a bright fire burned amid the tents under the pine trees; and the usual pow-wow made the evening hideous, and continued with the gayest of howling and the most festive treat-ment of the tom-tom until a late hour. But there were speeches besides the music that night: the young Chief "Four Sky" made an oration, in which he said he would go to Carrot River – to the land of rabbits, and stray cattle, and hen roosts, and settlers, and every other kind of game – to the land of good water, and lots of fish and all kinds of idleness. Then "The Lean Man" made a long and very stupid speech in which he said he would go too. Upon which the ancient and venerable big Chief "Stick-in-the-Mud," aided and abetted by "Resting Bird," the mother of "The Lean Man," made deprecations, and plati-tudes, and objections – all of which were overruled by the young men. "The Resting Bird," a few days after, retired in great gloom to a meadow some six miles up the river, with her brave and some other fogies.

Upon the morrow "Four Sky," with "The Lean Man," "Little Egg" with his son "Would-not-go-out," "Wandering Mule" and "Sat On," with their horses, their squaws, their dogs, their children, their dignity, and all that they had, went down to Carrot River to sojourn.

A short time afterwards "Would-not-go-out," the son of "Little Egg," was returning from an unsuccessful hunt after a lost *cayuse,* when he was overtaken by a settler driving an empty waggon, and asked for a lift. The white man grumbled out a surly refusal, which so far incensed the lad that he climbed up into the waggon from behind, and carried out the traditions of his name by refusing to climb out again. Thereupon the settler, greatly to the annoyance of his passenger, lashed out behind with the whip, and "Would-not-go-out" became very angry, and pointed his "shooting stick" at the enemy. Happening to remember that the old flintlock gun was not loaded, he relented, and proceeded to have satisfaction with a threat. He told the white man that he wouldn't trouble to kill him now. "Because we are going to kill all you whites in a few days anyhow." Having delivered himself of this very silly remark, and perceiving that he was now close to the tents, he jumped out of the waggon and walked home. But the settler went about with information "on the very best authority" that there was to be a general massacre of the whole settlement, and so much alarmed were the neighbors that a deputation was sent to beg for a detachment of Police.

The little group of lodges were placed among the aspens by a lake, in a sheltered, shadowy hollow in the plain. The wide rolling prairie whose yellow grass, starred with flowers, melted towards the greys and softest azures that lay against the sky; the beautiful still waters where the young ducks swam; the delicate shimmering poplars; the smoke shaded lodges; and ponies grazing in the meadow – this was the lovely scene where the Red Men dwelt, the happy abundant plain that the Good Spirit had given them.

In due course there came to the settlement a sergeant and four constables of the Mounted Police, bringing with them a tent or two in the waggon, and a general impression that they had come to stay. The people had seldom had the soldiers among them, and there was some idea among the women that they were queer animals with red coats and bad habits. The "Riders of the Plains," however, used, even as recently as that, to travel like bandits, often indeed being mistaken for horse-thieves; and soon won the hearts of the good wives by their liberal purchase of milk, eggs, and butter, by their quiet good humor and tendency towards a chat. To any one tired of the prosaic life of the cities of the East the very sight of these men would have been refreshment. Picturesque, liberal, unconventional, often highly educated, the Shermogonish have no flavor of the old tiresome life of the umbrella and the table-cloth, and I wish no man a better medicine than their company. Of course an early and rigorous examination was made into the causes that had given rise to such uneasiness among the people. Sergeant Monmouth had a chat with "Four Sky," whose people were found busy skinning rabbits; but there was some delay in producing the settler who had raised the alarm, he having gone to Fort a la Corne, from whence he could not be expected for a day or two. In the meantime nothing could be done, and there was no pressing necessity for action because everything was quiet.

Upon the third day some of the police were sitting in the little general store having a comfortable growl for want of something better to do. Steen having lit a very bad cigar, sat down on a barrel, and with his broad slouch hat jammed down on the back of his head, opened a discussion.

"Oh! it's all right," he said in reply to a general observation on the part of the storekeeper concerning the state of the country. "It's all right, if it warnt for them miserable 'nitchies' – who are no use anyhow – running the whole 'she-bang' with their confounded monkey business. 'Sif thar wasn't enough drills and fatigues to keep the whole darned outfit on the keen jump without their fooling around the country stealing horses, and killing cattle, and raising rackets from one year's end to another; and now there's that damn fool Garnett robbing the mails, and he'll give enough trouble by the time he's hanged to keep half the troop busy hunting him. I –" He was interrupted by Sergt. Monmouth; "Look here, I'll bet anyone a month's pay that there'll be a mounted escort for every mail in the country within this month – you jest see if there ain't!"

Constable Mercer took up the growl at this point, and made out a very bad case against the Canadian Government "for running a poor — of a buck policeman 'sif he was a navvy or suthin' worse."

Here Le Soeur broke in: "There was – wot you say – General Ordaire? Yes, General Ordaire, jest befor' we come away – er –"

Sergt. Monmouth: "O, give us a rest, 'nitchie' – go away back to yur reserve, man!"

At this moment Constable Anstaye burst into the store with a joke that could not be kept back a minute, but in a sad dilemma that he had not breath to tell it. The substance of his tale was gathered in the course of a few minutes, and was to the effect that he had been in one of the tepees talking to a squaw when a "nitchie" came in, and, when he saw him, looked as black as thunder and went out. Presently he heard a racket outside, and found the same Indian unmercifully thrashing a boy; but he was interrupted by "Four Sky" and another, who dragged him off and looked about as cheerful as a blizzard on a cold day.

"But which 'tepee' were you in – and what were you up to?"

"Oh, I dunno, it was the one next the trail, and the chap that raised the row was that lanky young cuss in a red blanket, and a top hat with the crown out."

Monmouth strolled down to the camp, but on his return said that everything was quiet enough there. No further notice was taken of the affair, and the next day it was forgotten; but Anstaye noticed that whenever he went down to the camp the Indian with the red blanket scowled upon him.

In course of time the man Brown, who had raised the alarm, returned from Fort a la Corne; and was taken by Sergt. Monmouth to the Indian camp. He felt uncomfortable about the result of his assertions; and being a mean man determined that instead of an open confession that he had been needlessly scared, he would justify himself at all costs. Unfortunately it happened that "Would-not-go-out" was absent; and when all the braves in the little band were brought before him, and he was asked to produce the bloodthirsty savage who had, as he said, attempted to murder him, the white man hesitated, and tried to excuse himself, and make light of it all in the most generous manner, saying that he would be very sorry to get the poor fellow into trouble.

"Come on – no fooling!" said Monmouth. Brown asked in Sioux whether all the band were there; and the Chief replied that they were all there except a lad who was not even full grown, and could scare nobody with any spirit.

Monmouth: "Well, which was it?"

Brown: "Oh, I don't want to get a poor miserable nitchie in jail!"

Monmouth: "Well, you're a pretty specimen, having us sent pretty near 200 miles to take the man who was going to kill you. You say that he attempted murder – by Jove, I'll arrest you if you don't take care, for trying to screen a murderer!"

Brown was now thoroughly cowed, and felt that he must do a dirty crime to save himself from public contempt. Pointing to a tall, surly-looking young man in a red blanket he said: "That one."

Monmouth asked the Chief what character the accused bore; and the reply was sorrowfully expressed that of late the evil spirit had been upon "The Lean Man," for only two days ago he had wantonly attacked and thrashed a lad in camp, named "Would-not-go-out," for no cause.

And so it came about that the detachment returned to Headquarters, and carried away "The Lean Man" a prisoner.

Chapter II

It was a pleasant sight to see a party of Mounted Police ride in from some command, bronzed, dusty and travel-stained, their harness rusted with the rough usages of the camp, their eyes bright with the reflected breath and freedom of the plains, while the horses pricked their ears to hear the whinny of a colt in the corrall, as they foresaw the quietude of the dim stables, or the sunny upland where the herd was grazing. Thus came home the party from Carrot River, and drew up sharp before the Guard House. The prisoner was sent into his allotted cell, the waggon unloaded at the Quartermaster's Store, the horses led to water, the bedding taken to the barrack rooms, the cook urged to be ready with the provisions. The arrivals shed their prairie dress, while a rapid discussion took place on the current news; and a Guard was told off, and having got into uniform its members made their way to the Guard House, growling not a little that a single prisoner should cause so much extra work. Until then the picquet had gone on solitary night rounds with his lantern, and dozed away the spare hours in the Guard Room; but this was only a pleasant reminiscence now. But the Indian, the restless unthinking child of the plains, had come to the weariness of an imprisoned spirit, and sank into the heavy lethargy of despair. The log walls of his prison, the iron bars of the door, the soldier sitting at the little table beyond, and what might be seen through a loop-hole in the wall, were now exchanged for the glorious horizon, with all the sweet sounds and sights of nature that people the broad tent of day. That loop-hole, pierced during the war, was now his only consolation, and he would sit for hours before it looking out upon the world. The sadness of his spirit seemed to weigh the atmosphere, for the air was dense for days with the smoke of prairie fires; and once at night he saw the sharp lines of flames coming down over the hills into the river flat, and hoped against hope that these would come down to release him.

"The Lean Man" was examined by the officer in command, but he was found so sullen and intractable that no evidence of his innocence could be come at: so he was committed for trial. One thing that he said to the interpreter was beyond the man's powers of translation, but was several times repeated among the men on the detachment in the words in which it was rendered: "The Good Spirit gave me the prairie for a bed, the trees to shelter me – but you Shermogonish have given me cold boards." And afterwards he said to Sergeant Monmouth, "You are going to kill me because I fought against you; be quick – kill me now – I am tired of waiting to die." He thought of the past – when he had gone through the tortures of the Sun Dance to come forth from the ordeal a warrior; he thought of all the excitement of the war, how he had seen the red flames of Fort Carlton leap up against the night, and had fought in the rifle pits of Batoche under Gabriel Dumont; he thought of his short happy married life before the dark cloud settled down upon him; and he brooded over what the Interpreter had said to him: "You will be tried next month."

Weeks passed outside the Guard House; and Change sat as usual on the wings of Time. The Mission people had ever since the war been as prompt in the matter of alarms as a fire brigade; and the Carrot River "scare," added to contemporary fictions about the Indians, had caused a general feeling of alarm. This was by no means mitigated by the departure of the Troop for the south by forced marches, to meet a great dignitary in the neighborhood of Long Lake; and by the rumored outbreak of an Indian war at Wood Mountain.

The band of "Four Sky" returned from Carrot River bringing the bereaved "Turkey Legs," who would sit for hours on the ground outside of the Guard House waiting for a casual glimpse of her lord; and comforted him much by her silent sympathy.

In due course the great dignitary returned to the East; and the Troop came home again, to the infinite regret of the little garrison, who by no means yearned for drill and discipline. The summer was ended, the harvest was gathered in, the winter began to send forth scouts to feel the way, and the full ripe year was waning to its close. And still "The Lean Man" knelt at the loop-hole, or made his little daily excuses for access to the free air of heaven. He lay through the long nights wondering what would be done to him after the trial, and feeling in his numbed sensibilities only the one terror – Disgrace. And he said within his heart, and whispered it to himself, and heard the winds whisper the words at night: "I will not be tried."

Three days after he arrived at this determination some of the men were spending a spare hour in the large barrack room engaged in "bed fatigue," and between the whiffs of a quiet smoke carrying on a desultory conversation. Burk, who was on guard that day, a tall, handsome, good-natured Englishman, sat on the edge of his bed fumbling in a kit-bag underneath for some tobacco, having permission to leave the Guard House for a few minutes.

"Well, Geometry," said Anstaye, "has the Nitchie been up to any of his games today?"

Burk: "I should just think he was! Why, I was just taking him over to the kitchen for the guard dinner at noon, when he made a break and got clean away past the Hospital."

Sergeant Monmouth: "Well, I hope you shot the –"

"Oh, it was no use shooting him; I just hollered out to the others and skinned after him."

"That is, you made use of your compasses, Geometry?"

"Oh shut up, Tribulation," said Burk; "Well, I caught up close to the Riding School and nabbed him. And then I ran him off to the kitchen and made him lay hold of the big tea pot without any more fooling."

"And did he buck?"

"I saw buck! No, you bet he was as quiet as – as – er – death. That's the third bolt he's made today; he must have a pretty bad conscience."

Indeed, "The Lean Man" had made several attempts to escape, but his escorts had each time seized him, and taken no extra precautions other than to show him the butt of a revolver or set forth some counsel. That evening, however, before he was sent with an escort for the supper, he was shackled with a "ball and chain," an instrument intended to restrain the most volatile of captives should he become too retiring. It must not be imagined that the prisoner was treated harshly, for if there is one virtue possessed by the rough soldiery of the prairies, it is their invariable kindness to the criminals committed to their charge.

"The Lean Man," thwarted in his attempts to escape, brought to the humiliation of chains, and filled with the darkest foreboding of evil, came to the black shadows of utter despair; and then, as man can do in the immediate presence of death, transcended his poor life as the day transcends night; he forgot the degradation of his people, and fought with all the magnificent courage and haughty endurance of his barbaric forefathers. He stood in the door of his cell when the time came that it was to be locked for the night, and, with his eyes aflame, his body trembling with the excitement, fought with the fury and the strength of madness for liberty. The whole guard hardly sufficed to cope with him and it was only after a long and furious struggle that the Indian, over-whelmed with the weight of numbers, fell back into the cell utterly exhausted. He had cast aside the dross that had come over the Indian character from ruinous contact with the ruling race; he had asserted for once the inalienable rights of heredity, the greater and manlier past. The change in him was inter-preted by the authorities as insanity.

Night deepened down upon the world, and the dim after-light waned through long hours into the north. The air was misty with smoke from the prairies; and, chilled in the shadowy day night of Indian summer, all the valley lay in mysterious silence.

The Indian sat long brooding in the intense stillness. Through the barred aperture in the door a stream of golden light poured into the cell; and under the lamp in the Guard Room the Sergeant of the Guard sat at the table writing. The two men off duty lay asleep on the sloping dais at the other side of the room, still in complete uniform, and wearing their heavy side-arms as they took their brief, uneasy hours of rest. There was no sound save their breathing, and the steady scratching of the Sergeant's pen, as he proceeded with his letters. Presently the "piquet" came in for the stable keys, saying that "the buckskin mare and Bulkeley's horse broke loose in the long stable – I can manage all right." Then he went out, and the prisoner watched him through the loop-hole as he went swinging his lantern towards the "corralls."

"The Lean Man" slowly unbound the sash from his waist, and knotted the ends together – he thrust the knot through the loop-hole – he drew the sash sharply back, catching the knot against the sides of a narrow gap between two logs – he pulled hard to make sure that the knot would hold. Then he sat a few moments in silence, and covered his face with his hands. He looked about him – the Sergeant of the Guard had taken a book and lay on the trestle bed beside his table reading, and the night around was infinitely still. Holding the loop of the sash the prisoner looked up towards heaven and prayed; then he placed his head within the loop and crouched down, leaning heavily with his throat against the sash. The Sergeant of the Guard was still reading – the two men were breathing quietly in their sleep – the "piquet" came out from the stables and went and stood on the bank of the river near by – the mist lay over the val-ley, and all was still.

The cold autumn day broke upon the world, and reveillé echoed from the wooded sides of the little valley, and rang melodiously against the banks of the broad river; the sun rose triumphant over the mists, and the waters were resplendent before his slanting rays – but the Indian had gone to the place of his fathers, and his sad stern eyes were closed forever in sleep. This man had dared the long agonies of torture in utter silence, had crushed with determined hands the life within him, and had gone down to the grave triumphant, with-out one sound to tell the watchful soldier, who was actually in the same room with him, that the last tragedy was being transacted in a lingering anguish of suffocation.

They buried him on the bank of the river, and one of the soldiers made two laths into a cross during an idle moment and set it over the grave. The Indian lay under the prairie flowers in the shadow of the cross; on the one side of him Humanity rattled down the long dusty trail, and on the other lay the still expanses of silver, the broad, silent waters of the great Saskatchewan.

BIBLIOGRAPHY - ROGER POCOCK

Criminous works

Captains of adventure. Indianapolis, Indiana: Bobbs-Merrill, 1913. Set: Canada. Mountie.
The blackguard. London: Beeman, 1896. Re-issued London: Murray – as: *The splendid blackguard.* Indianapolis, Indiana: Bobbs-Merrill – as: *The cheerful blackguard,* 1915. Also published as: *The beloved blackguard.* Set: Alberta in and around the 1885 Rebellion. Char: Jose de la Mancha, son of a Spanish father and an Irish mother. A humorous portrayal of the Mounties circa 1885. "A Canadian novel that is worthwhile: The novels of any merit that have to do with life in Canada are so few and far between that one is almost tempted to use too many superlatives in recommending *The cheerful blackguard.*" (Toronto *Mail,* 17 June 1916).
Jessie of Cariboo. London: Murray, 1911. Set: Canada.
A man in the open. Indianapolis, Ind.: Bobbs-Merrill, 1912. Set: Canada.

Other works

The Arctic night. London: Chapman, 1896.
Canada's fighting troops. [n.pl.: n.publ., 190?]
The chariot of the sun; a fantasy. London: Chapman, 1910.
Chorus to adventurers; being the later life of Roger Pocock, "a frontiersman." 1931.
Curly; a tale of the Arizona Desert. London: [n.publ.], 1904/Boston: Little, Brown, 1905.
The dragon slayer. London: Chapman, 1896. Repr.: London: Hodder & Stoughton – as: *Sword and dragon,* 1909.
Following the frontier. New York: McClure, Phillips, 1903/London: Gay & Hancock – as *A frontiersman,* 1904. autobiography.
Rules of the game.
Tales of Western life, Lake Superior and the Canadian Prairies. Ottawa: C. W. Mitchell, 1888.
The wolf trail. Oxford: Blackwell/New York: Appleton, 1923.
— (ed.) *The Frontiersman's pocket book.* Toronto: H. Frowde, 1909.

ROBERT W. SERVICE

The Shooting of Dan McGrew
Songs of a sourdough.
Toronto: Briggs/New York: Barse – as:
The spell of the Yukon; and other verses, 1907.

Clancy of the Mounted Police
Ballads of a cheechako.
Toronto: William Briggs/New York: Barse & Hopkins, 1909.

SERVICE, Robert W(illiam), 1874-1958

Some purists may question the inclusion of Robert W. Service as a "Canadian" crime writer, but his poetry has stamped him indisputably as Canadian, even earning him the sobriquet "The Canadian Kipling." To exclude him as being non-national would be to take parochialism beyond absurdity. Despite his stature as a major poet of the First World War, it is for his lyric portrayal of the Yukon that he is best known, loved, and remembered.

When he submitted the manuscript for *Songs of a sourdough* to the Methodist Book and Publishing House (later Ryerson Press) in 1907, he was prepared to pay for publication himself. But the typesetters enjoyed the book so much that the editor, the Rev. William Briggs, offered to have the firm bear the costs of publication. The book was a financial success, establishing Service's popularity. "Dangerous Dan McGrew" and "Sam McGee" entered the pantheon of immortal fictional characters, passing into Canadian and international folklore as the epitome of the Klondike Gold Rush.

Service was born in Preston, England, on the 16th of January, 1874. He was educated in Scotland, and his first job was with the Commercial Bank of Scotland in Glasgow. In 1894, in search of adventure, he immigrated to Canada, working on a farm and attending university before joining the Canadian Bank of Commerce (now melded with the former Imperial Bank of Canada into the Canadian Imperial Bank of Commerce). He worked for the bank in Whitehorse and Dawson City for six years. In 1909 he left the bank to devote his time to writing. His first novel, *The trail of '98; a Northland romance,* was published in 1910.

During World War I, Service was an ambulance driver on the Western Front. From his experiences came *Rhymes of a Red Cross man,* dedicated to the memory of his brother, who was killed in action with the Canadian infantry in France. Service is sadly neglected as one of the most evocative of the poets of the First World War, particularly in his imparting of the sense of being in the trenches.

> I see across the shrapnel-seeded meadows
> The jagged rubble-heap of La Boiselle;
> Blood-guilty Fricourt brooding in the shadows,
> and Thiepval's chateau empty as a shell.
> Down Albert's riven streets the moon is leering;
> The hanging Virgin takes its bitter ray;
> And all the road from Hamel I am hearing
> The silver rage of bugles over Bray.

After the First World War, Service settled in the south of France; here he wrote three crime thrillers, all set in France, ho-hum Wallace-esque clones of a type standard in the 1920s. But Service had already made an original contribution to criminous literature with "The Shooting of Dan McGrew."

Service and his family left France prior to the German occupation of World War II, eventually living on the Pacific coast of Canada. Late in life Service wrote two volumes of autobiography: *Ploughman of the moon* and *Harper of heaven; a record of radiant living,* published in 1945 and 1948. He died in 1958.

THE SHOOTING OF DAN McGREW

Songs of a sourdough. Toronto: Briggs/New York: Barse – as: *The spell of the Yukon; and other verses,* 1907.

If one accepts poetry as a narrative form, then the first criminous narrative by a Canadian set in the Klondike is "The shooting of Dan McGrew." Undoubtedly the best known of Service's books of verse, *Songs of a sourdough* contains his masterworks: in addition to "The shooting of Dan McGrew," there are "The cremation of Sam McGee," ("There are strange things done in the midnight sun/By the men who moil for gold;/The Arctic trails have their secret tales/That would make your blood run cold;/The Northern Lights have seen queer sights,/But the queerest they ever did see/Was that night on the marge of Lake Lebarge/I cremated Sam McGee."); "The law of the Yukon," ("This is the law of the Yukon, and ever she makes it plain;/"Send not your foolish and feeble; send me your strong and your sane."); and "The spell of the Yukon."

Service's narrative poetry made a vital and important contribution to the melange that made up the Great White North, the true North strong and free, as part of the mythic heritage of Canada.

The ancient Greeks said that a man is immortal as long as his name is remembered. Service will be immortal, not for his prose, but for those never-to-be-forgotten lines that begin "A bunch of the boys were whooping it up in the Malamute saloon ..."

THE SHOOTING OF DAN MCGREW

A bunch of the boys were whooping it up in the Malamute saloon;
The kid that handles the music-box was hitting a jag-time tune;
Back of the bar, in a solo game, sat Dangerous Dan McGrew,
And watching his luck was his light-o'-love, the lady that's known as Lou.

When out of the night, which was fifty below, and into the din and the glare,
There stumbled a miner fresh from the creeks, dog-dirty, and loaded for bear.
He looked like a man with a foot in the grave, and scarcely the strength of a
    louse,
Yet he tilted a poke of dust on the bar, and he called for drinks for the house.
There was none could place the stranger's face, though we searched ourselves
    for a clue;
But we drank his health, and the last to drink, was Dangerous Dan McGrew.

There's men that somehow just grip your eyes, and hold them hard like a spell;
And such was he, and he looked to me like a man who had lived in hell;
With a face most hair, and the dreary stare of a dog whose day is done,
As he watered the green stuff in his glass, and the drops fell one by one.
Then I got to figgering who he was, and wondering what he'd do,
And I turned my head – and there watching him was the lady that's known as
    Lou.

His eyes went rubbering round the room, and he seemed in a kind of daze,
Till at last that old piano fell in the way of his wandering gaze.
The rag-time kid was having a drink; there was no one else on the stool,
So the stranger stumbles across the room, and flops down there like a fool.
In a buckskin shirt that was glazed with dirt he sat, and I saw him sway;
Then he clutched the keys with his talon hands – my God! but that man could
    play!

Were you ever out in the Great Alone, when the moon was awful clear,
And the icy mountains hemmed you in with a silence you most could *hear;*
With only the howl of a timber wolf, and you camped there in the cold,
A half-dead thing in a stark, dead world, clean mad for the muck called gold;
While high overhead, green, yellow and red, the North Lights swept in bars –
Then you've a hunch what the music meant ... hunger and night and the stars.

And hunger not of the belly kind, that's banished with bacon and beans;
But the gnawing hunger of lonely men for a home and all that it means;

For a fireside far from the cares that are, four walls and a roof above;
But oh! so cramful of cosy joy, and crowned with a woman's love;
A woman dearer than all the world, and true as Heaven is true –
(God! how ghastly she looks through her rouge – the lady that's known as
   Lou).

Then on a sudden the music changed, so soft that you scarce could hear;
But you felt that your life had been looted clean of all that it once held dear;
That someone had stolen the woman you loved; that her love was a devil's lie;
That your guts were gone, and the best for you was to crawl away and die.
'Twas the crowning cry of a heart's despair, and it thrilled you through and
   through –
"I guess I'll make it a spread misere," said Dangerous Dan McGrew.

The music almost died away ... then it burst like a pent-up flood;
And it seemed to say, "Repay, repay," and my eyes were blind with blood.
The thought came back of an ancient wrong, and it stung like a frozen lash,
And the lust awoke to kill, to kill ... then the music stopped with a crash,
And the stranger turned, and his eyes they burned in a most peculiar way;
In a buckskin shirt that was glazed with dirt he sat, and I saw him sway;

Then his lips went in in a kind of grin, and he spoke, and his voice was calm;
And, "Boys," says he, "you don't know me, and none of you care a damn;
But I want to state, and my words are straight, and I'll bet my poke they're
   true,
That one of you is a hound of hell ... and that one is Dan McGrew."

Then I ducked my head, and the lights went out, and two guns blazed in the
   dark;
And a woman screamed, and the lights went up, and two men lay stiff and
   stark;
Pitched on his head, and pumped full of lead, was Dangerous Dan McGrew,
While the man from the creeks lay clutched to the breast of the lady that's
   known as Lou.

These are the simple facts of the case, and I guess I ought to know;
They say that the stranger was crazed with "hooch," and I'm not denying it's
   so.
I'm not so wise as the lawyer guys, but strictly between us two –
The woman that kissed him – and pinched his poke – was the lady that's
   known as Lou.

CLANCY OF THE MOUNTED POLICE
Ballads of a cheechako. Toronto: William Briggs/New York: Barse & Hopkins, 1909.

Service's poems were phenomenally popular following the publication of his first book of verse, *Songs of a sourdough.* As a result, probably no other fictional presentation of the Mounties did so much to increase their mythic stature in popular culture than this work.

The words may sound overblown to our jaded ears, but once those words rang sterling true – and still do for those who have not abandoned honour and decency.

CLANCY OF THE MOUNTED POLICE

In the little Crimson Manual it's written plain and clear
That who would wear the scarlet coat shall say good-bye to fear;
Shall be a guardian of the right, a sleuth-hound of the trail –
In the little Crimson Manual there's no such word as "fail" –
Shall follow on though heavens fall, or hell's top-turrets freeze,
Half round the world, if need there be, on bleeding hands and knees.
It's duty, duty, first and last, the Crimson Manual saith;
The Scarlet Rider makes reply: "It's duty – to the death."
And so they sweep the solitudes, free men from all the earth;
And so they sentinel the woods, the wilds that know their worth;
And so they scour the startled plains and mock at hurt and pain,
And read their Crimson Manual, and find their duty plain.
Knights of the lists of unrenown, born of the frontier's need,
Disdainful of the spoken word, exultant in the deed;
Unconscious heroes of the waste, proud players of the game,
Props of the power behind the throne, upholders of the name:
For thus the Great White Chief hath said, "In all my lands be peace,"
And to maintain his word he gave his West the Scarlet Police.

Livid-lipped was the valley, still as the grave of God;
    Misty shadows of mountain thinned into mists of cloud;
Corpselike and stark was the land, with a quiet that crushed and awed,
    And the stars of the weird sub-arctic glimmered over its shroud.

Deep in the trench of the valley two men stationed the Post,
    Seymour and Clancy the reckless, fresh from the long patrol;
Seymour, the sergeant, and Clancy – Clancy who made his boast
    He could cinch like a bronco the Northland, and cling to the prongs of the
        Pole.

Two lone men on detachment, standing for law on the trail;
    Undismayed in the vastness, wise with the wisdom of old –
Out of the night hailed a half-breed telling a pitiful tale,
    "White man starving and crazy on the banks of the Nordenscold."

Up sprang the red-haired Clancy, lean and eager of eye;
    Loaded the long toboggan, strapped each dog at its post;
Whirled his lash at the leader; then, with a whoop and a cry,
    Into the Great White Silence faded away like a ghost.

The clouds were a misty shadow, the hills were a shadowy mist;
    Sunless, voiceless and pulseless, the day was a dream of woe;
Through the ice-rifts the river smoked and bubbled and hissed;
    Behind was a trail fresh broken, in front the untrodden snow.

Ahead of the dogs ploughed Clancy, haloed by steaming breath;
    Through peril of open water, through ache of insensate cold;
Up rivers wantonly winding in a land affianced to death,
    Till he came to a cowering cabin on the banks of the Nordenscold.

Then Clancy loosed his revolver, and he strode through the open door;
    And there was the man he sought for, crouching beside the fire;
The hair of his beard was singeing, the frost on his back was hoar,
    And ever he crooned and chanted as if he never would tire:–

"I panned and I panned in the shiny sand, and I sniped on the river bar;
But I know, I know, that it's down below that the golden treasures are;
So I'll wait and wait till the floods abate, and I'll sink a shaft once more,
And I'd like to bet that I'll go home yet with a brass band playing before."

He was nigh as thin as a sliver, and he whined like a Moose-hide cur;
    So Clancy clothed him and nursed him as a mother nurses a child;
Lifted him on the toboggan, wrapped him in robes of fur,
    Then with the dogs sore straining started to face the Wild.

Said the Wild, "I will crush this Clancy, so fearless and insolent;
    For him will I loose my fury, and blind and buffet and beat;
Pile up my snows to stay him; then when his strength is spent,
    Leap on him from my ambush and crush him under my feet.

"Him will I rig with my silence, compass him with my cold;
    Closer and closer clutch him unto mine icy breast;
Buffet him with my blizzards, deep in my snows enfold,
    Claiming his life as my tribute, giving my wolves the rest."

Clancy crawled through the vastness; o'er him the hate of the Wild;
    Full on his face fell the blizzard; cheering his huskies he ran;
Fighting, fierce-hearted and tireless, snows that drifted and piled,
    With ever and ever behind him singing the crazy man.

    "Sing hey, sing ho, for the ice and snow,
      And a heart that's ever merry;

> Let us trim and square with a lover's care
>   (For why should a man be sorry?)
> A grave deep, deep, with the moon a-peep,
>   A grave in the frozen mould.
> Sing hey, sing ho, for the winds that blow,
>   And a grave deep down in the ice and snow,
>   A grave in the land of gold."

Day after day of darkness, the whirl of the seething snows;
   Day after day of blindness, the swoop of the stinging blast;
On through a blur of fury the swing of staggering blows;
   On through a world of turmoil, empty, inane and vast.

Night with its writhing storm-whirl, night despairingly black;
   Night with its hours of terror, numb and endlessly long;
Night with its weary waiting, fighting the shadows back.
   And ever the crouching madman singing his crazy song.

Cold with its creeping terror, cold with its sudden clinch;
   Cold so utter you wonder if 'twill ever again be warm;
Clancy grinned as he shuddered, "Surely it isn't a cinch
   Being wet-nurse to a loony in the teeth of an arctic storm."

The blizzard passed and the dawn broke, knife-edged and crystal clear;
   The sky was a blue domed iceberg, sunshine outlawed away;
Ever by snowslide and ice-rip haunted and hovered the Fear;
   Ever the Wild malignant poised and panted to slay.

The lead-dog freezes in harness – cut him out of the team!
   The lung of the wheel-dog's bleeding – shoot him and let him lie!
On and on with the others – lash them until they scream!
   "Pull for your lives, you devils! On! To halt is to die."

There in the frozen vastness Clancy fought with his foes;
   The ache of the stiffened fingers, the cut of the snowshoe thong;
Cheeks black-raw through the hood-flap, eyes that tingled and closed,
   And ever to urge and cheer him quavered the madman's song.

Colder it grew and colder, till the last heat left the earth,
   And there in the great stark stillness the balefires glinted and gleamed,
And the Wild all around exulted and shook with a devilish mirth,
   And life was far and forgotten, the ghost of a joy once dreamed.

Death! And one who defied it, a man of the Mounted Police;
    Fought it there to a standstill long after hope was gone;
Grinned through his bitter anguish, fought without let or cease,
    Suffering, straining, striving, stumbling, struggling on.

Till the dogs lay down in their traces, and rose and staggered and fell;
    Till the eyes of him dimmed with shadows, and the trail was so hard to
        see;
Till the Wild howled out triumphant, and the world was a frozen hell –
    Then said Constable Clancy: "I guess that it's up to me."

Far down the trail they saw him, and his hands they were blanched like bone;
    His face was a blackened horror, from his eyelids the salt rheum ran;
His feet he was lifting strangely, as if they were made of stone,
    But safe in his arms and sleeping he carried the crazy man.

So Clancy got into Barracks, and the boys made rather a scene;
    And the O.C. called him a hero, and was nice as a man could be;
But Clancy gazed down his trousers at the place where his toes had been,
    And then he howled like a husky, and sang in a shaky key.

"When I go back to the old love that's true to the finger-tips,
I'll say: 'Here's bushels of gold, love,' and I'll kiss my girl on the lips;
'It's yours to have and to hold, love.' It's the proud, proud boy I'll be,
When I go back to the old love that's waited so long for me."

BIBLIOGRAPHY - ROBERT W. SERVICE

Criminous works

The house of fear. New York: Dodd Mead/London: Unwin, 1927. Set: on the Brittany coast, France.

The master of the microbe; a fantastic romance. New York: Barse, 1926/London: Unwin, 1927. Set: Paris.

The poisoned paradise; a romance of Monte Carlo. New York: Dodd Mead, 1922.

The trail of '98; a Northland romance. Toronto: Briggs/New York: Dodd, Mead, 1910. Set: Klondike. Char: Athol Meldrum. Mountie.

Other works

Ballads of a Bohemian. New York: Barse; 1921.

Ballads of a cheechako. Toronto: William Briggs/New York: Barse & Hopkins, 1909.

Bar-room ballads; a book of verse. New York: Dodd, Mead, 1940.

Carols of an old codger. 1954.

Complete poetical works. New York: Barse, 1921. Repr. as: *Collected verse* – London: Benn, 1930/*Complete poems* – New York: Dodd, Mead, 1933.

Harper of heaven; a record of radiant living. 1948. autobiography.

Lyrics of a low brow. New York: Dodd, Mead, 1951.

More collected verse. 1956.

Ploughman of the moon; an adventure into memory. 1945. autobiography.

The pretender; a story of the Latin Quarter. New York: Dodd Mead, 1914.

Rhymes for my rags. 1956.

Rhymes of a rebel. 1952.

Rhymes of a Red Cross man. Toronto: Briggs/London: Unwin, 1916.

Rhymes of a rolling stone. Toronto: Briggs/New York: Dodd, Mead, 1912.

Rhymes of a roughneck. New York: Dodd, Mead, 1950.

The roughneck; a tale of Tahiti. New York: Barse, 1923.

Songs for my supper. 1953.

Songs of a sourdough. Toronto: Briggs/New York: Barse – as: *The spell of the Yukon; and other verses*, 1907.

Songs of a sun lover. London: Benn, 1949.

Songs of the high North. 1956.

Twenty bath-tub ballads. London: Francis, Day & Hunter, 1939.

Why not grow young?; or, Living for longevity. New York: Dodd, Mead, 1928. philosophy.

ARTHUR STRINGER

Running Out of Pay-Dirt

The man who couldn't sleep; being a relation of the divers strange adventures which befell one Witter Kerfoot when, sorely troubled with sleeplessness, he ventured forth at midnight along the highways and byways of Manhattan.
Indianapolis: Bobbs-Merrill/Toronto: McLeod, 1919.

STRINGER, Arthur (John Arbuthnot), 1874-1950

Stringer's place in Canadian literature rests on his enduring Prairie trilogy: *The Prairie wife; a novel, The Prairie mother,* and *The Prairie child.* They were based on his experiences in setting up a grain farm in southern Alberta about 1915. These books guarantee him a place as one of Canada's foremost regional novelists of the pioneer West.

Arthur Stringer was born on the 26th of January, 1874, in Chatham, Ontario. His father, a carriage maker, moved the family to London, Ontario, in 1884. At the age of twelve, young Stringer entered London Collegiate Institute with the highest entrance examination marks ever recorded. After studying at University of Toronto and Oxford, Stringer began a newspaper career with the Montreal *Herald.*

In Montreal he was initiated into the mysteries of literature through attendance at the soirées at the home of poet William Henry Drummond, whose residence was a literary meeting-place. Archibald Lampman was another regular. The habitués believed that they were part of the birth of a new Canadian literature.

Stringer moved to New York City in 1899 with fellow Canadian journalists and crime writers Harvey J. O'Higgins and Arthur E. MacFarlane. He became editorial director for the American Press Association from 1898 to 1901, and from 1903 to 1904 he was the literary editor of the magazine *Success.*

Stringer established himself as an author of popular fiction, especially crime stories, becoming one of the pacesetters of the mystery and suspense story of the underworld. His most important contribution to the genre is the collection of tales, *The man who couldn't sleep; being a relation of the divers strange adventures which befell one Witter Kerfoot when, sorely troubled with sleeplessness, he ventured forth at midnight along the highways and byways of Manhattan.*

Stringer returned to the Chatham district of his young boyhood in 1903 and purchased a fruit farm in Kent County on the north shore of Lake Erie, east of Leamington. Here he lived, despite frequent absences, until 1921, when he moved permanently to the United States. Most of the books that made Stringer popular during his lifetime were written at this farm, "Shadow Lawn." It was here in 1914 that he scripted the famous film serial, "The perils of Pauline."

Stringer set *Empty hands*

> North of The Pas and towards Hudson's Bay is Malign Canyon where a river breaks through miles of rock barrier in tempestuous rapids. The Indians say that the barrier is impassable and that no human being drawn into the rapids has a chance for life.

Stringer's frequent use of Canadian characters and settings, particularly the far North, contributed to a foreign understanding of Canada.*

Stringer died aged 76 at Mountain Lakes, New Jersey, on the 14th of September, 1950.

---

* *Canadian Bookman*, vol. 6, no.5, (May 1924), p.113.

RUNNING OUT OF PAY-DIRT
The man who couldn't sleep; being a relation of the divers strange adventures which befell one Witter Kerfoot when, sorely troubled with sleeplessness, he ventured forth at midnight along the highways and byways of Manhattan. Indianapolis: Bobbs-Merrill/Toronto: McLeod, 1919.

Set in New York City, the stories in this book feature Witter Kerfoot, a formerly successful, now insomniac Canadian writer of "blood and guts" yarns about Canada's North. His sleeplessness is caused by a writer's block when a friend points out that the inaccuracies in his novels cause great amusement to the people of the North. This is a neat piece of self-deprecating humour by Stringer, for not only did he write such novels, but he was often informing the reading public about the ludicrous errors made by such authors as Jack London and Richard Harding Davis in their novels about the North.

RUNNING OUT OF PAY-DIRT

To begin with, I am Canadian by birth, and thirty-three years old. For nine of those years I have lived in New York. And by my friends in that city I am regarded as a successful author.

There was a time when I even regarded myself in much the same light. But that period is past. I now have to face the fact that I am a failure. For when a man is no longer able to write he naturally can no longer be reckoned as an author.

I have made the name of Witter Kerfoot too well known, I think, to explain that practically all of my stories have been written about Alaska. Just why I resorted to that far-off country for my settings is still more or less a mystery to me. Perhaps it was merely because of its far-offness. Perhaps it was because the editors remembered that I came from the land of the beaver and sagely concluded that a Canadian would be most at home in writing about the Frozen North. At any rate, when I romanced about the Yukon and its ice-bound trails they bought my stories, and asked for more.

And I gave them more. I gave them blood-red fiction about gun-men and claim-jumpers and Siwash queens and salmon fisheries. I gave them supermen of iron, fighting against cold and hunger, and snarling, always snarling, at their foes. I gave them oratorical young engineers with clear-cut features and sinews of steel, battling against the forces of hyperborean evil. I gave them fist-fights that caused my books to be discreetly shut out of school libraries yet brought in telegrams from motion-picture directors for first rights. I gave them enough gun-play to shoot Chilcoot Pass into the middle of the Pacific, and was publicly denominated as the apostle of the Eye-Socket School, and during the three-hundred-night run of my melodrama, *The Pole Raiders,* even beheld on the Broadway sign-boards an extraordinarily stalwart picture of myself in a rakish Stetson and a flannel shirt very much open at the throat, with a cow-hide holster depending from my Herculean waist-line and a very dreadful-looking six-shooter protruding from the open top of that belted holster. My publishers spoke of me, for business reasons, as the Interpreter of the Great Northwest. And I exploited that territory with the industry of a badger. In my own way, I mined Alaska. And it brought me in a very respectable amount of pay-dirt.

But I knew nothing about Alaska. I had never even seen the country. I "crammed up" on it, of course, the same as we used to cram up for a third-form examination in Latin grammar. I perused the atlases and sent for governmental reports, and pored over the R.N.W.M.P. Blue Books, and gleaned a hundred or so French-Canadian names for half-breed villains from a telephone-directory for the city of Montreal. But I knew no more about Alaska than a Fiji Islander knows about the New York Stock Exchange. And that was why I could romance so freely, so magnificently, about it!

I was equally prodigal of blood, I suppose, because I had never seen the real thing flow – except in the case of my little niece, when her tonsils had been removed and a very soft-spoken nurse had helped me out of the surgery and given me a drink of ice-water, after telling me it would be best to keep my head as low as possible until I was feeling better. As for firearms, I abhorred them. I never shot off an air-rifle without first shutting my eyes. I never picked up a duck-gun without a wince of aversion. So I was able to do wonderful things with firearms, on paper. And with the Frozen Yukon and firearms combined, I was able to work miracles. I gave a whole continent goose-flesh, so many times a season. And the continent seemed to enjoy it, for those airy essays in iron and gore were always paid for, and paid for at higher and higher rates.

While this was taking place, something even more important was taking place, something which finally brought me in touch with Mary Lockwood herself. It was accident more than anything else, I think, that first launched me in what is so indefinitely and often so disparagingly known as society. Society, as a rule, admits only the lions of my calling across its sacred portals. And even these lions, I found, were accepted under protest or the wing of some commendable effort for charity, and having roared their little hour, were let pass quietly out to oblivion again. But I had been lucky enough to bring letters to the Peytons and to the Gruger-Philmores, and these old families, I will be honest enough to confess, had been foolish enough to like me.

So from the first I did my best to live up to those earlier affiliations. I found myself passed on, from one mysteriously barricaded seclusion to the other. The tea-hour visit merged into the formal dinner, and the formal dinner into the even more formal box at the Horse-Show, and then a call to fill up a niche at the Metropolitan on a Caruso-night, or a vacancy for an Assembly Dance at Sherry's, or a week at Tuxedo, in winter, when the skating was good.

I worked hard to keep up my end of the game. But I was an impostor, of course, all along the line. I soon saw that I had to prove more than acceptable; I had also to prove *dependable*. That I was a writer meant nothing whatever to those people. They had scant patience with the long-haired genius type. That went down only with musicians. So I soon learned to keep my bangs clipped, my trousers creased, and my necktie inside my coat-lapels. I also learned to use my wits, and how to key my talk up to dowager or down to débutante, and how to be passably amusing even before the champagne course had arrived. I made it a point to remember engagements and anniversaries, and more than once sent flowers and Millairds, which I went hungry to pay for. Even my *pourboires* to butlers and footmen and maids stood a matter, in those earlier days, for much secret and sedulous consideration.

But, as I have said, I tried to keep up my end. I *liked* those large and orderly houses. I liked the quiet-mannered people who lived in them. I liked looking at life with the hill-top unconcern for trivialities. I grew rather contemptuous of my humbler fellow-workers who haunted the neighborhood theaters and the red-inkeries of Greenwich Village, and orated Socialism and blank-verse poems to garret audiences, and wore window-curtain cravats and celluloid blinkers with big round lenses, and went in joyous and caramel-eating groups to the "rush" seats at *Rigoletto*. I was accepted, as I have already tried to explain, as an impecunious but dependable young bachelor. And I suppose I could have kept on at that rôle, year after year, until I developed into a foppish and somewhat threadbare old *beau*. But about this time I was giving North America its first spasms of goose-flesh with my demigod type of Gibsonian engineer who fought the villain until his flannel shirt was in rags and then shook his fist in Nature's face when she dogged him with the Eternal Cold. And there was money in writing for flat-dwellers about that Eternal Cold, and about battling claw to claw and fang to fang, and about eye-sockets without any eyes in them. My income gathered like a snow-ball. And as it gathered I began to feel that I ought to have an establishment – not a back-room studio in Washington Square, nor a garret in the Village of the Free-Versers, nor a mere apartment in the West Sixties, nor even a duplex overlooking Central Park South. I wanted to be something more than a number. I wanted a house, a house of my own, and a cat-footed butler to put a hickory-log on the fire, and a full set of *Sèvres* on my mahogany sideboard, and something to stretch a strip of red carpet across when the landaulets and the limousines rolled up to my door.

So I took a nine-year lease of the Whighams' house in Gramercy Square. It was oldfashioned and sedate and unpretentious to the passing eye, but beneath that somewhat somber shell nested an amazingly rich kernel of luxuriousness. It was good form; it was unbelievably comfortable, and it was not what the climber clutches for. The cost of even a nine-year claim on it rather took my breath away, but the thought of Alaska always served to stiffen up my courage.

It was necessary to think a good deal about Alaska in those days, for after I had acquired my house I also had to acquire a man to run it, and then a couple of other people to help the man who helped me, and then a town car to take me back and forth from it, and then a chauffeur to take care of the car, and then the service-clothes for the chauffeur, and the thousand and one unlooked for things, in short, which confront the pin-feather householder and keep him from feeling too much a lord of creation.

Yet in Benson, my butler, I undoubtedly found a gem of the first water. He moved about as silent as a panther, yet as watchful as an eagle. He could be ubiquitous and self-obliterating at one and the same time. He was meekness incarnate, and yet he could coerce me into a predetermined line of conduct as inexorably as steel rails lead a street-car along its predestined line of traffic. He was, in fact, much more than a butler. He was a valet and a *chef de cuisine* and a lord-high-chamberlain and a purchasing-agent and a body-guard

and a benignant-eyed old god-father all in one. The man *babied* me. I could
see that all along. But I was already an overworked and slightly neurasthenic
specimen, even in those days, and I was glad enough to have that masked and
silent
Efficiency always at my elbow. There were times, too, when his activities
merged into those of a trained nurse, for when I smoked too much he hid away
my cigars, and when I worked too hard he impersonally remembered what
morning horseback riding in the park had done for a former master of his. And
when I drifted into the use of chloral hydrate, to make me sleep, that dangerous little bottle had the habit of disappearing, mysteriously and inexplicably
disappearing, from its allotted place in my bathroom cabinet.

There was just one thing in which Benson disappointed me. That was in
his stubborn and unreasonable aversion to Latreille, my French chauffeur. For
Latreille was as efficient, in his way, as Benson himself. He understood his car,
he understood the traffic rules, and he understood what I wanted of him.
Latreille was, after a manner of speaking, a find of my own. Dining one night
at the Peytons', I had met the Commissioner of Police, who had given me a
card to stroll through Headquarters and inspect the machinery of the law. I had
happened on Latreille as he was being measured and "mugged" in the
Identification Bureau, with those odd-looking Bertillon forceps taking his cra-
nial measurements. The intelligence of the man interested me; the inalienable
look of respectability in his face convinced me, as a student of human nature,
that he was not meant for any such fate or any such environment. And when I
looked into his case I found that instinct had not been amiss. The unfortunate
fellow had been "framed" for a car-theft of which he was entirely innocent. He
explained all this to me, in fact, with tears in his eyes. And circumstances, when
I looked into them, bore out his statements. So I visited the Commissioner,
and was passed on to the Probation Officers, from whom I caromed off to the
Assistant District-Attorney, who in turn delegated me to another official, who
was cynical enough to suggest that the prisoner might possibly be released if I
was willing to go to the extent of bonding him. This I very promptly did, for I
was now determined to see poor Latreille once more a free man.

Latreille showed his appreciation of my efforts by saving me seven hundred
dollars when I bought my town car – though candor compels me to admit that
I later discovered it to be a used car rehabilitated, and not a product fresh from
the factory, as I had anticipated. But Latreille was proud of that car, and proud
of his position, and I was proud of having a French chauffeur, though my ardor
was dampened a little later on, when I discovered that Latreille, instead of hail-
ing from the *Bois de Boulogne* and the *Avenue de la Paix*, originated in the
slightly less splendid suburbs of Three Rivers, up on the St. Lawrence.

But my interest in Latreille about this time became quite subsidiary, for
something much more important than cars happened to me. I fell in love. I fell
in love with Mary Lockwood, head-over-heels in love with a girl who could

have thrown a town car into the Hudson every other week and never have missed it. She was beautiful; she was wonderful; but she was dishearteningly wealthy. With all those odious riches of hers, however, she was a terribly honest and above-board girl, a healthy-bodied, clear-eyed, practical-minded, normal-living New York girl who in her twenty-two active years of existence had seen enough of the world to know what was veneer and what was solid, and had seen enough of men to demand mental camaraderie and not "squaw-talk" from them.

I first saw her at the Volpi sale, in the American Art Galleries, where we chanced to bid against each other for an old Italian table-cover, a sixteenth century blue velvet embroidered with gold galloon. Mary bid me down, of course. I lost my table-cover, and with it I lost my heart. When I met her at the Obden-Belponts, a week later, she confessed that I'd rather been on her conscience. She generously offered to hand over that oblong of old velvet, if I still happened to be grieving over its loss. But I told her that all I asked for was a chance to see it occasionally. And occasionally I went to see it. I also saw its owner, who became more wonderful to me, week by week. Then I lost my head over her. That *apheresis* was so complete that I told Mary what had happened, and asked her to marry me.

Mary was very practical about it all. She said she liked me, liked me a lot. But there were other things to be considered. We would have to wait. I had my work to do – and she wanted it to be *big* work, gloriously big work. She wouldn't even consent to a formal engagement. But we had an "understanding." I was sent back to my work, drunk with the memory of her surrendering lips warm on mine, of her wistfully entreating eyes searching my face for something which she seemed unable to find there.

That work of mine which I went back to, however, seemed something very flat and meager and trivial. And this, I realized, was a condition which would never do. The pot had to be kept boiling, and boiling now more briskly than ever. I had lapsed into more or less luxurious ways of living; I had formed expensive tastes, and had developed a fondness for antiques and Chinese bronzes and those *objets d'art* which are never found on the bargain-counter. I had outgrown the Spartan ways of my youth when I could lunch contentedly at Child's and sleep soundly on a studio-couch in a top-floor room. And more and more that rapacious ogre known as Social Obligation had forged his links and fetters about my movements. More than ever, I saw, I had my end to keep up. What should have been a recreation had become almost a treadmill. I was a pretender, and had my pretense to sustain. I couldn't afford to be "dropped." I had my frontiers to protect and my powers to placate. I couldn't ask Mary to throw herself away on a nobody. So instead of trying to keep up one end, I tried to keep up two. I continued to bob about the fringes of the Four Hundred. And I continued to cling hungrily to Mary's hint about doing work, gloriously big work.

But gloriously big work, I discovered, was usually done by lonely men, living simply and quietly, and dwelling aloof from the frivolous side-issues of life, divorced from the distractions of a city which seemed organized for only the idler and the lotus-eater. And I could see that the pay-dirt coming out of Alaska was running thinner and thinner.

It was to remedy this, I suppose, that I dined with my old friend Pip Conners, just back to civilization after fourteen long years up in the Yukon. That dinner of ours together was memorable. It was one of the mile-stones of my life. I wanted to furbish up my information on the remote corner of the world, which, in a way, I had preempted as my own. I wanted fresh information, first-hand data, renewed inspiration. And I was glad to feel Pip's horny hand close fraternally about mine.

"Witter," he said, staring at me with open admiration, "you're a wonder."

I liked Pip's praise, even though I stood a little at a loss to discern its inspiration.

"You mean – this?" I asked, with a casual hand-wave about that Gramercy Square abode of mine.

"No, sir," was Pip's prompt retort. "I mean those stories of yours. I've read 'em all."

I blushed at this, blushed openly. For such commendation from a man who knew life as it was, who knew life in the raw, was as honey to my ears.

"Do you mean to say you could get them, up *there?*" I asked, more for something to dissemble my embarrassment than to acquire actual information.

"Yes," acknowledged Pip with a rather foolish-sounding laugh, "they come through the mails about the same as they'd come through the mails down here. And folks even read them, now and then, when the gun-smoke blows out of the valley!"

"Then what struck you as wonderful about them?" I inquired, a little at sea as to his line of thought.

"It's not *them* that's wonderful, Witter. It's *you*. I said you were a wonder. And you are."

"And why am I a wonder?" I asked, with the drip of the honey no longer embarrassing my modesty.

"Witter, *you're a wonder to get away with it!*" was Pip's solemnly intoned reply.

"To get away with it?" I repeated.

"Yes; to make it go down! To get 'em trussed and gagged and hog-tied! To make 'em come and eat out of your hand and then holler for more! For I've been up there in the British Yukon for fourteen nice comfortable years, Witter, and I've kind o' got to know the country. I know how folks live up there, and what the laws are. And it may strike you as queer, friend-author, but folks up in that district are uncommonly like folks down here in the States. And in the Klondike and this same British Yukon there is a Firearms Act which makes it against the law for any civilian to tote a gun. And that law is sure carried out. Fact is, there's no *need* for a gun. And even if you did smuggle one in, the Mounted Police would darned soon take it away from you!"

I sat staring at him.

"But all those motion-pictures," I gasped. "And all those novels about –"

"That's why I say you're a wonder," broke in the genial-eyed Pip. "You can fool *all* the people *all* the time! You've done it. And you keep on doing it. You can put 'em to sleep and take it out of their pants pocket before they know they've gone by-by. Why, you've even got 'em tranced off in the matter of every-day school-geography. You've had some of those hero-guys o' yours mush seven or eight hundred miles, and on a birch-bark toboggan, between dinner and supper. And if that ain't genius, I ain't ever seen it bound up in a reading-book!"

That dinner was a mile-stone in my life, all right, but not after the manner I had expected. For as I sat there in a cold sweat of apprehension crowned with shame, Pip Conners told me many things about Alaska and the Klondike. He told me many things that were new to me, dishearteningly, discouragingly, devitalizingly new to me. Without knowing it, he poignarded me, knifed me through and through. Without dreaming what he was doing, he eviscerated me. He left me a hollow and empty mask of an author. He left me a homeless exile, with the iron gates of Fact swung sternly shut on what had been a Fairy Land of Romance, a Promised Land of untrammelled and care-free imaginings.

That was my first sleepless night.

I said nothing to Pip. I said nothing to any one. I held that vulture of shame close in my arms and felt its unclean beak awling into my vitals. I tried to go back to my work, next day, to lose myself in creation. But it was like seeking consolation beside a corpse. For me, Alaska was killed, killed forever. And blight had fallen on more than my work. It had crept over my very world, the world which only the labor of my pen could keep orderly and organized. The city in which I had seemed to sit a conqueror suddenly lay about me a flat and monotonous tableland of ennui, as empty and stale as a circus-lot after the last canvas-wagon has rumbled away.

I have no intention of making this recountal the confessions of a neurasthenic. Nothing is further from my aims than the inditing of a second City of Dreadful Night. But I began to worry. And later on I began to magnify my troubles. I even stuck to New York that summer, for the simple reason that I couldn't afford to go away. And it was an unspeakably hot summer. I did my best to work, sitting for hours at a time staring at a blank sheet of paper, set out like tangle-foot to catch a passing idea. But not an idea alighted on that square of spotless white. When I tried new fields, knowing Alaska was dead, the editors solemnly shook their heads and announced that this new offering of mine didn't seem to have the snap and go of my older manner. Then panic overtook me, and after yet another white night I went straight to Sanson, the nerve specialist, and told him I was going crazy.

He laughed at me. Then he offhandedly tapped me over and tried my reflexes and took my blood pressure and even more diffidently asked me a question or two. He ended up by announcing that I was as sound as a dollar, whatever that may have meant, and suggested as an afterthought that I drop tobacco and go in more for golf.

That buoyed me up for a week or two. But Mary, when she came in to town radiant and cool for three days' shopping, seemed to detect in me a change which first surprised and then troubled her. I was bitterly conscious of being a disappointment to somebody who expected great things of me. And to escape that double-edged sword of mortification, I once again tried to bury myself in my work. But I just as well might have tried to bury myself in a butter-dish, for there was no effort and no activity there to envelope me. I was coerced into idleness, without ever having acquired the art of doing nothing. For life with me had been a good deal like boiling rice: it had to be kept galloping to save it from going mushy. Yet now the fire itself seemed out. And that prompted me to sit and listen to my works, as the French idiom expresses it, which is never a profitable calling for a naturally nervous man.

The lee and the long of it was, as the Irish say, that I went back to Doctor Sanson and demanded something, in the name of God, that would give me a good night's sleep. He was less jocular, this time. He told me to forget my troubles and go fishing for a couple of weeks.

I *did* go fishing, but I fished for ideas. And I got scarcely a strike. To leave the city was now more than ever out of the question. So for recreation I had Latreille take me out in the car, when a feverish thirst for speed, which I found it hard to account for, drove me into daily violations of the traffic laws. Twice, in fact, I was fined for this, with a curtly warning talk from the presiding magistrate on the second occasion, since the offense, in this case, was complicated by collision with an empty baby-carriage. Latreille, about this time, seemed uncannily conscious of my condition. More and more he seemed to rasp me on the raw, until irritation deepened into positive dislike for the man.

When Mary came back to the city for a few days, before going to the Virginia hills for the autumn, I looked so wretched and felt so wretched that I decided not to see her. I was taking veronal now, to make me sleep, and with cooler weather I looked for better rest and a return to work. But my hopes were ill-founded. I came to dread the night, and the night's ever-recurring battle for sleep. I lost my perspective on things. And then came the crowning catastrophe, the catastrophe which turned me into a sort of twentieth-century Macbeth.

The details of that catastrophe were ludicrous enough, and it had no definite and clear-cut outcome, but its effect on my over-tensioned nerves was sufficiently calamitous. It occurred, oddly enough, on Hallowe'en night, when the world is supposed to be given over to festivity. Latreille had motored me out to a small dinner-dance at Washburn's, on Long Island, but I had left early in the evening, perversely depressed by a hilarity in which I had not the heart to join. Twice, on the way back to the city, I had called out to Latreille for more speed. We had just taken a turn in the outskirts of Brooklyn when my swinging head-lights disclosed the figure of a man, an unstable and wavering man, obviously drunk, totter and fall directly in front of my car.

I heard the squeal of the brakes and the high-pitched shouts from a crowd of youths along the sidewalk. But it was too late. I could feel the impact as we struck. I could feel the sickening thud and jolt as the wheels pounded over that fallen body.

I stood up, without quite knowing what I was doing, and screamed like a woman. Then I dropped weakly back in my seat. I think I was sobbing. I scarcely noticed that Latreille had failed to stop the car. He spoke to me twice, in fact, before I knew it.

"Shall we go on, sir?" he asked, glancing back at me over his shoulder.

"*Go on!*" I shouted, knowing well enough by this time what I said, surrendering merely to that blind and cowardly panic for self-preservation which marks man at his lowest.

We thumped and swerved and speeded away on the wings of cowardice. I sat there gasping and clutching my moist fingers together, as I've seen hysterical women do, calling on Latreille for speed, and still more speed.

I don't know where he took me. But I became conscious of the consoling blackness of the night about us. And I thanked God, as Cain must have done when he found himself alone with his shame.

"Latreille," I said, breathing brokenly as we slowed up, "did we – *did we kill him?*"

My chauffeur turned in his seat and studied my face. Then he looked carefully back, to make sure we were not being followed.

"This is a heavy car, sir," he finally admitted. He said it coolly, and almost impersonally. But the words fell like a sledge-hammer on my heart.

"But we couldn't have killed a man," I clamored insanely, weakly, as we came to a dead stop at the roadside.

"Forty-two hundred pounds – and he got both wheels!" calmly protested my enemy, for I felt now that he was in some way my enemy.

"What in heaven's name are you going to do?" I gasped, for I noticed that he was getting down from his seat.

"Hadn't I better get the blood off the running-gear, before we turn back into town?"

"Blood?" I quavered as I clutched at the robe-rail in front of me. And that one word brought the horror of the thing home to me in all its ghastliness. I could see axles and running-board and brake-bar dripping with red, festooned with shreds of flesh, maculated with blackening gore. And I covered my face with my hands, and groaned aloud in my misery of soul.

But Latreille did not wait for me. He lifted the seat-cushion, took rubbing-cloths from the tool-box and crawled out of sight beneath the car. I could feel the occasional tremors that went through the frame-work as he busied himself at that grisly task. I could hear his grunt of satisfaction when he had finished. And I watched him with stricken eyes as he stepped through the vague darkness and tossed his telltale cloths far over the roadside fence.

"It's all right," he companionably announced as he stepped back into the car. But there was a new note in the man's demeanor, a note which even through that black fog of terror reached me and awakened my resentment. We were partners in crime. We were fellow-actors in a drama of indescribable cowardice, and I was in the man's power, to the end of time.

The outcome of that catastrophe, as I have already said, was indefinite, torturingly indefinite. I was too shaken and sick to ferret out its consequences. I left that to Latreille, who seemed to understand well enough what I expected of him.

That first night wore by, and nothing came of it all. The morning dragged away, and my fellow-criminal seemingly encountered nothing worthy of rehearsal to me. Then still another night came and went. I went through the published hospital reports, and the police records, with my heart in my mouth. But I could unearth no official account of the tragedy. I even encountered my good friend Patrolman McCooey, apparently by accident, and held him up on his beat about Gramercy Park to make casual inquiries as to street-accidents, and if such things were increasing of late. But nothing of moment, apparently, had come to McCooey's ears. And I stood watching him as he flatfooted his way placidly on from my house-front, with one of my best cigars tucked under his tunic, wondering what the world would say if it knew that Witter Kerfoot, the intrepid creator of sinewy supermen who snarl and fight and shake iron fists in the teeth of Extremity, had run like a rabbit from a human being he had bowled over and killed?

I still hoped against hope, however, trying to tell myself that it is no easy thing to knock the life out of a man, passionately upbraiding myself for not doing what I should have done to succor the injured, then sinkingly remembering what Latreille had mentioned about the weight of my car. Yet it wasn't until the next night, as I ventured out to step into that odiously ponderous engine of destruction, that uncertainty solidified into fact.

"*You got him,*" announced my chauffeur out of one side of his mouth, so that Benson, who stood on the house-steps, might not overhear those fateful words.

"Got him?" I echoed, vaguely resenting the man's use of that personal pronoun singular.

"Killed!" was Latreille's monosyllabic explanation. And my heart stopped beating.

"How do you know that?" I demanded in whispering horror. For I understood enough of the law of the land to know that a speeder who flees from the victim of his carelessness is technically guilty of manslaughter.

"A man I know, named Crotty, helped carry the body back to his house. Crotty's just told me about it."

My face must have frightened Latreille, for he covered his movement of catching hold of my arm by ceremoniously opening the car door for me.

"Sit tight, man!" he ordered in his curt and conspiratorial undertone. "Sit tight – for it's all that's left to do!"

I sat tight. It was all there was to do. I endured Latreille's accession of self-importance without comment. There promptly grew up between us a tacit understanding of silence. Yet I had reason to feel that this silence wasn't always as profound as it seemed. For at the end of my third day of self-torturing solitude I went to my club to dine. I went with set teeth. I went in the hope of ridding my system of self-fear, very much as an alcoholic goes to a Turkish-bath. I went to mix once more with my fellows, to prove that I stood on common ground with them.

But the mixing was not a success. I stepped across that familiar portal in quavering dread of hostility. And I found what I was looking for. I detected myself being eyed coldly by men who had once posed as my friends. I dined alone, oppressed by the discovery that I was being deliberately avoided by the fellow-members of what should have been an organized companionability. Then I took a grip on myself, and forlornly argued that it was all mere imagination, the vaporings of a morbid and chlorotic mind. Yet the next moment a counter-shock confronted me. For as I stared desolately out of that club window I caught sight of Latreille himself. He stood there at the curb, talking confidently to three other chauffeurs clustered about him between their cars. Nothing, I suddenly remembered, could keep the man from gossiping. And a word dropped in one servant's ear would soon pass on to another. And that other would carry the whisper still wider, until it spread like an infection from below-stairs to above-stairs, and from private homes to the very housetops. And already I was a marked man, a pariah, an outcast with no friendly wilderness to swallow me up.

I slunk home that night with a plumb-bob of lead swinging under my ribs where my heart should have been. I tried to sleep and could not sleep. So I took a double dose of chloral hydrate, and was rewarded with a few hours of nightmare wherein I was a twentieth-century Attila driving a racing-car over an endless avenue of denuded infants. It was all so horrible that it left me limp and quailing before the lash of daylight. Then, out of a blank desolation that became more and more unendurable, I clutched feverishly at the thought of Mary Lockwood and the autumn-tinted hills of Virginia. I felt the need of getting away from that city of lost sleep. I felt the need of "exteriorating" what was corroding my inmost soul. I was seized with a sudden and febrile ache for companionship. So I sent a forty-word wire to the only woman in the world I could look to in my extremity. And the next morning brought me a reply.

It merely said, "Don't come."

The bottom seemed to fall out of the world, with that curt message, and I groped forlornly, frantically, for something stable to sustain me. But there was nothing. Bad news, I bitterly reminded myself, had the habit of traveling fast. *Mary knew.* The endless chain had widened, like a wireless-wave. It had rolled on, like war-gas, until it had blighted even the slopes beyond the Potomac. For Mary *knew!*

It was two days later that a note, in her picket-fence script that was as sharp-pointed as arrow-heads, followed after the telegram.

"There are certain things," wrote Mary, "which I can scarcely talk about on paper. At least, not as I should prefer talking about them. But these things must necessarily make a change in your life, and in mine. I don't want to seem harsh, Witter, but we can't go on as we have been doing. We'll both have to get used to the idea of trudging along in single harness. And I think you will understand why. I'm not exacting explanations, remember. I'm merely requesting an armistice. If you intend to let me, I still want to be your friend, and I trust no perceptible gulf will yarn between us, when we chance to dine at the same table or step through the same *cotillion*. But I must bow to those newer circumstances which seem to have confronted you even before they presented themselves to me. So when I say good-by, it is more to the Past, I think, than to You."

That was the first night, I remember, when sleeping-powder proved of no earthly use to me. And this would not be an honest record of events if I neglected to state that the next day I shut myself up in my study and drank much more *Pommery-Greno* than was good for me. I got drunk, in fact, blindly, stupidly, senselessly drunk. But it seemed to drape a veil between me and the past. It made a bonfire of my body to burn up the debris of my mind. And when poor old patient-eyed Benson mixed me a bromide and put me to bed I felt like a patient coming out of ether after a major operation. I was tired, and I wanted to lie there and rest for a long time.

BIBLIOGRAPHY - ARTHUR STRINGER

Criminous works

The city of peril. New York: Knopf, 1923. Set: New York City.

The diamond thieves. Indianapolis, Ind.: Bobbs-Merrill, 1923/ London: Hodder & Stoughton, 1925.

The door of dread; a secret service romance. Indianapolis: Bobbs-Merrill, 1916/London: Amalgamated, 1925. Set: New York City.

Empty hands. Indianapolis: Bobbs-Merrill/London: Hodder & Stoughton/Toronto: McClelland & Stewart, 1924.

The ghost plane. Indianapolis: Bobbs-Merrill, 1940. Set: Canada.

The gun-runner; a novel. New York: Dodge, 1909.

The hand of peril. New York: Macmillan, 1915.

The house of intrigue. Indianapolis: Bobbs-Merrill, 1918. Set: New York City.

In bad with Sinbad. Indianapolis: Bobbs-Merrill, 1926.

The man who couldn't sleep; being a relation of the divers strange adventures which befell one Witter Kerfoot when, sorely troubled with sleeplessness, he ventured forth at midnight along the highways and byways of Manhattan. Indianapolis: Bobbs-Merrill/Toronto: McLeod, 1919.

Manhandled. With Russell Holman. New York: Grosset & Dunlap, 1924. Novelization of Paramount 1924 film.

Marriage by capture. Indianapolis: Bobbs-Merrill, 1933/ London: Methuen, 1934.

Night hawk; a novel. New York: McClure, 1908. Set: New York City.

Phantom wires. Boston: Little, Brown, 1907/London: Daily Mail, 1909.

The shadow. New York: Century, 1913. Also publ. as: *Never-fail Blake.* – New York: Burt, 1924.

Shadowed victory. New York: Bobbs-Merrill, 1943/London: Hodder & Stoughton, 1944.

Star in a mist; a novel. Indianapolis: Bobbs-Merrill, 1943.

The story without a name. With Russell Holman. New York: Grosset & Dunlap, 1924. Novelization of Paramount 1924 film.

Twin tales; Are all men alike? [and] The lost Titian. Indianapolis: Bobbs-Merrill, 1921/Toronto: McClelland & Stewart, 1922. Two novelettes: the first features Theodora Hayden and is set in New York City; the second is set in Western Ontario and features an art dealer named Conkling.

The under groove; a novel. New York: McClure, 1908.

The wire tappers. Boston: Little, Brown, 1906. Set: New York City. Espionage novel.

The wolf woman; a novel. Indianapolis: Bobbs-Merrill, 1928/London: Paul, 1929.

Other works

Alexander was great. New York: French, 1934. play.

The cleverest woman in the world; and other one-act plays. New York: Bobbs-Merrill, 1939. plays.

Confessions of an author's wife. New York: Bobbs-Merrill, 1927.

Cristina and I. Indianapolis: Bobbs-Merrill, 1929.

Dark soil. Indianapolis: Bobbs-Merrill, 1933. poetry.

The dark wing. New York: Bobbs-Merrill, 1939.

The devastator. Toronto: McClelland & Stewart, 1944.

Epigrams. London, Ontario: T. H. Warren, 1896. poetry.

Heather of the high hand; a novel of the North. New York: Bobbs-Merrill, 1937.

Hephaestus/Persephone at Enna/[and]Sappho in Leucadia. Toronto: Methodist Book Co., 1903. poetry. *Sappho in Leucadia* publ. as a separate – Boston: Little, Brown, 1907.

Intruders in Eden; a novel. Indianapolis: Bobbs-Merrill, 1942.

Irish poems. New York: Kennerley, 1911. Repr. as: *Out of Erin; songs in exile* – Indianapolis: Bobbs-Merrill, 1930.

The king who loved old clothes; and other Irish poems. New York: Bobbs-Merrill, 1941.

A lady quite lost; a novel. Indianapolis: Bobbs-Merrill, 1931.

The lamp in the valley; a novel of Alaska. New York: Bobbs-Merrill, 1938.

Lonely O'Malley; a story of boy life. Boston: Houghton Mifflin, 1905. an autobiographical novel of the author's early years.

The loom of destiny. Boston: Small Maynard, 1899. juvenile.

Man lost. Indianapolis: Bobbs-Merrill, 1934.

The mud lark. Indianapolis: Bobbs-Merrill, 1932. poetry.

New York nocturnes. Toronto: Ryerson, 1948.

The old woman remembers; and other Irish poems. Indianapolis: Bobbs-Merrill, 1938.

Open waters; (free verse). Toronto: Bell & Cockburn, 1912/New York: Lane, 1914.

Out of Erin; songs in exile. SEE *Irish poems* (supra).

Pauline; and other poems. London, Ontario: Warren, 1895.

Power. Indianapolis: Bobbs-Merrill, 1925.

The Prairie child. Indianapolis: Bobbs-Merrill, 1921.

The Prairie mother. Toronto: McClelland & Stewart, 1920.

Prairie stories. New York: Burt, 1936. Omnibus volume containing *The Prairie wife; The Prairie mother,* and *The Prairie child.*

The Prairie wife; a novel. Indianapolis: Bobbs-Merrill, 1915.

Red wine of youth; a life of Rupert Brooke. New York:[?], 1948. biography.

Shadowed victory. Indianapolis: Bobbs-Merrill, 1943. poetry.

The silver poppy; a novel. New York: Appleton, 1903/London: Methuen, 1904.

A study in 'King Lear.' New York: American Shakespeare Press, 1897. literary criticism.

Tooloona; a novel of the North. London: Methuen, 1936.

Watchers of the twilight; and other poems. London, Ontario: T. H. Warren, 1894.

White hands. Indianapolis: Bobbs-Merrill, 1927.

The wife traders; a tale of the North. Indianapolis: Bobbs-Merrill, 1936.

The wine of life. New York: Knopf, 1921.

A woman at dusk; and other poems. Indianapolis: Bobbs-Merrill, 1928.

The woman in the rain; and other poems. Toronto: McClelland & Stewart, 1949.

The woman who couldn't die. Indianapolis: Bobbs-Merrill, 1929.

Books about

Lauriston, Victor. *Arthur Stringer; son of the North: biography and anthology.* Toronto: Ryerson, 1941. (Makers of Canadian Literature series.) Victor Lauriston was also a Canadian crime writer.

—. *Postscript to a poet; off the record tales about Arthur Stringer, including some the censor should have suppressed.* Chatham, Ontario: Tiny Tree Club, 1941.

HARVEY O'HIGGINS

The Blackmailers
The adventures of detective Barney.
New York: Century, 1915.

The Marshall Murder
Detective Duff unravels it.
New York: Liveright, 1929.

O'HIGGINS, Harvey J(errold), 1876-1929

Harvey O'Higgins made two notable contributions to the detective story: *The adventures of detective Barney*, and *Detective Duff unravels it.*

A Canadian journalist, Harvey O'Higgins was born in London, Ontario, on 14 November 1876, the son of Joseph P. O'Higgins and Isabella (Stephenson) O'Higgins. At the London Collegiate Institute he became friends with Arthur Stringer, two years his junior. From 1893 to 1897, he attended the University of Toronto, but left without obtaining his degree to work as a reporter on the Toronto *Star.*

In 1898, he joined his high-school chum, Arthur Stringer, in trying their luck in the United States; O'Higgins became a reporter for the New York[City] *Globe.* He gave up newspaper work in 1901 to become a free-lance writer.

In the period before World War One, he collaborated with actress Harriet Ford on a series of melodramas and on the dramatization of Sinclair Lewis's *Main Street*, which was produced at the National Theater in New York City in 1921.

After a serious illness, O'Higgins became strongly influenced by the work of Sigmund Freud. He adapted Freud's work to a study of the American character: *From the life; imaginary portraits of some distinguished Americans*, published in 1919. His penultimate contribution to American letters was an iconoclastic attack on Walt Whitman, "Alias Walt Whitman," in *Harper's*, May 1929, exposing the poet as a homosexual and narcissist.

O'Higgins died of pneumonia at his home, "Doubleduck Farm," at Martinstown, New Jersey, on 28 February, 1929, leaving the posthumously published *Detective Duff unravels it.*

THE BLACKMAILERS
The adventures of detective Barney. New York: Century, 1915.

The adventures are seven stories set in New York City, and based on the real-life activities of the Burns Detective Agency. Barney Cook, the quintessential American boy, has been called the most believable and least offensive young detective in American literature. Barney also appears in *The Dummy,* a four-act play co-authored by O'Higgins and Harriet Ford in 1914. Through Barney's eyes, simple, realistic, private-eye work is depicted.

THE BLACKMAILERS

I

T he want ad – after the manner of want ads – had read simply: "Boy, over 14, intelligent, trustworthy, for confidential office work, references. Address B-67 *Evening Express.*"

Several scores of boys, who were neither very intelligent nor peculiarly trustworthy, exposed their disqualifications – after the manner of boys – in the written applications that they made. Of these scores, a dozen boys received typewritten requests to call next morning at room 1056, in the Cranmer Building, on Broadway, for a personal interview with "H.M. Archibald." But of the dozen, only one knew what sort of confidential office work might be waiting for him in room 1056.

He was little Barney Cook. And he kept his information to himself.

The directory, on the wall of the building's entrance, did not assign 1056 to any of the names on its list. The elevator boys did not know who occupied 1056. The door of 1056 had nothing on its glass panel but the painted number; and the neighboring doors were equally discreet. The "Babbing Bureau" was the nearest name in the corridor, but its doors were marked "Private. Entrance at 1070."

Nor was there anything in the interior aspect of 1056 to enlighten any of Barney Cook's competitors when they came there to be interviewed. It was an ordinary outer office of the golden-oak variety, with a railing of spindles separating a telephone switchboard and two typewriter desks from two public settles and a brass cuspidor. There were girls at the desks and the switchboard. The boys were on the settles or at the railing. The girls were busy, indifferent, chatty (among themselves) and very much at home. The boys, of course, were quite otherwise. They might have been suspected of having assumed a common expression of inert and anxious stupidity in order that each might conceal from all the others the required intelligence with which he hoped to win the "job."

Barney Cook alone betrayed the workings of a mind. He sat erect – stretching his neck – at the end of a settle nearest the gate of the railing, watching the door of an inner room and scrutinizing every one who came out of it. He paid no heed to the girls; he knew that they were merely clerks. But when he saw a rough-looking man appear, with a red handkerchief around his neck, he stared excitedly. Surely the bandanna was a disguise! Perhaps the black mustache was false!

Forty-eight hours earlier, in the uniform of a telegraph boy, Barney had been in the public office of the Babbing Detective Bureau; and he had been asked to deliver an envelope to the advertising department of the *Evening Express* as he went back. The envelope was not sealed. It did stick slightly in places – but it was not sealed. And it contained the want ad. "Confidential office work"! For the famous Walter Babbing!

Young Barney had been delivering telegrams to the Babbing Bureau for months, without ever getting past the outer office at 1070, and without so much as suspecting the existence of these operatives' rooms and inner chambers down the hall. He had seen Babbing only once, when "the great detective" came out with one of his men while Barney was getting his book signed. Babbing stood in the doorway long enough to say: "I'll meet you at the station. Get the tickets. I'll send Jim down with my suit-case." The operative replied: "All right, Chief." And Barney knew that this was Walter Babbing.

He was a brisk-looking, clean-shaven, little fat man – rather "a dude" to Barney – with a quietly mild expression and vague eyes.

Barney knew nothing of the scientific theory of "protective coloring" in detectives; he did not know that the most successful among them naturally look least like anything that might be expected of their kind. He went out, with his book open in his hand, absorbed in study of the picture of Babbing that had been photographed on his instantaneous young mind.

Subsequently, he decided that he had seen Walter Babbing without any make-up, in the private appearance that he reserved for office use among his men. And he was assisted to this conclusion by his knowledge of the adventures of Nick Carter which he read on the street cars, in the subways, on the benches in the waiting room of the telegraph office, or wherever else he had leisure. And it was the influence of these Nick Carter stories that had brought him now to 1056 in his Sunday best, with his hair brushed and his shoes polished, as guiltily excited as a truant, having lied to his mother and absented himself from his work in the wild hope of getting employment – confidential and mysterious employment – in the office of the great Babbing.

He was a rather plump and sturdy youth of sixteen, with an innocent brightness of face, brown-eyed, black-haired, not easily abashed and always ready with a smile. It was a dimpled smile, too; and he understood its value. In spite of his boyish ignorance of many things outside his immediate experience – such as famous detectives, for example – he knew his world and his way about in it; he met the events of the day with a practical understanding; and when he did not understand them he disarmed them with a grin. He was confident that he could get this job in the Babbing Bureau, in competition with any of the "boobs" who were waiting to dispute it with him, unless some one among them had a "pull." Being an experienced New Yorker, it was the fear of the pull that worried him.

He waited alertly on the edge of his settle, watching for an indication that the interviews with "H.M. Archibald" were to begin, and ready to rise and thrust himself forward as the first applicant. For a moment he did not recognize Babbing when the detective entered, from an inner office, in a spring overcoat and a light felt hat.

He had a small black satchel in his hand. He spoke to the telephone girl. Barney heard her ask: "The Antwerp?" Babbing added: "Until three o'clock."

He came towards the gate of the railing, and Barney rose to open it for him. Babbing did not appear to notice him, so Barney preceded him to the door and opened that also. Still Babbing did not heed. "I'll take your satchel, Mr. Babbing," Barney said, authoritatively. And Babbing gave it to him in the manner of an absent mind.

The whole proceeding had been a sudden inspiration on Barney's part, born of a desire to distinguish himself, in Babbing's eyes, from the other prospective office boys on the settles. Now, with Babbing's satchel in his hand, he followed the detective into a well-filled elevator, confident of Babbing's notice; but as they dropped in the cage together, he observed that the detective was looking over his head, occupied with his own thoughts.

Barney got out before him, preceded him to the entrance of the building, and stood at a revolving door for Babbing to go first. Babbing passed him without a glance. A taxi-cab was waiting at the curb, and he crossed the sidewalk to it, with Barney at his heels. While he was speaking in a low tone to the driver, Barney opened the cab door and held it open for him to get in; and he got in, without remark. Barney put the satchel at his feet; but the feet, too, were blind; they did not move. Barney shut the door, reluctantly; and the indifferent auto slowly started up Broadway, intent upon the internal uproar of its own convulsions.

Barney did not understand that if you are a detective, confronted by an incident which you do not understand, you pretend that you do not see it, so that you may observe it without putting it on its guard. He stood looking after his wasted opportunity, for a regretful moment. Then he turned and ran towards City Hall Park, to get an express train in the subway station at the Bridge.

He knew that the Antwerp – if it was the Hotel Antwerp that was meant – was around the corner from the subway station at 42nd Street.

Barney wanted that "job." Babbing had it, so to speak, in his pocket. And with the shrewd simplicity of youth Barney proposed to follow and put himself in the way until he was asked, impatiently: "Well, boy, what do you want?" Then he would say what he wanted – and probably get it.

Although the subway is not so expensive as a taxi-cab, it is speedier, in the long run; and Barney was standing near the door of the Antwerp – somewhat blown but cheerfully composed – when Babbing's car whirred around the corner and drew up to the sidewalk. Barney opened the cab door and took the satchel briskly, with a smile of recognition which the detective ignored. When the driver had been paid, Babbing turned into the hotel, apparently oblivious of his escort; and Barney followed undiscouraged, with the bag.

"Get away, kid," he said to the bell-boy who offered to carry it. "Er I'll bite your ankle."

Standing back at a respectful distance, he watched the detective get a letter and his room-key at the desk. When he went to the elevator, there was nothing for Barney to do but to go after him. In the elevator, Babbing said "Eighth," and busied himself with his letter, which he read and pondered on. He put it in his pocket and looked Barney over, for the first time, with an abstracted eye. Barney smiled at him, ingratiatingly. The smile met with no response.

And still Barney was not discouraged. He was not apprehensive. He was not even nervous. There was nothing forbidding in the mild reserve of the detective's face. He looked like a man of a kindly personality. He seemed easy-going and meditative. And Barney, of course, was not the first to get that impression of him. It was one of the things that explained Babbing's success.

He led the way down the padded carpet of the corridor to his room, and unlocked the door, and threw it open for Barney to enter one of the usual hotel bedrooms of the Antwerp's class, with the usual curly-maple furniture and elaborate curtains and thick carpeting. Barney put the satchel on the table, and waited in the center of stereotyped luxury. "When did Mr. Archibald take you on?" Babbing asked, aside, as he hung up his hat and overcoat.

"He hasn't taken me on – yet," Barney admitted.

Babbing put on a pair of unexpected spectacles and got out a ring of keys to unlock his bag. Occupied with that, he asked: "How did you know that I was coming here?"

Barney explained that he had overheard the instructions to the telephone girl.

The detective had begun to take, from his satchel, letters, telegrams, typewritten reports, and packages of papers strapped in rubber bands, which he proceeded to sort into little piles on the table, as they came. He appeared to be giving this business his whole attention, but while his hands moved deliberately and his eyes read the notations on the papers, he pursued Barney through an examination that ran: "How did you know who I was?"

"I delivered telegrams to your office an' –"

"For what company?"

"The Western Union."

"Why did you leave them?"

"I wanted to work fer you."

"How did you know we wanted a boy?"

"I saw the ad."

"How did you know it was ours?"

"I – I delivered it to the newspaper."

"Are you in the habit of opening letters that are given you to deliver?"

"No, sir."

"Don't smile so much. You overdo it," Babbing said, without looking up. And his merely professional tone of matter-of-fact advice sobered Barney as suddenly as if he had said: "I understand, of course, that you have found your smile very effective, but it doesn't deceive *me*. You're not so bland a child as you pretend, and I shall not treat you as if you were."

Barney shifted uncomfortably on his feet. The absent-minded ease with which Babbing had plied him with questions and caught up his answers made him fearful for the approach of the moment when the detective should give him a concentrated attention and begin forcibly to ransack him and turn him inside out.

Babbing asked unexpectedly: "How tall are you?"

"About five feet," Barney answered at a guess.

"How much do you weigh?"

"About a hundred – an' twenty-five."

Babbing glanced at him appraisingly, went on with his papers again, and said: "When you don't know a thing, say so. It saves time. What's your name?"

"Barney. Barney Cook."

"Where do you live?"

Barney gave the number of his home in Hudson Street.

"The Greenwich village quarter?"

"Yes, sir."

"Irish-Catholic?"

"Yes, sir."

"What does your father do?"

"He's dead. He was a policeman. He was killed."

"What was his name?"

"Robert E. Cook."

"Robert Emmet?"

"Yes, sir."

"When was he killed? How long ago?"

"About eight years."

Babbing was still at his papers. "Is your mother living?"

"Yes, sir."

"What does *she* do?"

"Looks after me an' my sister."

"What does she do for a living?"

"She rents furnished rooms. Her an' Annie. That's my sister."

"What does she do with your father's pension?"

"She puts it all in the bank."

"What bank?"

"I – I dunno."

"She doesn't own the house?"

"No, sir."

"Who owns it?"

"I – I forget."

"You went to the parochial school?"

"Yes, sir."

Babbing had found a typewritten report for which he had evidently been looking. As he crossed the room to the telephone, he asked: "Do you smoke cigarettes?"

"No, sir."

"Babbing took down the receiver from its hook. "When did you quit?"

Barney hesitated guiltily a moment. Then he answered: "This morning."

"Give me room eight-twenty," Babbing said, into the 'phone. He added, to Barney: "You can't work for me, if you're going to smoke. It will spoil your nerve." And while Barney, dumb with incredulous hope, was still staring at the implication of that warning, Babbing said: "Hello. This is eight-fourteen. Can you get in to see me for a few minutes?... Yes.... Have you received that uniform yet?... Bring it in with you."

He hung up the receiver but kept his hand on it. "Sit down," he said to Barney. He continued, to the telephone: "Get me one-seven-three-one Desbrosses.... Hello.... Archibald. Babbing.... You have an application there – in answer to our want ad – from a boy named Barney Cook. Have you looked up any of his references?... He says he delivered telegrams to us for the Western Union. His father was Robert Emmet Cook, a patrolman, killed about eight years ago. His mother lives in Hudson Street, where she rents furnished rooms. Run it out. 'Phone me right away, about the telegraph company and the police." He turned abruptly, to scrutinize Barney over his spectacles. And Barney, seeing himself engaged if his references proved satisfactory, did not attempt to suppress his triumphant grin.

"Well," Babbing said, "you don't look much like a plant –"

"No, sir," Barney admitted, not knowing in the least what was meant. He rose, at the end of a successful interview.

"Sit down," Babbing said, "your troubles have just begun. Come in!"

II

That last was in response to a knock at the door; and a man entered on the invitation, nonchalantly, with his hat on, carrying what proved to be a suit of black clothes on his arm. He was a large, dark, breezy-looking, informal sort of individual, about thirty-five; and Barney at once misplaced him as a Broadway type of "rounder" and race-track "sport." He ignored Barney and proceeded to drape the clothes over the foot of the bed, as if he had come merely to bring the suit. Barney did not guess that because of *his* presence the man did not speak to Babbing – until Babbing, by a question, indicated that it was all right to talk.

"Any one been to see him to-day?" Babbing asked.

"Not a soul," he answered. "He's been out, this morning, but he didn't connect."

"Snider has picked up some more telegrams." Babbing held out the report to him. "In cipher."

"Got their code yet?"

"No. If we had that, we'd have everything. We can figure out a word here and there. The names are easy. But that's as far as we can get."

They stood together beside the table, their feet in a patch of sunlight, their backs to Barney, interested in a page of the report which Babbing was showing to his operative. "'Kacaderm,' for instance. That's 'Murdock.' He's one of the men they've been bleeding, out there. They take the consonants 'm-r-d-c-k,' reverse them 'k-c-d-r-m,' and fill in vowels. But they do that only with the proper names. For instance, this last one: 'Thunder command wind kacaderm.' That can't be solved by reversing consonants."

The operative studied the page. "Search *me,*" he said. "Has Acker worked on it?"

"Yes. It was he that puzzled out the names. It's not a cryptogram. They have some simple method of writing one whole word for another. There's no use wasting time on it. We'll have to make our plant to catch him writing a message."

"I see."

Babbing took off his spectacles and began to walk up and down the room, twirling them by the ear bows. The operative sat on the side of the bed, leaning forward, with his hands clasped between his knees. He removed his derby and gazed thoughtfully into it, as if he hoped to find an idea there. It remained empty.

Babbing stopped in front of Barney. "Young man," he said, "I'm going to send you into the next room with a telegram. There's a man in there – registered as Marshall Cooper. Remember the name. You'll give the telegram to him and say 'Any answer?' Watch him. It will be a cipher telegram that will look as if it had been received downstairs. See what he does to make it out. He'll probably want to answer it; and if he does, you may have a chance to see how he makes up the answer. He has a writing table over at this window – here. If he sits down at it, he'll have his back to you. Try to see what he does. Don't try to do it by watching him quietly. He'd notice that. Move around and look at the pictures. Don't try to whistle – or anything of that fool sort. Try to act as you would if you were a bell-boy." He had taken the suit of clothes from the foot of the bed. "Go in the bathroom and try these on."

Afterward, when Barney thought of this moment, it seemed to him romantic and exciting beyond all his wildest young adventurous hopes. It seemed to him that he must have jumped to his feet with delight. As a matter of fact, he rose very soberly and took the clothes. His mind was busy with Babbing's directions which he was conning over and repeating to himself, so that he might be sure to make no mistakes. He was troubled about his ability to do what was expected of him. And he went into the bathroom and took off his Sunday twilled serge, and put on the black uniform of an Antwerp bell-boy mechanically, without thinking of himself as engaged in a Nick Carter exploit. Besides, the trousers were too long in the legs, and he had to pull them up until they were uncomfortable.

He heard Babbing answering the telephone, but he did not suspect that the detective was receiving a confirmatory report, from his office, upon Robert Emmet Cook's record at Police Headquarters and Barney Cook's service with the Western Union. Barney was not listening to what was going on around him, nor thinking of it. His thoughts were in Marshall Cooper's room. He was dramatizing a scene with the gentleman.

The voices of Babbing and his operative conferred together imperturbably:

"How are we going to send him a cipher telegram, Chief, if we don't know his code?"

"I'm going to repeat the one he got last night from Chicago. 'Thunder command wind kacaderm.' He hasn't answered it?"

"Unless by letter. And they wouldn't get that till to-night."

Babbing said: "He'll not go to the telegraph desk asking questions, because he won't care to identify himself to the man there. That's why he goes out to send his messages."

"Suppose he doesn't let the kid into the room at all."

"Well, he opens the door. The boy gives him the telegram and asks 'Any answer?' He reads it and sees it's the same message that he had last night. That'll make him forget the boy. He'll be trying to figure out what has happened. And the boy can stand at the door and watch him. It's worth trying anyway. Go and get the telegram ready, Jim."

"What is it, again?"

"'Thunder command wind kacaderm.' Unsigned."

"'Thunder – command – wind –– kacaderm.'"

"Have you the envelopes?"

"Yep. Billy has everything in there."

"Don't seal it till I've looked it over."

"All right, Chief."

The operative – whose name was Corcoran – departed with the unbustling celerity of a man accustomed to quick and noiseless movement. Babbing went to the bathroom door. "That's not so bad," he said of Barney's uniform. "Turn around." He settled the coat collar with a tug and a friendly pat. "Wipe off your shoes with a towel. The halls of the Antwerp aren't as dusty as all that." Barney looked up smiling, and found the detective's eyes kindly, amused, encouraging. "I ought to send you out to get a new pair," Babbing said, "but there isn't time. Come in here, now, and let's go over this again. I have an improvement to suggest."

He went to the window and stood looking out. Barney waited in the center of the room, excitedly alert. "You're a bell-boy recently employed here,"

Babbing said. "The man at the telegraph desk has said to you: 'Take this up to Mr. Cooper, room eight-eighteen, and see that he gets it, this time. It's a repeat.' That's not according to Hoyle, but it will have to do. Cooper won't know any better, anyway. So when you deliver the telegram at Cooper's door, you say: 'I was to be sure that you got this, this time. It's a repeat.' Step inside when you give him the message, so that he can't shut the door. And then watch him, as I told you before."

He stopped. He eyed Barney skeptically. "You couldn't possibly be as innocent as you look, could you? Because you'll have to do some quick lying, you know, if he suspects anything."

Barney looked sheepish.

"Here," Babbing said, suddenly. He took a letter from the table and gave it to the boy. "Go into the bathroom. No. The door opens in. I'll go in the bathroom, and you can come to the door and deliver this telegram. Let's see how you do it." And he went into the bathroom and shut the door on himself.

Barney turned the letter over in his hands. He frowned a moment at the door. Then he went up to it and rapped. There was no answer. He knocked more loudly. A voice, disconcertingly gruff, asked, "What is it?"

"A telegram, sir," Barney answered.

"Put it under the door."

Barney smiled to himself – the cunning smile of a child in a game. "They said I was to see that you got it, this time. It's a repeat."

The door was opened a few grudging inches. "What's that?"

"They said I was to see that Mr. Cooper got it, this time. It's a repeat."

"Well, I'm Mr. Cooper. Give it here." He put his hand out, still blocking the half-opened door. Barney gave him the letter. The door shut in his face.

Barney blinked at the panels. Then he knocked again sharply. Babbing opened the door.

"Well, what is it?"

"They didn't give me a receipt form," Barney said. "Will you sign the envelope an' give it back to me?"

"Have you a pencil?"

"No, sir," Barney said.

"Well, wait there till I find one."

Barney tried the door slyly. It opened. He edged in, over the threshold. "If you want to send an answer, sir," he said, "I can take it."

Babbing caught him by the "cowlick" that adorned his ingenuous young forehead. "Get out of here," he laughed, "or I'll have you arrested." And Barney, as startled as if he had been wakened from a dream, grinned confusedly. "That's all right," Babbing said. "If you do it as well as that."

"Was I all right?" Barney cried, exulting. "Was I?" He knew that he was; he could see it in Babbing's face; but he wanted to hear it. And he spoke in the voice of a boy playing with a boy.

Babbing changed his expression. "Yes, but this 'Nick Carter' stuff," he said, pointing to Barney's coat on a hook, "you mustn't destroy your mind with that sort of thing. That must stop with your cigarettes."

It returned Barney instantly to the hypocritical schoolroom manner of a pupil reproved by his teacher. "Yes, sir," he promised.

"Well, we'll see." Babbing was non-committal and unenthusiastic. "You've a lot to learn, yet."

Barney asked, shyly: "What's he been doin'?"

"Who?"

"Mr. Cooper."

Babbing turned back to the bedroom. "That's my business, not yours. You do what you're told – in my office – and don't ask questions. And don't discuss cases. That's another thing to learn.... Come in," he called to Corcoran's knock.

The operative came in, taking a telegraph envelope from his pocket. He gave it to Babbing, cheerfully silent. The detective put on his glasses and scrutinized it. He took out the telegram and read it. He compared the "time received" with his watch. "That looks convincing," he said. He moistened a finger tip and delicately wetted the gummed flap. "We can give it a couple of minutes to dry." He handed it to Barney. He went through his pockets for silver. "There are tips you've received. A dollar on account of salary. He may ask you for change.... Now don't be over-anxious. If this doesn't work, we'll find some other way. If he gets suspicious and telephones to the desk – or anything of that sort – just get in here as quickly as you can, and we'll protect you. Sit down a minute." He turned to the papers on his table. "Jim," he said, "You remember the disappearance case we had in Dayton – the little girl."

"Yes?"

"Our theory worked out all right. They've got a confession from the suspect and found the body in the bushes where he buried it. Here's Wally's report."

Corcoran took the paper and sat down to read it. "I hope they hang him," he said piously.

Babbing consulted his watch. "Mr. Bell-boy," he said at last, "You have a telegram for Mr. Cooper in eight-eighteen. Go ahead and deliver it."

Barney had a sensation of peculiar heaviness in the knees as he walked stiffly to the door. ("They said I was to see that you got it, this time.") Outside, he paused to close the door with unnecessary gentleness and make sure that the corridor was empty. ("It's a repeat.") Where was 818? He saw 819 across the hall to his left. He put a finger down the back of his neck, and eased his collar. He cleared his throat of nervousness. He walked boldly to 818, raised his small knuckles to a panel, and knocked.

There was no answer. He had put up his hand to knock again, when the door opened and a tall man in slippers and bathrobe asked, "Well?"

"A telegram for Mr. Cooper," Barney said steadily. "They tol' me to see that he got it, this time. It's a repeat."

Cooper stood back. "Come in." His voice was pitched low. "What did you say?"

Barney came across the threshold and Cooper closed the door on him. "It's a repeat," Barney said, "an' they told me to see that you got it, this time." He held out the telegram.

Cooper took it nervously. He was a gaunt-featured, long-nosed, lean man, with deep lines from his nostrils to the corners of his thin lips. There was a little patch of lather drying on one cheek-bone, and Barney understood that he had been shaving. He wiped his hand on his bathrobe before he took the telegram, and he fumbled over it. Barney found himself suddenly cool and confident. He noticed that Cooper's hands were very thin and very hairy; and he looked at them and then slowly looked Cooper over with a curious feeling of contempt. It was the contempt that accounts for half the daring of spies and detectives. People are so easily deceived, so easily outwitted. Their attention is so easily caught with one hand while the other goes unwatched. Barney was learning his trade.

"Why!" Cooper said. "I got this last night."

"Maybe you didn't answer it," Barney suggested. "It's a repeat."

He puzzled over it. "Well," he said, "I –" His voice faded out in the tone of abstraction. He turned and shuffled across the room to his writing desk, his eyes on the telegram. Unconscious of Barney's craning watchfulness, he took a small cloth-bound volume from an upper drawer of the little escritoire and turned the printed pages, comparing the words in the message with words in the book. The code book!

"If you want to send an answer," Barney said boldly, moving down towards him, "I could take it."

He did not reply. He sat down to the desk and took a pencil and wrote, and consulted the book carefully with his pencil point on the page, and came back again to the message, and returned to find another page in the book. "No, that's all right," he said, finally. He tore the telegram and retore it into tiny pieces. "There's no answer." He made as if to throw the torn paper into the waste basket, and then he checked himself. "Wait a minute," he said, rising; and Barney understood that he was to have a tip.

Cooper shuffled off to the bathroom in his slippers.

Barney, as pale as a thief, darted to the secretary and crammed the little code book into his pocket.

When Cooper returned to the room, the bell-boy was standing near the door looking up at a framed engraving. He took the dime that Cooper gave him, and said stiffly, "Thanks," but without raising his guilty eyes. As he went out, he glanced back and saw that Cooper was returning to the bathroom. Gee!

III

He was so obviously – so breathlessly – excited when he burst in upon the detectives that Corcoran came to his feet at sight of him. "What's the matter?"

Babbing jerked off his spectacles. "What has happened?"

"I go-got it," Barney stammered, tugging at the book that stuck in his pocket.

"Got what?"

"His – his book."

"What!" Corcoran grabbed him roughly by the shoulder and snatched the volume from his hand. He glanced at its brown cloth cover. *"What?"* he cried. And that second "What" expressed the extreme of incredulous disgust. He held out the book to Babbing who had not moved from his seat at the table. "He's swiped the man's dictionary!"

Babbing looked at it. It was a "pocket Webster," a cheap abridged edition, on cheap paper. "Where did you get this?" he asked; and there was no kindly personality showing in the cold malevolence of his flat eyes.

"On his desk. I –"

"Why did you bring it?"

"Oh, hell!" Corcoran muttered. "This *kid* business!"

"That'll do!" Babbing flared out at him. "I'm in charge of this case."

They glared at each other, as if they were old enemies, with old jealousies concealed and long injustices unforgiven. Corcoran turned with a shrug and sat down on the bed. Babbing rounded on the boy again.

"Why did you bring this?"

"Well, gee," Barney defended himself. "As soon as he got the telegram, he beat it to his desk an' yanked this book out of a drawer, an' began to hunt the words up in it, an' –"

"Wait a minute. Corcoran, get on watch out there. If you hear anything, come back for this boy. Take him in to Cooper and tell him you're the house detective – that you caught the boy with this book and he confessed he'd stolen it from eight-eighteen. Give it back and ask him not to prosecute – because it would hurt the hotel. He won't anyway. And that'll hold him quiet till we can get time to turn round. Otherwise, we've tipped our hand."

Corcoran was already at the door. He went out on the final word.

"Now," Babbing said, with perfect suavity, "take your time. Show me exactly what he did."

"Well, look-a-here!" Barney took the book. "He got this out o' the drawer, an' then he sat down this way, an' got a pencil, an' then he wrote down the telegram –"

"Wrote it down? Where? On what?"

"On a piece o' paper. An' then he looks in the book, this way, an' gets a word. An' then he looks at the telegram. An then he goes back to the book an' turns over the pages. An' then he –"

Babbing reached the dictionary from him. "Wait." He put on his spectacles and wrote on the back of an envelope: "Thunder command wind kacaderm." Below that he wrote it again, reversed, and then several times with the words transposed and permuted in all possible orders. He turned to the word "thunder" in the dictionary. It was at the bottom of the first of the three narrow columns that filled the page. He studied it. He studied the words around it. He turned the page, and his eyes widened thoughtfully on the word "through" at the bottom of the third column. The line read "Through, (throo) *prep.* from." And on the margin the point of a pencil had made a light indentation. He turned back to "Thunder"; and on the margin there, the pencil mark showed in a raised point.

He wrote, under the word "thunder" on his paper, the word "through."

He turned to the word "command" in the dictionary, but after a prolonged scrutiny he wrote nothing.

He turned to "wind." And he found, on the same page but in another column, the word "will" touched with a faint pencil mark. He sat back in this chair and his face became meditatively blank.

His eyelids constricted sharply. He wrote: "Murdock will come through." Turning back in the dictionary to the word "command," he found "come" standing directly beside it in the parallel column of print on the page. He looked at Barney and nodded. "Got it!" he said, grimly. "Go and bring Corcoran."

Barney, almost running – but on his tiptoes – with the secrecy and the excitement, saw himself vindicated to the surprised Corcoran. He saw himself the hero of the occasion. He had solved the mystery! He had discovered the cipher! He signaled imperiously to Corcoran in the hall. The operative came scowling.

When they returned to the room, Babbing said: "Sit down there, boy, and keep quiet. You scuttle like a rat.... Jim, I've got his method. I want you to send off some messages while I'm translating these. Wire our Chicago office: 'Case 11A393. Case completed. Immediately arrest Number Two on information in your files.' Wire Indianapolis in the same words to grab Pirie. He's Number Three. And have Billy 'phone the office to get papers and an officer up here, at once, for our friend next door. I'll hold him till they come. Go ahead. I'll finish this."

He settled down to his task studiously, copying out cipher telegrams, and writing between the lines the translated words as he found them in the dictionary. And in a room that was quiet and sunny, working with a little complacent pucker of the lips occasionally, or raising his eyebrows and adjusting his spectacles in a pause of doubt, he looked anything but sinister, anything but the traditional "bloodhound" on the trail in a man-hunt. There was something Pickwickian in his small rotundity. The nattiness of his business suit gave him an air of conventional unimportance.

Barney watched him fascinatedly. His plump little hands – his rather flat profile with its small beaked nose and the owlish spectacles – his dimpled chin – all reminded the boy of some one incongruous whom he could not place. When Babbing took out a white silk handkerchief to polish his glasses and buried his nose in it before he replaced it in his pocket, Barney remembered. It was a bishop who had once graced the closing exercises of the parochial school by conferring the prizes. He had given Barney a "Lives of the Saints."

"Now, young man," Babbing said, "get off that uniform. I'm going in to get a statement from your Mr. Cooper. If any one rings me up, take the number. If any of the men come in here, tell them where I am. I'm registered as A.T. Hume. Wait here till I come back." He had taken a small blue-metal "automatic" from his hip pocket and put it in the side pocket of his coat. He gathered up his notes and the dictionary. "Don't make the mistake again of exceeding your instructions. You've forced our hand, already."

"Yes, sir," Barney said, contritely. But the door had scarcely closed before he was capering. He did a sort of disrobing dance, his face fearfully contorted with grins that were a silent equivalent of whoops of delight. And it was an interpretative dance. It expressed liberation from drudgery and the dull commonplace. It welcomed rhythmically a life of adventure, in which a boy's natural propensity to lie should be not only unchecked but encouraged – that should give him, daily, games to play, hidings to seek, simple elders to hoodwink and masquerades to wear. He danced it, in his shirt sleeves, waving his coat – and in his shirt tails waving coat and trousers. It stopped as suddenly as it had begun, and he darted into the bathroom to be ready in case he should be called upon.

He was clothed and sober – rocking himself to an ecstatic croon in one of the Antwerp's bedroom rockers – when he heard a thudded report in the hall. It sounded to him as if two books had been clapped together. He sat listening.

Babbing came in. "Get out of here, boy. What have you done with that uniform? Put it in my valise. Snap it shut. Hurry. Report to the office to-morrow morning at eight-thirty." He was at the telephone. "Give me the house detective," he said. "What? Mr. Dohn, your house detective." He put his hand over the transmitter. "How much have you been earning?"

"Six dollars a week – with the tips."

"You'll start at twelve. Hurry up. Get out of here. To-morrow morning at eight-thirty."

Barney started for the door, reluctantly.

"Hello. Dohn? This is Babbing. Get up here as quick as you can with a doctor. That Chicago swindler in eight-eighteen has shot himself. Through the mouth. He's blown the back of his head out. Hurry up!"

Barney, slamming the door behind him, fled down the hall, frightened, aghast, but with a high exultant inner voice still crooning triumphantly: "I'm a de-*tec*-tive! I'm a de-*tec*-tive!" Through the mouth! The back of his head out! Even in his horror there was a pleasurable shudder, for he had all a boy's healthy curiosity about murder, shootings and affairs of bloodshed. "I'm a de-*tec*-tive!" And he hurried to tell his mother of his new job, aware that she would cry out against it – till he explained: "I start at twelve a week." That would settle it with her. "I'm a detective! I'm a detective!"

THE MARSHALL MURDER
Detective Duff unravels it. New York: Liveright, 1929.

This book introduces criminous literature's first psychoanalytical detective, John Duff, revealing the author's interest in and knowledge of Freud.

In the dust jacket blurb, the publisher said, "Every crime is committed in two places. It is committed at the scene of the crime, where the police investigate it, but what is far more important, it is also committed in the mind of the criminal. The old-fashioned detective followed the first trail, but Detective Duff tracked the psychological trail of the criminal through a labyrinth of haunting fears and hidden repressions and veiled passions. Duff ... discovered the guilty ones by the warm, believable tracing of a human being's motives."

"Ellery Queen" selected the book for his *Queen's quorum,* and considered it the anchor book of the year: "in many ways the most important book of its decade, [it] both symbolizes and epitomizes the First Moderns."* The first serious approach to psychoanalytical detection, John Duff follows the trail deep into the mind of the perpetrator.

---

* *Queen's quorum; a history of the detective-crime short story as revealed in the 106 most important books published in this field since 1845.* Boston: Little, Brown/Toronto: McClelland & Stewart, 1951/London: Gollancz, 1953/revised edition with Supplements through 1967 – New York: Biblo & Tannen, 1969.

THE MARSHALL MURDER

"This is Mr. Duff," the lawyer introduced them. "Miss Marshall, Mr. Duff." And Duff shook hands with a very small, a very dark, a very alert and fashionable spinster-lady of middle age, who looked up at him with a sweet and ironical smile.

"Well," she said softly, "you're big enough."

He was huge. He was nearly six feet tall; he weighed some two hundred pounds; and he was solid with muscle.

"It's a disguise," he assured her. "I use it to deceive people – the same as you do." And he met her smile with a shrewd, appraising twinkle.

"The same as I do?"

"Yes," he said. "They never suspect me of being a detective, any more than they suspect you of being an autocrat."

Her smile became sweeter than ever. "What makes you think I'm an autocrat?"

"The same thing in me that makes me think I'm a detective. Won't you sit down?"

She accepted a chair by the fireplace with a tiny dignity that was not unimpressive. "I only hope," she murmured, "that you're not equally deceived in us both."

She and Westingate, her lawyer, had come to consult Duff in his rooms, instead of at his office, because they wished to keep their visit to him a careful secret. His rooms were on the second floor of an old brownstone house on Eleventh Street near Sixth Avenue, and the living-room in which they found him, typical of the decayed gentility of the district, had a high ceiling, an old black marble mantelpiece, tall windows, and a hardwood floor. He had furnished it chiefly with a law library, descended from the days when he had been an unsuccessful young attorney. As a living-room, it looked studious and celibate. The chairs were all fat bachelor chairs, upholstered in dark leather, as severe as they were comfortable; and they were so burly that Alicia Marshall, for all her furs, sat in hers like a little fairy godmother in a giant's seat.

The lawyer, Westingate, took a chair on the same side of the fireplace as she, and frowned at the blaze with a forehead that was permanently corrugated. A somber and bilious-looking bald man, he seemed always to be brooding over the obscurities of the law behind a set and worried countenance. "I suppose you've guessed," he said, "that we wanted to see you about this" – he coughed – "murder."

Duff raised his heavy eyebrows, deprecatingly. "No," he admitted. "I wasn't sure."

"Well," Alicia Marshall said, "we *did*." She had unbuttoned her sealskin sacque. She threw it open, now, with a gesture of beginning the discussion. Duff sat down. The lawyer cleared his throat.

The murder – the Marshall murder – was one of those picturesque New Jersey murders that happen in the best-regulated families of a state that prides itself on its "swift Jersey justice" – murders of which no one is ever found guilty, so that they present the fascinating spectacle of an irresistible force meeting an insoluble mystery. The chief victim was a distinguished citizen, Senator Amos K. Marshall, a corporation lawyer and party politician; and his outrageous end may have been more shocking to the popular mind because, after all, the murder of a "big business" lawyer, who is also a machine senator, contains elements that do not wholly horrify, and it is necessary for many people to be volubly distressed at such a crime in order to overcome a contrary impulse, perhaps. In any case, the public outcry was tremendous, measured either by the amount of newspaper space that was filled with accounts of the Marshall murder, or by the amount of boxwood hedge that was carried away from the Marshall lawn by souvenir hunters.

There was killed with Senator Marshall, a young widow, named Mrs. Starrett, who was his housekeeper. When a man and a woman are murdered together, scandal seems inevitable; and in this case, the scandal traveled fast because no evidence was found to support it. It moved as freely as a flying column that lives off the countryside without any need for a base of supplies. And it was followed by the rumor that the man accused of the murder had been in love with the housekeeper, though there was no discoverable basis in fact for that report either.

The man accused was an ex-soldier named Andrew Pittling – a young veteran of the Argonne, suffering from shell-shock – whom Marshall had employed as general utility-man around his suburban home in Cold Brook. Pittling had been voluble in his support of President Wilson's League of Nations, and Marshall had conspicuously helped to defeat Wilson's policies. Hence, many arguments about the murder were warm with the animation of political sympathy.

Hence, also, Alicia Marshall – before her lawyer could get his cleared throat into action – broke out gently to Duff: "We've decided that there's no use leaving it to the local authorities any longer. They're a lot of Democratic politicians. I believe they're capable of protecting the man who killed Amos, if they knew who he was."

"You were not in the house, that night?" Duff asked, meaning the night of the murder.

"No, I was not."

She lived, she explained, in the original Marshall homestead, on Marshall Avenue, in Cold Brook. Her dead brother Amos, when he married, bought an estate in the hills behind the town; he rebuilt magnificently an old Dutch farmhouse on the property and he had lived there ever since. There had been no one in the house on the night of the murder except his daughter, Martha – so ill in bed with influenza that she was too weak to lift her head from the pillow, and a number of servants, all women except this one man, the ex-soldier, Pittling.

"What is the actual evidence against Pittling, do you know?" Duff asked the lawyer.

Well, to tell the truth, there was none. Senator Marshall had been killed, evidently with a hatchet, as he lay asleep in his bed. His housekeeper, Mrs. Starrett, had been struck down, apparently with the same hatchet, in the hall outside his door. In the morning, a bloody hatchet was found lying among some rose bushes under an open window that looked out from the dining-room on a side lawn. Either the murderer had dropped his weapon there, as he escaped out the window, or he had tossed it out the window and remained in the house himself. In neither case was there anything to cast suspicion on Pittling except the fact that the hatchet was his. He kept it in the furnace-room of the basement to use when he was building fires; and he had used it earlier in the day to split kindling for a fire in the bedroom of the daughter, Martha. The weather had turned suddenly colder that afternoon, and Martha had complained that her room was chilly even with the furnace on full draught. Pittling and the housemaid built a fire of cannel coal in her bedroom grate, to satisfy her; but neither of them could remember whether Pittling had brought the hatchet up out of the basement then, or whether if he *had* brought it up, he had failed to return it to the cellar. No distinguishable fingerprints were on it when it was found in the morning. There were no footprints outside the window, because the ground was frozen hard and bare of snow. And no one but the dead housekeeper knew whether the window had been left unlocked the night before, or whether it had been opened from the inside after she had locked it. It was her duty to make the rounds at night and see that all the doors and windows were closed and fastened before she went to bed.

"And no one," Duff asked, "heard any noise whatever during the night?"

No one. No one could be expected to, except Martha, the sick girl. Her room was next to her father's. The housekeeper was killed in the hall between her father's door and hers. But she had gone through the crisis of her fever that afternoon; she fell asleep, in a weak perspiration, late that evening; and she did not wake till the following dawn. Her door had been closed after she fell asleep, evidently by the housekeeper, to protect her slumber; and she heard nothing. The women servants – that is to say, the cook and the two maids – slept in the kitchen wing, out of hearing of anything that might happen in the main portion of the house. The chauffeur slept over the garage. Pittling, the ex-soldier, had fixed himself a room in the basement, where he lived as if he were in a cement dugout. He was peculiar.

"I see," Duff said. "And he heard nothing either?"

"Nothing," the lawyer replied, "of any importance."

"No? What was it?"

Westingate explained impatiently: "Senator Marshall's home is not supplied with water from the waterworks in Cold Brook. It's too far outside the town. It has its own pumping plant – an air pump, in a driven well, at some distance from the house. Compressed air is stored in a tank in the pumphouse, and the pump is quiet except when any of the faucets in the house are opened; then, as water flows out of the pipe, the mechanism of the pump trips off with an audible stroke. Pittling complains that he was wakened in the night by this sound of the pump working. The main supply pipe to the house runs through the basement just outside his room, and the sound of the pump travels quite loudly along that pipe. It prevented him from sleeping. For half an hour at least, he says, he was kept awake by it. Then it stopped."

"He doesn't know at what hour this was?"

"No. He thinks he'd been asleep for some time, but of course he can't be sure. It may have happened before all the others had gone to bed."

"Of course. And he heard nothing else?"

"Nothing until the housemaid screamed when she found Mrs. Starrett dead in the hall. Pittling had been up for some time. He'd dressed and tended the furnace –"

"Oh, never mind all that," Miss Marshall broke in, with a mild impatience. "You can't possibly suspect poor Pittling. He's the last man in the world to murder anyone. He had enough of that in France."

Duff had been listening, very much at his ease, his eyes on the fire, asking questions in a voice that was almost absent-minded, his big hands at rest on the massive arms of his comfortable chair. He already knew many of the details of the Marshall murder; he had pieced them together, with a professional interest, from the newspaper accounts. And he had been listening less to what Alicia Marshall and her lawyer said than to the state of mind about the murder which they unconsciously expressed.

Thus far, the most striking fact that he had learned was this: Alicia Marshall was not as deeply concerned about her brother's death as she was about "poor Pittling."

"He's been arrested, has he? – Pittling?"

"Yes. He's in the county jail."

"Has he a lawyer?"

"I'm his lawyer," Westingate replied.

"I see. I may have to get a talk with him, if you don't mind. And the other servants? Where are they?"

"They're with me," Miss Marshall said. "At my house."

"And the daughter, Martha?"

"She is, too. She's still in bed. We had her moved, the next day. It was impossible for anyone to remain in that house, with the crowds that gathered."

"Naturally. I suppose you've left some one there to see that they don't carry the house away piecemeal."

"Yes. The chauffeur has moved in from the garage."

Duff nodded. "I'll put in a caretaker and his wife – if you don't object – and relieve the chauffeur." He turned benignly to Miss Marshall. "And I'd like to send you a trained nurse, supposedly for your niece, so as to have some one in touch with those servants. They may know something they haven't reported because they don't realize that it's significant. If I tried to cross-examine them myself, I'd only frighten them. I'll not send a detective," he added, seeing her reluctance in her eyes. "I have a very nice girl who goes out for me, now and then, on confidential cases – a girl of good family. She's had training as a convalescent nurse. You'll like her."

"Have you any suspicion," she asked warily, "about who did it?"

"No," he said. "None. None whatever. If it were a murder of revenge, committed by some enemy from the outside, he'd have brought a weapon with him. He wouldn't've had to use that hatchet – whether he carried it up from the basement or found it somewhere upstairs. On the other hand, if it was a burglar whom Mrs. Starrett surprised, he might have killed her, naturally enough, but why should he kill your brother in his bed? And I understand that nothing was stolen?"

"Nothing whatever."

"If it were Pittling, he'd have taken the hatchet back downstairs and cleaned it off, probably, or concealed it. It's not likely that he'd direct suspicion against himself by leaving his hatchet, covered with blood, lying around where it would be found at once. No. That suggests, perhaps, an attempt to cast suspicion on Pittling."

"Exactly," Miss Marshall agreed.

"Or, the whole thing may be just an insane accident. Some madman may have broken in, and found the hatchet, and dropped it again as he ran away."

"That would be my theory," the lawyer said.

"I suppose this Mrs. Starrett has been looked up? – to see whether *she* had any enemies."

"Yes, thoroughly. They've found nothing."

"And Senator Marshall's relations with Mrs. Starrett? They've gone into that?"

He asked it casually, reflectively, looking at the fire. The lawyer did not reply. Duff turned to Miss Marshall and found her regarding her shoe tips with a sarcastic smile.

"Well," she said, "my brother was no fool. If there was anything going on between him and Mrs. Starrett, no one will ever find it out."

"You think there *was* something, then?"

"It's the last thing I should think. Senator Marshall had about as much private life as the Statue of Liberty."

"He was a very religious man," Westingate put in, "very strict with his family, a leader in the law-and-order movement, and most severe on all this modern – er – laxity."

"And the daughter? Is *she* religious?"

"Ah, poor Martha," Miss Marshall sighed. "She's a saint."

"I see. Well," Duff decided, "I'll start work on it at once. If I send a care-taker and his wife to you, to-morrow morning, you can install them in the house?"

"Certainly," the lawyer promised.

"And my nurse may come to you, Miss Marshall, to-morrow afternoon?"

"If you wish it."

"Thanks. I'll arrive in Cold Brook, probably, to-morrow evening, and stop for a few days with the caretaker. That'll make it easier for me to consult with you both the moment I get any sort of clew. If anyone notices me and asks questions, we can explain that Senator Marshall's estate is in the hands of a New York trust company, as his executors, and I'm their agent, appraising the property and making an inventory of the estate. My name is Duffield."

"Very good."

They all rose.

"You'll not tell the truth about me, or my operatives, to anyone – the ser-vants, the chauffeur, nor even your niece?"

"Certainly not."

They shook hands on it.

"I'm beginning to think you really are a detective," Miss Marshall said.

"Then, at least, I'm not deceived in us *both*," replied Duff.

II

Cold Brook did not remark the arrival, next day, of a new caretaker at the Marshall home, installed by order of the executors of the estate. The nurse whom Miss Marshall engaged, from New York, to take care of her invalid niece, came unnoticed, in the afternoon, and went silently to work. Duff drove out by automobile, after dark, spent the night in one of Senator Marshall's guest rooms, and appeared next morning, as the agent of the executors, to look over the other properties which Marshall had owned in Cold Brook, and to consult Alicia Marshall and her lawyer, Westingate. He ate dinner, that evening, with Westingate and the County Prosecutor at Westingate's home; and the following morning a tramp, arrested for drunk-enness, was put in the cell that adjoined Pittling's in the county jail. Duff drove back to New York in the afternoon, and no one seemed any the wiser. Not even he.

Cold Brook, with its tree-lined residential avenues and its suburban homes, was a commuters' town that had no public opinion of its own outside of its one business street of shopkeepers, lawyers, real estate and insurance agents, plumbers, barbers and such. Its commuters read the New York papers and smiled with the New York reporters at the provincial animosity of the local authorities to the metropolitan newspaper men. The business district resented those smiles. Duff might have walked the streets of Cold Brook openly, for a week, and none of the reporters would have known that he was a stranger in the town, because none of the real townsfolk would have tipped them off. He was not recognized as a detective anywhere, except in those circles in which he found his clients. He did not, as he said, "Hunt criminals with a brass band" – that is to say, he never advertised. He had served with Military Intelligence during the war – especially around airplane factories and shipyards – and some of his war-time friends had urged him to set up a detective agency of his own when the war ended, and one of those friends was an automobile manufacturer who happened to be a client of Westingate's. The automobile man advised Westingate to see Duff about the Marshall murder. That was how he came into the case.

When, after two days of a peculiar dawdling sort of inconspicuous diligence in Cold Brook, he returned to his office near Union Square, he telephoned to Westingate: "I'll have something to report in about a week, I think. My operatives are busy. I believe we're on the trail of something."

"What's your theory?" the lawyer asked.

"Well," Duff said, "this murder, you understand, occurred in two places."

"In two places?"

"Yes."

"How so?"

"It occurred in Cold Brook, in the home of ex-Senator Marshall, but before that, it occurred somewhere else."

"Somewhere else?"

"Yes. It occurred first in somebody's mind, because it was evidently a premeditated murder."

"Oh. I get you."

"And it left a trail in that mind."

"I suppose it did."

"And while the County Prosecutor is trying to find its actual trail, I'm going after its mental trail."

"In whose mind?"

"I'm not yet sure, but I can tell you this much: I don't believe it was Pittling's."

"I'm glad of that. Then I may expect to hear something definite from you in a week?"

"Or two," Duff promised.

And it was two.

The tramp who had been shut up with Pittling wormed his way into the ex-soldier's confidence and obtained nothing but indications of innocence. The caretaker and his wife did as much for the chauffeur, with the same result. Mrs. Starrett, the murdered housekeeper, had had no enemies, apparently. She had been a respectable young widow who had lived all her life in Cold Brook. Her only surviving relative, an older sister, kept a boarding house; and an operative who went to live there found nothing on which to base a suspicion that there had been anything illicit in Mrs. Starrett's relations with her employer, or that there was anyone to resent such relations if they had existed. The nurse, at Miss Marshall's, made friends with the dead man's servants and discovered nothing startling from them. The county authorities were beginning to believe that the crime had been committed by some insane yeggman who had broken into the house to burglarize it and killed two people in a homicidal mania; and they were holding Pittling, merely as a matter of form, until the popular excitement passed.

All these confessions of failure were received cheerfully by Duff in daily conversations over the telephone and in the daily reports which his operatives wrote for his office files. He motored out twice to Cold Brook and consulted with the members of his little field force at night, in Senator Marshall's library, looking blankly meditative and saying nothing. He called on Alicia Marshall to admit that he was making no progress, and he talked with her chiefly about her father, Jeremiah Marshall, with whom she had lived for years in the Marshall homestead. He had died of heart disease, in 1909, at the age of 71, in Senator Marshall's house, where he had gone to live after a quarrel with his spirited daughter. "My brother always gave way to him," she said. "I'm afraid I irritated him. At any rate, the doctor declared his heart was so weak that the excitement of living with me was too much for him. He was too old to live alone. So he went to Amos. And he died there in about a month." She smiled at Duff placidly. "You don't think *he* was in any way connected with Amos's death, do you?"

Duff returned the smile. "Yes," he said, "I'm beginning to suspect so."

She accepted the statement with an air of humorously resigning herself to the fantastic. "Well," she sighed, "I hope you can prove it – he's so safe from the police."

III

He proved it on the following Sunday night. He proved it to Alicia Marshall and to Westingate, in an after-dinner conversation that took place in the picture gallery which Miss Marshall had added to the old Marshall homestead, in Cold Brook. She had been much abroad after her father's death. She had brought back a collection of Italian primitives and housed them in a gallery that was furnished with medieval chairs, antique carved tables, Oriental rugs, bronzes of the Rodin school and church vestments. In this room that looked like the showroom of a Fifth Avenue picture-dealer, by the light of electric bulbs that had been wired into church candelabra and seven-branched candlesticks, Duff made his report to Miss Marshall and her lawyer, over their after-dinner coffee. And it was a report as grotesque as any utterance of the mind of man that Miss Marshall's curiosities had ever heard in their long association with human life and its dramatic emotions.

He locked the big carved door of the gallery, He looked around to see that there were no windows at which anyone could listen. He warned them: "I don't want you to worry over anything I tell you. It can't possibly make trouble for anyone, simply because it can't possibly be proved." He drew from his pocket a modern octavo volume bound in green boards. "This is my case," he said, and handed the book to Miss Marshall.

She was sitting, very erect and diminutive, in a pontifical carved chair beside the heavy library table on which their coffee had been served. She was in an evening gown of silver brocade and crimson, and she looked at the volume with the aid of a lorgnette. It was called "The Roosevelt Myth," a book published by the author, James Clair Billings, in 1908 and dedicated to "the enlightenment of all loyal subjects of Theodore, Rex." On the flyleaf was written, in a girlish hand: "In memory of my beloved Chester, Dec. 1909."

Miss Marshall said: "This is Martha's handwriting."

Duff replied: "Yes. It's her book."

Westingate drew up a Savonarola chair beside her and studied the inscription silently.

"Your father," Duff said to her, "your father, Jeremiah Marshall, was a great Roosevelt fan, you remember. This book is an attack on Roosevelt. It's the book that he was reading, the night he died."

Alicia Marshall turned to him with her sweetest smile. "Yes? And who was Chester?"

"Chester was a cat."

"A cat? Well! And that's your case?"

"That's the beginning of it." He indicated the book with a nod to her to go on. She turned over the pages till she came to a photograph, a snapshot that had been pasted into the book like an extra illustration. It was a faded picture of a young man and a girl in a canoe. "The girl," Duff said, "is your niece, Martha. The man is a young minister, named Keiser, who left Cold Brook some years ago."

"I'll have to take your word for it," Miss Marshall replied. "It's too dim for me to make out."

"She was in love with him, wasn't she?"

"I believe so."

"And Senator Marshall interfered."

"Yes. I'm afraid he did."

Duff nodded at the book again. She turned the pages to another insertion, a folded letter pasted in like a map – a letter from Senator Marshall to his daughter Martha, telling her that the household expenses were too high and that he intended to employ a housekeeper who was to oversee all expenditures in the future. Miss Marshall read it slowly. "Yes," she said, with a sigh, "it was very foolish. Very foolish." The letter was dated July of the previous year.

"There's one more exhibit," Duff said.

She went through the book without finding it. He turned to the inside of the back cover and showed them that something was concealed under the final page of paper that had been pasted down on the cover-lining. He drew out a typewritten note, unsigned, which read, "I shall arrive, my dear, for our anniversary." He handed it to Miss Marshall.

"That's my whole case," he concluded.

She gave the book and its contents to Westingate, with the air of resigning a puzzle to an expert. "That's your whole case?"

"Yes."

"But," she complained, cheerfully, "I don't at all understand what it means."

"Well," he said, "Let's take the first exhibit, the book itself. Jeremiah Marshall, your father – Martha's grandfather – died of heart disease in your brother's house on the fifteenth of December, 1909. Is that correct?"

"I believe it is."

"The doctor had warned you all that any excitement would be likely to kill him. That was the reason why he left your house. He was always quarreling with you."

"Always."

"When he went to live with your brother, your niece Martha was about seventeen years old. Her mother had been dead about ten years. She was a solitary, eccentric child, with a stern father and an irritable grandfather. The only living thing in the world for which she seemed to have any affection was a pet cat, named Chester. Do you remember that the grandfather had a great aversion to cats?"

"Yes, I do."

"Did you know that he had Martha's pet cat poisoned?"

"I didn't know. I vaguely remember something of the sort."

"That's the meaning of the inscription in the front of the book. In order to annoy him, to persecute him for killing her cat, she took into his sickroom and left on his bedside table at night, this attack on his idol, Roosevelt. She may have heard him arguing with Senator Marshall about Roosevelt. Or she may have known that Senator Marshall refused to argue with him about it, for fear of exciting him too much. At any rate, she knew that if he read the book it might irritate him dangerously. And it did. He may have thought that his son had put it there to plague him. He was furious. He jumped out of bed, in a rage, and threw up the window, and flung the book out on the lawn. And the strain of that violent action killed him. They found him dead, next morning, on the floor, with the window open, and his reading lamp still burning at his bedside. One of the servants picked up the book, outside, later in the day, and no one knew where it had come from. When Martha finally got it back, she wrote in it: 'In memory of my beloved Chester, Dec. 1909.'"

Alicia Marshall spread her hands in an eloquent gesture which said, "Well, even so! Supposing it's true. What of it?"

Westingate asked suspiciously: "Who told you all this?"

"The girl told my nurse."

"You mean to say that she told the nurse, in so many words, that she had killed her grandfather?"

"No. She described a nightmare that's been persecuting her – a nightmare of a Cheshire cat that showed its teeth in a grin like Theodore Roosevelt's. My nurse asked her if she had ever had a cat, and she recalled a pet cat which her grandfather had poisoned. Subsequently, she asked the nurse to go to her father's house and get this book out of her room. The nurse pretended that she couldn't find it and sent it to me. Later we learned, from Senator Marshall's old cook, about how the grandfather had died in the night beside an open window. She's superstitious about the coincidence, in both cases, of an open window – and in one case a book, and in the other case a hatchet, flung outdoors."

Miss Marshall drew back in her chair, in an attitude of obstinate defensiveness. "Well, if Martha really did this to her grandfather," she said, "I, for one, can quite understand it. It was time that some one retaliated on him. He'd been making life impossible for everybody, for forty years, to *my* knowledge."

"Quite so," Duff agreed. "And you and I can understand how an angry child could give him that book, with no clear idea of killing him, though with a sort of furious hope that it might pay him back for killing her cat. Quite so. But do we realize what it would mean to her to succeed, and accept her success definitely, and inscribe a book with her triumph, as a Westerner cuts a notch in his gun?"

Alicia Marshall, for the first time, frowned at him. The lawyer rose and put the book on the table and pushed it away from him nervously, as if he were legally refusing any responsibility for its possession.

Duff went on: "Nothing's as satisfying to one's ego as the death of an enemy. Any soldier can tell you what a godlike feeling of power it gives you. You can't in a moment, and with a wave of the hand, create a human being, but you can destroy one, that way. And the effect on you is almost as great as an act of creation. This girl had already a very sturdy sense of her own importance. She was solitary and eccentric, but she was not timid and depressed. She was an only child. I judge that her mother had been devoted to her and proud of her. I understand that her father thought her spoiled and obstinate. Well, here was this old man, the grandfather, who had been persecuting her with his bad temper. And by a sort of magic act, she had simply wiped him out of the world. That is the sort of youthful experience that makes a unique personality. From this time on, we have to reckon with a human being who has had an experience that may make her superhuman."

"That," Miss Marshall said flatly, "is all nonsense. Martha has never been anything but a devout and simple girl —"

"She became devout," Duff cut in, "She became religious, after the death of her grandfather."

"She became religious, as I did, when she should have been falling in love. If you knew anything about women, you'd know that half of us are like that."

"Naturally." Duff leaned forward on the arms of his chair, with a slowly genial smile. "But — did you ever notice how often religious fanatics are killers? It's my experience that whenever there's a mysterious murder in a decent, respectable family, it's a safe bet that the thing was done by the most religious member of the household. And why? A religious person hates himself. He knows that he's a hateful animal in the sight of heaven, full of low animal impulses that are sinful and nasty. He hates those things in himself, and so he hates himself. An emotion of that sort — an emotion of love or hatred — is almost like a charge of electricity in a person. It either gets drained off naturally in expressions of love or hatred for somebody else, or it stores up as if it were electricity in a storage battery until it's a tremendous charge of suppressed emotion. A religious person can't drain off his hatred freely on people around him because hatred of others is a sin. So he goes on storing up hatred until he's charged full with it. And then — something happens. The hated person blunders into circumstances that make the electric connection, and there's a flash that's murderous, and the thing's done."

Westingate asked hoarsely: "Are you trying to prove that this girl killed her father — and the housekeeper — with a hatchet?"

"I'm not trying to prove anything," Duff smiled. "I'm trying to tell you privately how this case looks to me."

"I never heard anything more absurd in my life," Miss Marshall said.

"Good!" He seemed actually relieved. "I was afraid I might worry you. I appreciate how absurd it looks, and how safe the girl is from any charge of the kind, but I wasn't sure you'd feel that way about it. Now that you understand how ridiculous the whole thing sounds, I can go ahead with it, more frankly."

Neither of them replied. The lawyer, having seated himself with the table between them, was staring at Duff with eyes that saw only too clearly the possible implications of his charge. Alicia Marshall, sitting as if her back were against a wall, watched him silently, intent and frowning.

"Let me go ahead," Duff proposed, "and tell you the whole story as I see it, without any reservations, or apologies, or anything like that. This girl, Martha, after the grandfather's death was at first defiant, as her inscription in that book shows. Then she began to feel guilty and remorseful, and she fell ill. When she recovered, she became religious, and that annoyed her father. You've spoken of him as a religious man. He wasn't religious. He attended church. And for many years he helped to take up the collection, I know. But that was merely part of his routine of life as a respectable citizen, a leader in the community who had to set a good example to the ungodly and keep himself high in the estimation of his clients and his constituents. He had no patience with his daughter's excess of piety. And when she fell in love with the minister – this young Keiser – he objected to the match. He refused to settle any money on her – so as to keep her from marrying. He used his influence to get Keiser transferred. He told her that Keiser only wanted to marry her for her money. And when Keiser went away, and stopped writing to her, she blamed her father.

"As far as my nurse has been able to find out, this was her only love affair. She was taken ill again after Keiser left, and when she recovered she was more religious than ever, but now her religion began to take a bitter turn. She read mostly the Old Testament, and that's bad reading for anyone who's full of hate; there's too much revenge and murder in it. She became an active worker in all the leagues and associations for the enforcement of Sunday observance laws and prohibition and such – or, at least, she contributed to them every cent she could get from her father or save out of the money he gave her for household expenses. I find that she made herself conspicuous by her opposition to the war and by her refusal to help the Red Cross or the Liberty Loans or anything of the sort. That's significant."

"Of what?" Westingate asked.

"War," Duff replied, "is murder."

Miss Marshall dropped her eyes, and she did not raise them again. She continued looking at the floor, without a word, her head up obstinately, grasping the arms of her chair.

"Her father quarreled with her about her attitude to the war. He quarreled with her about scrimping on the household expenses so as to give money to the societies in which she was so active. He stopped her allowance, and allowed her to purchase only on charge accounts, paying the monthly bills by check, himself. That was a serious matter for her. She was a proud young woman, silent, repellent in her manner, with none of the magnetism that makes friends. Her ability to contribute money to the causes in which she was interested – that brought people to her, made her important, won her praise. Without that power, she was cut off from everybody. She knew it. She shut herself up in the house. She gave up all her committees, her meetings, her outside work. Then in desperation, she attempted to jockey her accounts, and he found it out. And he wrote her that letter in which he announced that he was putting in a housekeeper who was to have charge of all her expenditures. Did you know that she had to have even her personal accounts – for clothes and books – endorsed by Mrs. Starrett?"

Miss Marshall did not answer. She did not look up.

"This long struggle between her and her father was carried on, you understand, in silence. She never spoke to anyone about it. She never remonstrated with him. She set her will against his, obstinately, and never bent to him once. He had deprived her of her lover, of her friends, of her station in life, of everything that a human being – Well, there you are. She began to have these long periods of illness, headaches, attacks of nervous exhaustion. She kept herself shut up in her room, with her thoughts. She expressed them, as far as I've been able to learn, to no one. The servants report of her exactly what you report, Miss Marshall – that she was a saint."

Miss Marshall raised her hand from the chair arm and dropped it despairingly. "I had no idea," she said, "and my brother could have had no idea. I merely thought her – a peculiar girl. She never told me –"

"Quite so. She never told anyone. And I have no means of knowing what her relations with Mrs. Starrett were, or whether she suspected that there was anything going on between Mrs. Starrett and her father. I believe she did. I believe that when she got hold of that letter to Mrs. Starrett, about their 'anniversary,' it only confirmed a suspicion that needed no confirmation."

"You mean," Westingate asked, "that this note is from Senator Marshall to Mrs. Starrett?"

"Yes. Senator Marshall wrote it on a typewriter himself and left it unsigned, in case it went astray. He addressed the envelope himself on a typewriter, but he made a mistake, absent-mindedly, in the address. He addressed it to 'Mrs. Agnes Starrett, Brook Farm, New York City.' He didn't notice the mistake until he was about to drop the envelope in a mail box, I presume. It was evidently then too late to type another envelope. He struck out the 'New York City' with lead pencil and wrote in 'Cold Brook, N.J.' as you see." Duff had taken an envelope from his pocket and passed it to Westingate. "That's Senator Marshall's handwriting. The note was still in its envelope when I found it concealed in the back cover of the book."

The lawyer offered the envelope to Miss Marshall. She shook her head without looking at it, her eyes averted.

Duff rose from his chair and began to pace slowly up and down the room, as if he were dictating a report. "The postmark on that envelope shows that it probably arrived at Senator Marshall's home some thirty-six hours before the murder. I judge that the girl intercepted it. She recognized her father's writing in lead pencil and read the note. The fact that it was typewritten and unsigned was sufficient indication that it was a guilty note of assignation. She hid it in the back of the book in which she kept her case against her father, and then she went to bed, ostensibly ill with the grippe, and remained there brooding, in a state of mind that you can imagine. Her father returned on the following forenoon, and found her, as usual, ill in her room. She had been pleading illness, whenever he was in the house, to avoid seeing him. So far, there was nothing unusual.

"But now the circumstance occurred that brought the deadly flash. She complained of being cold. She was probably shaking with a chill of hate and despair. And Pittling was ordered to build a fire in her bedroom fireplace. He brought up a basket of kindling, and in it, I believe, he brought the hatchet that he'd used to split the kindling. It's my theory that he put the hatchet aside as he took the kindling out of the basket and he forgot the hatchet when he returned with the basket to the basement.

"Have you seen that hatchet? It's a real woodsman's broad 'razor-blade' of forged steel. I believe that the girl saw it, standing against the fender, after her fire was lit, when she turned in her bed to stare at the blaze. And I believe that when the housemaid came back into her room, she had concealed the hatchet between the mattresses of the bed on which she was pretending to be sleeping in a weak exhaustion."

Westingate asked, in a shaken whisper, "Did Pittling tell you –"

"No," Duff said. "Pittling won't admit that the hatchet was ever in the girl's room. All he'll admit is the business about the pump. It wakened him, in the middle of the night, and he heard it working slowly, with long intervals between the strokes, as if some one were drawing water in a very small flow. But that flow continued for a long time – for so long that he thought some one must have risen to get a drink and left a faucet running. Then it stopped. The faucet had been turned off. I believe that this water was used by the murderer to wash in. And I'm sure that Pittling suspects it. In the morning when the hatchet was found, outside the open window, he was sure that some one in the house had committed the murder, and this secret suspicion gave him the guilty manner that led the police to arrest him. I don't believe that he suspects the daughter. He doesn't know what to think, so he keeps his mouth shut, and pretends that he doesn't remember whether or not he carried the hatchet upstairs. Or perhaps he doesn't really remember now. He's in a bad state mentally.

"I have no evidence of how the murders actually occurred. I believe that the girl intended to lie in wait for Mrs. Starrett and her father and confront them together and threaten them with exposure and disgrace, unless her father gave in to her and discharged Mrs. Starrett and ceased to tyrannize over her. She probably seized on the hatchet as a weapon of defense, or perhaps she intended to threaten them with it. While she was waiting to waylay them, she heard Mrs. Starrett tiptoeing past her door, and she darted out, under an ungovernable impulse of rage and hatred, and struck the woman from behind. I don't believe she knew the blow was fatal, but her murderous frenzy was now beyond her control She rushed into her father –"

Miss Marshall suddenly reached forward to the table and caught up the Roosevelt book. "It's impossible," she said, harshly. "Impossible! I don't believe a word of it. I'll never believe it. Never."

"Quite so," Duff said. "However, you'd better burn that book."

"Burn it," she defied him. "You may be sure I'll burn it."

He turned to Westingate. "There's nothing here for the prosecution to base a case on – even if they knew about it. And they'll never find out anything from her. When my nurse first asked her about her cat, she seemed really to have forgotten about it. I believe she'll forget all this in the same way. She'll

THE MARSHALL MURDER 203

probably behave about it as if she had a double personality. She'll become, perhaps, even more fanatically religious than she's been in the past. She'll be more proud and inaccessible than ever, with this secret buried in the back of her mind, but she'll bury it, and she'll keep her thoughts away from its grave. She's a very tough-minded young woman, with a Napoleonic ego, and she may break down physically, and become an invalid, but I don't believe she'll ever break down mentally, and though she may be peculiar, I don't believe she'll go insane."

Westingate asked: "Do your detectives –? Does your nurse –?"

"No," Duff assured him. "The nurse may suspect, but she knows nothing."

Miss Marshall rose, to end the interview. "I don't believe a word of it."

"Good," Duff congratulated her. "Then nobody else will. As a matter of fact, so many people kill their parents, in one way or another, that there's a natural resistance to believing a girl like this guilty. If wishes could have killed *your* father, for instance, Miss Marshall –"

"Stop!" She confronted him, in a sort of frightened rage, her head held high but trembling. "You're a fiend!"

Duff bowed, ponderously. "I'm a detective."

She turned and unlocked the door and flung it open. "You're a monster. I'll not hear another word against my niece."

"No," Duff agreed. "You probably never will."

And as far as anyone knows she never did. She heard nothing, certainly, from Duff, who closed the case then and there – nor from his nurse who left her charge next morning and never mentioned her again – nor from Pittling who was released from custody a few weeks later and went back to his home in Ohio, discreetly silent. By that time, Miss Marshall had taken her invalid niece to the south of France, and though she herself returned to Cold Brook at various times to attend to selling Senator Marshall's property and storing his goods, her niece has never come back. It is understood that she has joined some sort of lay sisterhood and devoted her fortune to works of piety. And the Marshall murder remains still a mystery.

BIBLIOGRAPHY - HARVEY J. O'HIGGINS

Criminous works

The adventures of detective Barney. New York: Century, 1915.
Detective Duff unravels it. New York: Liveright, 1929.
With Harriet Ford. *The dummy.* New York: French, 1925. play.

Other works

Clara Barron. New York: Harper, 1922.
Don-a-dreams; a story of love and youth. New York: Century, 1906. The author's first novel,
    it is an autobiographical story about student life at the University of Toronto.
From the life; imaginary portraits of some distinguished Americans. New York: Harper,
    1919/London: Harper/Toronto: Hodder & Stoughton – as: *Some distinguished
    Americans; imaginary portraits,* 1922. biography.
A grand army man. New York: Century, 1908.
His mother. Toronto: Press Agency, 1909.
Julie Cane. New York: Harper/Toronto: Musson, 1924. novel.
Old clinkers; a story of the New York Fire Department. Boston: Small Maynard, 1909.
The secret springs. New York: Harper, 1920.
Silent Sam; and other stories of our day. New York: Century, 1914.
The smoke-eaters; the story of a fire crew. New York: Century, 1905.
With F.J. Cannon. *Under the prophet in Utah.* New York, 1911.
With Harriet Ford. *On the firing line.* New York, 1909. play.
With Harriet Ford. *Polygamy.* 1914.
With Harriet Ford. *Main Street.* 1921. play.
With B.B. Lindsey. *The beast and the jungle.* 1910. A study of city-bred youth, controversial
    at the time.
With B.B. Lindsey. *The doughboy's religion.* New York, 1920.
With E.H. Reade. *The American mind in action.* New York, 1924.

FRANK L. PACKARD

Shanley's Luck
and
The Builder
On the iron at Big Cloud. New York: Crowell, 1911.

PACKARD, Frank L(ucius), 1877-1942

Frank Lucius Packard was born in Montreal, Quebec, on February 2, 1877, to Lucius Henry Packard and Frances (Joslin) Packard, both American émigrés. Packard grew up in Montreal and studied at McGill University, where he took his B.Sc. in Engineering in 1897. He undertook post-graduate work at the L'Institut Montefiore, Université de Liège, in Belgium, then practised as a civil engineer in the United States and in the Canadian Pacific Railroads Workshops.

In 1910, he married Marguerite Pearl Macintyre, a Canadian. They settled in Lachine, Quebec, on the north shore of the St. Lawrence River west of Montreal. Here they brought up their three sons and one daughter; here he began his prolific writing career as, in his day, a highly popular novelist; and here he lived until his death in 1942 on February 17th.

Packard's early work was about railroads, now a forgotten genre, but he is best remembered, if remembered at all, for his criminous novels, which he began in 1917 with *The adventures of Jimmie Dale*. Jimmie Dale, featured in five novels, was the forerunner of those masked avengers, The Shadow and The Spider, and one of those engaging gentleman-crooks on the side of justice who have illuminated crime fiction since the days of Maurice LeBlanc's Arsène Lupin.

The *Canadian Bookman* noted, "Packard is not only Canada's greatest crime-story writer but he is one of the most successful authors of this kind of fiction in the English-speaking world. His Jimmie Dale series of novels have had, deservedly, an immense vogue." *

"Over a period of twenty-five years, [Packard] wrote many novels. The detective thriller was his chosen field and in it he won an enviable reputation. Possessed of the logical mind and scientific training which are the necessary equipment of the mystery writer, Mr. Packard was a specialist in adding the bizarre touch to give his work an extra fillip of fascination for the reader. His most successful stories star 'Jimmie Dale', the wealthy play-boy detective. With the aid of his beautiful helper he solves crimes with easy skill and adds his name to the list of immortal sleuths." **

---

* *Canadian Bookman*, vol. 14: no. 1, (January 1932), p.11.
** Clara Thomas. *Canadian novelists, 1920-1945*. Toronto: Longmans, Green, 1946.

SHANLEY'S LUCK and THE BUILDER
On the iron at Big Cloud. New York: Crowell, 1911.

Despite the accolades for Packard's detective fiction, we have decided to pass on Jimmie Dale and present an example of Packard's railroad fiction, partially because it is set in Canada during the construction of the transcontinental line, and partially because of the importance the railroads have to Canada. We also have a fondness for this now forgotten sub-genre and feel that it should be honoured with an example.

Railroad fiction was a field in which Packard excelled, according to the Toronto *Daily Star* in 1919: "There are few authors nowadays who can make us realize with such vividness as Mr. Packard does how sentient, how living and responsible a thing a railroad is."

Readers should not make the mistake of thinking that the events in the second of the two linked stories are exaggerated. The story is based on an actual riot in March 1885, at Beavermouth, British Columbia, on the west bank of the Columbia River, when hundreds of strikers armed with revolvers terrorized the work gangs and put a halt to construction of the CPR.

The day was saved by the action of Sam Steele, the Mounted Police Inspector in charge, "Mr. Mountie" himself, the embodiment of the stalwart red-coat mythologized in popular culture. Sam Steele's life from trooper to Commissioner of the Mounted Police, commanding officer of Lord Strathcona's Horse in the Boer War, the man who almost singlehandedly policed the Yukon during the Klondike Gold Rush and provided law and order during the construction of the CPR through the Rockies, is one long boys' adventure novel. His autobiography, *Forty years in Canada; reminiscences of the Great North-West, with some account of his services in South Africa,* is the best known memoir of service with the Force.* And it's all true!

From Frank Packard, two haunting tales of building the National Dream and of accidental and deliberate heroism ...

---

* Sir Samuel Benfield Steele. *Forty years in Canada; reminiscences of the Great North-West, with some account of his services in South Africa.* Toronto: McClelland, Goodchild & Stewart/London: Herbert Jenkins, 1915.

SHANLEY'S LUCK

Generally speaking, Carleton, the super, was a pretty good judge of human nature, and he wasn't in the habit of making many breaks when it came to sizing up a man – not many. He did sometimes, but not often. However –

Shanley came out from the East, third class, colonist coach, billed through to Bubble Creek, B.C. Not that Shanley had any relatives or friends, there, nor, for that matter, any particular reason for wanting to go there – it was simply a question of how far his money would go in yards of pink-colored paper, about two and one-half inches wide, stamped, printed, countersigned, and signed again to obviate any possible misunderstanding that might arise touching the company's liability for baggage, the act of God, dangers foreseen and unforeseen, personal effects or resultant personal defects whether due to negligence or not – it was all one. The colonist ticket was a bill of lading, and the "goods" went through "O.R.," owner's risk.

This possibly may not be strictly legal, but it is strictly safe – for the company. Furthermore, the directors didn't have to sit up very late at night to figure out that if they got the colonists' money first there would be none left for legal advice in case of eventualities, and that's the way it was with about nine hundred and ninety-nine out of every thousand colonists. The company, of course, did take *some* risk – they took a chance on the one-thousandth man. The company had sporting blood.

If Shanley had only known what was going to happen, he could have saved some of his money on that ticket. As it stands now, he has still got transportation coming to him from Little Dance on the Hill Division to Bubble Creek, B.C. That may be an asset, or it may not – Shanley never asked for it.

Third class, colonist, no stop over allowed, red-haired, freckle-faced, an uptilt to the nose, a jaw as square as the side of a house, shoulders like a bull's, and a fist that would fell an ox – that was Shanley. That was Shanley until the sprung rail that ditched the train at Little Dance caused him the loss of two things – his erstwhile status in the general passenger agent's department, and a well-beloved and reeking brier.

Both were lost forever – his status partly on account of the reasons before mentioned, and partly because Shanley wasn't particularly interested in Bubble Creek; his brier because it became a part, an integral part, of that memorable wreck, as Shanley, who was peacefully smoking in the front-end compartment of the colonist coach when the trouble happened, left the pipe behind while he catapulted through the open door – it was summer and sizzling hot – and landed, a very much dazed, bewildered, but not otherwise hurt Shanley, halfway up the embankment on the off side of a scene of most amazing disorder.

The potentialities that lie in a sprung rail are something to marvel at. Up ahead, the engine had promptly turned turtle, and, as promptly giving vent to its displeasure at the indignity heaped upon it, had incased itself in an angry, hissing cloud of steam; behind, the baggage and mail cars seemed to have vied with each other in affectionate regard for the tender. Only the brass-polished, nickel-plated Pullmans at the rear still held the rails; the rest was just a crazy, slewed-edgeways, up-canted, toppled-over string of cars, already beginning to smoke as the flames licked into them.

The shouts of those who had made their escape, the screams of those still imprisoned within the wreckage, the sight of others crawling through the doors and windows brought Shanley back to his senses. He rose to his feet, blinked furiously, as was his habit on all untoward occasions, and the next instant he was down the embankment and into the game – to begin his career as a rail-road man. That's where he started – in the wreck at Little Dance.

In and out of the blazing pyre, after a woman or a child; the crash of his ax through splintering woodwork; the scorching heat; prying away some poor devil wedged down beneath the débris; tinkling glass as the heat cracked the windows or he beat through a pane with his fist – it was all hazy, all a dream to Shanley as, hours afterward, a grim, gaunt figure with blackened face, his clothes hanging in ribbons, he rode into the Big Cloud yards on the derrick car.

Some men would have hit up the claim agent for a stake; Shanley hit up Carleton for a job. But for modesty's sake, previous to presenting himself before the superintendent's desk, he borrowed from one of the wrecking crew the only available article of wearing apparel at hand – a very dirty and disreputable pair of overalls. Dirty and disreputable, but – whole.

"I want a job, Mr. Carleton," said he bluntly, when he had gained admittance to the super.

"You do, eh?" replied Carleton, looking him up and down. "You do, eh? You're a pretty hard-looking nut, h'm?"

Shanley blinked, but, being painfully aware that he undoubtedly did look all if not more than that, and being, too, not quite sure what to make of the super, he contented himself with the remark:

"I ain't a picture, I suppose."

"H'm!" said Carleton. "Been up at the wreck, I hear – what?"

"Yes," said Shanley shortly. No long story, no tale of what he'd done, no anything – just "Yes," and that was what caught Carleton.

"What can you do?" demanded the super.

"Anything. I'm not fussy," replied Shanley.

"H'm!" said Carleton. "You don't look it." And he favored Shanley with another prolonged stare.

Shanley, at first uncomfortable, shifted nervously from one foot to the other; then, as the stare continued, he began to get irritated.

"Look here," he flung out suddenly. "I ain't on exhibition. I come for a job. I ain't got any letters of recommendation from pastors of churches in the East. I ain't got anything. My name's Shanley, an' I haven't even got anything to prove *that*."

"You've got your nerve," said Carleton, leaning back in his swivel chair and tucking a thumb in the armnhole of his vest. "Ever worked on a railroad?"

"No," answered Shanley, a little less assertively, as he saw his chances of a job vanishing into thin air, and already regretting his hasty speech – a few odd nickels wasn't a very big stake for a man starting out in a new country, and that represented the sum total of Shanley's worldly wealth. "No, I never worked on a railroad."

"H'm," continued Carleton. "Well, my friend, you can report to the train-master in the morning and tell him I said to put you on breaking. Get out!"

It came so suddenly and unexpectedly that it took Shanley's breath. Carleton's ways were not Shanley's ways, or ways that Shanley by any peradventure had been accustomed to. A moment before he wouldn't have exchanged one of his nickels for his chances of a job, therefore his reply resolved itself into a sheepish grin; moreover – but of this hereafter – Shanley back East was decidedly more in the habit of having his applications refused with scant ceremony than he was to receiving favorable consideration, which was another reason for his failure to rise to the occasion with appropriate words of thanks.

Incidentally, Shanley, like a select few of his fellow creatures, had his failings; concretely, his particular strayings from the straight and narrow way, not having been hidden under a bushel, were responsible, with the advice and assistance of a distant relative or two – advice being always cheap, and assistance, in this case, a marked-down bargain – for his migration to the West, as far West as the funds in hand would take him – Bubble Creek, B.C., the distant relatives saw to that. They bought the ticket.

Shanley, still smiling sheepishly and in obedience to the super's instruction to "get out," was halfway to the door when Carleton halted him.

"Shanley!"

"Yes, sir?" said Shanley, finding his voice and swinging around.

"Got any money?"

Shanley's hand mechanically dove through the overalls and rummaged in the pocket of his torn and ribboned trousers – the pocket had not been spared – the nickels, every last one of them, were gone. The look on his face evidently needed no more interpretation.

Carleton was holding out two bills – two tens.

"Cleaned out, eh? Well, I wouldn't blame any one if they asked you for your board bill in advance. Here, I guess you'll need this. You can pay it back later on. There's a fellow keeps a clothing store up the street that it wouldn't do you any harm to visit – h'm?"

With gratitude in his heart and the best of resolutions exuding from every pore – he was always long on resolutions – Shanley being embarrassed, and therefore awkward, made a somewhat ungraceful exit from the super's presence.

But neither gratitude nor resolutions, even of steel-plate, double-riveted variety, are of much avail against circumstances and conditions over which one has absolutely, undeniably, and emphatically no control. If Dinkelman's clothing emporium had occupied a site between the station and MacGuire's Blazing Star saloon, instead of the said Blazing Star saloon occupying that altogether inappropriate position itself, and if Spider Kelly, the conductor of the wrecked train, had not run into Shanley before he had fairly got ten yards from the super's office, things undoubtedly would have been very different. Shanley took that view of it afterward, and certainly he was justified. It is on record that he had no hand in the laying out of Big Cloud nor in the control of its real estate, rentals, or leases.

Railroad men are by no stretch of the imagination to be regarded as hero worshipers, but if a man does a decent thing they are not averse to telling him so. Shanley had done several very decent things at the wreck. Spider Kelly invited him into the Blazing Star.

Shanley demurred. "I've got to get some clothes," he explained.

"Get 'em afterward," said Kelly; "plenty of time. Come on; it's just suppertime, and there'll be a lot of the boys in there. They'll be glad to meet you. If you're hungry you'll find the best free layout on the division. There's nothing small about MacGuire."

Shanley hesitated, and, proverbially, was lost.

An intimate and particular description of the events of that night are on no account to be written. They would not have shocked, surprised, or astonished Shanley's distant relatives – but everybody is not a distant relative. Shanley remembered it in spots – only in spots. He fought and whipped Spider Kelly, who was a much bigger man than himself, and thereby cemented an undying friendship; he partook of the hospitality showered upon him and returned it with a lavish hand – as long as Carleton's twenty lasted; he made speeches, many of them, touching wrecks and the nature of wrecks and his own particular participation therein – which was seemly, since at the end, about three o'clock in the morning, he slid with some dignity under the table, and, with the fond belief that he was once more clutching an ax and doing heroic and noble service, wound his arms grimly, remorselessly, tenaciously, like an octopus, around the table leg – and slept.

MacGuire before bolting the front door studied the situation carefully, and left him there – for the sake of the table.

The sunlight next morning was not charitable to Shanley. Where yesterday he had borne the marks of one wreck, he now bore the marks of two – his own on top of the company's. Up the street Dinkelman's clothing emporium flaunted a canvas sign announcing unusual bargains in men's apparel. This seemed to Shanley an unkindly act that could be expressed in no better terms than "rubbing it in." He gazed at the sign with an aggrieved expression on his face, blinked furiously, and started, with a step that lacked something of assurance, for the railroad yards and the trainmaster's office.

He was by no means confident of the reception that awaited him. If there is one characteristic over and above any other that is common to human nature, it is the faculty, though that's rather an imposing word, of worrying like sin over something that *may* happen – but never does. Shanley might just as well have saved himself the mental worry anent the trainmaster's possible attitude. He did not report to the trainmaster that morning, never saw that gentleman until long, very long afterward. Instead, he reported to Carleton – at the latter's urgent solicitation in the shape of a grinning call-boy, who intercepted his march of progress toward the station.

"Hi, you, there, cherub face!" bawled the urchin politely. "The super wants you – on the hop!"

Shanley stopped short, and, resorting to his favorite habit, blinked.

"Carleton. Get it? Carleton," repeated the messenger, evidently by no means sure that he was thoroughly understood; and then, for a parting shot as he sailed gaily up the street: "Gee, but you're pretty!"

Carleton! Shanley had forgotten all about Carleton for the moment. His hand instinctively went into his pocket – and then he groaned. He remembered Carleton. But worst of all, he remembered Carleton's twenty.

There were two courses open to him. He could sneak out of town with all possible modesty and dispatch, or he could face the music. Not that Shanley debated the question – the occasion had never yet arisen when he hadn't faced the music – he simply experienced the temptation to "crawl," that was all.

"It looks to me," he ruminated ruefully, "as though I was up against it for fair. Just my luck, just my blasted luck, always the same kind of luck. that's what. 'Tain't my fault neither, is it? *I* ain't responsible for that darned wreck – if 'twasn't for that I wouldn't be here. An' Kelly, Spider he said his name was, if 'twasn't for him I wouldn't be here neither. What the blazes did *I* have to do with it? I always have to stand for the other cuss. That's me every time, I guess. An' that's logic."

It was. Neither was there any flaw in it as at first sight might appear, for the last test of logic is its power of conviction. Shanley, from being a man with some reasonable cause for qualms of conscience, became, in his own mind, one deeply sinned against, one injured and crushed down by the load of others he was forced to bear.

He explained this to Carleton while the thought of his burning wrongs was still at white heat, and before the super had a chance to get in a word. He began as he opened the office door, continued as he crossed the room, and finished as he stood before the super's desk.

The scowl that had settled on Carleton's face, as he looked up at the other's entrance, gradually gave way to a hint of humor lurking around the corners of his mouth, and he leaned back in his chair and listened with an exaggerated air of profound attention.

"Just so, just so," said he, when Shanley finally came to a breathless halt. "Now perhaps you will allow *me* to say a word. It may not have occurred to you that I sent for you in order that *I* might do the talking – h'm?"

This really seemed to require no answer, so Shanley made none.

"Yesterday," went on Carleton, "you came to me for a job, and I gave you one, didn't I?"

"Yes," admitted Shanley, licking his lips.

"Just so," said Carleton mildly. "I hired you then. I fire you now. Pretty quick work, what?"

"You're the doctor," said Shanley evenly enough. He had, for all his logic, expected no more nor less – he was too firm a believer in his own particular and exclusive brand of luck. "You're the doctor," he repeated. "There's a matter of twenty bucks – "

"I was coming to that," interrupted Carleton; "but I'm glad *you* mentioned it. I'll be honest enough to admit that I hardly expected you would. A man who acts as you've acted doesn't generally – h'm?"

"I told you 'twasn't my fault," said Shanley stubbornly.

Carleton reached for his pipe, and struck a match, surveying Shanley the while with a gaze that was half perplexed, half quizzical.

"You're a queer card," he remarked at last. "Why don't you cut out the booze?"

"'Twasn't my fault, I tell you," persisted Shanley.

"You're a pretty good hand with your fists, what?" said Carleton irrelevantly. "Kelly's no slouch himself."

Shanley blinked. It appeared that the super was as intimately posted on the events of the preceding evening as he was himself. The remark suggested an inspection of the fists in question. They were grimy and dirty, and most of the knuckles were barked; closed, they resembled a pair of miniature battering-rams.

"Pretty good," he admitted modestly.

"H'm! About that twenty. You intend to pay it back, don't you?"

"I'm not a thief, whatever else I am," snapped Shanley. "Of course, I'll pay it back. You needn't worry."

"When?" insisted Carleton coolly.

"When I get a job."

"I'll give you one," said Carleton – "Royal" Carleton the boys called him, the squarest man that ever held down a division. "I'll give you one where your fists will be kept out of mischief, and where you can't hit the high joints quite as hard as you did last night. But I want you to understand this, Shanley, and understand it good and plenty and once for all, it's your last chance. You made a fool of yourself last night, but you acted like a man yesterday – that's why you're getting a new deal. You're going up to Glacier Cañon with McCann on the construction work. You won't find it anyways luxurious, and maybe you'll like McCann and maybe you won't – he's been squealing for a white man to live with. You can help him boss Italians at one seventy-five a day, and you can go up on Twenty-nine this morning, that'll take care of your transportation. What do you say?"

Shanley couldn't say anything. He looked at the super and blinked; then he looked at his fists speculatively – and blinked.

Carleton was scribbling on a piece of paper.

"All right, h'm?" he said, looking up and handing over the paper. "There's an order on Dinkelman, only get some one else to show you the way this time, and take the other side of the street going up. Understand?"

"Mr. Carleton," Shanley blurted out, "if ever I get full again, you –"

"I will!" said Carleton grimly. "I'll fire you so hard and fast you'll be out of breath for a month. Don't make any mistake about that. No man gets more than two chances with me. The next time you get drunk will finish your railroad career for keeps, I promise you that."

"Yes," said Shanley humbly; and then, after a moment's nervous hesitation: "About Kelly, Mr. Carleton. I don't want to get him in bad on this. You see, it was this way. He left early – that's what started the fight. I called him a – a – quitter – or something like that."

"H'm, yes; or something like that," repeated Carleton dryly. "So I believe. I've had a talk with Kelly. You needn't let the incomprehensible workings of that conscience of yours prick you any on his account. Kelly knows when to stop. His record is O.K. in this office. Kelly doesn't get drunk. If he did, he'd be fired just as fast as you will be if it ever happens again."

"If I'm never fired for anything but that," exclaimed Shanley in a burst of fervent emotion, "I've got a job for life. I'll prove it to you, Mr. Carleton. I'm going to make good. You see if I don't."

"Very well," said Carleton. "I hope you will. That's all, Shanley. I'll let McCann know you're coming."

Shanley's second exit from the super's presence was different from the first. He walked out with a firm tread and squared shoulders. He was rejuvenated and buoyant. He was on his mettle – quite another matter, entirely another matter, and distinctly apart from the paltry consideration of a mere job. He had told Carleton that he would make good. Well, he would – and he did. Carleton himself said so, and Carleton wasn't in the habit of making many breaks when it came to sizing up a man – not many. He did sometimes, but not often.

Shanley did not take the other side of the street on the way to Dinkelman's – by no means. He deliberately passed as close to the Blazing Star saloon as he could, passed with contemptuous disregard, passed boastfully in the knowledge of his own strength. A sixteen-hundred class engine with her four pairs of forty-six-inch drivers can pull countless cars up a mountain grade steep enough to make one dizzy, but Shanley would have backed himself to win against her in a tug of war over the scant few inches that separated him from MacGuire's dispensary as he brushed by. None of MacGuire's for him. Not at all. Red-headed, freckle-faced, barked-knuckled, bulwarked-and-armor-cased-against-temptation Shanley dealt that morning with Mr. Dinkelman, purveyor of bargains in men's apparel.

The dealings were liberal – on the part of both men. On Shanley's part because he needed much; on Mr. Dinkelman's part because it was Mr. Dinkelman's business, and his nature, to sell much – if he could – safely. This was eminently safe. Carleton's name in the mountains stood higher than guaranteed, gilt-edged gold bonds any time.

The business finally concluded, Shanley boarded Twenty-nine, local freight, west, and in due time, well on in the afternoon, righteously sober, straight as a string, cleaned, groomed, and resplendent in a new suit, swung off from the caboose at Glacier Cañon as the train considerably slackened speed enough to give him a fighting chance for life and limb.

He landed safely, however, in the midst of a jabbering Italian labor gang, who received his sudden advent with patience and some awe. A short, squint-faced man greeted him with a grin.

"Me name's McCann," said he of the squint face. "This is Glacier Cañon, fwhat yez see av ut. Them's the Eyetalians. Yon's fwhere I roost an' by the same token, fwhere yez'll roost, too, from now on. Above is the shack av the men. Are yez plased wid yer introduction? 'Tis wan hell av a hole ye've come to. Shanley's the name, eh? A good wan, an' I'm proud to make the acquaintance."

Shanley blinked as he stretched out his hand and made friends with his superior, and blinked again as he looked first one way and then another in an effort to follow and absorb the other's graphic description of the surroundings.

The road foreman's summary was beyond dispute. Glacier Cañon was as wild a piece of track as the Hill Division boasted, which was going some. The right of way hugged the bald gray rock of the mountains that rose up at one side in a sheer sweep, and the trains crawled along for all the world like huge flies at the base of a wall. On the other side was the Glacier River with its treacherous sandy bed that had been the subject of more reports and engineer's gray hairs than all the rest of the system put together. The construction camp lay just to the east of the Cañon, and at the foot of a long, stiff, two-mile, four-per-cent grade. That was the reason the camp was there – that grade.

Locking the stable door when the horse is gone is a procedure that is very old. It did not originate with the directors of the Transcontinental – they never claimed it did. But their fixed policy, if properly presented before a court of arbitration, would have gone a long way toward establishing a clear title to it. If they had built a switchback at the foot of the grade in the first place, Extra Number Eighty-three, when she lost control of herself near the bottom coming down, would have demonstrated just as clearly the necessity for one being there as she demonstrated most forcibly what would happen when there wasn't. All of which is by way of saying that rock or no rock, expense or no expense, the door was now to be locked, and McCann and his men were there to lock it.

McCann explained this to Shanley as he walked him around, up the track to the men's shanties, over the work, and back again down the track to inspect the interior of the dwelling they were to share in common – a relic of deceased Extra Number Eighty-three in the shape of a truckless box-car with dinted and bulging sides – dinted one side and bulged the other, that is.

"But," said Shanley, "I dunno what a switchback is."

"Who expected it av ye?" inquired McCann. "An' fwhat difference does ut make? Carleton sint word ye were green. Ye've no need to know. So's ye can do as yez are told an' make them geesers do as they are told, *an'* can play forty-foive at night – that's the point, the main point wid me, an' it's me yez av to get along wid – 'twill be all right. Since Meegan, him that was helpin' me, tuk sick a week back, I've been alone. Begad, playin' solytare is – "

"I can play forty-five," said Shanley.

McCann's face brightened.

"The powers be praised!" he exclaimed. "I'll enlighten ye, then, on the matter av switchbacks, me son, so as ye'll have an intilligent conception av the work. A switchback is a bit av a spur track that sticks out loike the quills av a porkypine at intervuls on a bad grade such as the wan forninst ye. 'Tis run off the main line, d'ye mind, an' up contrariwise to the dip av the grade. Whin a train comin' down gets beyond control an' so expresses herself by means av her whistle, she's switched off an' given a chance to run uphill by way av variety until she stops. An' the same holds true if she breaks loose goin' up. Is ut clear?"

"It is," said Shanley. "When do I begin work?"

"In the mornin.' 'Tis near six now, an' the bhoys'll be quittin' for the night. Forty-foive is a grand game. We'll play ut to-night to our better acquaintance. I contind 'tis the national game av the ould sod."

Whether McCann's contention is borne out by fact, or by the even more weighty consideration of public opinion, is of little importance. Shanley played forty-five with McCann that night and for many nights thereafter. He lost a figure or two off the pay check that was to come, but he won the golden opinion of the little road boss, which ethically, and in this case practically, was of far greater value.

"He's a bright jool av a lad," wrote McCann across the foot of a weekly report.

And Carleton, seeing it, was much gratified, for Carleton wasn't in the habit of making many breaks when it came to sizing up a man – not many. He did sometimes, but not often. Shanley was making good. Carleton was much gratified.

Of the three weeks that followed Shanley's advent to Glacier Cañon, this story has little to do in a detailed way; but, as a whole, those three weeks are pointed, eloquent, and important – very important.

Italian laborers have many failings, but likewise they have many virtues. They are simple, demonstrative, and their capacity for adoration – of both men and things – is very great.

From Jacko, the water boy, to Pietro Maraschino, the padrone, they adored Shanley, and enthroned him as an idol in their hearts, for the very simple reason that Shanley, not being a professional slave-driver by trade, established new and heretofore undreamed-of relations with them. Shanley was very green, very ignorant, very inexperienced – he treated them like human beings. That was the long and short of it. Shanley became popular beyond the popularity of any man, before or since, who was ever called upon to handle the "foreign element" on the Hill Division.

And the work progressed. Day by day the cut bored deeper into the stubborn mountain-side; day by day the Glacier River gurgled peacefully along over its treacherous sandy bed, one of the prettiest scenic effects on the system, so pretty that the company used it in the magazines; day by day regulars and extras, freights and passengers, east and west, snorted up and down the grade, the only visitations from the outside world; night after night Shanley played forty-five with McCann in the smoky, truckless box-car.

Also the camp was dry, very dry, dryer than a sanitarium – that is, than *some* sanitariums. Carleton had been quite right. There was no opportunity for Shanley to hit the high joints quite as hard as he had that night in Big Cloud – there was no opportunity for him to hit the high joints *at all.* Shanley had not seen a bottle for three weeks. Therefore Shanley felt virtuous, which was proper.

Some events follow others as the natural, logical outcome and conclusion of preceding ones; others, again, are apparently irrelevant, and the connection is not to be explained either by logic, conclusion, or otherwise. Rain, McCann's departure for Big Cloud, and Pietro Maraschino's birthday are an example of this.

When it settles down for a storm in the mountains, it is, if the elements are really in earnest, torrential, and prolonged, and has the effect of tying up construction work tighter than a supreme court injunction could come anywhere near doing it.

McCann had business in Big Cloud, whether personal or pertaining to the company is of no consequence, and the day the storm set in – the morning having demonstrated that its classification was not to be considered as transient – he seized the opportunity to flag the afternoon freight eastbound. This was natural and logical, and an opportunity not to be neglected.

That this day, however, should be the anniversary of the day the padrone's mother of blessed memory had given birth to Pietro Maraschino in sunny

Naples fifty-three years before is, though apparently irrelevant, far from being so; and since its peculiar and coincident happening cannot be laid at the door of either logical, natural, scientific, or philosophical conclusions, and since it demands an explanation of some sort, it must, perforce, be attributed to the metaphysical – which is a name given to all things about which nobody knows anything.

"Yez are in charge," said McCann grandiloquently, waving his hand to Shanley as he swung into the caboose. "Yez are in charge av the work, me son. See to ut. I trust ye." As the work at the moment was entirely at a standstill and bid fair to remain so until McCann's return on the morrow, this was very good of McCann. But all men like words of appreciation, most of them whether they deserve them or not, so Shanley went back into the box-car out of the rain to ponder over the tribute McCann had paid him, and to ponder, too, over the new responsibility that had fallen to his lot.

He did not ponder very long; indeed, the freight that was transporting McCann could hardly have been out of sight over the summit of the grade, when a knock at the door was followed by the entrance of the dripping figure of the padrone.

Shanley looked up anxiously.

"Hello, Pietro," he said nervously, for the weather wasn't the kind that would bring a man out for nothing, and he was keenly alive to that new responsibility. "Hello, Pietro," he repeated. "Anything wrong?"

Pietro grinned amiably, shook his head, unbuttoned his coat, and held out – a bottle.

Shanley stared in amazement, and then began to blink furiously.

"Here!" said he. "What's this?"

"Chianti," said Pietro, grinning harder than ever.

"Key-aunty." Shanley screwed up his face. "What the devil is key-aunty?"

"Ver' good wine from Italia," said the beaming padrone.

"It is, is it? Well, it's against the rules," asserted Shanley with conviction. "It's against the rules. McCann 'u'd skin you alive. He would. Where'd you get it? What's up, eh? It's against the rules. I'm in charge."

Pietro explained. It was his birthday. It was very bad weather. For the rest of the afternoon there would be no work. They would celebrate the birthday. Meester McCann had taken the train. As for the wine – Pietro shrugged his shoulders – his people adored wine. Unless they were very poor his people would have a little wine in their packs, perhaps. He was not quite sure where they had got it, but it was very thoughtful of them to remember his birthday. Each had presented him with a little wine. This bottle was an expression of their very great good estime of Meester Shanley. Perhaps, later, Meester Shanley would come himself to the shack.

"It's against the rules," blinked Shanley. "McCann 'u'd skin you alive. Maybe I'll drop in by and by. You can leave the bottle."

Pietro bobbed, grinned delightedly, handed over the bottle, and backed out into the storm.

Shanley, still blinking, placed the bottle on the table, and gazed at it thoughtfully for a few minutes – and his thoughts were of Carleton.

"If 'twere whisky," said he, "I'd have no part of it, not a drop, not even a smell. I would not. I would not touch it. But as it is – " Shanley uncorked the bottle.

Not at all. Once does *not* get drunk on a bottle of Chianti wine. A single bottle of Chianti wine is very little. That is the trouble – it is *very* little. After three weeks of abstinence it is very little indeed – so little that it is positively tantalizing.

The afternoon waned rapidly – and so did the Chianti. Outside, the storm instead of abating grew worse – the thunder racketing through the mountains, the lightning cutting jagged streaks in the black sky, the rain coming down in sheets that set the culverts and sluiceways running full. It was settling down for a bad night in the mountains, which, in the Rockies, is not a thing to be ignored.

"'Tis no wonder McCann found it lonely," muttered Shanley, as he squeezed the last drop from the bottle. "'Tis very lonely, indeed" – he held the bottle upside down to make sure that it was thoroughly drained – "Most uncommon lonely. It is that. Maybe those Eyetalians'll be thinkin' I'm stuck up, perhaps – which I am not. It's a queer name the stuff has, though it's against the rules, an' I can't get my tongue around it, but I've tasted worse. For the sake of courtesy I'll look in on the birthday party."

He incased himself in a pair of McCann's rubber boots, put on McCann's rubber coat, and started out.

"An' to think," said he, as he sloshed and buffeted his way up the two hundred yards of track to the construction shanties, "to think that Pietro came out in cruel bad weather like this all for to present his compliments an' ask me over! 'Twould be ungracious to refuse the invitation; besides my presence will keep them in due bounds an' restraint. I've heard that Eyetalians, being foreigners, do not practice restraint – but, being foreigners, 'tis not to be held against them. I'm in charge, an' I'll see to it."

They greeted him in the largest of the three bunkhouses. They greeted him heartily, sincerely, uproariously, and with fervor. They were unfeignedly glad to see him, and if he had not been by nature a modest man he would have understood that his popularity was above the popularity ever before accorded to a boss. Likewise, their hospitality was without stint. If there was any shortage of stock – which is a matter decidedly open to question – they denied themselves that Shanley might not feel the pinch. Shanley was lifted from the mere plane of man – he became a king.

A little Chianti is a little; much Chianti is to be reckoned with and on no account to be despised. Shanley not only became a king, he became regally, imperially, royally, and majestically drunk. Also there came at last an end to the Chianti, at which stage of the proceedings Shanley, with extravagant dignity and appropriate words – an exhortation on restraint – waddled to the door to take his departure.

It was very dark outside, very dark, except when an intermittent flash of lightning made momentary daylight. Pietro Maraschino offered Shanley one of the many lanterns that, in honor of the festive occasion, they had commandeered, without regard to color, from the tool boxes, and had strung around the shack. Further, he offered to see Shanley on his way.

The offer of assistance touched Shanley – it touched him wrong. It implied a more or less acute condition of disability, which he repudiated with a hurt expression on his face and forceful words on his tongue. He refused it; and being aggrieved, refused also the lantern Pietro held out to him. He chose one for himself instead – the one nearest to his hand. That this was red made no difference. Blue, white, red, green, or purple, it was all one to Shanley. His fuddled brain did not differentiate. A light was a light, that was all there was to that.

The short distance from the shanty door to the right of way Shanley negotiated with finesse and aplomb, and then he started down the track. This, however, was another matter.

Railroad ties, at best, do not make the smoothest walking in the world, and to accomplish the feat under some conditions is decidedly worthy of note. Shanley's performance beggars the English language – there is no metaphor. For every ten feet he moved forward he covered twenty in laterals, and, considering that the laterals were limited to the paltry four feet, eight and one-half inches that made the gauge of the rails, the feat was incontestably more than worthy of mere note – it was something to wonder at. He clung grimly to the lantern, with the result that the gyrations of that little red light in the darkness would have put to shame an expert's exhibition with a luminous dumb-bell. The while Shanley spoke earnestly to himself.

"Queshun is am I drunk – thash's the queshun. If I'm drunk – lose my job. Thash what Carleton said – lose my job. If I'm not drunk – s'all right. Wish I knew wesser I'm drunk or not."

He relapsed into silent communion and debate. This lasted for a very long period, during which, marvelous to relate, he had not only reached a point opposite his box-car domicile, but, being oblivious of that fact, had kept on along the track. Progress, however, was becoming more and more difficult. Shanley was assuming a position that might be likened somewhat to the letter C, owing to the fact that the force of gravity seemed to be exerting an undue influence on his head. Shanley was coming to earth.

As a result of his communion with himself he began to talk again, and his words suggested that he had suspicions of the truth.

"Jus' my luck," said he bitterly. "Jus' my luck. Allus same kind of luck.

What'd I have to do wis Peto Mara – Mars – Marscheeno's birthday? Nothing. Nothing 'tall. 'Twasn't my fault. Jus' my luck. Jus' my – "

Shanley came to earth. Also his head came into contact with the unyielding steel of the left-hand rail, and as a result he sprawled inertly full across the right of way, not ten yards west of where the Glacier River swings in to crowd the track close up against the mountain base.

Providence sometimes looks after those who are unable to look after themselves. By the law of probabilities the lantern should have met disaster quick and absolute; but instead, when it fell from Shanley's hand, it landed right side up just outside the rail between two ties, and, apart from a momentary and hesitant flicker incident to the jolt, burned on serenely. And it was still burning when, five minutes later, above the swish of leaping waters from the Glacier River, now a chattering, angry stream with swollen banks, above the moan of the wind and the roll of the thunder through the mountains, above the pelting splash of the steady rain, came the hoarse scream of Number One's whistle on the grade.

Sanderson, in the cab, caught the red against him on the right of way ahead, and whistled insistently for the track. This having no effect, he grunted, latched in the throttle, and applied the "air." The ray of the headlight crept along between the rails, hovered over a black object beside the lantern, passed on again and held, not on the glistening rain-wet rails – *they* had disappeared – but on a crumbling road-bed and a dark blotch of waters, as with a final screech from the grinding brake-shoes Number One came to a standstill.

"Holy MacCheesar!" exclaimed Sanderson, as he swung from the cab.

He made his way along past the drivers to where the pilot's nose was inquisitively poked against the lantern, picked up the lantern, and bent over Shanley.

"Holy MacCheesar!" he exclaimed again, straightening up after a moment's examination. "Holy MacCheesar!"

"What's wrong, Sandy?" snapped a voice behind him, the voice of Kelly, Spider Kelly, the conductor, who had hurried forward to investigate the unscheduled stop.

"Search me," replied Sanderson. "Looks like the Glacier was up to her old tricks. There's a washout ahead, and a bad one, I guess. But the meaning of this here is one beyond me. The fellow was curled up on the track just as you see him with the light burning alongside, that's what saved us, but he's as drunk as a lord."

As Kelly bent over the prostrate form, others of the train crew appeared on the scene. One glance he gave at Shanley's never-under-any-circumstances-to-be-forgotten homely countenance, and hastily ordered the men to go forward and investigate the washout ahead. Then he turned to the engineer.

"The man is not drunk, Sandy," said he.

"He is gloriously and magnificently drunk, Kelly," replied the engineer.

222 CRIME IN A COLD CLIMATE

"What would he be doing here, then? He is not drunk."

"Sleeping it off. He is disgracefully drunk."

"Can ye not see the bash on his head where he must have stumbled in the dark trying to save the train and struck against the rail? He is *not* drunk."

"Can ye not *smell?*" retorted Sanderson. "He is dead drunk!"

"I have fought with him and he licked me. He is a man and a friend of mine" – Kelly shoved his lantern into Sanderson's face. *"He is not drunk."*

"He is *not* drunk," said Sanderson. "He is a hero. What will we do with him?"

"We'll carry him, you and me, over to the construction shanty, it's only a few yards, and put him in his bunk. He works here, you know. McCann's in Big Cloud, for I saw him there. After that we'll run back to the Bend for orders and make our report."

"Hurry, then," said the engineer. "Take his legs. What are you laughing at?"

"I was thinking of Carleton," said Kelly.

"Carleton? What's Carleton got to do with it?"

"I'll tell you later when we get to the Bend. Come on."

"H'm," said Sanderson, as they staggered with their burden over to the box-car shack. "I've an idea that bash on the head is more dirt than hurt. He's making a speech, ain't he?"

"Jus' my luck," mumbled the reviving Shanley dolefully. "Jus' my luck. Allus same kind of luck."

"Possibly," said Kelly. "Set him down and slide back the door. That's right. In with him now. We haven't got time to make him very comfortable, but I guess he'll do. I can fix him up better at the Bend than I can here."

"At the Bend? What d'ye mean?" demanded Sanderson.

"You'll see," replied Kelly, with a grin. "You'll see."

And Sanderson saw. So did Carleton – in a way.

Kelly's report, when they got to the Bend, was a work of art. He disposed of the nature and extent of the washout in ten brief, well-chosen words, but the operator got a cramp before Kelly was through covering Shanley with glory. The passengers, packed in the little waiting-room clamoring for details, yelled deliriously as he read the message aloud – and promptly took up a collection, a very generous collection, because all collections are generous at psychological moments – that is to say, if not delayed too long to allow a recovery from hysteria.

At Big Cloud, the dispatcher, because the washout was a serious matter that not only threatened to tie up traffic, but *was* tying it up, sent a hurry call to Carleton's house that brought the super on the run to the office. By this time the collection had been counted, and the total wired in, as an additional detail – one hundred and forty dollars and thirty-three cents. The odd change being a contribution from a Swede in the colonist coach who could not speak English, and who paid because a man in uniform, a brakeman acting as canvasser, made the request. A Swede has a great respect for a uniform.

"H'm," said Carleton, when he had read it all. "I know a man when I see one. Tell Shanley to report here. I guess we can find something better for him to do than bossing laborers. What? Yes, send the letter up on the construction train. One hundred and forty, thirty-three, h'm? Tell him that, too. He'll feel good when he sees it in the morning."

But Shanley did not feel good when he saw it in the morning, for he was nursing a very bad headache and a stomach that had a tendency to squeamishness. The letter was lying on the floor, where some one had considerately chucked it in without disturbing him. His eyes fell on it as he struggled out of his bunk. He picked it up, opened it, read it – and blinked. His face set with a very blank and bewildered expression. He read it again, and again once more. Then he went to the door and looked out.

A construction train was on the line a little below him, and a gang of men, not his nor Pietro Maraschino's men, were busily at work. As he gazed, his face puckered. The problem that had so obsessed him on his return journey from the birthday celebration the night before was a problem no longer.

"I *was* drunk," said he, with conviction. "I *must* have been."

He went back to the letter and studied it again, scratching his head.

"Something," he muttered, "has happened. What it is, I dunno. I was drunk, an' I'm not fired. I was drunk, an' I'm promoted. I was drunk, an' I'm paid well for it, very well. I was drunk – an' I'll keep my mouth shut."

Which was exactly the advice Kelly took pains to give him half an hour later, when Number One crawled down to the Cañon and halted for a few minutes opposite the dismantled box-car, while the construction train put the last few touches to its work.

THE BUILDER

There are two sides to every story – which is a proverb so old that it is in the running with Father Time himself. It is repeated here because there must be *some* truth in it – anything that can stand the wear and tear of the ages, and the cynics, and the wise old philosophical owls without getting any knock-out dints punched in its vital spots must have some sort of merit fundamentally, what? Anyway, the company had their side, and the men's version differed – of course. Maybe each, in a way, was more or less right, and, equally, in a way, more or less wrong. Maybe, too, both sides lost their tempers and got their crown-sheets burned out before the arbitration pow-wow had a chance to get the line clear and give anybody rights, schedule or otherwise. However, be that as it may, whoever was right or whoever was wrong, one or the other, or both, it is the strike, not the ethics of it, that has to do with – but just a moment, we're over-running our holding orders.

From the time the last rail was spiked home and bridging the Rockies was a reality, not a dream – from then to the present day, there isn't any very much better way of describing the Hill Division than to call it rough and ready. Coming right down to cases, the history of that piece of track, the history of the men who gave the last that was in them to make it, and the history of those who have operated it since isn't far from being a pretty typical and comprehensive example of the pulsing, dominating, dogged, go-forward spirit of a continent whose strides and progress are the marvel of the world; and, withal, it is an example so compact and concrete that through it one may see and view the larger picture in all its angles and in all its shades. Heroism and fame and death and failure – it has known them all – but ever, and above all else, it has known the indomitable patience, the indomitable perseverance, the indomitable determination against which no times, nor conditions, nor manners, nor customs, nor obstacles can stand – the spirit of the New Race and the Great New Land, the essence and the germ of it.

Building a road through the Rockies and tapping the Sierras to give zest to the finish wasn't an infant's performance; and operating it, single-track, on crazy-wild cuts and fills and tangents and curves and tunnels and trestles with nature to battle and fight against, isn't any infant's performance, either. The Hill Division was rough and ready. It always was, and it is now – just naturally so. And Big Cloud, the divisional point, snuggling amongst the buttes in the eastern foothills, is ever more so. It boasts about every nationality classified in certain erudite editions of small books with big names, and, to top that, has an extra anomaly or two left over and up its sleeve for good measure; but, mostly, it is, or rather was – it has changed some with the years – composed of Indians, bad Americans, a scattering of Chinese, and an indescribable medley of humans from the four quarters of Europe, the Cockney, the Polack, the Swede, the Russian and the Italian – laborers on the construction gangs. Big Cloud was a little more than rough and ready – it wasn't exactly what you'd call a health resort for finicky nerves.

So, take it by and large, the Hill Division, from one end to the other, wasn't the quietest or most peaceful locality on the map even before the trouble came. After that – well, mention the Big Strike to any of the old-timers and they'll talk fast enough and hard enough and say enough in a minute to set you wondering if the biographers hadn't got mixed on dates and if Dante hadn't got his material for that little hair-stiffener of his no further away than the Rockies, and no longer back than a few years ago. But no matter —

The story opens on the strike – *not* the ethics of it. There's some hard feelings yet – too much of it to take sides one way or the other. But then, apart from that, this is not the story of a strike, it is the story of men – a story that the boys tell at night in the darkened roundhouses in the shadow of the big ten-wheelers on the pits, while the steam purrs softly at the gauges and sometimes a pop-valve lifts with a catchy sob. They tell it, too, across the tracks at headquarters, or on the road and in construction camps; but they tell it better, somehow, in the roundhouse, though it is not an engineer's tale – and Clarihue, the night turner, tells it best of all. Set forth as it is here it takes no rank with him – but all are not so fortunate as to have listened while Clarihue talked.

Just one word more to make sure that the red isn't against us anywhere and we'll get to Keating and Spirlaw – just a word to say that Carleton, "Royal" Carleton, was superintendent then, and Regan was master mechanic, Harvey was division engineer, Spence was chief dispatcher, and Riley was trainmaster. Pretty good men that little group, pretty good railroaders – there have never been better. Some of them are bigger now in the world's eyes, heads of systems instead of departments – and some of them will never railroad any more. However —

If you haven't forgotten Shanley you will recall the Glacier Cañon, and, most of all, you will recall the Glacier River with its treacherous sandy bed that snuggled close to the right of way and forced the track hard against the rocky walls of the mountain's base. The havoc the Glacier played with the operating department on the night of Shanley's memorable heroism was not the first time it had misbehaved itself, nor was it the last – that was the trouble. It washed out the road-bed with such consistent persistency, on so little provocation, and did it so effectually as to stir at last to resentment even the torpid blood of the directors down East. So they voted the sum, though it hurt, and solaced themselves with the thought that after all it was economy – which was true.

There was only one thing to do against that over-hospitable and affectionate little stream, and that was to get away from it; but, before proceeding to do so – in order to get elbow room to work so that the flyers and the fast mails and the traffic generally wouldn't be hung up every time a Polack swung a pick – they pushed the track out over the chattering river on a long, temporary, hybrid trestle of wood and steel. That done, the rest was up to Spirlaw – up to Spirlaw and Keating.

The plans called for the shaving down of the mountain-side, the barbering, mostly, to be done with dynamite, for the beard of the Rockies is not the down of a youth. So, when the trestle was finished, Spirlaw with a gang of some thirty Polacks moved into construction camp, promptly tore up the old track, and set themselves to the task in hand. A little later, Keating joined them.

Spirlaw was a road boss, and the roughest of his kind. Physically he was a giant; and which of the three was the hardest, his face, his fist, or his tongue, would afford the sporting element a most excellent opportunity to indulge in a little book-making with the odds about even all round. His hair was a coarse mop of tawny brown that straggled over his eyes; and his eyes were all black, every bit of them – there didn't seem to be any pupil at all, which gave them a glint that was harder than a cold chisel. Take him summed up, Spirlaw looked a pretty tough proposition, and in some ways, most ways perhaps, he was – he never denied it.

"What the blue blinding blazes, d'ye think, h'm?" he would remark, reaching into his hip pocket for his "chewing," as he swept the other arm comprehensively over the particular crowd of sweating foreigners that happened to be under his particular jurisdiction at the time. "What d'ye think! You can't run cuts an' fills with an outfit like this on soft soap an' candy sticks, can you? Well then – h'm?"

That last "h'm" was more or less conclusive – very few cared to pursue the argument any further. At a safe distance, the Big Fellows on the division, as a salve to their consciences when humanitarian ideas were in the ascendancy, would bombard Spirlaw with telegrams which were forceful in tone and direful in threat – but that's all it ever amounted to. Spirlaw's work report for a day on anything, from bridging a cañon to punching a hole in the bitter hard rock of the mountain-side, was a report that no one else on the division had ever approached, let alone duplicated – and figures count perhaps just a little bit more in the operating department of a railroad than they do anywhere else in the world. Spirlaw used the telegrams as spills to light a pipe as hard-looking as himself, whose bowl was down at the heels on one side from much scraping, and on such occasions it was more than ordinarily unfortunate for the sour-visaged Polack who should chance to arouse his ire.

Some men possess the love of a fight and their natures are tempestuous by virtue of their nationality, because some nationalities are addicted that way. This may have been the case with Spirlaw – or it may not. There's no saying, for Spirlaw's nationality was a question mark. He never delivered himself on the subject, and, certainly, there was no figuring it out from the derivation of his name – that could have been most anything, and could have come from most anywhere.

To say that "opposites attract" isn't any more original, any less gray-bearded, than the words at the head of these pages. Generally, that sort of thing is figured in the worn-out, stale, familiarity-breeds-contempt realm of platitude, and at its unctuous repetition one comes to turn up his nose; but, once in a while, life has a habit of getting in a kink or a twist that gives you a jolt and a different side-light, and then, somehow, a thing like that rings as fresh and virile as though you had just heard it for the first time. As far as any one ever knew, Keating was the only one that ever got inside of Spirlaw's shell, the only one that the road boss ever showed the slightest symptoms of caring a hang about – and yet, on the surface, between the two there was nothing in common. Where one was polished the other was rough; where one was weak the other was strong. Keating was small, thin, pale-faced, and he had a cough – a cough that had sent him West in a hurry without waiting for the other year that would have given him his engineer's diploma from the college in the East.

When the boy, he wasn't much more than a boy, dropped off at Big Cloud, and Carleton read the letter he brought from one of the big Eastern operators, the super raised his eyebrows a little, looked him over and sent him out to Spirlaw. Afterwards, he spoke to Regan about him.

"I didn't know what to do with him, Tommy; but I had to do something, what? Any one with half an eye could tell that he had to be kept out of doors. Thought he might be able to help Spirlaw out a little as assistant, h'm? Guess he'll pick up the work quick enough. He don't look strong."

"Mabbe it's just as well," grinned the master mechanic. "He won't be able to batter the gang any. One man doing that is enough – when it's Spirlaw."

Spirlaw heard about it before he saw Keating, and he swore fervently.

"What the hell!" he growled. "Think I'm runnin' a nursery or an outdoor sanitarium? I guess I've got enough to do without lookin' after sick kids, I guess I have. Fat lot of help he'll be – help my eye! I don't need no help."

But for all that, somehow, from the first minute when Keating got off the local freight, that stopped for him at the camp, and shoved out his hand to Spirlaw it was different – after that it was *all* Keating as far as the road boss was concerned.

Queer the way things go. Keating looked about the last man on earth you would expect to find rubbing elbows with an iron-fisted foreman whose tongue was rougher than a barbed-wire fence; the last man to hold his own with a slave-driven gang of ugly Polacks. He seemed too quiet, too shy, too utterly unfit, physically, for that sort of thing. The blood was all out of the boy – he got rid of it faster than he could make it. But his training stood him in good stead, and, within his limitations, he took hold like an old hand. That was what caught Spirlaw. He did what he was told, and he did what he could – did a little more than he could at times, which would lay him up for a bad two or three days of it.

"Good man," Spirlaw scribbled across the bottom of a report one day – a day that was about equally divided between barking his knuckles on a Polack's head and feeding cracked ice to Keating in his bunk. Cracked ice? No, it wasn't on the regular camp bill of fare – but the company supplied it for all that. Spirlaw, with supreme contempt for the dispatchers and their schedules and their trainsheets, held up Number Twelve and the porter of the Pullman for a goodly share of the commodity possessed by that colored gentleman. That's what Spirlaw thought of Keating.

For the first few weeks after he struck the camp Keating didn't have very much to say about himself, or anything else for that matter; but after he got a little nearer to Spirlaw and the mutual liking grew stronger, he began to open up at nights when he and the road boss sat outside the door of the construction shanty and watched the sun lose itself behind the mighty peaks, creep again with a wondrous golden-tinted glow between a rift in the range, and finally sink with ensuing twilight out of sight. Keating could talk then.

"Don't see what you ever took up engineerin' for," remarked Spirlaw one evening. "It's about the roughest kind of a life I know of, an' you –"

"I know, I know," Keating smiled. "You think I'm not strong enough for it. Why, another year out here in the West and I'll be like a horse."

"Sure, you will," agreed Spirlaw, hastily. "I didn't mean just that." Then he sucked his briar hard. Spirlaw wasn't much up on therapeutics, he knew more about blasting rock, but down in his heart there wasn't much doubt about another year in the West for the boy, and another and another, *all of them* – only they would be over the Great Divide that one only crosses once when it is crossed forever. Six months, four, three – just months, not years, was what he read in Keating's face. "What I meant," he amended, "was that you don't have to. From what you've said, I figur' your folks back there would be willin' to stake you in most any line you picked out, h'm?"

"No, I don't have to," Keating answered, and his face lighted up as he leaned over and touched the road boss on the sleeve. "But, Spirlaw, it's the greatest thing in all the world. Don't you see? A man does something. *He builds.* I'm going to be a builder – a builder of bridges and roads and things like that. I want to do something some day – something that will be worth while. That's why I'm going to be an engineer; because, all over the world from the beginning, the engineers have led the way and – and they've left something behind them. I think that's the biggest thing they can say of any man when he dies – that he was a builder, that he left something behind him. I'd like to have them say that about me. Well, after I put in another year out here – I'm a heap better even now than when I came – I'm going back to finish my course, and then – well, you understand what I want to do, don't you?"

There were lots of talks like that, evening after evening, and they all of them ended in the same way – Spirlaw would knock out his pipe against a stone or his boot heel, and "figur'" he'd stroll up the camp a bit an' make sure all was right for the night."

A pretty hard man Spirlaw was, but under the rough and the brutal, the horny, thick-shelled exterior was another self, a strange side of self that he had never known until he had known Keating. It got into him pretty deep and pretty hard, the boy and his ambitions; and the irony of it, grim and bitter, deepened his pity and roused, too, a sense of fierce, hot resentment against the fate that mocked in its pitiless might so defenseless and puny a victim. To himself he came to call Keating "The Builder," and one day when Harvey came down on an inspection trip, he told the division engineer about it – that's how it got around.

Carleton, when he heard it, didn't say anything – just crammed the dottle in his pipe down with his forefinger and stared out at the switches in the yards. They were used to seeing the surface of things plowed up and the corners turned back in the mountains, there weren't many days went by when something that showed the raw didn't happen in one way or another, but it never brought callousness or indifference, only, perhaps, a truer sense of values.

They had been blasting in the Cañon for a matter of two months when the first signs of trouble began to show themselves, and the beginning was when the shop hands at Big Cloud went out – the boiler-makers and the blacksmiths, the painters, the carpenters and the fitters. The construction camp, that is Spirlaw, didn't worry very much about this for the very simple reason that there didn't appear to be any reason why it, or he, should – that was Regan's hunt. But when the train crews followed suit and stray rumors of a fight or two at Big Cloud began to come in, with the likelihood of more hard on the heels of the first, it put a different complexion on things; for the rioting, what there had been of it, lay, not at the door of the railroad boys, but with the town's loafers and hangers-on, these and the foreign element – particularly the foreign element – the brothers and the cousins of the Polacks who were swinging the picks and the shovels under the iron hand of Spirlaw, their temporary lord and master – the Polacks, as pungently urgentle, when amuck, as starved pumas.

Then the Brotherhood said "quit," and the engine crews followed the trainmen. Things began to look black and headquarters began to find it pretty hard to move anything. The train schedule past the Cañon was cut better than in half, and the faces of the men in the cabs and the cabooses were new faces to those in camp – the faces of the men the company were bringing in on hurry calls from wherever they could get them, from the plains East or the coast West.

Every day brought reports of trouble from one end of the line to the other, more rioting, more disorder at Big Cloud; and, in an effort to nip as much of it in the bud as possible, Carleton issued orders to stop all construction work – all except the work in Glacier Cañon, for there the temporary trestle lay uneasy on his mind.

The day the stop orders went out elsewhere a letter went out to Spirlaw. Spirlaw read it and his face set like a thunder cloud. He handed it to Keating.

Keating read it – and looked serious.

"I guess things aren't any too rosy down there," he commented; then slowly: "I've noticed our men seemed a bit sullen lately. They don't care anything much about the strike, it must be a sort of sympathetic movement with the rest of their crowd that's running wild at Big Cloud – only I don't just figure how they can know very much about what's going on. We don't ourselves, for that matter."

Spirlaw smiled grimly.

"I'll tell you how," he said. "I caught a Polack in the camp last night that didn't belong here – and I broke his head for the second time, see? He used to work for me about a year ago – that's when I broke it the first time. He's one of their influential citizens – name's Kuryla. Sneaked in here to stir up trouble – guess he's sorry for it, I guess he is."

"That's the first I've heard of it," said Keating, his eyes opening a little wider in surprise.

"You was asleep," explained Spirlaw tersely.

Keating stared curiously at the road boss for a minute, then he glanced again at the super's letter which he still held in his hand.

"Carleton says he is depending on you to put this work through if it's a possible thing. You don't really think we'll have any serious trouble here though, do you?"

Spirlaw bit deeply into his plug before he answered.

"Yes, son; I do," he said at last. "And there's a good many reasons why we will, too. Once start 'em goin' an' there's no worse hellions on earth than the breed we're livin' next door to. Furthermore they don't *love* me – they're just afraid of me as, by the holy razoo, I mean 'em to be. Let 'em once get a smell of the upper hand an' it would be all day *an'* good-by. Let 'em get goin' good at Big Cloud an' they'll get goin' good here – they'll kind of figur' then that there ain't any law to bother 'em – an', unless I miss my guess, Big Cloud's in for the hottest celebration in its history, which will be goin' some for it's had a few before that weren't tame by a damn sight."

"Well," inquired Keating, "what do you intend to do?"

"H'm-m," drawled Spirlaw reflectively, and there was a speculative look in his eyes as they roved over his assistant. "That's what I've been chewin' over since I caught that skunk Kuryla last night. As far as I can figur' it the chance of trouble here depends on how far those cusses go at Big Cloud. If I knew that, I'd know what to expect, h'm? I thought I'd send you up to headquarters for a day. You could have a talk with the super, tell him just where we stand here, an' size things up there generally. What do you say?"

"Why, of course. All right, if you want me to," agreed Keating readily.

"That's the boy," said Spirlaw, heartily. "Number Twelve will be along in half an hour. I'll flag her, an' you can go an' get ready now. I'll give you a letter to take along to Carleton."

As Keating, with a nod of assent, turned briskly away, Spirlaw watched him out of sight – and the hint of a smile played over the lips of the road boss. He pulled a report sheet from his pocket, and on the back of it scrawled laboriously a letter to the superintendent of the Hill Division. It wasn't a very long letter even with the P.S. included. His smile hardened as he read it over.

"Supt., Big Cloud," it ran. "Dear Sir:– Replying to yours 8th inst., please send a couple of good .45s, and *plenty of stuffing*. ('Plenty of stuffing' was heavily underscored.) Yrs. Resp., H. Spirlaw. P.S. *Keep the boy up there out of this.*" (The P.S. was even more heavily underscored than the other.)

Wise and learned in the ways of men – and Polacks – was Spirlaw. Spirlaw was not dealing with the *possibility* of trouble – it was simply a question of how long it would be before it started. He folded the letter, sealed it in one of the company's manilas, and, as he watched Number Twelve disappear around the bend steaming east for Big Cloud with Keating aboard her and the epistle reposing in Keating's pocket, he stretched out his arms that were big as derrick booms and drew in a long breath like a man from whose shoulders has dropped a heavy load.

That day Spirlaw talked from his heart to the men, and they listened in sullen, stupid silence, leaning on their picks and shovels.

"You know me," he snapped, and his eyes starting at the right of the group rested for a bare second on each individual face as they swept down the line. "You know *me*. You've been actin' like sulky dogs lately – don't think I haven't spotted it. You saw what happened to that coyote friend of yours that sneaked in here last night. I meant it as a lesson for the bunch of you as well as him. The yarns he was fillin' you full of are mostly lies, an' if they ain't it's none of your business, anyhow. It won't pay you to look for trouble, I promise you that. You can take it from me that I'll bash the first man to powder that tries it. Get that? Well then, wiggle them picks a bit an' get busy!"

"The man that hits first," said Spirlaw to himself, as he walked away, "is the man that usually comes out on top. I guess them there few kind words of mine'll give 'em a little something to chew on till Carleton sends that hardware down, I guess they will, h'm?"

The camp was pretty quiet that night – quieter than usual. The cook-house and the three bunk-houses, that lay a few hundred yards east of the trestle, might have been occupied by dead men for all the sounds that came from them. Occasionally, Spirlaw, sitting out as usual in front of his own shanty, that was between the trestle and the gang's quarters, saw a Polack or two skulk from one of the bunk-houses to the other – and he scowled savagely as he divided his glances between them and the sky. It looked like a storm in the mountains, and a storm in the mountains is never by any possibility to be desired – least of all was it to be desired just then. The men at work was one thing; the men cooped up for a day, or two days, of enforced idleness with the temper they were in was another – Spirlaw turned in that night with the low, ominous roll of distant thunder for a lullaby.

Once in the night he woke suddenly at the sound of a splitting crash, and once, twice, and again, like a fierce, winking stream of flame, the lightning filled the shack bright as day, while on the roof the rain beat steadily like the tattoo of a corps of snare drums. Spirlaw smiled grimly as the darkness shut down on him again.

"Got the little builder out just about the right time, h'm?" he remarked to himself; and, turning over in his bunk, went to sleep again – but even in his sleep the grim smile lingered on his lips.

The morning broke with the steady downpour unabated. Everything ran water, and the rock cut was filled with it. Work was out of the question. Spirlaw ate his breakfast, that the dripping camp cook brought him, and then, putting on his rubber boots and coat, started over for the track. Number Eleven was due at the Cañon at seven-thirty, and she would have the package of "hardware" he had asked Carleton for.

But though seven-thirty came, Number Eleven did not – neither did any other train, east or west. The hours passed from a long morning to drag though a longer afternoon. Something was wrong somewhere – and badly wrong at that. Spirlaw's face was blacker than the storm. Twice, once in the morning and once in the afternoon, he started down the track in the direction of Keefer's Siding, which was just what its name proclaimed it to be – a siding, no more, no less, only there was an operator there. Each time, however, he changed his mind after getting no further than a few yards. The Polacks could be no less alive to the fact than himself that something out of the ordinary was in the air, and second considerations swung strongly to the advisability of sticking close to the camp, so that his presence might have the effect of dampening the ardor of any mischief that might be brewing.

It was not until well on toward eight o'clock in the evening and the last of the twilight that the hoarse screech of a whistle sounded down the cañon grade – a long blast and three short ones. It was belated Number Eleven whistling for the camp – she wouldn't stop, just slow down to transact her business. Spirlaw, who was in his shanty at the time, snatched up his hat, dashed out of the door, and headed for the bend of the track. As he did so, out of the tail of his eye, he caught sight of the Polacks clustered with out-poked heads from the open doors of the bunk-houses.

As he reached the line, Number Eleven came round the curve, and the door of the express car swung back. The messenger dropped a package into his hand that the road boss received with a grim smile, and a word into his ear that caused Spirlaw's jaw to drop – nor was that all that dropped, for, from the rear end, as the train rolled by – dropped Keating.

White-faced and shaky the boy looked – more so than usual. Spirlaw stared as though he had seen an apparition, stared for a minute in silence before he could lay tongue to words – then they came like the out-spout of a volcano.

"What the hell's the meanin' of this?" he roared. "Who in the double-blanked blazes let you out of Big Cloud, h'm? I'll have some –"

"Let's get in out of the wet," broke in Keating, smiling though a spell of coughing that racked him at that moment. "You can growl your head off then, if you like" – and he started on a run for the shack.

Once inside, Spirlaw rounded on the boy again, and he stopped only when he was out of breath.

"Didn't Carleton tell you to stay where you was?" he finished bitterly.

"Oh yes," said Keating, "that's about the first thing he *did* say after he had read your letter, when I gave it to him yesterday. Then I tumbled to why you had sent me out of camp. You're about as square as they make them, Spirlaw. You needn't blame Carleton, *he* had about all he could do without paying any attention to me or any one else. Had any wires or news in here?"

Spirlaw shook his head.

"No; but I knew something was up, because Number Eleven is the first train in or out to-day. The express messenger just said they'd cut loose in Big Cloud and wrecked about everything in sight, but I guess he was puttin' it on a bit."

"He didn't put on anything," said Keating slowly. "My God, Spirlaw, it was an awful night! The freight-house and the shops and the roundhouse, what's left of them are ashes. They cut all the wires and then they cut loose themselves – the Polacks and that crowd, you know. Yes, they wrecked everything in sight, and there's a dozen lives gone out to pay for it." Keating stopped suddenly, and again began to cough.

Spirlaw looked at the boy uneasily, and mechanically fumbled with the cords of the package he had laid upon the table. By the time he had removed the wrappers and disclosed two ugly, businesslike looking .45s and a half-dozen boxes of cartridges, Keating's paroxysm had passed.

"I guess it was exciting enough for *me*, anyhow" – Keating tried hard to make his laugh ring true. "I'm a little weak from it yet."

"If you weren't sick," Spirlaw burst out, "I'd make you sick for comin' back here. You know well enough we'll get it next – you knew so well you came back to help –"

"I told Carleton he ought to send some help down here," Keating interrupted hastily; "and he just looked at me like a crazy man – he was half mad anyhow with the ruin of things. 'Help!' he flung out at me. 'Where's it coming from? Let Spirlaw yank up his stakes and pull out if things get looking bad!'"

"Pull out!" shouted Spirlaw, in a sudden roar. "Pull out! *Me!* Not for all the cross-eyed, ham-strung Polacks on the system!"

"I think you'd better," said Keating quietly. "After what I saw last night, I think you'd better. There was no holding them – they were like savages, and the further they went the worse they got. They were backed up by whisky and the worst element in town. I was in the station with Carleton, Regan, Harvey, Riley and Spence and some of the other dispatchers. It was a regular pitched battle, and in spite of their revolvers the station would have gone with the rest if, along toward morning, the striking trainmen and the Brotherhood hadn't taken a hand and helped us out. I don't know that it's over yet, that it won't break out again to-night; though I heard Carleton say there'd be a detachment of the police in town by four o'clock. I wish you would pull out, Spirlaw. You said yourself that all these fellows here needed to start them sticking their claws into you was a little encouragement from the other end. They've been afraid of you, but they hate you like poison. Once started, they'll be worse than the crowd at Big Cloud, for hate is a harder driver than whisky. Then besides, I really think you'd be of more use in Big Cloud. You could do some good there no matter what the end was, while here you're alone and you stand to lose everything, and gain nothing. I wish you would pull out, Spirlaw, won't you?"

Spirlaw reached out his hand and laid it on Keating's shoulder, as he shook his head.

"I've got a whole *lot* to lose," he answered, his hard face softening a little. "A whole lot. I can't say things the way you do, but I guess you'll understand. You got something that means a whole lot to you, that you'd risk anything for – what you want to do and what you want to leave behind you when it comes along time to cash in. Well, I guess most of us have in one way or another, though mabbe it don't rank anywheres up to that. I reckon, too, a whole lot of us don't never think to put it in words, an' a whole lot of us couldn't if we tried to, but it's there with any man that's any good. I'd rather go out for keeps than pull out – I'd rather they'd plant me. D'ye think I'd want to live an' have to cross the street because I couldn't look *even a Polack* in the eyes – a man would be better dead, what?"

For a moment Keating did not answer, he seemed to be weighing the possibility of still shaking the determination of the road boss before accepting it as irrevocable: then, evidently coming to the conclusion that it was useless to argue further, he pointed to the revolvers.

"Then the sooner you load those the better," he jerked out.

Spirlaw looked at him curiously, questioningly.

"Because," went on Keating, answering the unspoken interrogation, "when I dropped off the train I saw that fellow Kuryla – he was pointed out to me in Big Cloud yesterday – and three or four more drop off on the other side. I didn't know they were on the train until then, of course, or I would have had them put off. There isn't much doubt about what they are here for, is there?"

"So that's it, is it?" Spirlaw ripped out with an oath. "No, there ain't much doubt!"

He snatched up a cartridge-box, slit the paper band with his thumb nail, and, breaking the revolvers, began to cram the cartridges into the cylinders. His face was twitching and the red that flushed it shaded to a deep purple. Not another word came from him – just a deadly quiet. He thrust the weapons into his pockets, strode to the door, opened it, stepped over the threshold – and stopped. An instant he hung there in indecision, then he came back, shut the door behind him, sat down on the edge of his bunk, and looked at Keating grimly.

"There's been one train along, there'll be another," he snapped. "An' the first one that comes you'll get aboard of. I hate to keep those whinin' coyotes waitin,' but –"

"I'll take no train," Keating cut in coolly; "but I'll take a revolver."

Spirlaw growled and shook his head.

"Why didn't you tell me about Kuryla at first?" he demanded abruptly.

"You know why as well as I do," smiled Keating. "I wanted to get you away from here if I could. There wouldn't have been any use trying at all if I'd begun by telling you that. Wild horses wouldn't have budged you then. As for a train, what's the use of talking about it, there probably won't be another one along under an hour. In the meantime, give me one of the guns."

"Not m—"

Spirlaw's refusal died half uttered on his lips, as he sprang suddenly to his feet; then he whipped out the revolvers and shoved one quickly into Keating's hand.

Carried down with the sweep of the wind came the sound of many voices raised in shouts and discordant song. It grew louder, swelled, and broke into a high-pitched, defiant yell.

"Whisky!" gritted Spirlaw between his teeth. "That devil Kuryla and the coyotes that came with him knew the best an' quickest way to start the ball rollin.' Well, son, I reckon we're in for it. The only thing I'm sorry about is that you're here; but that can't be helped now. You were white clean through to come – Holy Mother, listen to that!" – another yell broke louder, fiercer than before over the roar of the storm.

Spirlaw stepped to the door and peered out. It was already getting dark. The rain still poured in sheets, and the wind howled down the gorge in wild, furious, spasmodic gusts. Thin streaks of light strayed out from the doors of the bunk-houses, and around the doors were gathered shadowy groups. A moment more and the shadowy groups welded into a single dark mass. Came a mad, exultant yell from a single throat. It was caught up, flung back, echoed and re-echoed by a score of voices – and the dark mass began to move.

"Guess you'd better put out that light, son," said Spirlaw coolly. "There's no use makin' targets of our –"

Before he ended, before Keating had more than taken a step forward, a lump of rock shivered the little window and crashed into the lamp – it was out for keeps. A howl followed this exhibition of marksmanship, and, following that, a volley of stones smashed against the side of the shack thick and fast as hail – then the onrush of feet.

Spirlaw's revolver cut the black with a long, blinding flash, then another, and another. Screams and shrieks answered him, but it did not halt the Polacks. In a mob they rushed the door. Spirlaw sprang back, trying to close it after him; instead, a dozen hands grasped and half wrenched it from its hinges.

"Lie down on the floor, Spirlaw, *quick!*" – it was Keating's voice, punctuated with a cough. The next instant his gun barked, playing through the doorway like a gatling.

From the floor the road boss joined in. The mob wavered, pitched swaying this way and that, then broke and ran, struggling with each other to get out of the line of fire.

"Hurrah!" cried Keating. "I guess that will hold them."

"'Tain't begun," was Spirlaw's grim response. "Where's them cartridges?"

"On the table – got them?"

"Yes," said Spirlaw, after a minute's groping. "Here, put a box in your pocket."

"What are they up to now?" asked Keating, as, in the silence that had fallen, they reloaded and listened.

"God knows," growled Spirlaw; "but I guess we'll find out quick enough."

As he spoke, from a little distance away, came the splintering crash of woodwork – then silence again.

"That's the storehouse," Spirlaw snarled. "They're after the bars an' anything else they can lay their hands on. Guess they weren't countin' on our havin' anything more than our fists to fight with, guess they weren't."

Keating's only reply was a cough.

The minutes passed, two, three, five of them. Once outside sounded what might have been the stealthy scuffle of feet or only a storm-sound so construed by the imagination. Then, from the direction of the river-bed, sudden, sharp, came a terrific roar.

"My God!" yelled Spirlaw. "There's the trestle gone – they've blown it up! They're sure to have laid a fuse here, too. Get out of here quick! Fool that I was, I might have known it was the *dynamite* they were after."

Both men were scrambling for the door as he spoke. They reached it not an instant too soon. The ground behind them lifted, heaved; the walls, the roof of the shack rose, cracked like eggshells, and scattered in flying pieces – and the mighty, deafening detonation of the explosion echoed up and down the gorge, echoed again – and died away.

The mob caught sight of them as they ran and, foiled for the moment, sent up a yell of rage – then started in pursuit.

"Make for the cut," shouted Spirlaw. "We can hold them off there behind the rocks."

Keating had no breath for words. Panting, sick, his head swimming, a fleck of blood upon his lips, he struggled after the giant form of the road boss; while, behind, coming ever closer, ringing in his ears, were the wild cries of the maddened Polacks. The splash of water revived him a little as they plunged along the old right of way where the river, flooded by the storm, had again claimed its own. The worst of it was up to his armpits. A grip on his shoulder and a pull from Spirlaw helped him over. They gained the other side with a bare two yards separating them from the mob behind, went on again – and then Spirlaw caught his foot, tripped and pitched headlong, causing Keating, at his heels, to stumble and fall over him.

Like wild beasts the Polacks surged upon them. Keating tried to regain his feet – but he got no further than his knees as a swinging blow from a pick-handle caught him on his head. Half-stunned, he sank back and, as consciousness left him, he heard Spirlaw's great voice roar out like the maddened bellow of a bull, saw the giant form rise with, it seemed, a dozen Polacks clinging to neck and shoulders, legs and body, saw him shake them off and the massive arms rise and fall – and all was a blur, all darkness.

The road boss lay stretched out a yard away from him when he opened his eyes. He was very weak. He raised himself on his elbow. From the camp down the line he could see the lights in the bunk-houses, hear drunken, chorused shouts. He crept to Spirlaw, called him, shook him – the big road boss never moved. The Polacks had evidently left both of them for dead – and one, it seemed, was. He slid his hand inside the other's vest for the heart beat. So faint it was at first he could not feel it, then he got it, and, realizing that Spirlaw was still alive he straightened up and looked helplessly around – and, in a flash, like the knell of doom, Spirlaw's words came back to him: *"There's the trestle gone!"*

Sick the boy was with his clotting lungs, deathly sick, weak from the blow on his head, dizzy, and his brain swam. *"There's the trestle gone!"* – he coughed it out between blue lips.

"There's the trestle gone!"

Keefer's Siding was a mile away. Somehow he must reach it, must get the word along the line that the *trestle was out,* get the word along before the stalled traffic moved, before the first train east or west crashed through to death, before more wreck and ruin was added to the tale that had gone before. He bent to Spirlaw's ear and three times called him frantically: "Spirlaw! Spirlaw! *Spirlaw!"* There was no response. He tried to lift him, tried to drag him – the great bulk was far beyond his strength. And the minutes were flying by, each marking the one perhaps when it would be too late, too late to warn any one that the trestle was out.

Just up past the rock cut, a bare twenty yards away where the leads to the temporary track swung into the straight of the main line, was the platform handcar they had used for carrying tools and the odds and ends of supplies between the storehouse and the work – if he could only get Spirlaw there!

He called him again, shook him, breathing a prayer for help. The road boss stirred, raised himself a little, and sank down again with a moan.

"Spirlaw, *Spirlaw,* for God's sake, man, try to get up! I'll help you. You must, do you hear, *you must!*" – he was dragging at the road boss's collar.

Keating's voice seemed to reach the other's consciousness, for, weakly, dazed, without sense, blindly, Spirlaw got upon his knees, then to his feet, and, staggering, reeling like a drunken man, his arm around Keating's neck, his weight almost crushing to the ground the one sicker than himself, the two stumbled, pitched, and, at the end, *crawled* those twenty yards.

"The handcar, Spirlaw, the handcar!" gasped Keating. "Get on it. You must! Try! Try!"

Spirlaw straightened, lurched forward, and fell half across the car with outflung arms – unconscious again.

The rest Keating managed somehow, enough so that the dangling legs freed the ground by a few inches; then, with bursting lungs, far spent, he unblocked the wheels, pushed the car down the little spur, swung the switch, dragged himself aboard, and began to pump his way west toward Keefer's Siding.

No man may tell the details of that mile, every inch of which was wrung from blood that oozed from parted, quivering lips; no man may question from Whom came the strength to the frail body, where strength was not; the reprieve to the broken lungs, that long since should have done their worst – only Keating knew that the years were ended forever, that with every stroke of the pump-handle the time was shorter. The few minutes to win through – that was the last stake!

At the end he choked – fighting for his consciousness, as, like dancing points, switch lights swam before him. He checked with the brake, reeled from the car, fell, tried to rise and fell back again. Then, on his hands and knees, he crept toward the station door. It had come at last. The hemorrhage that he had fought back with all his strength was upon him. He beat upon the door. It opened, a lantern was flashed upon him, and he fell inside.

"The trestle's out at the Glacier – hold trains both ways – Polacks – Spirlaw on – handcar – I –"

That was all. Keating never spoke again.

"I dunno as you'd call him a builder," says Clarihue, the night-turner, when *he* tells the story in the darkened roundhouse in the shadow of the big ten-wheelers on the pits, while the steam purrs softly at the gauges and sometimes a pop-valve lifts with a catchy sob, "I dunno as you would. It depends on the way you look at it. Accordin' to him, he was. He left something behind him, what?"

BIBLIOGRAPHY - FRANK L. PACKARD

Criminous works

The adventures of Jimmie Dale. New York: Doran/Toronto: Copp Clark, 1917/London: Cassells, 1918.

The beloved traitor. Toronto: Copp Clark, 1915.

The big shot. New York: Doubleday/London: Hodder & Stoughton/Toronto: Copp Clark, 1929. Set: New York City.

Broken waters. New York: Doran/Toronto: Copp Clark, 1925/London: Hodder & Stoughton, 1927.

The Devil's mantle. New York: Doran, 1927/London: Hodder & Stoughton, 1928.

Doors of the night. New York: Doran/London: Hodder & Stoughton/ Toronto: Copp Clark, 1922. Set: St. Lawrence North Shore.

The dragon's jaws. New York: Doran/London: Hodder & Stoughton, 1937. Set: China.

The four stragglers. New York: Doran/London: Hodder & Stoughton/ Toronto: Copp Clark, 1923. Set: Florida.

From now on. New York: Doran/Toronto: Copp Clark, 1919. Set: California.

The further adventures of Jimmie Dale. New York: Doran, 1919/London: Hodder & Stoughton, 1926.

The gold skull murders. New York: Doubleday (Crime Club)/London: Hodder & Stoughton/Toronto: Doubleday, Doran & Gundy, 1931. Set: in the Malay Archipelago and the China Coast. Char: Dr. Ronald Ward.

Greater love hath no man. New York: Doran/London: Hodder & Stoughton/Toronto: Copp Clark, 1913.

The hidden door. New York: Doubleday (Crime Club)/London: Hodder & Stoughton, 1933. Set: Labrador. Char: Colin Hewitt, criminologist.

Jimmie Dale and the Blue Envelope Murder. New York: Doubleday/Toronto: Doubleday, Doran & Gundy/London: Hodder & Stoughton, 1930. Set: New York City.

Jimmie Dale and the missing hour. New York: Doubleday/London: Hodder & Stoughton, 1935.

Jimmie Dale and the phantom clue. New York: Doran/Toronto: Copp Clark, 1922/London: Hodder & Stoughton, 1923. Set: New York City.

The locked book. New York: Doran/London: Hodder & Stoughton/Toronto: Copp Clark, 1924.

The miracle man. New York: Doran/London: Hodder & Stoughton/Toronto: Copp Clark, 1914.

More knaves than one. New York: Doubleday/London: Hodder & Stoughton, 1938. ss.

The night operator. New York: Doran/Toronto: Copp Clark, 1919. Railroad fiction. Some of the stories are set in the Canadian Rockies.

On the iron at Big Cloud. New York: Crowell, 1911. Railroad fiction.

Pawned. New York: Doran/London: Hodder & Stoughton/Toronto: Copp Clark, 1921. Set: New York City.

The purple ball. New York: Doran, 1933/London: Hodder & Stoughton, 1934.

The red ledger. New York: Doran/London: Hodder & Stoughton, 1926.

Running special. New York: Doran/Toronto: Copp Clark, 1925/London: Hodder & Stoughton, 1926. Railroad fiction.

Shanghai Jim. New York: Doubleday/London: Hodder & Stoughton, 1928. Set: Far East. Four stories.

The sin that was his. New York: Doran/Toronto: Copp Clark, 1917/ London: Hodder & Stoughton, 1926. Set: Canada. The epitome of Frozen North fallen-sinner redemption novels.

Tiger claws. New York: Doran, 1928/London: Hodder & Stoughton, 1929. Set: New York City.

Two stolen idols. New York: Doran, 1927/London: Hodder & Stoughton —. as: *The slave junk*, 1927. Set: Far East.

The white moll. New York: Doran/London: Hodder & Stoughton/Toronto: Copp Clark, 1920. Set: New York City.

The wire devils. New York: Doran/Toronto: Copp Clark, 1918.

HULBERT FOOTNER

The Legacy Hounds
The velvet hand; new Madame Storey mysteries.
London: Collins/New York: Doubleday 1928.

FOOTNER, (William) Hulbert, 1879-1944

Born in Hamilton, Ontario, 2 April 1879, the son of Harold John Footner and Frances Christine (Mills) Footner, Hulbert Footner was educated at evening high school, New York City. A journalist in New York City in 1905 and in Calgary, Alberta, in 1906, he then became a full-time free-lance writer.

Footner lived for most of the latter part of his life in the State of Maryland. He was highly respected as a local historian of the Maryland tidewater, which he wrote about in *Maryland Main and the eastern Shore* and *Rivers of the Eastern Shore*, published as part of the important Rivers of America series. His home was a seventeenth century mansion which he lovingly restored; he wrote of its history and of the renovation in *Charles' gift; salute to a Maryland house of 1650*. He died in his beloved home on 25 November 1944.

Footner made a minor contribution to the fiction of the Canadian Northwest, the setting for his first novel, *Two on the trail*. His 1,200 mile trek through the region is also described in his book *New rivers of the north; a yarn of two amateur explorers on the head waters of the Fraser, Peace River, the Hay River, Alexandra Falls*. Despite this experience, Footner was one of the writers of "Northerns" mocked by Arthur Stringer in *The man who could not sleep*.

Prolific is an apt descriptor for his output: in the late 1920s and early 1930s he often produced three books a year. Most of his mystery stories are set in New York City, where he was part of the literati in the roaring twenties, hobnobbing with writers such as Christopher Morley. His best stories feature the intriguing Madame Rosika Storey.

THE LEGACY HOUNDS

The velvet hand; new Madame Storey mysteries. London: Collins/New York: Doubleday 1928

Despite the number of his published books and stories, Hulbert Footner did not make a lasting impression on the criminous literary scene. What slight reputation he does have rests on his tales of the exploits of Madame Rosika Storey, whom he introduced in 1926 as "a practical psychologist - specializing in the feminine." In Madame Storey Footner created an admirable feminist role model: a woman making her own way on her own terms in a man's world. The following, an excerpt from *The legacy hounds,* is a typical example of her sleuthing.

THE LEGACY HOUNDS

When the very wealthy – and miserly – Mrs. Genevieve Brager was murdered, all the occupants of her house were suspects. And a strange lot they were, these "legacy hounds": Madame Rose La France, a fat blonde with a face you could break rocks on; The Honourable Shep Chew, a big man, fashionably dressed, but with false and greedy black eyes; Signor Raymondo Oneto, lounge lizard, sheik, his face slinking, mean and cruel. These were Mrs. Brager's "friends" – and all were certain they had been named prime beneficiary in Mrs. Brager's will.

So different from the other inmates of that weird household was the housekeeper, Mrs. Marlin, a handsome young woman of thirty; everything about her bespoke character, resolution, and decency. Yet all the evidence pointed to her and her fiancé Dr. Brill, inventor of clarium gas, as the murderers. In fact, the prosecutor, Mr. Dockra, had just ordered the pair taken into custody when Madame Storey, the feminist detective, intervened:

After the scene I have just described Mme Storey took charge of the proceedings. Mr. Dockra never ventured to oppose her. One could not help but feel a little sorry for the deflated young prosecutor. He was not a bad fellow at heart; but he had been carrying too much pressure. Imagine the small-town attorney thinking he could show Mme Storey a thing or two! She softened the blow as much as she could by making believe to consult him at every point, etc. Everybody remained in the room, and my mistress turned from one to another as questions occurred to her. It was much simpler.

"Mrs. Marlin," she said, "when you went out, was it your custom to lock your door?"

"No, Madame, it never occurred to me to do so. In fact, I had no key to the lock."

"Thank you." My mistress picked up the fateful kettle and tapped it reflectively with her finger nail. "Dr. Brill," she said, handing it over, "look at this again, please. It is a cheap kettle, you see, the metal is very thin. If this kettle, not having any water in it, were suspended over a flame, how long would it be before the metal fused?"

"It would depend upon the flame, Madame."

"I am referring to the flame of the alcohol lamp that goes with it."

Dr. Brill lighted the little lamp and put it out again. "Between six and eight minutes, Madame. The bottom of the kettle is badly discoloured and warped. Another minute and it would have burned out."

"Thank you. How long would you have to cook the clarium powder before it began to give off its gas?"

"No time at all. As soon as the heat penetrated it the gas would be released."

"I see. When the gas is released, how long a time must pass before it becomes innocuous?"

"Fifteen minutes, Madame."

Mme Storey turned to Mr. Dockra. "An elementary sum in arithmetic," she remarked. "If Mrs. Marlin carried the kettle into that room and lighted it, unless she went back in eight minutes to put out the flame, the bottom of the kettle would burn out. Yet it has not burned out, you see. On the other hand, if she went back inside of fifteen minutes, the fumes would kill her too. It won't work out."

The young man's face became longer and longer, seeing his case crumble to the ground. "According to that, nobody could have done it, then," he said sullenly.

"But somebody did do it," said Mme Storey, "for Mrs. Brager lies dead in there."

"How did they get the gas in there, then?" said Mr. Dockra. "Mrs. Brager didn't come out of the room, because the birds are dead in there with her."

"The hot-air flue from the furnace," said Mme Storey softly.

A little sound of astonishment went around the circle of listeners. The prosecutor gaped at my mistress. We all did.

She turned to Mme La France without pausing. "Will you please give an account of your movements this morning?"

"Certainly, Madame." The fat woman had by now succeeded in concealing the rage that gnawed her vitals. During one of her absences from the room she had fixed her hair and repaired her make-up. She faced Mme Storey with a hard smile. "After breakfast I sat in the dining room reading the paper," she began.

"Waiting for the mail?" put in Mme Storey pleasantly.

"We all were. When it came we went out into the hall to see what there was. I seen the little package addressed to Mrs. Marlin –"

"You have already testified as to that. Was there anything for you?"

"No, Madame. Afterwards I went upstairs and put on my things, and left the house. I went down to Ye Gilded Lily Shoppe – that's a beauty parlour in the town – where I had an appointment for a head shampoo."

"At what hour was your appointment?"

"Ten o'clock."

"That leaves a whole hour to be accounted for."

"Well, I didn't hurry none. I took my time about getting my things on. I suppose it would be about nine twenty when I left the house."

"But it only takes ten minutes to go downtown on the car. Less than that by taxi."

"I walked, Madame. I am reducing."

"Oh, I see. Did you leave the house before or after the gentlemen?"

"I can't say. I didn't see them when I went out."

"Then nobody saw you leave the house?"

"Nobody that I know about."

"Did you meet anybody you knew on the way downtown?"

"No, Madame."

"I suppose you are known at the beauty parlour?"

"Oh, yes, Madame, they all know me there."

"What time did you leave there?"

"Eleven. And come right home by car. You was already here then."

"You were wearing a cape when I saw you. Is that your custom?"

"No, Madame. Only when I'm walking. It gives me more freedom, like."

"That is all, thank you," said Mme Storey. "Now, Mr. Oneto."

The young man faced her with a look at once nervous and sulky. His eyes quailed; he passed his handkerchief over his face. This looked hopeful.

"You, too, were waiting in the dining room after breakfast?" suggested my mistress with an ironical air.

"Yes."

"Reading the paper?"

"No, she had it."

"What were you doing?"

"Nothing."

"Waiting for the mail?"

"Oh, I don't look for much in the mail. I'm no hand to write letters."

"But you went out in the hall when it came?"

"Yes."

"Get anything?"

"No."

"Then what did you do?"

"My hat and coat were downstairs. I took them and went out. Mr. Chew saw me go."

"Where did you go?"

The young man scowled ever more blackly, and his eyes darted from side to side like something trapped. "Went to see a friend," he muttered.

"Who?"

He hesitated. "I won't say," he muttered.

"Hm!" said Mme Storey. "You understand what that implies?"

"Aah, what difference does it make?" he burst out. "Chew saw me go out right after the mail came; and you all saw me come in again after eleven o'clock. It couldn't have been me."

"How do we know that you didn't come back in between?" suggested Mme Storey quietly.

"I didn't have a latchkey."

"It would have been a simple matter to leave the door on the latch."

"Well, I didn't," he muttered.

"There is a door opening from the side yard directly onto the cellar stairs," Mme Storey went on. "It has not been used in many years; not since the house was last painted, in fact. But this morning it was opened, and somebody entered that way, after having put down a board over the soft earth outside to avoid leaving a footprint."

Oneto stared at her. "Well, it wasn't me," he said sullenly, "and you can't hang it on me."

"You will be under suspicion until you can account for your movements."

"Aah, I went to see a lady friend," he said with a hang-dog air. "It wouldn't do any good for me to give her name, because she'd deny I was there if you asked her."

"Why should she deny it?"

"Because her husband don't know me."

A smile travelled around the circle at this answer. But Oneto had no intention of being funny; he was sweating. To my disappointment, Mme Storey let him go for the moment.

"Mr. Chew," she said.

There was no hesitancy about this witness. He was too eager to testify, too full of virtuous protestations. "After the mail came I went back into the dining room to look at the paper," he said. "Nobody gets a chance at it when Mme La France is around. I didn't see Oneto leave the house. He may have done so, but he can't prove it by me, because I wasn't taking any notice of him. I didn't read the paper long – only the headlines. The dining room door was closed to keep in the heat, and I didn't see Mme La France go out. Maybe she did. My hat and coat were up in my room, and after a few minutes I got them and went out."

"Where did you go?"

"Well, you'll think it's funny, Madame Storey, but I got on a car and went down to a sort of little club that I know of called the Acme Social Club, and played pool with some men there. I assure you it's not my custom. But this morning I was to talk over some business matters with Mrs. Brager, and when the housekeeper told us at breakfast that she was indisposed it left me at a loose end, so to speak, and I –"

"Quite so," said Mme Storey, cutting him short. "With whom did you play pool?"

"Well, there was quite a crowd: a fellow they call Fred, and a fellow they call Spike, and Dan – you see I don't know then outside the club, and I'm not sure about their last names; Dan's last name is Potter, I think."

"But they could be found at the club?"

"Certainly, Madame Storey."

"At what time did you enter the club?"

"I couldn't tell you exactly. It would be about twenty-five past nine."

"Mr. Chew, can you produce a witness who will swear that he saw you enter the club before half-past nine?"

A panicky look came into the greedy, darting black eyes. "How do I know if I can?" he gobbled. "There was a crowd there; fellows always coming and going. I don't know if anybody noticed me particularly coming in or could tell the time to a minute." He darted off on a new tack. "Nobody who ever saw me and Mrs. Brager together would ever suspect me of meaning harm to her!" he cried with tears in his voice. "Why, we were like brother and sister together, like mother and son; a hundred times she has termed me her son."

Those of us who knew the old lady and her pretensions to youthfulness smiled at this.

"Why, when a fellow come into the club and said that a rumour was going around town that Mrs. Brager was dead, I almost dropped where I stood. Ask any of them how I took it! My friend! My benefactor! I rushed out of the place and jumped in a taxi and came right here. I am still so overcome by this shocking event, I scarcely know what I'm saying!"

My mistress was bored by these protestations. "I noticed, when you came in, that you were wearing your overcoat across your shoulders," she said. "Why was that?"

"It is just a way I have got into," he said.

"Madame La France," said my mistress, "have you seen Mr. Chew wearing his overcoat in that manner?"

"No," was the blunt answer.

"That's a lie!" cried Mr. Chew excitedly. "That woman has it in for me. She –"

"Oh, please!" said Mme Storey, holding up her hand. "No recriminations. That is all, thank you, Mr. Chew."

Things began to happen then.

A battered figure appeared in the doorway. It was Crider, the best man we have; one of his eyes was puffed up and beginning to blacken; his cheek was cut; his collar was torn open. I gasped at the sight; but my imperturbable mistress never batted an eye.

"Did you get your man?" she asked coolly.

"Yes, Madame," he said grimly.

"Good!"

The room had become so crowded we could scarcely breathe. Mme Storey suggested that it be partly cleared; and the flock of lawyers was requested to wait in the hall. Mr. Dockra also sent his men outside, except the one who was taking notes. The door had to be left open for air; and during the subsequent proceedings there was a whole bouquet of heads there, peering and listening. Even for those who remained in the room there were not seats enough, though some sat on the bed and some on the couch. I doubt if any of those who stood ever became conscious of weariness, for minute by minute the tension increased, as one might slowly screw the strings of an instrument higher and higher. It became almost unbearable.

Crider was looking at Mme Storey for further instructions. "Speak out," she said; "the Public Prosecutor is waiting to hear what you have to say."

"From the cook downstairs," Crider began, "I got a tip that the man you sent me after would be going to St. Agnes' school after leaving here. He visits the school four times a day. I followed by the route he would naturally take. According to your instructions, I searched all places that would likely suggest themselves as hiding places for a small object he might want to dispose of. I found that my route carried me across the Stanfield River, and I realized, of course, that that would be the place, if any. It is a small tidal stream, and at the time I crossed the bridge was just a narrow creek flowing out between mud flats. I did not feel that I ought to take the time myself, so I hired some boys to drag the water under the bridge, and I went on.

"From having to stop so many times, I found the man gone when I got to the school. But they had his address, and I went there. It was a lodging house in a poor quarter. I found him at home. He had just got there. He refused to come back with me. In fact, I had considerable trouble with him. He was a heavier man than me. But I managed to hold him until the people in the house, who were scared by the racket, sent out for a policeman. I told the officer who I was and took the liberty of adding that the Public Prosecutor wanted the man at Mrs. Brager's house, and the officer took him in charge for me. I searched his room but did not find any of the things you told me to look for. I followed behind to make sure he did not throw anything away in the street.

"When we approached the bridge, I saw that the boys had found something, so I let the officer and his man walk on ahead. The boys gave me this, which they had found in the water. The man does not know that we have it. He is down in the kitchen under guard."

Crider handed Mme Storey a crumpled piece of tin. It had the look of a small box which had been squeezed flat so that it would sink when thrown into the water. Mme Storey, pulling the sides apart, examined it all over, while everybody in the room waited in a breathless silence.

"Dr. Brill," she said at last, "do you smoke Demiopolis cigarettes?"

"Why, yes, Madame," he said, astonished.

"Do you buy them in boxes of one hundred?"

"Yes, Madame."

"Did you use one of the empty boxes to mail the clarium powder to Mrs. Marlin?"

"Yes, Madame," he said, with rising excitement.

"This will be it, then, I fancy," she drawled. "You had better take charge of it, Mr. Dockra." She handed it over. "You will find the name of the maker stamped in the tin."

A little sound of wonder travelled around the room.

Amid an electrical silence, the mysterious man in the case was led into the room and told to sit down in the chair at the foot of the bed. I shivered with repulsion at the sight of the murderer, as I then supposed him to be. He looked like a murderer, which murderers seldom do: a Hercules of a man, now some-what gone to fat, with a ridged, bony head and completely brutalized features. The sort of man whose only retort is a guffaw of coarse laughter. His little swimming pig eyes held no expression whatever. The coarse and dirty clothes betrayed his occupation. He wore no overcoat.

"What is your name?" asked Mme Storey mildly.

"Henry Hafner," he growled.

Instantly Dr. Brill cried out: "That is the voice I heard over the telephone!"

It was on my tongue's tip to echo him. I too recognized that growling voice! But Mme Storey has taught me to restrain my impulses at such moments. I could see that she was annoyed by Dr. Brill's cry. She looked at Mr. Dockra meaningly. He said:

"There must be no interruptions, or we will have to clear the room."

In order to lull his suspicions, my mistress was adopting a painstakingly friendly attitude toward the brute. "Married, single, or widowed?" she asked.

"Single, 'm."

"Age?"

"Fifty-one."

"I shouldn't have thought it," said Mme Storey politely. "How long have you lived in Stanfield?"

"Eight months, 'm."

"Then you're not well known here?"

"No, 'm. I keeps to myself."

"What is your occupation?"

"Sort of odd jobs, 'm. In the winter I tends furnaces. Summers I gardens and mows lawn.... Can I make a statement?" he asked.

"I'd be glad to hear it," said Mme Storey.

"Well? 'm," he began with an aggrieved air, "when this guy here" – a jerk of the dirty thumb in Crider's direction – "come to my room and says, 'Come with me,' I says, 'What t' hell,' I says, 'a man's got his rights. A man's house is his castle,' I says, 'who are you to come buttin' in here?' He says: 'I'm Madame Storey's man,' or some such name. Well, I don't know who Madame Storey is, and I tell him so. 'Show me your badge,' I says. And he ain't got no badge. 'Nothin' doin',' I says, 'get the hell out of here.' Then he tried to drag me, and I pasted him one and we mixed it up, sort of, till the cop come. The guy tells the cop the Public Prosecutor wants me. He din't tell me that. Soon as he says

Public Prosecutor, I goes with him like a lamb. I just want you to get me right, lady: I don't set up to resist no lawful authority."

"That's all right," said Mme Storey; "your resistance to my agent will not be counted against you. Let us get on. I understand that you attend to the furnace in this house?"

"Yes, 'm."

"How long have you been working here?"

"Since the fire was lighted last fall."

"Who got you the job?"

"I got it by astin' at t' kitchen door."

"What time do you come here every day?"

"A little before seven in the morning, and again between nine and ten at night. At this house they won't give no key, so I has to wait for the cook to let me in mornings."

"Then you enter by the kitchen?"

"Yes, 'm."

"Why don't you use the door direct from the yard into the cellar?"

"Is there a door from the yard?" he said with a cunning look. "Oh, sure, I mind seein' that door on the cellar stairs. But that there door has been bolted up since before my time. I suppose the missus wants the kitchen help to keep tab on all who comes and goes in the cellar."

"You came back a second time this morning, didn't you?" said Mme Storey carelessly.

The little eyes darted an uneasy look in her face; but he answered readily: "Yes, 'm."

"What for?"

"Well, you see, 'm, the first time I come the fire was so near out I couldn't fill her up. I just had to put a little on and wait for it to catch good. So I told Mis' Morris, that's the cook here, that I'd be back."

"What time did you come back?"

"Some'eres about nine."

"Where had you been in the meantime?"

He named three houses that he had visited.

"But it wouldn't take you two hours to fix three furnaces."

"No, 'm, I was waitin' round to give the fire time to burn up good."

"It wouldn't take two hours for the fire to come up."

"Not if the dampers was opened right, 'm. But they won't let me do that here. Burn too much coal. They buy it every month, and I gotta make two ton last out. They ought to burn four."

"I want to fix the exact time of your return, if I can," said Mme Storey. "Did you meet the letter carrier making his first round?"

"Not that I rec'lect."

"Are you sure?"

252 CRIME IN A COLD CLIMATE

It evidently occurred to Hafner that the letter carrier might have been questioned. "Sure, that's right, I met him," he said. "I just forgot for the moment. Fella name of Smitty. Me and him's well acquainted."

"Had he been to this house, or was he on the way here?"

"He'd been."

"Had you been waiting for him?" asked Mme Storey slyly.

But she didn't catch him. "Why should I?" he asked with an innocent air.

"I don't know," said Mme Storey, just as innocent. "What did you do when you came back?"

From this point on he weighed every word of his answers. As you have perceived, he was by no means as stupid as he looked. That debased exterior concealed a world of low cunning. He made a good witness for himself.

"I went down cellar."

"Did you find anything out of the way there?"

"No, 'm, nothin' out of the way. The fire was still sulkin'. I opened all the drafts and went up to the kitchen while she burned up."

"Right away?"

"No, 'm. I can't say as it was right away. I fooled around a bit, watching her – drawing out a clinker or two. Then I went up."

"What did you do in the kitchen?"

"I sat down and talked to cook and the girl."

"Oh, you sat down and talked. What about?"

"'Deed, I can't tell you that, 'm. Nothin' particular. Just talkin' like." Then, reflecting, no doubt, that the cook was at hand to corroborate this part, he added: "But I remember one thing."

"What was that?"

"While I was sittin' there cook wanted to send the girl down cellar for potatoes and I stopped her."

"Why?"

"Because of the coal gas. The furnace was givin' out gas somepin' fierce. I had opened everything up to drawr it off, and I opened the cellar window, too. I told the girl she better wait awhile."

"But you just told me you'd been fooling around down there."

"Oh, I'm used to the gas. Don't notice it a-tall."

"Did the furnace often give off gas?"

"Yes 'm. Plumb wore out that furnace was. Weren't no use to complain. Wild horses wouldn't have drug the price of a new furnace out of the old missus."

"Then you went down cellar again?"

"Yes, 'm, I went down again."

"Closing the cellar door after you."

"That was along of the gas."

"Oh, I see. Did the girl go down with you?"

"No, 'm. She didn't come down till I hollered up that the gas was out."

"How was the fire then?"

"Not so good. I fooled around awhile yet, waitin' for it, then I couldn't wait no longer, so I fixed it up the best I could and left."

"Did the girl get her potatoes?"

"Oh, yes, 'm, she got her potatoes all right."

At this point the questioning was interrupted by the entrance of Stephens, the second operative, who had come out from town with Crider. He stood just within the door, waiting to catch his mistress's eye.

"Well, that's fine!" Mme Storey said to Hafner: "Just excuse me a minute while I speak to this gentleman."

Stephens handed her a slip of paper on which was a written memorandum. After reading it Mme Storey folded it and kept it in her palm during what followed. I guessed by that that it was something of first-rate importance. Hafner's little eyes watched her with an agonized curiosity. He would have given something to know what was written on that paper. Mme Storey then whispered further instructions close in Stephens's ear, and he left the room again.

Up to this moment Mme Storey had shepherded Hafner along so gently that he thought he was picking his own way. He was cunning, but not cunning enough. He thought he was getting along fine; but I who knew Mme Storey so well, could see that by the apparently plausible answers she was drawing out of him she was making him weave the rope that would later hang him.

I say hang him, but of course I could see by this time that he could not be the principal in this affair. He had no access to the upper part of the house; and he had nothing to gain directly by the death of Mrs. Brager. He was a tool in the hands of one of the three interested persons. I glanced at that precious trio where they sat in a row on the couch near the door: La France, Oneto, Chew. Each face showed the same wary mask, each was awaiting Hafner's answers with the same secret tenseness. Were they all in it? I wondered.

Mme Storey now changed her tactics. With an unexpectedness that caused the witness visibly to jump she said: "Hafner, for what reason did you follow my car back to New York night before last?"

He made his eyes as big as possible with astonishment. "I never followed you, lady," he said in an aggrieved voice. "I never seen you before I come into this room."

"I saw you." (This was not so, of course.)

"Maybe you did, but I wasn't follerin' you.... What kind of a car was I in?"

My mistress bit her lips to control a smile. Brute though the man was, his readiness of wit pleased her. "Never mind that," she said. "You followed me and my secretary to the Restaurant Lafitte on Park Avenue. You then went to a pay station near by and called me up."

"You're mistaken, lady. If somebody called you up, it wasn't me."

"You should butter your voice before you call up folks on the 'phone," remarked Mme Storey dryly. "...Who pointed me out to you and told you to follow me?"

"Nobody, 'm, because I didn't foller you. I ain't been to New York since Christmas."

"Well, let's get back to the cellar," said Mme Storey. "You say the second time you went down you didn't see anything out of the way."

"No, 'm. Nothin' out of the way."

"Well, that's funny," said Mme Storey carelessly, "because when I went down I immediately noticed that the tops of all the hot-air pipes leading out of the furnace had been dusted off."

Hafner's eyes flickered with fear; but he answered without hesitating: "You don't say. Must 'a' been done after I come up, for that would be a thing I'd notice. Everything down cellar was covered with dust."

"Yes. Seems funny anybody would go to the trouble of dusting off all those old pipes."

"You're right, lady." She had him sweating now; but his answers still came out pat. He started to pull a handkerchief out of his back pocket and then shoved it back again.

Mme Storey's voice rang out: "Give me that handkerchief!"

Jumping to his feet with a snarl, he clapped his hand over the spot. But resistance was useless, of course, in that crowd. The handkerchief was taken from him and handed to my mistress. It showed the unmistakable dark brown stains of thick dust. Mme Storey give it a flirt, and a little cloud of fresh dust flew out of it.

"How did it get so dusty, Hafner?" she asked softly.

His tongue failed him then. "I – I – I –" he stammered – "I used it to dust my room with this morning. I hadn't nothin' else to use."

"Your room must have needed it," remarked Mme Storey, looking at the thick brown accumulations on the handkerchief. "Mr. Dockra," she said, brusquely raising her voice, "I would like to have this man searched."

Hafner crouched; showed his teeth like a trapped animal; glanced desirously toward the door. Useless to think of escape. Mr. Dockra called two of his men in.

Mme Storey said carelessly: "I expect to find on him a pair of pliers, a pair of gloves of some sort, a knife – of course, the knife won't prove anything, because every workman carries a knife. If you can also find some scraps of rubber and wire, it will help prove my case."

While the man was being frisked, she turned indifferently away. One after another the objects she had named were thrown on the table: the pliers; a pair of coarse cotton gloves, new, but stained on the palms with the same brown dust; a penknife; two pieces of rubber which looked as if they might have been cut from an old inner tube. Only the wire was missing.

Mme Storey glanced over these things. "We can do without the wire," she said.

Everybody else in the room looked on open mouthed, like a crowd of yokels at a side show.

"These gloves I think were worn for the first time this morning," said Mme Storey, calling attention to their clean backs. "What did you want gloves for, Hafner?"

"To protect my hands," he muttered.

If you could have seen those dirty, calloused hands! A laugh travelled around the room.

Hafner sat down again, breathing hard; but he was not yet beaten; for when Mme Storey said: "Has there been anything wrong with the heating flue leading to Mrs. Brager's bedroom?" he answered readily:

"Not as I knows of."

"Because the next thing I noticed in the cellar," she went on, "was that that flue had been disconnected and joined up again. There was an edge of bright tin showing at the joining of the old pipe. It was at the point where the horizontal flue from the heating chamber joins the vertical flue which runs up through the walls. There is a sort of square tin box there, which receives the round pipe from the furnace."

My mistress's quiet, matter-of-fact voice was too much for Hafner's nerves. "What's all this about?" he suddenly burst out. "What you gettin' at, anyway? A man's got the right to know what he's suspected of!"

Mme Storey stepped to the door into Mrs. Brager's room. We all held our breath. The key had been left in the lock; she opened the door. "Come here and see," she said quietly to Hafner.

His face turned greenish. Showing all his teeth, he strained away, like an animal on a leash. "I won't!" he cried hoarsely. "None of your tricks! I asked you a plain question – can't you give me a plain answer?"

Mr. Dockra looked at his man. "Make him look in there," he said.

But Mme Storey held up her hand. "It's not necessary," she said. "He knows what's in there." She closed the door.

Hafner dropped into his chair again. You could not help but pity the wretch.

"I disconnected the pipe again," Mme Storey resumed, "and looked inside that square box. That had not been dusted out – a fatal oversight! In the bottom of it was collected the dust of thirty years which has sifted down through the register in Mrs. Brager's room. It was, I suppose, a quarter of an inch thick. And in the dust I found three fresh marks in the shape of a triangle, three marks which correspond to the three legs of the standard which supports this kettle. I was careful not to disturb these marks; they are still there."

She paused to flick the ash off her cigarette, and one could hear a little sigh travel around the room as the pent-up breath was released.

"Hafner," asked Mme Storey, "how do you suppose those marks came there?"

"How do I know?" he said. "I couldn't have come up here to get that kettle."

"How did you know that kettle belonged in this room?" she asked quickly.

"I didn't know it," he retorted. "That was just in the way of speaking."

There was an interruption here. The servant Maud pushed through the crowd at the door to say that Miss Rose Schmalz was wanted on the telephone. Mme Storey looked inquiringly at Mrs. Marlin.

"Never heard of such a person," said the housekeeper.

The maid was instructed to say that there was nobody of that name in the house, and she returned downstairs. At the moment I saw nothing in this incident but what appeared on the surface; but it was to have an important bearing on the result, as you will see.

Mme Storey resumed: "I'll tell you how I have figured out what happened, Hafner. Set me right if I go wrong.... The same person who instructed you to follow me into town two days ago told you to watch this house this morning for the first call of the letter carrier and to come back after he'd gone...."

"It's not so," muttered Hafner. He kept interrupting Mme Storey throughout with denials, but I need not set them all down.

"On your way down cellar, you opened the door into the yard – I could see where the old film of paint on the outside had been freshly broken. You then disconnected the flue leading to Mrs. Brager's room. You wore the gloves to avoid leaving finger prints on the pipes. In working over the pipe you disturbed the dust, therefore you were obliged to dust all the pipes alike. Your companion joined you, entering from the yard, and bringing the little brass kettle and the tin box containing the powder."

Mme Storey held up the two pieces of rubber. One piece, a rough ring, had obviously been cut out of the other. "The ring was for a washer to make the lid of the kettle fit snugly. In this manner." She showed how the rubber ring had been snapped around the lid of the kettle. "After the powder had been emptied into the kettle," she resumed, "the lid was wired down. Here are the marks of the wires on the kettle. The wire itself came from one of the supports of the flues. All this business of making the lid tight was perfectly unnecessary, by the way; for the gas would have puffed right up the flue even if the lid had been off; but you and your friend were not chemists enough to know that.

"You were in momentary fear of being surprised by one of the servants in the kitchen," she went on; "therefore you left your companion to light the flame under the kettle and to blow it out before the bottom of the kettle burned through. You went up into the kitchen and stood guard over the cellar door. When you heard your companion pass out into the yard by the door on the cellar stairs, you returned. You bolted up the door into the yard. You connected up the heating flue again. Your companion had taken the kettle, and you concealed the other evidences of your activities. You then called up to the kitchen that the gas was out.... The gas *was* out," she gravely concluded, "and so was the spark of life in the old woman who lies in the next room."

Hafner was breaking fast now. "It's not true!" he panted. "I know nothing about it!"

"Then how came you in possession of the tin cigarette box in which the poison was mailed?" asked Mme Storey. "You tossed it into Stanfield River when you crossed the bridge this morning." She held out her hand, and Mr. Dockra passed the box back.

Hafner's nerve went completely. A strangled cry broke from him. He held out his hands toward Mr. Dockra as if inviting the handcuffs. "Take me away!" he bellowed. "Take me away from that woman! Lock me up! Send me to the chair! I don't care what you do to me!... Take me away from her! She's not a natural woman. Nothing can be hid from her!"

It was a horrible and grotesque sight. The sweat was pouring down his face in drops as big as tears; his eyes were devoid of all sense; his brutal mouth was working like an idiot's. I turned away my head from that sight. "Take me away from her!" he kept shrieking.

"One moment," said the prosecutor coldly; "you have not yet told us the name of your companion in the cellar."

"I'll never tell you that!" cried Hafner. "I don't care what you do to me. Send me to the chair! Won't that satisfy you?"

"Oh, I guess we know how to make you tell," said Mr. Dockra grimly.

Mme Storey turned quickly. "Don't do it," she said with a note of compassion in her voice. "It's his last shred of decency. Give him credit for it. I know who his companion was."

"Who?"

Mme Storey pointed to the fat woman sitting on the end of the couch. "There is the real murderer," she said quietly.

"Madame La France!" cried Mr. Dockra.

"If you like," said Mme Storey. "She goes by several names. She is most commonly known as Rose Schmalz. She betrayed herself when I caused that name to be spoken at the door awhile ago." She unfolded the slip of paper that she kept in her hand all this time. "I had previously been informed that Rose Schmalz and Henry Hafner were married in South Norwalk on October 24th last."

I do not know if the woman had seen this coming. She got to her feet. There was a hard peasant strength in her, and she uttered no sound; her face remained composed. But that ghastly mottled look returned to her skin, and her hand stole to her throat.

"That was how she secured to herself the accomplice she was in need of, by marrying him," Mme Storey went on – there was no compassion in her voice now. "She herself takes marriage lightly. According to the reports of my agent she has been married at least three times before. That was as far as he could go into her past in two hours' telephoning. Her room adjoins this, you remember. It was she who stole out of the house, carrying the kettle under her cape; and stole back with it later, knowing that the men had gone out."

The woman, still without having uttered a sound, suddenly swayed forward, crashed against the bed opposite, and collapsed in a huddle on the floor. A heart attack. How like man and woman, I thought – his frantic self-pitying cries, and her collapse without a sound. That ended the proceedings.

I must say that Walter Dockra took his humiliation at the hands of my mistress very handsomely. After the excitement was over he marched up to her like a man saying:

"Madame Storey, that was the finest piece of work I ever saw in my life. I consider it a privilege that I was there to see the whole thing worked out. Allow me to congratulate you and to express my regret that I ventured to differ from you, even for a moment."

"Oh, you give me far too much credit," said my mistress, smiling. "In this case, as it happened, I enjoyed an exceptional advantage through having been introduced to the house before the tragedy occurred. It was what I learned then that gave me my line. It was obvious that the three legacy hounds hated Mrs. Marlin poisonously. When I found the kettle with the remains of the poison in her room, I knew it was a plant."

"Why did they hate her?" he asked.

"Because her decency and good feeling were a perpetual reproach to them."

"Nevertheless, it was a wonderful piece of logical reasoning," he insisted.

My mistress smiled suddenly and merrily. "I'm afraid I don't think as much of logic as you do," she said.

"Why not?"

It would have been useless to try to explain. She just smiled on.

Dockra was a young man, and I think the lesson did him permanent good. I have never seen a trace of bumptiousness in his manner since. He remains our very good friend, and sometimes comes to consult my mistress concerning the knotty points that rise in his practice.

When the Schmalz woman and Hafner came to trial, they had not a leg to stand on. Both pleaded guilty and threw themselves on the mercy of the court. But as it had come out that they had been plotting the old woman's death for months, they did not receive much mercy. There is a prejudice against executing a woman; and as they could not execute the lesser criminal and let her live, both received life sentences.

They had first planned to lead common illuminating gas into the heating flue, but gave it up because the odour would have betrayed them. They next prepared to suffocate her with coal gas from the furnace. By tampering with the rusted smoke flue where it passed through the heating chamber, Hafner had already worked a hole in it. Then, if the smoke flue had been stopped up and all the heating flues shut off in the cellar except the one leading to Mrs. Brager's room, the old woman would certainly have suffocated before morning, and it could have been made to appear an accident. However, before they had time to carry this out, they learned of clarium gas.

As for the Hon. Shep Chew and Raymondo Oneto, they quietly disappeared, and I have never heard of them since. No doubt they have gone sleuthing after other legacies. I understand it is quite a business.

As a result of this case we also added Dr. Brill and Mrs. Marlin to our circle of friends – or Dr. and Mrs. Brill as they now are. Their happiness was beautiful to see. Under the last will signed by Mrs. Brager Mrs. Marlin inherited practically her entire fortune, and it seemed as if nothing could be more just and right. But that ridiculous and high-minded pair were one in refusing to touch the money; and this in spite of the fact that Dr. Brill was actually evicted from his laboratory and Mrs. Marlin had lost her job. The money must be disposed of according to the terms of the last will drawn up by Mrs. Brager's orders, though not yet signed by her, they insisted. In other words, the aged gentlewomen were to benefit. There was a legacy to Mrs. Marlin in this will, but not sufficient to support her.

Well, the trustees accepted the money, but I'm happy to say that their first act was to set aside a trust fund that will relieve Dr. Brill and his wife of the necessity of worrying during the rest of their lives. Perhaps they are happier than if they had the millions. Clarium gas has not yet been rendered harmless, and I do not know if it ever will be; but I do know that the Brills' is one of the most delightful houses that I am privileged to visit. There is nothing like having escaped a hideous danger to give one an edge for joy.

BIBLIOGRAPHY - HULBERT FOOTNER

Criminous works

The almost perfect murder; more Madame Storey mysteries. London: Collins, 1933/Philadelphia: Lippincott, 1937 – with sub-title: a case book of Madame Storey. Set: New York City. Char: Madame Rosika Storey. ss.

Anybody's pearls. London: Hodder & Stoughton, 1929/New York: Doubleday, 1930. Set: England.

At mile ninety-two. [?]: Ridgeway, 1913. This may be an alternate title of a book already listed.

A backwoods princess. London: Hodder & Stoughton/New York: Doran, 1926. Set: Canada.

Cap'n Sue. London: Hodder & Stoughton, 1927/New York: Doubleday, 1928.

The casual murder. London: Collins, 1932/Philadelphia: Lippincott, 1936 – as: *The kidnapping of Madame Storey; and other stories.* US ed. lacks orig. title story of UK ed. ss.

The chase of the 'Linda Belle'. London: Hodder & Stoughton, 1925.

Dangerous cargo. London: Collins/New York: Harper, 1934. Char: Madame Storey.

The dark ships. London: Collins/New York: Harper, 1937.

Dead man's hat. London: Collins/New York: Harper, 1932. Set: New York City.

The death of a celebrity. London: Collins/New York: Harper, 1938. Set: New York City. Char: Amos Lee Mappin.

Death of a saboteur. New York: Harper, 1943/London: Collins, 1944. Set: New York City. Char: Amos Lee Mappin.

The Deaves affair. London: Collins/New York: Doran, 1922.

The doctor who held hands; a Madame Storey novel. London: Collins/New York: Doubleday, 1929. Repr. as: *The murderer's challenge* – London: Collins, 1932. Char: Madame Rosika Storey.

Easy to kill. London: Collins/New York: Harper, 1931. Char: Madame Rosika Storey.

The folded paper mystery. London: Collins/New York: Harper as – *The mystery of the folded paper,* 1930. Char: Amos Lee Mappin. Features the American author and literati and close personal friend of Footner, Christopher Morley, as a character. In return, Morley wrote a biographical tribute of Footner in the latter's posthumously published *Orchids to murder,* (infra).

The fugitive sleuth. London: Hodder & Stoughton, 1918. Set: New York City.

The fur bringers; a tale of Athabasca. London: Hodder & Stoughton, 1916/New York: James A. McCann – as: *The fur-bringers; a story of the Canadian Northwest,* 1920. Mountie.

The house with the blue door. New York: Harper, 1942/London: Collins, 1943. Char: Amos Lee Mappin.

The huntress. London: Hodder & Stoughton, 1917/New York: Coward McCann, 1922.

The island of fear. London: Cassell/New York: Harper, 1936.

Jack Chanty; a tale of Athabasca. New York: Doubleday, 1913/London: Hodder & Stoughton, 1917.

Madame Storey. London: Collins/New York: Doran, 1926. ss.

Murder of a bad man. London: Collins, 1935/New York: Harper, 1936.

Murder runs in the family. London: Collins/New York: Harper, 1934.

The murder that had everything. London: Collins/New York: Harper, 1939. Char: Amos Lee Mappin.

Murderer's vanity. New York: Harper, 1940/London: Collins, 1941. Char: Amos Lee Mappin.

The nation's missing guest. London: Collins/New York: Harper, 1939. Set: Washington, D.C. Char: Amos Lee Mappin.

The obeah murders. New York: Harper, 1937/London: Collins – as: *Murder in the sun,* 1938.

Officer! London: Collins/New York: Doran, 1924. Set: New York City.

On Swan River. London: Hodder & Stoughton, 1919/New York: Coward McCann – as: *The woman from "Outside",* 1921. Set: Canada.

Orchids to murder. London: Collins/New York: Harper, 1945. Published posthumously, with biographical tribute by Christopher Morley.

The owl taxi. New York: Doran, 1921/London: Collins, 1922.

The queen of clubs. New York: Doran, 1927/London: Collins, 1928.

Ramshackle House. New York: Doran, 1922/London: Collins, 1923. Also published as: *Mystery at Ramshackle House* – London: Collins, 1932.

The ring of eyes. London: Collins/New York: Harper, 1933.

Scarred jungle. New York: Harper/London: Cassell, 1935. Set: Brazil.

The sealed valley. New York: Doubleday, 1914/London: Hodder & Stoughton, 1915. Set: Canada.

A self-made thief. London: Collins/New York: Doubleday, 1929.

The shanty sled. London: Hodder & Stoughton, 1925/New York: Doran, 1926. A novel of the Canadian Northland.

Sinfully rich. London: Collins/New York: Harper, 1940.

The substitute millionaire. New York: Doran, 1919/London: Collins, 1921.

Thieves' wit; an everyday detective story. New York: Doran, 1918/ London: Hodder & Stoughton, 1919.

Tortuous trails. London: Collins, 1937. Char: Madame Storey. ss.

Trial by water. London: Hodder & Stoughton, 1930/New York: Farrar, 1931.

Two on the trail; a story of the far Northwest. London: Methuen/New York: Doubleday, 1911.

The under dogs. London: Collins/New York: Doran, 1925. Char: Madame Storey.

Unneutral murder. London: Collins/New York: Harper, 1944. Set: Lisbon, Portugal. Char: Amos Lee Mappin.

The velvet hand, new Madame Storey mysteries. London: Collins/New York: Doubleday, 1928. ss.

The viper. London: Collins, 1930. Contains three stories, two of which are from his *The velvet hand,* (supra). ss.

The whip-poor-will mystery. New York: Harper/London: Collins – as: *The new made grave,* 1935.

Who killed the husband? London: Collins/New York: Harper, 1941. Char: Amos Lee Mappin.

The wild bird. London: Hodder & Stoughton/New York: Doran, 1923.

Other works

Antennae. New York: Doran, 1926/London: Faber – as: *Rich man, poor man,* 1928. novel.

Charles' gift; salute to a Maryland house of 1650. New York: Harper, 1939/London: Faber, 1940.

Country love. London: Hodder & Stoughton, 1921. novel.
Maryland Main and the Eastern Shore. New York: Appleton Century, 1942.
More than bread. Philadelphia: Lippincott/London: Faber, 1938. novel.
A new girl in town. London: Hodder & Stoughton, 1927. novel.
New rivers of the north; a yarn of two amateur explorers on the head waters of the Fraser, Peace River, the Hay River, Alexandra Falls. New York: Outing, 1912/London: Unwin, 1913.
New York, city of cities. Philadelphia: Lippincott, 1937.
Rivers of the Eastern Shore, seventeen Maryland rivers. New York/ Toronto: Farrar & Rinehart, 1944. (Rivers of America series.)
Roger Manion's girl. London: Hodder & Stoughton, 1925. novel.
Sailor of fortune; the life and adventures of Commodore Barney, U.S.N.. New York: Harper, 1940.
Shirley Kaye. [play, produced, New York, 1916].

ROBERT STEAD

The Squad of One
Why don't they cheer? poems.
London: T. Fisher Unwin, 1918.

STEAD, Robert J(ames) C(ampbell), 1880-1959

Robert Stead was born in Middleville in Lanark County, twenty miles north of Perth, Ontario, on 4 September 1880. His family moved West and he was raised on a homestead farm near Cartwright, Manitoba. He was educated at local public schools, leaving at fourteen to attend the Winnipeg Business College. From his return in 1898 until 1909 he published a weekly newspaper, which was called, successively, the *Rock Lake Review, Rock Lake Review and Cartwright Enterprise,* and *Southern Manitoba Review.*

Stead sold his paper and other business interests in 1910 and moved to High River, Alberta. In 1912 he joined the staff of the *Albertan* newspaper in Calgary, Alberta. A year later he became local publicist for the Canadian Pacific Railway, and was eventually promoted to publications director for the railway.

In 1919, Stead returned to Ontario to take up an Ottawa post as publicity director for the federal Department of Immigration and Colonization. In 1936 he transferred to become superintendent of information and publicity for parks and resources for the Department of Mines and Resources, where he worked until his retirement in 1946.

During his seventeen year term with Immigration and Colonization, Stead took the unusual step of commissioning James Oliver Curwood to write novels popularizing Canada. Stead was active in the founding of the Canadian Authors' Association in 1921, following John Murray Gibbon as its second national president. He also served on the editorial board of *Canadian Geographic* from 1942 until his death in Ottawa aged 78, on 26 June 1959.

Stead was at his best in his realistic portrayal of life on the Prairies, and built a reputation as a Western novelist in a regional, not a genre, sense. He ceased productive writing in 1931, but his one masterpiece, *Grain,* based on his Prairie experiences, assures him his place in Canadian literature.

THE SQUAD OF ONE
Why don't they cheer? poems. London: T. Fisher Unwin, 1918.

The inclusion of this little gem is an admitted piece of self-indulgence. It's just too precious to waste – besides, it's good fun. Stead's poems are of interest since the attitudes and ideas they express reflect the moderately educated, moderately well-to-do Westerners of British background among whom he grew up.

This eulogy is a perfect example of the mythic stature which the Mounties attained, and a window on how they were viewed and even revered, especially by Westerners in the late nineteenth century.

Because both Ontario and Quebec have provincial police forces and therefore do not see the RCMP on a daily basis, residents in central Canada may have lost sight of just how important the Force was to the creation of Canada. The Mounties were especially important in the years following Confederation in the Northwest Territories, which did not become provinces until the early years of the twentieth century.

Canada is the only nation that has a policeman as a national symbol – and Sergeant Blue could well be the model.

THE SQUAD OF ONE

SERGEANT BLUE of the Mounted Police was a so-so kind of guy;
He swore a bit, and he lied a bit, and he boozed a bit on the sly;
But he held the post at Snake Creek Bend for country and home and God,
And he cursed the first and forgot the rest – which wasn't the least bit odd.

Now the life of the North-West Mounted Police breeds an all-round kind of
    man;
A man who can jug a down-South thug when he rushes the red-eye can;
A man who can pray with a dying bum, or break up a range stampede –
Such are the men of the Mounted Police, and such are the men they breed.

The snow lay deep at the Snake Creek post and deep to east and west,
And the Sergeant had made his ten-league beat and settled down to rest
In his two-by-four that they call a "post," where the flag flew overhead,
And he took a look at his monthly mail, and this is the note he read:

"To Sergeant Blue, of the Mounted Police, at the post at Snake Creek Bend;
From U.S. Marshal of County Blank, greetings to you, my friend:
They's a team of toughs give us the slip, though they shot up a couple of
    blokes,
And we reckon they's hid in Snake Creek Gulch, and posin' as farmer folks.

"They's as full of sin as a barrel of booze, and as quick as a cat with a gun,
So if you happen to hit their trail be first to start the fun;
And send out your strongest squad of men and round them up if you can,
For dead or alive we want them here. Yours truly, Jack McMann."

And Sergeant Blue sat back and smiled, "Ho, here is a chance of game!
Folks 'round here have been so good that life is getting tame;
I know the lie of Snake Creek Gulch – where I used to set my traps –
I'll blow out there to-morrow, and I'll bring them in – perhaps."

Next morning Sergeant Blue, arrayed in farmer smock and jeans,
In a jumper sleigh he had made himself set out for the evergreens
That grew on the bank of Snake Creek Gulch by a homestead shack he knew,
And a smoke curled up from the chimney-pipe to welcome Sergeant Blue.

"Aha, and that looks good to me," said the Sergeant to the smoke,
"For the lad that owns this homestead shack is East in his wedding-yoke;

There are strangers here, and I'll bet a farm against a horn of booze
That they are the bums that are predestined to dangle in a noose."

So he drove his horse to the shanty door and hollered a loud "Good-day,"
And a couple of men with fighting-irons came out beside the sleigh,
And the Sergeant said, "I'm a stranger here and I've driven a weary mile;
If you don't object I'll just sit down by the stove in the shack awhile."

Then the Sergeant sat and smoked and talked of the home he had left down
    East,
And the cold and the snow, and the price of land, and the life of man and
    beast,
But all of a sudden he broke it off with, "Neighbours, take a nip?
There's a horn of the best you'll find out there in my jumper, in the grip."

So one of the two went out for it, and as soon as he closed the door
The other one staggered back as he gazed up the nose of a forty-four;
But the Sergeant wasted no words with him, "Now, fellow, you're on the rocks,
And a noise as loud as a mouse from you and they'll take you out in a box."

And he fastened the bracelets to his wrists, and his legs with some binder-
    thread,
And he took his knife, and he took his gun, and he rolled him on to the bed;
And then as number two came in, he said, "If you want to live
Put up your dukes and behave yourself, or I'll make you into a sieve."

And when he had coupled them each to each and laid them out on the bed,
"It's cold, and I guess we'd better eat before we go," he said.
So he fried some pork, and he warmed some beans, and he set out the best he
    saw,
And they ate thereof, and he paid for it, according to British law.

That night in the post sat Sergeant Blue, with paper and pen in hand,
And this is the word he wrote and signed and mailed to a foreign land:
"To U.S. Marshal of County Blank, greetings I give to you;
My squad has just brought in your men, and the squad was

                                                    SERGEANT BLUE.

There are things unguessed, there are tales untold, in the life of the great lone land,
But here is a fact that the prairie-bred alone may understand,
That a thousand miles in the fastnesses the fear of the law obtains,
And the pioneers of justice were the "Riders of the Plains."

BIBLIOGRAPHY - ROBERT STEAD

Criminous works

The bail jumper. Toronto: Briggs/London: Unwin, 1914. Set: Canada.
The copper disc. New York: Doubleday (Crime Club), 1931. Set: England. Char: Morley
 Kent.
The homesteaders; a novel of the Canadian West. Toronto: Musson/London: Unwin, 1916.
 Mountie.

Other works

Canada's playgrounds. Ottawa: King's Printer, 1941.
The cow puncher. New York: Harper/Toronto: Musson, 1918.
Dennison Grant; a novel of today. Toronto: Musson, 1920. Revised and re-issued as: *Zen of
 the Y.D.; a novel of the Foothills* – London: Hodder & Stoughton, 1925.
Dry water; a novel of Western Canada. Ottawa: Tecumseh, 1983. (published posthumously.)
The empire builders; and other poems. Toronto: Briggs, 1908.
Grain. Toronto: McClelland & Stewart, 1926.
Kitchener; and other poems. Toronto: Musson, 1917.
Neighbours. Toronto: Hodder & Stoughton, 1922.
Prairie born; and other poems. Toronto: Briggs, 1911.
The smoking flax. Toronto: McClelland & Stewart, 1924.
Songs of the Prairie. Toronto: Briggs, 1911.
Why don't they cheer?; poems. London: Unwin, 1918.

R.T.M. SCOTT

The Crushed Pearl
Aurelius Smith – detective.
New York: Dutton, 1927/London: Heinemann, 1928.

SCOTT, R(eginald) T(homas) M(aitland), 1882-1966

Born in the Ontario town of Woodstock on 14 August 1882, R.T.M. Scott was educated at Baptist's College there and at the Royal Military College of Canada in Kingston, Ontario, from 1901 to 1904. From 1908 until 1912, he worked as an engineer for the International Marine Signal Company installing a new system of marine lighting for the various Governments in Italy, Arabia, India, Burma, Ceylon, and Australia. In 1914, he accepted a captain's commission with the 21st Battalion, Canadian Expeditionary Force, and saw active service on the Western Front in Belgium, latterly attaining the rank of Major.

After the war, Scott lived in New York City and took up writing. He created a New York-based amateur detective, Aurelius Smith, who appeared in a series of short stories and novels with a psychic element. Scott also contributed to many of the "slick" magazines of the period. He died in New York City on 5 February 1966.

In the 1930s, his son, R.T.M. Scott II, wrote for the pulps about Richard Wentworth, The Spider, a character he shared with Grant Stockbridge (the pseudonym of Norvell W. Page [1904-1961]). These works are often attributed erroneously to the father. R.T.M. Scott II served with the 48th Highlanders of Toronto in the Second World War.

THE CRUSHED PEARL
Aurelius Smith – detective. New York: Dutton, 1927/London: Heinemann, 1928.

The roaring twenties was the age of extravagant amateur sleuths, and Aurelius Smith lives up to the mark. The detective is a lean and lanky pipe-smoker who began his career as a secret service agent in India and later retired to reside as a dilettante criminologist in a "travel-littered" apartment near Washington Square in New York City. He is ably assisted by his beautiful secretary, Bernice Asterly, a gifted mimic, and his Hindu man-servant, Langa Doonh. Aurelius Smith also appeared on radio as 'Secret Service Smith' in 1935.

Barzun and Taylor credit the short stories in Scott's *Aurelius Smith – detective* with managing "a trick or two worthy of Holmes" and offering "amusing sidelights on the New York of 1925."* Scott's writing was not without merit, as demonstrated in the superb "Bombay Duck," a triumphant exercise in psychological manipulation which merits reviving, and in this collection's story, "The crushed pearl."

---

* Jacques Barzun and Wendell Hertig Taylor. *Catalogue of crime; [being a reader's guide to the literature of mystery, detection & related genres]* (2nd imp. corr.). New York: Harper & Row, 1971.

THE CRUSHED PEARL

Aurelius Smith, lean and lanky criminal investigator, pressed dark, shredded tobacco into the bowl of a black briar with a slender finger. He regarded thoughtfully the result of the careful operation. Perhaps much of his success came because, like Aurelius of old, he believed that everything, no matter how small, should be done as though the entire universe depended upon the doing of it. It was very seldom that he seemed to hurry and the result was that most people thought him the laziest man in New York. Yet he could act with staccato swiftness when time pressed.

Across the big work-table from Smith, in his travel-littered diggings on tiny Fenton street down near Washington Square, sat a very large man upon whose round face, so suitable for laughter, there was a strained expression. Over the bowl of his pipe the detective gazed at his client with the lazy eyes of an old and experienced physician. Smith's eyes held something of the philosopher – and something of a child. Age seemed mixed. The suns and winds of distant places had played upon his face. Life, ever changing life, had intimately surrounded him. The man might have been anything from thirty to fifty years of age.

"I have had a ten thousand dollar pearl necklace stolen," had announced Mr. Budden upon entering, "and the police have failed as usual."

It was not until after the pipe had been so carefully filled and lighted that Smith replied.

"You mean," he said finally, "that Mr. Average Voter has failed as usual. There are about twelve thousand police in New York and they are an excellent body of men – much better than the intelligence of the average voter deserves. Of course, among so many men, there must be some corruption and some inefficiency but, on the whole, the New York police are unusually clever and courageous. Their weakness lies chiefly in their numbers. Consider that London, with an equal population of a less dangerous character, possesses a police force of about twenty-two thousand."

"You do not find fault with our police?" asked Budden in some surprise.

"Of course not," returned Smith. "The high percentage of crime in this city is due to the fewness of the police and to the sentimentally low sentences which are meted out to criminals. The average voter has the power to change these things but he doesn't know enough to use that power. Since most criminals are under thirty years of age it might prove to be a solution if the right to vote were taken away from all citizens under the same age."

Mr. Budden drummed nervously upon the table with his fingers.

"I suppose you are right," he admitted, "but since you praise the police so highly, do you consider that you have much chance to succeed when they have failed?"

"Certainly," answered Smith. "A police detective may be forced to carry half a dozen cases in his mind. I only accept one case at a time and I give it my entire personal attention. Has your recent financial embarrassment anything to do with your reason for calling upon me?"

The large man started suddenly in his chair.

"Yes and no," he answered quickly enough but in open astonishment. "How in thunder did you know that I had recently become pressed for money? You never saw me before."

Smith chuckled, which was his nearest approach to laughter.

"You would not be surprised," he retorted, "if a strange doctor were able to tell you that you were bilious. That would be in accordance with his profession. My profession allows me to discern other things. My clients are my patients, and, like sick people, they sometimes do not know what ails them. I try to learn their real trouble and to set things right, but, to do so, I must study each client as carefully as a doctor studies a patient."

"And you are talking now in order to give yourself more time for observation?" asked Budden.

"Your college mind has penetrated my design," said Smith.

"How do you know I am a college man?" asked Budden.

For answer Smith leaned forward and touched, with a long index finger, his client's partly exposed fraternity pin.

"It is fortunate that I have nothing to conceal," said Budden, smiling slightly at the simplicity of the explanation.

"Very few men have nothing to conceal," remarked Smith rather grimly. "As a matter of fact I am not sure that I have ever met one. I will compliment you by saying that a man of your type would have a minimum to conceal intentionally but he might conceal a maximum unintentionally. You are a married man and you have illness in the family. As yet I do not know whether or not that illness bears upon the case that you have brought me."

Budden's great body went limp in his chair as he gazed in frank amazement across the table.

"My wife!" he almost gasped. "It is really because of her that I have come to you. How could you possibly know that she was ill or even that I was married?"

"You credit me with a little too much," returned Smith. "I did not say that your wife was ill but merely that there was illness in your family which, in the face of your own healthy appearance, I deduced from the little slip of paper which peeps from your vest pocket and exposes the letters 'M.D.' No doubt it is a medical prescription. I said that you were married because you have that peculiar air which is possessed by almost every married man, indescribable but easily distinguished through practice."

Budden shook his head helplessly.

"If I weren't so worried," he said, "I would laugh at my own stupidity."

An expression of sympathy passed over Smith's lean face.

"These worries will pass," he said in a softened voice, "just as the mud and blood of the World War passed away from you."

"Yes," said Budden, also in a softened voice, "I thought it would never end when I was in the trenches. Have I, then, the air of the old soldier?"

"No," returned Smith, "you went into the army from civilian life and are not the type of professional soldier. The army stamped you slightly but not indelibly and the army will fade in the course of another year or so. I deduced your war service from your character, your age, your short hair-cut and the handkerchief up your sleeve – an example of cross observation."

"I had no idea that any man could reason so accurately from such trifling things," said Budden very much impressed. "I shall waste no more of your time if you will only explain how you knew that I have recently been hard pressed for money."

"You are not wasting time," returned Smith assuringly. "I should like to go on a fishing trip with each of my clients before accepting his case. The better I knew him the better I could work for him.

"About your recent financial trouble? My dear sir, every article of your clothing, while modest in appearance, is of the best and most expensive quality and yet, when you crossed your legs in sitting down, I observed that your shoe had been *half-soled*. A man of your manner of dressing does not usually have his shoes resoled, and *never half-soled*, unless he suddenly finds it necessary to save his ready cash in every possible way."

"Incredible and yet absurdly simple!" exclaimed Budden.

"Everything not understood," replied Smith, "is incredible. Everything misunderstood is absurd and everything understood is simple. I am ready. Please state your case."

For answer Budden drew an envelope from his pocket, extracted several pages of typewritten matter and laid them upon the table. For all his apparent laziness of manner Smith read the typewritten statement with rapidity.

"Comprehensive and clearly expressed," he remarked, folding the sheets and placing them in his pocket. "I compliment you. The circumstance of the crushed pearl is extremely interesting. It probably holds the solution."

"Yes," replied Budden, looking hopefully across the table. "The police detective thinks that it indicates a very cool and clever thief. The necklace was broken and, in order to be certain that the pearls were genuine, the thief deliberately crushed one of them on the marble top of my wife's antique dressing-table."

"Humph!" grunted Smith. "Maybe and maybe not. Just how ill is Mrs. Budden?"

Budden's face clouded.

"She is very ill," he answered. "It is Spanish influenza and the doctor thinks that the loss of the necklace is worrying her so that she is not making a good fight. It – it may mean her life and that is the real reason I have come to you in something that is very near to desperation."

The tall, lanky detective rose slowly to his feet and glanced at his watch.

"You know," he said, leading his client to the door, "you have interested me. A wife in trouble and a crushed pearl are worth fighting for. Undoubtedly it is my first crushed pearl. Go home and wait till I arrive."

Aurelius Smith did not disguise himself nor do anything spectacular. He did not rent a room opposite Mr. Budden's apartment house so that he could watch the entrance under cover. He did not even carry a revolver, handcuffs or magnifying glass. All such he could do, and had done – but very rarely. His tools were a quick wit, a keen power of observation, a knowledge of 1925 and common sense. Neither did he summon several "operatives" and send them out on various shadowing expeditions as would have been done by some commercial agencies. Instead, he used common sense and called on the police.

It was a police station, local to Mr. Budden's apartment house, that Smith entered and spoke a few words to the desk sergeant before sauntering back to the detectives' room in rear. Half a dozen men, in civilian clothes, cluttered up a bare and rather messy room. They were busy with pencils and note-books and a couple of telephones. One of the detectives recognized Smith and introduced him to a man named Sullivan.

"Yes," said Sullivan and spoke willingly enough, "I have the Budden case – six other cases too and mighty little sleep for a week. Glad you came around. Wish everybody would turn detective. We need 'em all in this city."

"Just so," said Smith. "How far did you get on the Budden case?"

"Nowhere at all," replied Sullivan. "The thief left no trace. Same as three other robberies in the same building. Only one or two valuable things taken and nothing disturbed – no marks of entrance. I dope it out that one of the hall boys is in cahoots with the thief and tips him off when an apartment is empty for a few hours. The hall boy then stands guard down stairs and rings the house telephone in the apartment from the hall switch-board if the tenants happen to return accidentally while the thief is busy. In that case the thief walks out of the apartment and down the stairs while the tenants go up in the elevator. We are watching the hall boys but can't get anything on 'em."

"Excellent!" commented Smith. "Probably the way it was done. You have given me great help. Now, about the other robberies in the same building, you are sure that they bear earmarks similar to Mr. Budden's case?"

"Exactly the same," answered Sullivan, "except that Mr. Budden had no insurance and the others did."

"And the pearl that was crushed on the marble top of the dressing-table?" asked Smith. "What do you make of that?"

"It means that the thief was an old hand at the game," replied Sullivan confidently. "He deliberately tested one of the pearls to see if it was an indestructible imitation. He was as cool and clever as they make 'em any place between the Bronx and the Battery."

"How do you know he crushed it deliberately?" questioned Smith.

"Takes a lot of pressure to crush a pearl," retorted Sullivan a little sharply. "They don't just drop and smash."

The tall investigator lighted a cigarette without comment.

"You don't agree with me?" demanded Sullivan.

"I think," drawled Smith, "that a very cool and clever thief would know a genuine pearl by *looking* at it."

Suddenly the police detective slipped a finger in first one vest pocket and then another before holding out a lustrous sphere on the palm of his hand.

"Is it a genuine pearl or an imitation?" he queried.

"Imitation," remarked Smith after a mere glance through his cigarette smoke.

"But how could you tell?" asked Sullivan. "It's the best imitation on the market and you hardly looked at it."

"My dear chap," replied Smith, "you are not a fool and only a fool would carry a five thousand dollar stone loose in his pocket – and even forget which pocket."

Aurelius Smith left the police station after having learned all that the police knew about the Budden robbery. They admitted that they knew very little but they did know who else had been similarly robbed in the same building and Smith entered those names and apartment numbers in his note-book before leaving.

The apartment house in which Mr. Budden lived was a huge structure overlooking the Hudson River and the Budden apartment was upon the top floor. Before entering this building Smith telephoned his client and warned him that he was about to call but that there might be some delay after he was announced before he reached the apartment. At seven o'clock the hall boy sent the name of Smith – a most excellent name for a detective – to the Budden apartment by means of the house telephone system. At eight o'clock Smith reached the apartment having, in the interval, wandered about the apartment house by means of the stairs and interviewed the other tenants who had been robbed. Neither hall boy nor elevator attendant had the least suspicion that the serious and rather indolent visitor, after being taken to the top floor, had wandered at large about the building. The tenants, upon whom he had called, met an earnest and ingratiating man who represented himself as a special investigator of the insurance companies. They found themselves talking very freely in answer to succinct questions which were most searching without being in the least offensive.

It was in the Budden apartment that Smith came face to face with his task. He was admitted by a woman, an elderly servant, whose eyes were red from crying. A nurse brushed by him in the hall and in a front room, striding restlessly up and down, he found the master of the household with drawn and haggard face.

"Mrs. Budden is worse?" asked Smith.

"There isn't much change," answered Budden, "but she is very low and the doctor has asked for a consultation tonight. In her weakened state he thinks that the loss of the necklace is unduly affecting her mind."

"Why not tell her that the police have captured the thief?" asked Smith. "You might add that they have to retain the pearls for a few days as evidence."

Budden smiled grimly.

"I am blessed with a wife to whom I cannot lie," he explained. "She can read my mind like an open book. Even in her weakened state she would know the truth."

"Some wives are like that," returned Smith, "and they can be wonderful partners in life. Let me see her photograph."

Budden pointed to a picture in an oval frame upon a table and Smith carried it to a light where he studied the face for a full minute.

"Now show me a picture of her mother," was the next request.

This time Budden indicated an oil painting upon one of the walls and the detective scrutinized the larger face which closely resembled the smaller one in the oval frame.

"Thoroughbred through generations," was the quietly spoken verdict. "Notice the delicate lips, the ear lobes, the high forehead, the separated eyebrows and much more. Mr. Budden, you are a particularly fortunate man."

"That or – or one damned!" replied the big man allowing himself to sink disconsolately into a chair.

Smith's next move was to examine the house telephone in the kitchen. A heavy rubber band over the bells drew his attention and the cook assured him that the band had not been removed for months. He struck one of the bells sharply with a pencil and listened to the muffled sound.

"Couldn't hear that bell outside of the kitchen," he commented, after returning to the front room with Budden. "I scarcely think that the hall boy used the house telephone as a signal to warn the thief. Still, he may have been careless and failed to see that the bell was not muffled before depending upon it. I suppose that Mrs. Budden is in the bedroom from which the pearls were stolen?"

"No," answered Budden, "she was moved to a small dressing-room – her favorite room – which opens off the bedroom."

"Good!" said Smith. "Let me see the dressing-table where the necklace was last kept."

In the large bedroom the investigator stood for quite a long time without speaking. Behind him was the door through which he had entered. To his left was a door leading into the dressing-room which was being used as the sick room. In front of him was an antique dressing-table – evidently an heirloom –

massive, with old carving and backed by a large mirror. To his right was a door leading into a bathroom. As he stood there, he referred briefly to the typewritten statement which Budden had given him earlier in the day.

"I see how it was done," he said finally to Budden who was standing by his side. "You left the apartment with Mrs. Budden at eight o'clock but your wife felt ill and you returned unexpectedly at nine o'clock. When you opened the front door the thief was standing before that mirror with the necklace in his hand. When you and Mrs. Budden entered this bedroom the thief was standing in the bathroom doorway. As you came into the room he went through the bathroom into the hall and out the front door."

"How do you know?" asked Budden.

"Well," said Smith, "that is what I would have done if I had been the thief. He stole the pearls between eight and nine. He was surprised. If he had not been surprised he would have taken more. There was nothing else for him to do."

Without further speech Smith took the chair before the dressing-table and looked at the old-fashioned marble slab which was covered with the usual articles of toilet. He seemed to be immersed in thought rather than to be paying much attention to the toilet articles beneath his eyes. Finally he dropped a hand and delicately touched some whitish substance with a slender finger.

"The crushed pearl," he commented to Budden who was standing behind him. "It has not been disturbed. Good! And the toilet articles? They have been moved, I suppose?"

"Yes," said Budden. "My wife used the dressing-table when she came home. The theft was not discovered until the next morning."

"It doesn't matter," returned Smith, gazing into the mirror so that he could examine the rest of the room without the effort of turning around. "This broken pearl tells the story. In the end every thief makes a slip and faces the sordid, dreary days of jail. Your thief has made a slip which is positively unique in my experience."

"Have you discovered something?" questioned Budden.

"Yes," said Smith. "I can return the pearls to you."

"And – and the thief?" asked Budden, perhaps a trifle nervously.

Smith turned slowly in his chair and regarded his big client somewhat curiously.

"Such a delicate case needs thought," he said. "I would like to sit here, quite alone, and – think."

It was perhaps ten minutes later that Smith returned to the front room and found Budden pacing anxiously up and down. Before speaking, he again took up the picture in the oval frame and carefully studied the delicate, aristocratic features of Mrs. Budden. Finally he asked an unexpected question.

"Mr. Budden," he asked, "what does Mrs. Budden think of your business ability?"

"How can that possibly bear upon the theft of the pearls?" demanded Budden in surprise.

"I am not sure that it does," returned Smith, "but you have given me so delicate a case that I must probe. Please answer the question."

"Well," answered Budden visibly embarrassed, "she thinks I am a colossal business genius and that I cannot be beaten."

"I thought she would think that," replied Smith, putting down the framed picture. "She is not worrying about a business smash for you – a smash that might possibly have been averted had you been able to use the pearls for the purpose of raising money."

A slow red mounted to Budden's face and Smith spoke a little sharply.

"Mr. Budden," he exclaimed, "you said that you had nothing to conceal. I can see that you *have*. What is it?"

"These family matters cannot possibly help you," returned Budden with annoyance. "I don't wish to talk about them."

"Permit me to say that you are not capable of judging," said Smith quietly. "You have held back something in connection with the pearls and I must know what it is."

For a moment Budden hesitated but the expression in the eyes of the tall man seemed to reassure him.

"I'll tell you," he said at last. "My wife has a brother who is rather wild. He got into trouble and asked her to send him five thousand dollars. I told her that I could only do it by raising the money on the pearls."

"And what makes you think Mrs. Budden is not worrying about her brother?" asked Smith.

"Because I met an old friend on the way home tonight," remarked Budden dryly. "Because he wrote me a check for more than enough to see me through my difficulties. Because, an hour ago, I mailed Bob a check that will pay his gambling debt. Because my wife was scarcely interested when I told her the check was mailed. I am positive she is not worrying about her brother."

"Have you asked her what is worrying her?" demanded Smith.

Budden shook his had sadly.

"If she wanted me to know, she would tell me," he replied. "I – I dare not force the question on her. She is very weak. I asked her if she would be more comfortable if I applied for burglary insurance again and she just looked at me wistfully without answering."

"Again?" queried Smith sharply. "You *did* apply for burglary insurance?"

"Why, yes," answered Budden. "About a month ago I applied for burglary insurance and had a binder for a couple of days. I was so pressed for money that I canceled the application."

"And when the insurance company sent up their investigator, did he find all the locks and window fastenings in good shape?" asked Smith.

"Yes," said Budden.

"The name of the insurance company?"

Budden named it.

"Man!" exclaimed Smith. "I have solved the case. I know where the pearls are. I know who the thief is. I know what worries Mrs. Budden."

"What is worrying my wife?" asked Budden breathlessly.

"Something," drawled Smith, "which you have failed to conceal from me."

Budden regarded his cool companion with a mixture of embarrassment and anger. Before he could reply a servant entered with a telegram which he tore open, allowing the envelope to fall to the floor. As his eyes ran over the message a rapid change came into his face. His features seemed to harden and his eyes appeared to deaden as they lost focus upon the objects in the room. When he spoke, his voice was toneless.

"The case is ended," he said at last. "How much is your fee?"

Smith placed a hand upon his shoulder.

"Won't you explain?" he asked gently.

"Yes," returned the big man listlessly. "I, too, know where the pearls are and I, too, know what worries my wife."

"And do you know the – thief?" demanded Smith very slowly.

"There is no thief, damn you!" was the angry retort.

"Mr. Budden," returned Smith, still very gently, "all your happiness in life depends upon your handing me that telegram immediately."

"It is only a business wire," was the cold reply.

"You lie!" said Smith.

The big man moved forward abruptly with upraised fist and undoubtedly would have struck the detective had not the latter quickly picked up the fallen envelope and extended it. Above the window, which the address had partly missed, appeared the name of *Mrs.* Budden. The upraised fist dropped weakly and Budden sank into a chair with his head in his hands.

Again Smith asked for the telegram but Budden slowly shook his head without looking up and remained silent. After a pause Smith's voice became severe.

"Mr. Budden," he said, "If you give me the telegram I promise to take no action without your consent. If you refuse, the name of the thief will be in every newspaper within twenty-four hours."

Perhaps a full minute passed before Budden silently placed the telegram upon the stable and Smith read:

THANKS TO STRING OF PEARLS EVERYTHING ALL RIGHT. BOB.

There was no immediate speech from either man. Undoubtedly the telegram plunged Smith into the deepest thought. Motionless he stood at the table gazing down at the yellow sheet. Nor did he speak until he had again picked up the oval frame and gazed long at the face of Mrs. Budden; and, when he spoke, he addressed the picture.

"I'm damned if I believe it!"

Budden whirled in his chair.

"What do you mean?" he demanded.

"I mean," returned Smith, speaking earnestly, "that I have more faith in her than you have. That woman never deceived her husband by the slightest action or thought. She is incapable of the least degree of dishonesty – yet you suspected her a little from the start and now you do more than suspect. It is your suspicion that has touched the telepathic sensitiveness of her mind. She is too proud to combat your suspicion and, in her weakened state, it is the knowledge of your suspicion which stands between life and death for her."

"The pearls were hers," murmured Budden brokenly," and she had a perfect right to send them to her brother. She *must* have sent them. How else can you explain the telegram?"

"I can't explain it," admitted Smith. "It won't fit my theory. I think your wife could explain it but she is too ill. Let me test my deductions a bit more. Before the robbery, can you remember being called uselessly to the telephone on a number of evenings about eight o'clock? Did you take down the receiver only to find nobody on the wire?"

"Ye-es," returned Budden. "I believe that is true."

"That was the thief calling to learn if the apartment was empty," said Smith. "I *must* be right."

Then the end came with unexpected suddenness.

Down the hall sounded running steps and the old servant, with reddened eyes, burst into the room. Mrs. Budden was worse and the nurse wanted the doctor at once. Budden, thrusting downward with his hands, smashed both arms of his chair as he rose to his feet before rushing from the room. The old servant, about to follow, felt a hand upon her shoulder and turned to look into Smith's serious face.

"You were listening in the hall when I was talking to Mr. Budden," he said. "Was I right?"

Slowly the old woman nodded her head.

"I've been with her ever since she was a baby," she replied, "and no man ever understood her till you came."

A bell sounded and the servant moved away in the direction of the front door. At that instant Smith's eye fell upon a small desk of the dainty kind which is used by ladies. Quickly he approached it and swiftly his fingers searched drawers and tiny pigeonholes with a skill that would have been the envy of any thief. It was only a matter of seconds before he slipped a night telegram into his pocket with distinct satisfaction and left the room.

In the hall Smith saw the nurse pass rapidly from the kitchen to the sickroom with a hot water bag. He heard Budden's voice speaking urgently to the doctor over the telephone. He was quite near the front door when the old servant opened it and a man spoke.

"I am a detective investigating the robberies in this building."

Smith stood motionless.

"I come from an insurance company and would like Mr. Budden to let me examine this apartment," added the man at the door.

Swiftly Smith stepped forward.

"My name is Smith," he said. "I am Mr. Budden's cousin. Perhaps I can help you."

The old servant looked gravely at the tall man who had taken her place at the door and accepted the new relative of the family by walking silently away.

The newly arrived detective was short but heavily built with shrewd eyes and a hard face. Smith conducted him to the front room but turned back for a minute and found the old servant watching, with grave eyes, near the kitchen. Quickly he bent and spoke softly to her.

"Lock the door between the sick-room and the large bedroom."

In the front room Mr. Budden's "cousin" and the insurance detective talked the case over at length. Smith showed much interest in the profession of a detective and expressed considerable admiration for the clever way in which his companion explained the methods of thieves and described his own methods of catching them.

"Dear me!" exclaimed Smith. "You must run great risks."

"Yes," admitted the insurance detective in an off hand manner, "but we get used to it. Besides, we carry our little gat."

As he spoke the man drew a revolver from a side pocket.

Smith sucked in his breath.

"Is it loaded?" he asked.

"Sure!" answered the man with a laugh as he returned his pistol. "Now I've doped it out that the superintendent of this building is the guilty bird. I have worked on the three other apartments that have been robbed and I'm going to nail this super. Now what I want to do is to make a professional study of this apartment and I want to start in on the room in which the theft was committed."

Smith's ear caught the door bell again and he heard the entrance of a man. No doubt it was the doctor. As the steps in the hall ceased he replied to his companion.

"Certainly," he said very affably. "I shall take you to the bedroom."

If Smith's words had been affably spoken his actions seemed even more friendly. Indeed he placed a hand upon the shorter man's shoulder and led him down the hall in a way that would indicate the best of good fellowship.

"Just make yourself at home," he said when they reached the bedroom. "You don't mind excusing me for a minute or two?"

Smith nearly closed the door behind him as he left the room. It remained open just sufficiently to allow a crack where it hinged to the wall. Budden, leaving the sick-room by the hall door, found Smith standing with his eye to the crack. Without a word Smith pushed open the door. In the bedroom, *standing upon the dressing-table,* was the man who had represented himself as an insurance company detective.

The tableau lasted but a second before the man on the dressing-table jumped to the floor and rushed into the bathroom. From the bathroom he entered the hall through its outer door and, finding his way to the front door blocked by Smith and Budden, fled into the front room.

"I don't understand!" exclaimed Budden. "Who is he?"

"The thief," answered Smith. "Let's examine him."

In the front room a short, heavy man stood before an open window twelve stories above the street. His face was nervous, puzzled, irritated, partly vicious. He did not speak as the two men entered.

"Now," said Smith, standing by the door which was the only exit to the room, "the case is ended. There were four similar robberies in this building. All four owners of the robbed apartments had applied for burglary insurance from the *same* company. So far as I could learn the only man who had access to all four apartments was the preliminary investigator of that insurance company. Mr. Budden, is that the man who came up to examine this apartment when you applied for insurance about a month ago?"

"Yes," said Budden.

Fear and anger spread over the face of the man at the window but he remained silent.

"You gave him the key to your front door when he tested the lock," went on Smith. "He took an impression of the key and had a duplicate made. By telephoning he discovered when the apartment was empty and walked boldly through your front door. You returned unexpectedly and nearly caught him in the act. Rather than chance being caught with the goods on him, he hid the necklace before he escaped. The crushed pearl told me the hiding place."

Budden looked inquiringly at Smith but the latter never took his eyes off the man at the window.

"You will remember that the necklace was broken," continued Smith. "One pearl fell off and was crushed upon the marble top of the dressing-table. I reasoned that this pearl had been crushed accidentally and I could think of no way for the thief to do it except by *stepping* on it. What would induce him to stand on the dressing-table? The answer is that he wished to reach up high and the only thing for him to reach was the picture molding – *along which he laid the necklace.*"

As Smith finished speaking, the man at the window drew a gleaming necklace from his pocket. Suspending the string he allowed the pearls to slip off the silk thread into his other hand.

"Ten thousand dollars," he said sullenly. "I go free or they go out the window."

Smith took a step forward but Budden put out a detaining hand.

"You promised to take no action without my consent," interposed Budden. "My wife is fond of those pearls. If they were mine it would be different."

"Will you *never* have confidence in me?" asked Smith and took another step.

The man at the window flung a shower of shining orbs into the darkness of the night.

"That will count against you at your trial," remarked Smith dryly and took from his own pocket another necklace. "These are the genuine pearls. When I heard about the crushed pearl I bought an imitation necklace so that, if my theory proved right, I could substitute it and catch the thief red handed without any risk."

"You still have some risk," growled the thief, shooting a hand into his side pocket where something hard poked outward. "One more step and I'll plug you. Hands up!"

Smith coolly handed the pearls to Budden and faced the thief again.

"You haven't the courage to fire," he taunted.

The man at the window stood tensely without speaking.

Again Smith took a step forward and the hand in the thief's pocket convulsed as a loud click was heard.

"So you are a would-be murderer also," commented Smith, walking rapidly forward while two more clicks came from the pocket. "My dear chap, you shouldn't let strangers walk down halls with their arms around you. It was quite a simple matter for me to take your gun away, unload it and return it to your pocket."

Later that evening, after the police had taken away the thief and after the doctor had reported that the nurse had been unduly alarmed, Budden tried to express his gratitude.

"You have been wonderful," he said to Smith. "You have cleared up everything except – except the telegram."

"And that reminds me of something," answered Smith. "While Mrs. Budden is ill you really should read all her telegrams."

Quietly the lanky investigator, now sprawled in a huge chair and smoking one of his client's best cigars, extended the night telegram which he had taken from the lady's writing desk. He watched lazily while Budden read it.

YOUR BROTHER MAY BE A ROTTER BUT HE IS NOT ROTTEN STOP DO NOT WORRY ABOUT ME ANY MORE STOP HAVE BET MY LAST MONEY AT THE RACES ON TWO LONG SHOTS STOP IF WHITE STAR OR STRING OF PEARLS WINS I SHALL BE ALL RIGHT STOP WIN OR LOSE I AM GOING TO SETTLE DOWN AND GO TO WORK STOP LOVE STOP BOB.

The night telegram fluttered from Budden's fingers and his eyes wandered to the photograph of his wife.

"I shall never doubt her again," he said softly, "but how can I ever remove the hurt from her mind – the hurt of having suspected her?"

Smith reached for the photograph and held it before him.

"Do you really want the answer to that question?" he asked.

"Yes," said Budden earnestly.

"Why, you great, over-grown puppy," replied Smith, "she is the kind of woman who will *enjoy* forgiving a man like *you.* "

And all this explains the presence of a lady's photograph upon Smith's desk – a photograph signed by both the lady and her husband.

BIBLIOGRAPHY - R.T.M. SCOTT

Criminous works

Aurelius Smith – detective. New York: Dutton, 1927/London: Heinemann, 1928.

The agony column murders; a Secret Service Smith novel. New York: Dutton, 1946. Set: New York City. Char: Aurelius Smith.

Ann's crime. New York: Dutton, 1926/London: Heinemann, 1927. Also publ as: *Smith of the Secret Service* – London: Amalgamated, 1929. Set: New York City. Char: Aurelius Smith.

The black magician. New York: Dutton, 1925/London: Heinemann, 1926. Set: New York City. Char: Aurelius Smith.

The mad monk. New York: Kendall, 1931/London: Rich, 1933. Set: Russia.

Mammoth Secret Service Smith stories. 1926. ss.

Murder stalks the mayor. London: Rich, 1935/New York: Dutton, 1936. Set: New York City. Char: Aurelius Smith.

The nameless ones; a Secret Service Smith novel. New York: Dutton, 1947. Set: New York City. Char: Aurelius Smith.

Secret Service Smith. New York: Dutton, 1923/London: Hodder & Stoughton, 1924. Set: India; with some stories set in the United States of America, mostly New York City.

Bibliography - R.T.M. SCOTT II

The Spider; [Master of men]. New York: Berkley, 1969. 2 vols. (Vol. 1: *The Spider strikes!*, Vol. 2: *The wheel of death.*) Reprinted from 1930s pulp magazines. Set: New York City. Char: Richard Wentworth, "The Spider." Criminals needed "Flit" instead of guns, with so many insectoid crime-busters harassing them, such as "The Spider" and "The Green Hornet"!

SKENE-MELVIN, Lewis David St Columb

David Skene-Melvin is well known in the world of Canadian crime — Canadian crime literature, that is. He is a former executive director of the Crime Writers of Canada, and has researched and taught courses in the genre; his M. Phil. thesis was on the history and development of the spy novel. With his wife Ann, he compiled the important reference book, *Crime, detective, espionage, mystery, and thriller fiction and film; a comprehensive bibliography of critical writing through 1979.*

A qualified librarian, Skene-Melvin has been an infantry officer in the Canadian Army, an academic and scholar of popular culture, and an antiquarian bookdealer specializing in out-of-print, old and rare hardcover crime fiction and true crime and military history. A noted Sherlockian scholar, his contributions to the study of the Master have been rewarded by investiture in the Baker Street Irregulars. Among other activities, he is an aileurophile, an active bird watcher, and a member of the Arts & Letters Club of Toronto.

David Skene-Melvin has called upon skills learned in all of these different vocations and avocations to select, locate, research, and compile the fascinating collection for *Crime in a Cold Climate.*

Bibliography - Criminous works

With Ann Skene-Melvin. *Crime, detective, espionage, mystery, and thriller fiction and film; a comprehensive bibliography of critical writing through 1979.* Westport, Conn.: Greenwood Press, 1980.
"The secret eye: the spy in literature; the history and development of espionage fiction." *Pacific Quarterly,* vol. 3: no. 1 (January 1978). Special criminous literature issue; also guest editor of this issue.
"Crime writers with a past." In *The 23rd annual Anthony Boucher memorial mystery convention souvenir programme book.* Toronto: Bouchercon XXIII, 1992. Repr. in Arthur Ellis Awards, souvenir programme book, May 19, 1993.
"The 1992 Canadian crime fiction scene in review." In *The 24th Annual Anthony Boucher Memorial Mystery Convention, October 1-3, 1993 souvenir program book.* Omaha, Neb.: BoucherCon XXIV, 1993.
"Canadian crime fiction." Tokyo: Canadian Embassy, 1993. Descriptive brochure to accompany an exhibition of Canadian crime fiction, Canadian Embassy, Tokyo, September 1993. [translated into Japanese].
"Criminal clefs; crime fiction based on true crime" [tripartite article]. In *The Mystery Review,* vol. 2: nos 1-3 (Fall and Winter 1993, Spring 1994).
"Pushing crime." In *Books in Canada,* vol. 23: no. 2 (March 1994).
"Canadian crime writing." In *Oxford Companion to Crime and Mystery Writing.* New York: Oxford University Press, 1995.
Northern crimes; a comprehensive bibliography of Canadian crime fiction and biographical dictionary of Canadian crime writers (in preparation).

Other works

Biography and autobiography; training course for bookstore employees. Toronto: Canadian Booksellers Association, 1964.
How to find out about Canada. London (Eng.): Pergamon, 1967 (co-author).
The Longship Review no. 1. Toronto: The Arts & Letters Club, 1990 (editor).